The Regiment

THE
REGIMENT

Christopher Nicole

St. Martin's Press
New York

Library of Congress Cataloging-in-Publication Data

Nicole, Christopher.
    The regiment / Christopher Nicole.
        p.   cm.
    ISBN 0-312-03418-0
    I. Title.
    PR9320.9.N5R44   1989
823'.914—dc20   89-35073
                            CIP

First published in Great Britain by Century Hutchinson Ltd.

10 9 8 7 6 5 4 3 2

This book is dedicated to GEORGE GREENFIELD, who suggested the idea.

Contents

Prologue

MAY, 1983

'You'll be for the regimental dinner,' remarked the doorman at the Savoy Hotel, holding his umbrella above the young man as he got out of his taxi; the May evening, still light, was obscured by the persistent London drizzle. Hastily the new arrival was escorted into the warm comfort of the lobby, where he stood for a moment, water dripping from his dark blue overcoat and from the burnished helmet he carried under his arm. The elegantly dressed men and women moving to and fro before him paid little attention as he removed his greatcoat and revealed the sky-blue shell jacket, dark blue breeches, high polished black boots, lacking spurs, and the cavalry sabre hanging at his side. If he appeared as a relic from a long-forgotten imperial past, the hotel guests and staff had already seen too many exactly like him this evening.

One of the under-managers was waiting for him. 'It's down the stairs and on the left, sir,' he explained confidentially.

'Thank you.' The second lieutenant crossed the floor, disturbingly aware of the noise his boots were making, and descended the stairs. He breathed a sigh of relief as he saw the sergeant-major, also wearing full dress uniform, standing before one of the doors. 'Lieutenant Wilson,' he murmured diffidently.

The sergeant-major came to attention. 'Lieutenant Wilson, sir,' he repeated, as if he did not already know the newcomer by sight. 'Colonel Mackinder is waiting, sir.'

'The taxi was late,' Lieutenant Wilson explained, pausing as he stepped inside. The large room was festooned with bunting, dominated by the huge light blue regimental flag, but surrounded by others, ensigns and standards

11

representing the battle honours won by the Royal Western Dragoons during their remarkable history. Sedgemoor – the regiment had been raised by Sir William Lord of Taunton in 1683 just to oppose Monmouth's rebellion – and Blenheim, Minden and Busaco, Salamanca and Vittoria, Waterloo and Chilianwalah, Kabul and the Modder River, Le Cateau and the Somme, Dunkirk and El Alamein, the list was endless. Beneath the flags, the long tables sagged under the weight of the regimental silver; there were four tables, a top and three arms stretching away from it, with the centre arm slightly longer than the others. Along the near wall there ran another long table, on which all the helmets of the diners were arrayed.

The room was also filled with officers, past and present, from youthful second lieutenants like Wilson himself, more at home inside a tank than on the back of a horse, to active captains and retired majors, all wearing the unique sky-blue jacket – a reminder of the Peninsular War, when the original red tunics wore out. No replacements were available, so the then lieutenant-colonel had obtained permission from the Duke of Wellington to clothe his men out of his own pocket; the only material obtainable in sufficient quantity was sky-blue. Already known as 'Lord's Own', from the name of their founder, the nickname had promptly been changed to 'Heaven's Own' by the rest of the army, and had been worn with distinction and pride ever since.

'Wilson! Thank God you've arrived. The old man is expected at any moment.'

Lieutenant Wilson faced his commanding officer, Lieutenant-Colonel Ian Mackinder, a tall, powerfully built man with clipped features and piercing blue eyes, who, Wilson had already discovered, was not quite so fierce as he sometimes appeared; but he was looking fierce enough this evening. 'The taxi was late, sir,' he explained.

'You know what you have to do?' Mackinder inquired, ignoring the stammered excuse.

'I think so, sir.'

'Think so? Damn it, boy, you have to know it. Come with me.'

Other officers stepped aside as the colonel led the junior lieutenant through their ranks to the huge painting which hung immediately behind the top table; some looked sympathetic, some looked amused; most had had to undergo this ordeal early in their own careers, when they had first joined the regiment.

'Now,' Colonel Mackinder said. 'Tell me about that picture.'

Lieutenant Wilson swallowed. He was staring at the most famous episode in the entire history of the Royal Western Dragoons. The picture depicted an enormous number of turbaned warriors, some on horseback, most on foot, milling about a sunbaked Indian plain beneath a brilliantly blue sky, and being charged by about four hundred helmeted horsemen, armed with swords and wearing sky-blue jackets, weapons pointed in front of them as they followed their commander into what seemed certain death.

'Well?' Mackinder demanded.

Wilson swallowed again. 'That was April 1843, sir,' he said. 'Just after the Battle of Hyderabad, when Sir George Napier completed the conquest of Sind. Two squadrons of the Royal Westerns were detailed to carry out a reconnaissance towards the Baluchi position. Their commanding officer was Major Ian Mackinder. . . .' He paused to glance at the man beside him, but Mackinder's face was impassive. 'A Scottish officer who had only recently been seconded to the regiment, but was now in command owing to the illness of the lieutenant-colonel. The regiment was led into a trap by their guides, and found itself surrounded by fifteen thousand Baluchis, who summoned Major Mackinder to surrender.' Again he paused, having run out of breath.

'Well?' Colonel Mackinder demanded.

'Major Mackinder refused to surrender,' Wilson went on. 'Instead, he led his men in prayer, and then drew his sword and gave the order to charge. The Baluchis broke and fled, and Major Mackinder took his men to safety with the loss of but thirty casualties.'

'Now, do you feel capable of repeating that prayer?'

'Yes, sir,' Wilson said, and drew a long breath. ' "May the great – " '

'Not now, boy,' his colonel admonished. 'When the time comes. Just remember it. I think the old man is here.'

The sergeant-major had appeared in the doorway and was signalling urgently. Mackinder, followed by his adjutant and the regimental majors, hurried across as several men entered the room. They all wore the sky-blue jackets of the Westerns, and three of them looked remarkably alike, except for differences in ages. They also looked remarkably like Lieutenant-Colonel Mackinder, who was now greeting them. Wilson knew that they were in fact all Mackinders; with one or two very brief exceptions, the Royal Western Dragoons had always had a Mackinder on their roster since that fateful day in 1843, and the three men who had just arrived, father, son, and grandson, were all past lieutenant-colonels.

Like everyone else in the room, Wilson had eyes only for the man in the centre of the group; because if Major Ian Mackinder had been the founder of a legend, this man, his great-grandson, was the most famous soldier ever to wear the sky-blue jacket of the regiment. It was not merely his exalted rank – Lieutenant-General (retired) Sir Murdoch Mackinder, VC, KCMG, DSO and bar, Légion d'honneur, followed by a host of other honours and decorations which were all displayed upon his breast tonight – which made him memorable; nor even the fact that he was still alive, at the age of one hundred and two, and still stood erect, and moved firmly, if slowly, smiling a greeting here, nodding another there, clearly remembering many of the faces. What had made him into an immortal was the legend of his life, the manner in which he had gained all those decorations. And now, having handed over his helmet to a waiting orderly to be placed beside the others on the table along the wall, he was coming closer. Wilson braced himself and stood to attention, trying to keep himself from shaking with apprehension.

Murdoch Mackinder's own great-grandson, the lieutenant-colonel, stood beside the famous old man. 'May I

14

present Second Lieutenant Wilson, sir,' he said. 'Just joined.'

Wilson gazed at a tall, very spare man, clean shaven and not, at the moment, anyway, wearing glasses – nor was it easy to suppose that the cool blue eyes ever needed them. His features had the family clipped regularity, which tended again to create an impression of coolness, perhaps even aloofness, but he was smiling as he extended his hand. 'The new sub,' he remarked. 'Are you nervous, Mr Wilson?'

'I . . . ah . . . yes, sir,' Wilson said.

Murdoch Mackinder nodded. 'If you weren't, you'd have reason to worry. We were all nervous when we had to utter the prayer.' The smile broadened. 'I imagine even the first Ian Mackinder was nervous.'

'Were you nervous, sir?' Wilson could not believe his ears.

'When I had to utter the prayer? My dear boy, I was shivering like a kitten,' General Mackinder told him. 'And many times afterwards, I can tell you. No nerves, no performance. Remember that.' He turned to his great-grandson. 'Well, Colonel Mackinder, shall we begin? Dr Crossfield says I have to be in bed by midnight.'

'Of course, sir. Take your place, Wilson,' Colonel Mackinder said, and escorted his great-grandfather, flanked by his father and grandfather, to the head of the table, where the old gentleman was seated exactly beneath the picture of the first Ian Mackinder's charge. The other officers took their places, and the sergeant-major stood to attention at Wilson's shoulder, at the foot of the longer centre arm, facing both Murdoch Mackinder and the picture, with the regimental standard in his right hand.

'Gentlemen, the regimental prayer.'

Every officer stood to attention, and then, with a single movement, each drew his sword and pointed it at the ceiling. There were some seventy men present, and Lieutenant Wilson, gazing at the swords held aloft, his own amongst them, had a sudden concept that this was indeed a recreation of the scene on that hot and dusty Pakistani plain,

15

a hundred and forty years before, when Ian Mackinder and his men had accepted the simple choice: victory, or death.

'Mr Wilson, sir.' The voice was quiet, as the room was absolutely still.

Lieutenant Wilson took the longest breath of his life. ' "May the great God of battle," ' he said, in a high, clear voice, ' "who has guided the fate of this famous regiment on many a hard-fought field, and never failed to lead it to distinction, grant that on this day, faced as we are with a host of enemies of our Queen and our country, every man will do his duty, so that should we fail in our ordained task, it will yet be said of us, they were the Royal Western Dragoon Guards, who fought and died according to the ancient valour of their regiment and their blood." '

There was a moment of silence, then Wilson remembered, and added, speaking quietly as he had been instructed, ' "Gentlemen, there is your enemy." '

There was a burst of applause as the swords were sheathed with a scintillating rasp, and the orderlies moved forward to relieve the diners and stack the weapons against the wall. The assembly then sat down, but Murdoch Mackinder remained standing. 'That was well said, Mr Wilson. Well said. The regiment is proud of you.'

There was another ripple of applause, and the old gentleman took his seat, while the waiters immediately began carrying in the meal.

'When you said the prayer, Great-grandpa,' Ian Mackinder wondered, 'where was the dinner held?'

'Oh, down in Bath, in the mess,' Murdoch Mackinder replied. 'It was a much smaller, more intimate affair in those days. Besides, we were under orders to sail for the Cape the next week.'

'My God, to fight the Boers,' Ian Mackinder said. 'That seems. . . .' He checked himself.

Murdoch Mackinder smiled. 'A long time ago? It *was* a long time ago. Different men, different weapons, different enemies. Perhaps a different concept of life. But the same regiment.'

'I imagine these dinners take you back,' his great-grandson ventured.

'They do,' Murdoch Mackinder agreed. 'All of those eighty-four years.' His eyes were misty as he looked into his wineglass.

Part One

THE SUBALTERN

1

Cape Town, 1899

The hansom cab rolled to a halt at the gates of the military depot outside the city of Bath, and the young officer stepped down. He wore a sky-blue jacket and dark blue breeches, black boots, and a burnished gilt helmet with a nodding plume. His sword was tucked under his arm. His boxes were lifted down by the cabby, watched with interest by the soldier on guard duty, who also wore light and dark blue. 'Who goes there, sir?' he inquired, coming to attention.

'Second Lieutenant Mackinder, reporting for duty,' Murdoch Mackinder told him. 'Is there someone to help with my gear?'

'Yes, sir,' the sentry said. 'Sergeant,' he called, without turning his head.

The sergeant emerged from the guardhouse and swung the gate in. 'Mr Mackinder, sir.' He stood to attention and saluted. 'We was not expecting you before tomorrow.'

'I found an earlier train,' Murdoch Mackinder told him. 'My gear?'

'Of course, sir. Look alive there,' the sergeant shouted, and four other troopers hurried from the guardhouse to stand to attention before the officer. Murdoch looked past them at the barracks, and the parade ground, and the stables, and the flags – and drew a deep breath. This depot had already played a large part in his life, but he had never actually been here before. As a Mackinder, all his life he had been destined for just this moment, when he would report for duty to the regiment which his father, his grandfather, and his great-grandfather had all commanded in turn. And which he would in turn one day command? That was looking too far ahead. But he could feel the weight of history descending on his shoulders.

'Well, sir, welcome to Bath,' the sergeant said. 'Colonel Edmonds will be pleased to see you.'

He gave instructions to his men, who collected the two suitcases and the various other personal pieces of equipment – the saddle and the bag of golf clubs, the small cased travelling library and the revolver holster – which were all indications of the young English officer and gentleman in the sixty-second year of the reign of Queen Victoria, Queen of England, Empress of India, and head of the greatest empire the world had ever seen. They would take the baggage directly to the bachelor officers' quarters; Murdoch followed the sergeant round the central parade ground, where a troop of recruits were undergoing the basic training of mounting – and falling off – a line of patient horses, towards the headquarters building, where the pale blue regimental standard and the Union Jack waved together above the red brick and the creeping wisteria.

Here there were more sentries, and the regimental mascot – a Shetland pony called Morag, who almost seemed able to stand to attention like her human companions at the approach of an officer. The door at the top of the steps was opened for him, and he stepped into an office, where another sergeant and two corporals immediately stood to attention behind their desks, and a languid-looking young man with a pale moustache glanced up from his desk with tremendous disinterest.

'Second Lieutenant Mackinder, sir, reporting for duty,' the sergeant said.

The officer, who also wore the single pip – or star – of a subaltern on his epaulette, raised his eyebrows. 'Bit early, aren't you, old man? Weren't expecting you until tomorrow.'

'Well, I found I had a day to spare. . . .'

'And you're keen as mustard. Because your name's Mackinder.'

'My name is Mackinder, yes,' Murdoch said. He was beginning to bridle, and when he did that he suddenly looked older than his eighteen years. He was tall for his age and somewhat slenderly built, but there was clearly ample strength in the narrow frame, and he carried himself with the peculiar erectness that marks the born professional soldier. But it was his face which always attracted attention. It was a thin face, matching the body beneath, with unusually clipped features which made an attractive whole. His mouth was flat and strong, his complexion good, if a trifle pale, his hair was black and lank, and his eyes were a pale blue – normally cool, but occasionally, as now, distinctly cold.

'You can see the resemblance,' said his new acquaintance, glancing at the portrait which hung on the wall, opposite that of the Queen.

Murdoch followed his example and looked at his great-grandfather, General Sir Ian Mackinder, the hero of the famous charge in Baluchistan in 1843. A print of the same portrait hung in his mother's house.

'Hobbs is the name,' said the lieutenant, holding out his hand. 'Glad to have you with us, Mackinder. Forgive the chaff, but Mackinder is not a name we are ever allowed to forget about in this regiment.'

'Well, I apologise for that,' Murdoch said.

'Why should you? If my family virtually owned the regiment, I wouldn't complain.' Second Lieutenant Hobbs knocked on the inner door, waited a moment and then opened it. 'Mackinder is here, sir.'

'Mackinder?' asked a voice from inside. 'We weren't expecting him until tomorrow.'

Murdoch felt that his blood was about to crawl.

'Well, he's a keen type, sir,' Hobbs explained. 'Naturally.'

'Oh, show him in.'

Hobbs stepped aside and jerked his head towards the door.

Murdoch replaced his helmet, adjusted the chin strap, stepped through, came to attention and saluted. 'Second Lieutenant Murdoch Mackinder, sir, reporting for duty.'

'Hm,' remarked the man behind the desk. His moustache was bushy and wide and dark, and appeared to be his principal characteristic; now that he stood up he could be seen to be short and running to stomach. Like everyone else he wore the sky-blue uniform jacket of the regiment. 'Yes, you're Mackinder, all right. I knew your father.'

'Yes, sir.' Murdoch remained at attention; he knew he would have to accept this from virtually everyone he met.

'At ease. Craufurd's the name. Glad to have you with us, Mackinder.'

Murdoch removed his helmet and shook hands with the major; Craufurd wore a crown on his shoulder straps. 'Glad to be here, sir.'

The adjutant looked him up and down. 'The old man will see you in a minute. You knew we were under orders?'

'No, sir.' Murdoch was mystified, but at the same time immediately excited. 'Are we being sent back to India?'

'Hm,' Craufurd said again, not replying. 'How was Sandhurst?'

'I enjoyed it, sir.'

'I imagine you did. Sword of Honour, was it?'

'I was lucky, sir.'

Craufurd returned behind his desk, sat down and pointed. 'We don't believe in false modesty in this regiment, Mackinder.' He tapped himself on the left breast, where he wore the ribbon of the Military Cross. 'I won this for gallantry in the Khyber Pass. Under the command of your father, incidentally. If you won the Sword of Honour at Sandhurst, it was because you were the best damned officer in your class. Luck had nothing to do with it. And it is for that reason we are glad to have you here – not because your name happens to be Mackinder. Understood?'

Murdoch returned to attention. 'Yes, sir.'

'So come along and meet Colonel Edmonds.'

Another inner door was opened, and Murdoch found himself in an altogether larger office. Lieutenant-Colonel Claude Edmonds was as tall and slim as himself, although a good deal older. His left arm was stiff, a relic of a spear-thrust in the Afghan wars, and he was quite bald, but he looked fit and vigorous, and his handshake was firm. 'Murdoch Mackinder,' he said. 'Do you remember me?'

'I think so, sir,' Murdoch answered truthfully.

24

'Twelve years,' Edmonds said thoughtfully. 'You would have been . . . ?'

'I was six years old, sir, when you visited Broad Acres. You were Father's adjutant.'

'Indeed I was.' Edmonds looked him up and down. 'You've grown even more than I expected. How is your mother?'

'Well, sir. Lonely.'

'Quite,' Edmonds agreed. 'And your sisters? Ah, Philippa and . . . ?'

'Rosemary, sir. Rosemary is engaged to be married.'

'Of course she is, to Phillips of the Guards. I read it in *The Times*. Good fellow, Phillips. You must be pleased.'

'I was not actually consulted, sir.'

Edmonds raised his eyebrows. 'Difficult, I imagine, discovering yourself the head of the family when your sisters are older than yourself.'

'It can be, sir,' Murdoch agreed.

'Hm. Sit down. Cigarette?'

'Thank you, no, sir.' Murdoch carefully lowered himself into one of the straight chairs before the desk, his helmet on his knees. Major Craufurd had returned to the outer office.

'I was with your father on the march to Kandahar,' Edmonds said. 'I remember Bobs shaking him by the hand and congratulating him on the charge we carried out before Kabul.'

Murdoch waited. He could remember his father's pride at having been so singled out by the immortal 'Bobs' – Field Marshal Sir Frederick Roberts – now Lord Roberts – the idol of the British Army. But he knew what was coming next.

'And then I was with him when he died,' Edmonds said. 'Had no idea I would eventually inherit the regiment, of course. Damned nasty business, enteric fever. I want you to know he died as a Mackinder should, without fear, without regret. Save at not seeing you and your mother and the girls again, of course.'

'Thank you, sir,' Murdoch said.

'Damned unfortunate,' Edmonds went on. 'Forty-six years old, his whole career in front of him . . . India is a curse.'

He paused, and Murdoch waited. He had mixed emotions about his father's death four years before, while he was still at Wellington College, only a few miles from where he now stood; until he went to Sandhurst he had spent almost his entire life in the broad acres of Somerset, after which, indeed, his family home was named.

His father's personality, and the fact that he belonged to the Mackinder family, overshadowed his every moment. It meant that from the day of his birth he had not only been destined for the Army, but for this particular regiment – a fact of which he had been made aware while still in the nursery. His boyhood had been spent surrounded by the relics of the Mackinders' famous past: Grandfather Murdoch Mackinder's sword and helmet, Great-grandfather Ian Mackinder's medals for his Indian service, together with his sword and pistol and sky-blue jacket – the house had been like a museum. And of course there had been the famous prayer, which had been intoned on birthdays and other anniversaries. But Father himself, Lieutenant-Colonel Fergus Mackinder, had been a distant figure in every sense, most of the time with the regiment in India or Egypt or some other remote post of empire, only returning at long intervals to spend a few days with his family before setting off again. There had been little intimacy between father and son.

His death had made more of an impact because of the awesome responsibility it thrust on Murdoch's youthful shoulders. Immediately he had been reminded that he was the last male Mackinder, and that it was his duty to emulate and if possible surpass the great deeds of his ancestors. Driven by such a spur he had excelled himself at Sandhurst, gaining himself at the same time the reputation of being something of a loner who made friends with difficulty and preferred to work than to play. It was not a reputation that had concerned him. Play to Murdoch Mackinder had always been something to do in between periods of work, not the

26

other way around. His sole aim had been to achieve his rightful place in the regiment; that his single-minded devotion to his study and his duty had gained him the highest honour open to a cadet had seemed largely irrelevant at the time. As it seemed irrelevant now, in the euphoria of having actually arrived at his goal.

'You know we've been posted to the Cape?' Edmonds was asking.

'No, sir,' Murdoch replied. 'The Cape?'

'Makes a change from India, eh? It appears the Boers are still up in arms, literally, over the Jameson Raid and may need overaweing, so an army corps is being got together for despatch to South Africa. An army corps! Do you know that Great Britain has never put an army corps into the field before in all her history? Not for the Peninsular, and not for the Crimea. We are talking about forty thousand men or more – horse, foot, guns, medical and commissariat units, all combined as a single force. Redvers Buller will command. And all to overawe a few Dutch farmers.'

Murdoch made no comment. From what he knew of the subject, and it had been studied at Sandhurst, he considered that the Boers, the Dutch inhabitants of the South African republics of the Transvaal and the Orange Free State, had every reason to be up in arms. The absurd invasion of the Transvaal by five hundred men in 1895, led by Cecil Rhodes' friend Leander Starr Jameson, had been an act of naked aggression designed to create rebellion amongst the 'Uitlanders', the non-Boer, and chiefly British, labour force which had flooded to Johannesburg in response to the discovery of gold there ... no one could doubt that the eventual aim of the raid had been to foment a situation in which British interference on behalf of its nationals would have been justified, and annexation would have probably followed. That the rising had not materialised had proved what a haphazard and ill-considered venture the raid had been. The fact that the British Government, while officially condemning the act, had not actually punished the perpetrators must have increased the Boers' suspicions. Nor did he feel that the Boers, after their amazing victory over

27

a British force at Majuba Hill in 1881, could summarily be dismissed as mere farmers. But it was not his place to argue with his commanding officer.

'We are the advance guard of Buller's corps, you could say,' Edmonds continued. 'We sail in three weeks. I'm afraid it's all been rather sudden. But I don't imagine there will be much glory to be won marching across the veldt, while South Africa has just as much fever as India.' He looked embarrassed. 'If you would care to remain at the depot until you have found your feet, as it were, and come out with the first batch of replacements, I should regard that as a very wise decision.' His embarrassment grew visibly. This was the only son of his oldest friend and much revered commander, whom he was desperate not to lead to his death. But who was also a Mackinder.

'I would like to remain with the regiment, sir,' Murdoch said. 'But thank you.'

'Oh, quite. I never doubted you would wish to be with us. Well, then.' He became suddenly brisk and efficient. 'Your first responsibility will be to get yourself fitted out with tropical kit. Then you will take command of B Troop of the second squadron. That is Tom Holt's. He is an excellent man. And you'll have Sergeant Bishop. Another excellent man. Troop B is composed almost entirely of India veterans. They all knew your father. Well, most of them.'

'Yes, sir,' Murdoch said, with just a trace of uneasiness. If he had known, and accepted, that he would have to exist in the shadow of a dead man for at least the first half of his career, this seemed to be rather forcing the issue.

'You'll be given leave before we sail to return to Broad Acres and say goodbye to your mother and your sisters, of course. Oh, and I should mention that the regimental dinner has been brought forward. As the junior subaltern you'll have to make the toast. I suppose you do know the prayer?'

' "May the great God of battle," ' Murdoch said, looking across the faces of past and present officers of the regiment seated in the mess, ' "who has guided the fate of this famous regiment on many a hard-fought field, and never failed to lead it to distinction, grant that on this day, faced as we are with a host of enemies of our Queen and our country, every man will do his duty, so that should we fail in our ordained task, it will yet be said of us, they were the Royal Western Dragoon Guards, who fought and died according to the ancient valour of their regiment and their blood." ' He slightly lowered his sword to point it at the picture hanging on the wall behind Colonel Edmonds' head. ' "Gentlemen, there is your enemy." '

The swords were sheathed and the conversation became general. The evening was attended by a special air of conviviality because of the imminent departure of the regiment for service overseas.

'I'll wager you have repeated that prayer every day of your life,' remarked Second Lieutenant Hobbs.

'Why, yes, I have, almost,' Murdoch agreed.

'Which is why you were word perfect,' said Lieutenant Fielder. 'When I had to do it, my dear fellow, it was an absolute bloody shambles. Forgot the whole thing. Had to be prompted by the sergeant-major.'

'Ah,' Lieutenant Chapman said. 'But your name wasn't Mackinder, now was it?'

'No such luck,' Fielder agreed.

'Now, I have a wizard idea for after dinner. We're off in a week, right?' Chapman looked around the wine-reddened faces. 'I say, let's pool all the funds we've got and go into Bath, and knock up Kitty and her girls. Take the whole place over and have the lot. Have a real smash send-off.'

'Oh, indeed,' agreed Lieutenant Morton. 'I had that in mind anyway. But it'll be more fun in a group. How about it, Mackinder? Game for a quick in and out? You won't see a white fanny again for a good while.'

Morton was lieutenant in command of A Troop in Captain Holt's squadron, and had therefore assumed a rather proprietorial air towards the junior subaltern. But at the same time, the two men had taken an instant dislike to each other. Morton, short and stocky and moustached, had been taken aback – as had all the junior officers – by Murdoch's steely disinclination to accept any of the hazing

29

usual when a subaltern joined a regiment straight from military school; while Murdoch had quickly come to the conclusion that Morton did not take his duties seriously enough.

Therefore Murdoch had no doubt that the invitation was in the nature of a snare to create a joke at the expense of his inexperience. So he said, 'Thank you, no.'

Morton raised his eyebrows and glanced at his fellows. 'A cavalryman not interested in the fair sex?'

Hobbs shrugged. He and Murdoch had adjoining rooms in the bachelor quarters. 'He sits up most nights, reading.'

'Not Sherlock Holmes, I bet,' Chapman laughed.

'A book on Africa!' Hobbs said.

'Good Lord!' Fielder commented.

'It happens to be where we are going,' Murdoch pointed out. 'Don't you suppose it might be of some use to learn something about it?'

'Just Boers and blackamoors, old boy,' Chapman told him. 'Boers and blackamoors.'

'And bush and bugs,' Morton put in.

'But no bitches.'

'Oh, black bitches, old boy. Black bitches.'

'Have you ever had one?'

'Can't say I have.'

'But you were with the regiment in India, Morton,' Chapman said.

'Oh, quite. But they were brown, old boy. Brown. Mind you, how they could move their little arses. . . .'

'And they clapped you out,' Fielder laughed.

'Why, so they did. So they did. Which is why I'm for Kitty tonight. She's never given anyone the clap. How about it, Mackinder?'

'The answer is no,' Murdoch said again.

'Damn it, I do believe you're a virgin.'

'Is that criminal?'

Morton stared at him for a moment, then changed the subject, and Murdoch was pointedly excluded from the conversation.

This caused him less concern than might have been

30

supposed. Quite apart from Johnnie Morton, he had not been very taken with any of his fellow officers during his three weeks at the depot – at least the junior ones. A good many of his fellow cadets at Sandhurst seemed not to have realised they were no longer schoolboys, and that there were more important things in life than cricket or beer or women. But he expected better of those who had actually begun their careers, and even more of men, like Morton, who had been overseas with the regiment and presumably seen action. Certainly Morton seemed an efficient soldier, rode well, had his troop well in hand – but yet appeared to regard the daily grind as no more than that, to be got through so that the evenings could be enjoyed with cards and beer – and whenever possible, a visit to Bath. But he, like every officer in the regiment, was a young man with a career to make. Since the Cardwell reforms of a generation earlier, which had transformed the British Army into a modern fighting force, the old, iniquitous system of purchasing commissions had been swept away. Although several of the officers had the benefit of a private income to supplement their service pay, promotion was nowadays only to be had by hard work and ability. Which was probably why Morton was still a lieutenant despite being several years older than his friends; if he had the ability, he was too lazy to make use of it. But perhaps he would reveal a different, more positive side, once they were in the field.

On the other hand, Murdoch had quickly become impressed by the men under his command. Most of them, as Colonel Edmonds had indicated, were veterans of India, and some had indeed served under Fergus Mackinder. Murdoch knew they had not yet accepted him, and that he would have a good deal of proving to do. He did not doubt he would succeed; he had total confidence in himself, in his horsemanship, and in his knowledge of the military art, which he had studied as a hobby all of his life.

This understandably made him a dull boy to his fellows. He suspected he would be a dull boy to the famous Kitty as well, and knew he would probably have declined the invitation to visit the brothel even had he and Morton been

31

the best of friends. His upbringing had been distinctly Achillean; while surrounded by warlike instruments and memories, his daily company had been entirely that of his mother and sisters. As a result he had conceived an idealistic view of the female sex. He *was* a virgin, and had never considered altering that status before his wedding night, which, under army regulations, could not take place – except in the most exceptional circumstances and with the permission of his commanding officer – until he was thirty years old. That was a long twelve years off; before then he intended to do a lot of soldiering, and not change his direction just for the sake of personal popularity.

The dinner over, he began to walk back to the bachelor quarters, and suddenly found Colonel Edmonds beside him.

'You said the prayer splendidly, Mackinder.'

'Thank you, sir.'

'Mind you, I never doubted you would. And Holt seems pleased with you.'

'Does he, sir?' Murdoch was astonished. Captain Holt, a lean, saturnine man, had hardly addressed half a dozen words to him, except of command, during the three weeks he had been with the regiment.

'Oh, indeed. You're a soldier through and through. Well, you have to be; you're a Mackinder. But you know, Murdoch . . . soldiering, well, it's composed of camaraderie even more than discipline and ability and courage. When you're surrounded by enemies, it's reassuring to know that the chap standing next to you isn't just wearing the same uniform, but that he's also a friend who has shared your life at every level for the past few years. That kind of shared background is necessary to command, too. It's something none of us should ever forget. By the way, my wife would like you to come to tea tomorrow afternoon.'

'Thank you, sir.'

'Yes. Goodnight, Mackinder. You spoke the prayer splendidly.'

The colonel walked off towards his house, leaving Murdoch gazing after him. He had just been read a lecture because the old blighter had undoubtedly overheard some of the conversation at the foot of the table. Go out and visit the whores, the colonel had been telling him, because your fellow officers are doing that, and comradeship is everything. He wondered if Father, had he still been alive and therefore colonel of the regiment, would have told him to do that?

He went to bed.

The regimental band played the march from *Aida* as the Royal Western Dragoon Guards disembarked in Cape Town. For two days they had had the spectacular beauty of Table Mountain in view, and had been given an opportunity to recover somewhat from a very rough passage down the African coast, while preparations were made for their arrival. A long sea voyage with horses, especially when there was bad weather, was a trying business. Murdoch thought it was a tribute to Colonel Edmonds' efficiency that only half a dozen animals had been lost. The colonel might be a little too much of a father figure to inspire confidence in his ability to take hard decisions in battle; but that he was an experienced and capable soldier could not be doubted.

Officers and men and horses were all sorely in need of exercise; yet they put on a brave show, clad in their khaki tunics and topees – with the regimental flash stuck in the hatband – over their blue breeches and black boots, as they led their horses down the gang-plank. Each mount was fully accoutred, sword hanging on the left-hand side in a brown leather scabbard, rifle in a matching scabbard on the right, for the dragoons had begun life as mounted infantry, and even nowadays were trained to fight on foot with a facility equal to charging behind levelled swords. The troopers had bayonets on their hips, as the officers carried holstered revolvers at their waists, and they looked what they were: six hundred highly trained professional soldiers who had campaigned wherever the British Army had been employed during the previous two hundred years. Only the regimental ensign was missing; since the disaster of Majuba Hill in 1881, when the colours had been lost, the ensigns were never taken by regiments serving abroad; those of the

Western Dragoons had been stored for safe-keeping in Bath Abbey.

Murdoch, standing to attention in front of his men, was very aware of the huge crowd which had turned out on the quayside to watch the disembarkation. There were men, women and children, white, black and brown; and a good number of them, judging by the heavy beards of the men and the plump fairness of the women and children, were of Dutch extraction. Whether they were Boers and therefore qualified as potential enemies it was impossible to say.

'Prepare to mount.'

The men turned to their horses.

'Mount.'

The regiment swung into its saddles, and the crowd clapped its appreciation of the precision with which the manoeuvre was carried out. The band struck up another march, Colonel Edmonds raised his arm and in a long double column the three squadrons walked their horses on to the road and began their parade through the streets of the city. These too were lined with people, most cheering now at the sight of these first representatives of the might of Great Britain arriving to protect them from any invaders. Outside Government House it was eyes right for a salute to the Governor himself. Then, mercifully – for now it was all but noon and the sun was blazing down – they were beyond the houses and into the encampment. The long rows of orderly white tents gleaming in the sun had been organised by Craufurd and Hobbs and the regimental commissariat, who had gone ashore the previous day.

Here Murdoch surveyed the eighty-odd men of his command. 'That was smartly done,' he said. 'My congratulations, Sergeant Bishop.'

'Sir!' The sergeant came to attention. He was a large, heavy man with considerable service behind him, and in the beginning he, like the troopers under his command, had been more than a little suspicious of the young officer, a tyro with a famous name who would no doubt wish to behave in a famous way.

There had been little time for the men to get to know

their new officer before leaving England, but on the voyage out they had begun to appreciate some of his worth, at any rate. They could not help but respond to his care for them, the way he minutely inspected every aspect of their quarters and their food, listened to their complaints, spent a large part of every day with their horses making sure all was well and, in the storm they had encountered off the Guinea Coast, had indeed spent two whole days helping to calm the terrified animals. They had been less appreciative of his insistence that every day the whole troop should turn out for physical exercises on the well deck, pointing out in low grumbles that none of their comrades were exposed to quite such treatment. But Murdoch had refused to be deflected from his determination to have the fittest troop in the regiment, and they had had to accept the situation.

Now that they were ashore, and actually on a campaign, however, they were again regarding him somewhat quizzically; they knew more about this business than he did.

'Once the horses have been rubbed down and staked, sergeant, the men will take their tents,' Murdoch said. 'I will hold an inspection this afternoon at four. Commencing tomorrow morning at dawn, we will exercise the horses.'

'At dawn, sir?'

'The coolest part of the day, sergeant. Rifle practice and sword drill can come later. Understood?'

'Sir.'

'Very good. Troop dismissed.'

He saluted his men as they turned to their left and fell out, leading their horses to the water troughs and then the picket lines. Murdoch's batman, Trooper Reynolds, was waiting to take his mount.

'Don't know what living conditions are going to be like here, Mr Mackinder,' he said. He was a small man with a huge moustache, who, having served under Fergus Mackinder, had virtually adopted Murdoch from the moment of their first meeting. With his experience and his innate good humour and common sense he was a very valuable man to have around, Murdoch discovered; he was, he supposed somewhat ruefully, the nearest thing to a friend he possessed in the regiment. 'There seems an awful lot of creepy-crawlies,' he remarked.

Bugs and Boers and black bottoms, Murdoch thought, recalling the regimental dinner. 'I imagine we will have to learn to live with the bugs, Reynolds,' he said, and went across to the large headquarters tent, above which the Union Jack was already flying. Here Colonel Edmonds was surveying his officers and, beyond them, the country, which was undulating, green and altogether attractive.

'It won't be like this up-country,' he warned, somewhat gloomily. 'From all accounts it is brown and arid, and very hilly. Now, gentlemen, our original orders were to proceed to the rail junction at De Aar, close to the frontier of the Orange Free State, in order to reinforce the garrison there, just as rapidly as possible. However, the Governor has seen fit to countermand these; he wishes us to remain here for a while, both to reassure the population and because he is afraid that any strengthening of the garrison at De Aar would offer provocation to the Boers. I have to say that I would have thought provoking the Boers is the very last thing we should be worrying about, but there it is; we must keep the civil authorities happy. And a short stay here will enable us to get the men and the horses back into peak condition.'

'What is the news, sir?' asked Lieutenant Morton. 'Is there going to be a war?'

'I doubt it,' the colonel replied. 'I don't see even Kruger being fool enough to take on the British Army. But this is not to say that we can regard ourselves as being on holiday. I want every troop in the field tomorrow, exercising those horses. Understood?'

'Yes, sir,' they chorused.

'But for the time being,' Edmonds grinned, 'it will be permitted to take a look at Cape Town.'

'Which is what I am going to do this evening,' Johnnie Morton confided as the junior officers dispersed. 'Some of those girls cheering us this morning, damn it, they were just juicy. I don't suppose you noticed, Mackinder.'

'No,' Murdoch said. 'I didn't.'

36

Morton walked away with Chapman and Fielder; Murdoch went towards Trooper Reynolds, who was waiting with his gear before the tiny tent that he was apparently to call home for the foreseeable future.

Murdoch understood that he had become an object of contempt to his fellow officers, even if he felt he was beginning to earn the respect of his men. But that respect remained grudging, even on the part of Sergeant Bishop, because he had not yet led them into action. Did he wish to do that? As a professional soldier he would have to, eventually, so probably the sooner the better. Yet he felt an odd reluctance actually to engage the Boers. He tried to remind himself that this was because there would hardly be any glory, as Colonel Edmonds had suggested, in leading his men against a handful of farmers who knew nothing of modern warfare and wished only to preserve their lands and their way of life – even if they had once destroyed a poorly led British army. Had it been the Afghans now, traditional enemies of the British in India, or the Dervishes in the Sudan, or even a European enemy, like the French . . . he wasn't sure that he would be able to attack the Boers with the certainty and determination that would be required. On that test would lie his ability to win his men.

And his place amongst his fellow officers? That he doubted. He had set out to establish himself as a person from the first moment inside the depot near Bath, but he would admit that he had chosen a hard and sometimes despairing, path to follow. Being entirely friendless in the midst of several hundred men was an intensely lonely business. He was not given to too much introspection, feeling that it led to depression, but it was none the less galling to be deliberately left out of all group activities shared by his brother officers – even those he would have enjoyed – simply because he would not partake in those he felt distasteful.

The colonel's remarks on the evening of the regimental dinner had stuck in his mind. When they finally went into action it would certainly be a splendid thing to feel that

Johnnie Morton would be thinking with the same mind. Professionally, of course, they would do so. They had both gone through the same training, studied the same books. And Morton was certainly respected by his men; he had been with them in India and had been under fire, too. Yet it was impossible to feel any affinity for him, as either a man or an officer; he left the care of his people to his sergeant and seemed interested in soldiering only as a means to enjoy life.

Yet he was the most popular officer in the regiment, so no doubt Colonel Edmonds was right after all.

That evening Murdoch almost surrendered and asked if he could accompany Morton, Chapman, Hobbs and Fielder when they set off for the city. He didn't, partly because he still did not wish to compromise his principles – and in any event had no desire to be thrust forward as a sacrificial virgin by his fellows – and partly because he suspected they might refuse his company. So he remained in the camp and read his history of South Africa, and tried to envisage what the country to the north of Cape Town, with its 'drifts' and 'kopjes' might be like ... and found himself wondering what the happy, jolly, plump Dutch girls of Cape Town might be like as well. It was the first time in his life he had ever really had a yen to go out and find himself a woman. And he simply did not know how to begin.

Over the next few days, exercising the troop and the mounts, he was keenly aware that he was under the constant, distant, supervision of both Colonel Edmonds and Captain Holt. It was hot, exhausting work in the semi-tropical sun, but he kept his men at it longer than any other subaltern. Quite apart from wishing to occupy himself, he was certain they were going to need absolute fitness to campaign in the rough country that lay up north. The men grumbled, but he just smiled at them and made them do it all one more time.

He was surprised at the end of the first week when he found Captain Holt waiting for him as he finally dismissed the troop. 'I would take things just a little more easily, Mackinder,' Holt remarked. 'You have a fine body of men

38

there, but it is possible to hone them to too sharp an edge, as one can do with a sword; the blade begins to wear away.'

Although Colonel Edmonds had suggested back in Bath that Holt was pleased with his work, this was the first time that the captain had ever addressed more than half a dozen consecutive words to him, and Murdoch was considerably taken aback. He knew, of course, that Holt seldom spoke to anyone. Nevertheless, he had been just a little disconcerted at his captain's apparent lack of interest, and now, to be told off for working his men. . . .

'We must assume we are here to fight a war, sir,' he said. 'That is hardly a matter one can take lightly.'

Holt frowned at him. 'We're not at war yet, Mackinder,' he pointed out. 'But *you* want to take it more lightly, certainly. Next thing you'll be down with heat exhaustion, and we can't replace officers all that easily. Not good ones,' he added.

Murdoch turned his head sharply.

Holt grinned at him. 'I gather you prefer your own company,' he said. 'However, if you can stand it, I'm going into Cape Town this evening for a jar or two. Care to join me?'

Murdoch hesitated only a moment; Holt was as different as could be from Morton, therefore his tastes would be different too. 'I'd be delighted, sir.'

'Then have a shave and put on your undress, and meet me at the gate in an hour.'

They rode remounts. Murdoch had had to come to grips with a strange horse when he joined the regiment and settled for Edward IV, a powerful black gelding who rode like a steeplechaser; but Edward had been out all day with the troop and needed a rest. Besides, they were going to explore Cape Town, not take it by assault.

Holt led him on a tour of the saloons, less interested in drink than in conversation about the place and the people and their prospects. Cape Town was still very much a frontier town, although with some pretensions to beauty, and with some long-established residential areas as well. These apparently did not attract Holt, who preferred to investigate the commercial centre, surveying the various bar patrons they encountered with his sardonic expression.

'It seems odd,' he remarked, 'that we should have been sent here to fight against the Boers, perhaps, and here we are surrounded by them. Of course, you have the same thing in India, where you never really know whether the johnnie you are speaking to in the street is an Afghan or a Pathan waiting to stab you in the back. But somehow one expects it to be different, where white people are concerned. I wonder how loyal these people would be if it were to come to blows.'

'Do you think it'll come to blows?' Murdoch asked.

'I think it very well might,' Holt said. 'We're not inclined to learn by our mistakes, unfortunately. We provoked the American colonists to armed resistance, a hundred and twenty-five years ago, and got a bloody nose. Of course, we seem to be taking things a little more seriously this time, and when Buller gets his army corps assembled here in the Cape things may look different, but it's entirely possible the Boers do not realise the force that is being mustered against them.'

'So if they start something, it'll be murder,' Murdoch suggested. 'I mean, I know they licked Colley at Majuba Hill in eighty-one, but, well. . . .'

Holt grinned. 'Don't be too afraid to speak ill of your betters. Colley was incompetent. Oh, indeed he was. Let us hope Buller is not.'

'I understand Buller is very highly thought of.'

'Oh, indeed he is. Victoria Cross, experience in Africa, but fighting darkies armed with spears and muzzle loaders, unfortunately . . . we shall have to see. Have another beer.'

'Mine this time.' Murdoch signalled the waiter, feeling more at home than at any moment since he had first joined the regiment. He noticed a young man looking at him, only a couple of years older than himself, he estimated, tall and powerfully built, with broad, strong features topped by a mass of curly yellow hair. Now the young man realised he had been discovered, and gave a brief bow, moving his feet almost as if he would have clicked his heels.

'Forgive me,' he said, speaking English with just a hint of an accent. 'I was admiring your uniforms.' Both Murdoch and Holt wore the pale blue undress jacket of the regiment. 'May I say that they do not look British?'

'Well, they are,' Holt said.

The young man came closer. 'So I have heard. The Royal Western Dragoon Guards, recently arrived from England. A very famous regiment. My name is Paul Reger.'

'Murdoch Mackinder,' Murdoch said.

'Tom Holt,' Holt grunted. 'Are you Dutch, sir?'

'No, captain. I am German. But I am on my way to Johannesburg.'

'To earn your fortune,' Murdoch suggested.

'I hope so. But really, my uncle has a share in a gold mine there,' Reger told them. 'Which I have been appointed to look into. But I am interested in military matters. I have done my service with the colours. Do you mind if I join you?' He signalled the waiter to bring more drinks.

Holt shrugged his agreement. Murdoch was more obviously welcoming; he rather liked the look of this young man.

Reger sat down, and paid for the next round. 'I too served with the cavalry, in Germany,' he said. 'The 9th Uhlans. Perhaps you have heard of them.'

'I have heard of the Uhlans,' Holt said. 'A famous body of men.'

'But you have left them?' Murdoch asked.

'Well, I have done my service. Now I am in the reserve.'

'Oh, I see; you were a conscript.' The concept was foreign to his way of thinking. 'Then you mean that if there was a war, you would be recalled to the colours?'

'Of course.'

'Yet you have been allowed to go off to remote corners of the globe, like Johannesburg?'

Reger smiled. 'Why not? Germany is not at war. Nor likely to be, in our lifetimes.'

'Oh, quite.'

'Do you suppose it would be possible to visit your camp?' Reger asked. 'I should very much like to see the British cavalry at work.'

Murdoch looked at Holt, who gave another shrug. 'We have nothing to hide, mein Herr. If you are going up to the Transvaal, perhaps you'll tell the Boers of the strength we possess down here.'

'I shall certainly do that, Captain Holt,' Reger agreed.

They spent a convivial evening, with the young German proving the best of companions, able to discuss music and art, drama and politics with as much facility as he talked about military matters. Murdoch suspected that there might be a good deal more to him, and his background, than he was prepared to admit. He spoke of his uncle's estate in East Prussia, and mentioned several well known German personalities as if he had met them – but he was also totally unlike the average British concept of a Prussian junker, friendly and outgoing rather than stiff and formal, and not in the least offended by some of Holt's rather blunt remarks or questions as the beer flowed. 'If you were at university, mein Herr,' the captain remarked after his tenth pint, 'why do you not have a duelling scar? I thought all German students carried a duelling scar.'

Reger gave one of his easy smiles. 'Simply because I never encountered anyone sufficiently my superior with the sabre to give me one, captain.'

Holt raised his eyebrows at Murdoch. But Murdoch was inclined to believe their new friend.

Next day Reger arrived at the camp, riding a hired horse, and after being introduced to Colonel Edmonds, went out with Murdoch to watch the troop being exercised. Colonel Edmonds seemed very pleased to see him; like most Englishmen in 1899, he regarded the close friendship between Germany and Britain, based on the relationship between Kaiser Wilhelm II and the British royal family – he was grandson of Queen Victoria and nephew of the Prince of Wales – as the ultimate factor in preserving the peace of Europe, and thus the world.

Murdoch was also delighted to see him; he had seldom enjoyed an evening more, and from being friendless, had suddenly acquired two very good friends indeed, both men he could respect and admire. That morning he really put the troop through its paces. It was a rifle exercise, in which the entire squadron galloped to an appointed place, halted at the blast of a trumpet, drawing their rifles from the saddle holsters as they did so, and sought shelter along the banks of a stream, falling into their places with the minimum of orders as they had been taught to do in England, and lying prone, delivered a first volley of blank shot. Holt stood over them, stop-watch in hand; Morton and Murdoch actually manoeuvred with their troops, but joined the captain after the volley.

'Three minutes, B Troop,' Holt said. 'Three and a half minutes, A Troop. You have some work to do, Morton. But I would like it down to two and a half minutes for each troop, if you don't mind, from the moment the order to dismount is given to the firing of the first volley. Fall out your men for ten minutes, then we'll try it again.'

Their batmen poured coffee, and they sat on the dry grass while Holt and Morton smoked cigarettes; the squadron was brewing up a hundred yards away, and the farriers were busy with nosebags for the horses.

'An interesting manoeuvre,' Reger commented. 'I have never seen cavalry double as infantry before.'

'Ah, but that is what being a dragoon is all about,' Murdoch explained. 'We were raised in the first instance as mounted infantry. That's why we carry swords instead of sabres, and rifles instead of carbines. What weapons do the Uhlans carry?'

'Lances and swords,' Reger said. 'The German army has no equivalent of your dragoons.' He grinned. 'Perhaps I shall recommend the adoption of such tactics to General von Schlieffen when next I am in Berlin. And these are all professional soldiers?'

'Oh, indeed,' Morton told him. 'No conscripts in the British Army, mein Herr.'

Morton did not take to the young German, any more than he had appreciated being told his troop had been slow to manoeuvre. But Murdoch continued to find Reger a most pleasant companion, and over the next few weeks saw a great deal of him. Reger invited him to the house at which he was staying in Cape Town. It belonged to a merchant named Dredge, who had apparently had dealings with Germany in the past, and Reger had been given a letter of introduction to him by a friend of his family. William Dredge had a Yorkshireman's eye for making a profit, and had done very well for himself in South Africa; his house was large and comfortable, and had an extensive garden at the back.

His wife, considerably larger than her husband, was also a comfortable woman, and they possessed an attractive daughter, Rosetta, who was plump and cheerful like her mother, and clearly delighted to find herself in the company of two handsome young men. Rosetta Dredge, however, soon made it clear she had eyes only for the handsome blond German, who was at once older and more knowledgeable than Murdoch.

Murdoch did not begrudge him his conquest. He liked him too much. And the feeling was apparently reciprocated. Reger even pretended envy. 'To belong to such a family,' he said, 'why, I would like that more than anything else in the world.'

'To have to live your entire life in the shadow of your ancestors?' Murdoch smiled.

'Don't we all do that, anyway?' Reger countered. 'It is better at least to know and admire them, and have goals at which to aim in emulating them, than to exist adrift from the past, like a rudderless ship at the mercy of every change of current, every gust of wind. It is purpose which matters in this life, my friend. Purpose.'

Murdoch was quite sorry when, three days later, Reger took his leave. 'You have been most kind to me, Murdoch,' he said. 'I am grateful. If you are ever in Johannesburg, please visit me. I shall endeavour to repay your hospitality. But now I must be on my way.'

'I don't know how soon I will get to Johannesburg,' Murdoch said. 'It depends on how the situation develops here. But I would like to keep in touch. If you will write me from Johannesburg, giving me your address, I will certainly reply.'

Reger clasped his hand. 'Why, I shall do that. I have promised to write to Rosetta in any event. Expect to hear from me within a month.'

But before the month had elapsed the Boers had issued an ultimatum, demanding that the British cease building up their military establishment in South Africa, and two days later, no satisfactory reply having been received, they declared war.

2

The Modder River, 1899

There was tremendous excitement in Cape Town as the news came through that the Boers had made several simultaneous attacks, both to the east and west of their centrally placed republics, had invested the towns of Kimberley and Mafeking, and were even invading Natal. 'Of course, Sir George White commands in Natal,' Colonel Edmonds told his officers. 'With a strong force of regulars. He'll stop them, no doubt about that.'

'Are we going there, sir?' Chapman asked.

'No. Our business is to defend Cape Colony until the arrival of General Buller and the rest of the corps. The plan, as I understand it, will then be to invade the Orange Free State from the south and west, relieve Mafeking and Kimberley, and simply roll up the Boers against White's force in Natal.'

'But if Sir George White really smashes them and they make peace,' Morton protested, 'we won't even get a look in.'

'You'll get your look in,' Edmonds promised him. 'When General Buller gets here. It is his intention to dictate peace in Johannesburg. You'll get your look in.'

Murdoch wondered where Reger was, if he had reached his destination before hostilities had commenced, and what he would feel about a British army marching into Johannesburg to dictate peace. He decided to see if Rosetta had heard anything of him and took himself into town.

He found Mrs Dredge in a state of high indignation. 'That President Kruger,' she declared, 'I always knew he was not to be trusted. You can see it in his face. I mean, going to war like this. Giving *us* an ultimatum! I hope they put him in prison.'

'They have to catch him first,' her husband remarked.

'Will the Boers invade Cape Colony, Murdoch?' Rosetta asked, her huge eyes glooming at him.

'There's little chance of that,' he promised her. 'Not with us here.'

'It is so reassuring, having an English regiment actually camped outside the town,' Mrs Dredge agreed. 'Why don't you take Mr Mackinder for a walk in the garden, Rosetta?'

Murdoch took the hint and escorted the young lady outside, into the cool of the evening, when within seconds they were out of sight of the house behind a stand of tall cypresses. 'Have you heard from Paul?' he asked.

'Oh, no. I did not really expect to, whatever he promised. Have you?'

'No. I suppose there is no way a letter could get through, now. I hope he is all right.'

'Why should he not be?'

'Well, he's in an alien country, in time of war. . . .'

'You liked him, didn't you?' she asked, gazing at the ground as they walked.

'Why, yes, I did, very much. Didn't you?'

'Oh.' She gave a little shiver. 'He frightened me.'

'Frightened you?'

'He could be so intense. So. . . .' She glanced at him, blushing prettily. 'Not like you.'

'You don't find me intense?' He had always thought of himself as a most intense person.

Rosetta gave a pretty little laugh. 'You? Oh, you are just sweet.'

'Oh,' he said, somewhat disconcerted.

'And far too handsome to be a soldier.'

'Oh,' he said again, more disconcerted yet.

'Now I have been improper. It's just that . . . will you really have to go and fight, Murdoch?'

'Well, I sincerely hope so. I mean, this is what we came all this way for.'

'But isn't it better not to fight?'

'Well . . . I suppose, if the other fellow surrenders. But

47

if he always did that, where would one get any glory? Achieve any fame?'

'Oh, you men!' She threw both arms round his neck and kissed him on the mouth. For a moment he was too surprised to react, then his arms went round her and he held her against him, discovering for the first time in his life all the beauty of a woman in his arms. She stayed there for several seconds, moving her body against his, making him more aware of himself than he had ever been before, then she pulled away, her cheeks pink. 'Will you come to see me again tomorrow?' she asked, panting.

'Well, of course. If I can. But. . . .'

'If you could come in the afternoon,' she said, 'Mother goes to her whist game every Tuesday afternoon. And Father will be at the office.' Her cheeks were pinker yet, and her breasts were heaving.

'Oh, I. . . .' He didn't know what to say. He hadn't expected anything quite so sudden and so determined, and he was in any event utterly confused.

'You might be going to get killed,' she pointed out.

'Oh. Yes, I suppose I might. But what about Paul?'

'Oh, him . . . he's a German. He can get killed any time he likes.' She kissed him again. 'Tomorrow,' she said. 'About three. Don't worry about the servants. I'll send them away.'

He returned to camp in a mood half of euphoria and half of alarm. It was not merely the newness of the experience for him, the amazing realisation that he had indeed taken a giant step beyond the ken of Messrs Morton, Hobbs and Chapman, so much as the revelation that this delightful bundle of femininity actually seemed to find him more attractive than Paul Reger – something he could never have believed had he not had the evidence of his own senses. And now she wanted . . . he was not at all sure *what* she wanted. But he couldn't help feeling that she was going to get it, and that once she had she would regard him as entirely hers. He went to bed uncertain what he wanted most, to ride up to the frontier as quickly as possible to fight the Boers, or remain here and enjoy Rosetta Dredge.

The decision was made for him the following morning, when the officers were assembled by Colonel Edmonds to hear some very grave news.

'Word has just been received from Natal,' the colonel told them, 'that the situation there is extremely serious. The so-called victories which Sir George White claimed at Elandslaagte and Talana were mirages. The Boers were apparently not actually beaten, but merely withdrew and regrouped. It seems that they possess some keen tactical brains under those slouch hats. Anyway, the long and the short of it is that Sir George White, far from driving the invaders out of the colony, has reported that he is himself now bottled up in Ladysmith by superior Boer forces.' He raised his head to look at the faces in front of him. 'In fact, gentlemen, apart from some isolated units in Natal, and the small garrisons at De Aar and Belmont along the railway line, this regiment is the only British force in South Africa which possesses any freedom of movement. In these circumstances, I have been instructed by the Governor of Cape Colony to revert to my original orders, and proceed to De Aar as rapidly as possible, both to reinforce the garrison there, and to repel the Boer invasion, which can be expected at any moment, following their success in the east. The regiment will therefore move out at dawn.'

'But shouldn't we be moving to Natal, to help Sir George White?' inquired Lieutenant Chapman.

'Sir George White is quite confident of holding Ladysmith until the arrival of reinforcements,' Edmonds told him. 'He commands several thousand men. No, no, despite these temporary Boer victories, I have no doubt that Sir Redvers Buller, who will be in the Cape any day now, will hold to the original plan and use his army corps to attack the Boers from the west. That is the quickest and surest way to relieve the pressure on Natal. Our immediate duty is to secure the railway and the border, and await the arrival of the rest of the corps. Prepare your commands, gentlemen. And as of this moment, all leave is cancelled.'

'You won't be able to say goodbye to your little friend,' Morton remarked as they walked back to their tents.

'I have already done so,' Murdoch lied. He had had no idea Morton even knew where he went on his visits to town.

'Quite a dark horse, aren't you, old man,' Morton commented. 'Where do you suppose your German friend is now?'

'Probably with the Boers.'

'Well, then, I may have the pleasure of putting a bullet through his brain. Or would you rather have that privilege?'

'I am sure you will do it very well,' Murdoch replied, determined to be quite as relaxed about the whole thing as his more experienced compatriot.

The journey north was to be undertaken by the Cape Railway. Several armoured trucks had been provided in which men and horses could be sheltered from any Boer sharpshooters. The procedure was that five troops were taken in the train, and one troop, rotated daily, rode out ahead as an advance guard and to make sure no one interfered with the track.

It took the regiment ten days to reach De Aar junction, as they covered no more than sixty miles a day, owing to the required stoppages for water and to exercise the horses – but of course even this was far faster than they could have ridden and still arrived in a fit state for action. And it was a most delightful journey. The first two days, where the line from Cape Town took an odd turn up to Gouda in the north-west, were through rolling grasslands, such as the country in which they had spent the last month, but as they reached Worcester on the second afternoon, they were already nearly a thousand feet above sea level, with much higher mountains – the Hexrivierberge to their left and the peak of Keeromsberg to their right – towering above them. Wherever they passed a settlement or a station there were cheering crowds gathered by the line to wave them on, but they could never forget, both from the names of most of the villages and the complexions of most of the people, that they were already in Boer country, even if these Boers were living in apparent contentment under British rule.

Next day the line crawled up into the mountains proper, and there were fewer people to be seen. Now they looked up at great peaks such as the Matroosberg of more than twenty thousand feet. On the fifth day, after leaving Laingsburg, they emerged on to the plain of the Great Karroo, well over a thousand feet above sea level, ringed by far higher peaks, and yet a totally monotonous carpet of grassland which seemed to stretch forever. Here humanity was almost non-existent, as was fresh water, although they saw huge areas of salt-pans shimmering in the midday heat. The horses suffered badly.

Murdoch was surprised by the scarcity of game, although he realised that the scrub-like vegetation would hardly support any large numbers of animals. He had hoped to see some lion, but if there were any on the high veldt, they were keeping away from the railway track and the puffing train. In any event, he was more concerned with the coming day, when, as junior subaltern, he would finally lead his troop out as the advance guard.

They spent the fifth night at Beaufort West Station, where the mountains before them seemed to form a solid wall, and next morning, when the train had been watered, B Troop was called out by bugle and stood to their horses.

'Your orders are as before, Lieutenant Mackinder,' said Major Craufurd. 'You will proceed ten miles in front of the train, with flankers out, and you will ascertain that the track remains in good order and that there are no enemy forces in the vicinity.'

'Yes, sir.' Murdoch saluted, and faced his men. 'Prepare to mount.' The troop turned. 'Mount.'

The men swung into the saddle, Sergeant Bishop closed up behind him, and in column of twos they walked out of the little village, followed for the first half a mile by several small black boys and an equal number of yapping dogs. 'Send your flankers out, Sergeant Bishop,' Murdoch said.

'Yes, sir,' Bishop acknowledged, and fell back to give the necessary orders, while Murdoch gazed at the scrub and the rising land in front of him in a sudden thrill of excitement. This was the first time he had been in independent command of his troop, other than on a field exercise. He watched two vultures soar out of some rocks perhaps half a mile away, and felt an immediate tightening of his muscles, an increase in his heartbeat. Of course they had not seen a sign of an enemy since leaving Cape Town, but they were certainly approaching closer to the frontier with every day, and no one knew for certain where the Boers actually were; this line stretched all the way to Kimberley and then Mafeking, following as it did the western boundary of the Orange Free State. If the Boers were considering an invasion of Cape Colony, and had pushed out their patrols south of the Orange River, there was no telling when he might be fired on; he kept mentally rehearsing all the drill he had learned and committed to memory, over and over again.

He was quite startled to hear the drumming of hooves behind him, and turned to see Tom Holt cantering up. 'Do you mind if I ride along with you, Mackinder?' the captain asked. 'Strictly for the exercise; it's your show. But I find that train unbearably warm.'

'I'd be obliged, sir,' Murdoch said, even if he knew Holt was really here just to oversee his progress on this first day. Well, he was not altogether sorry to have his senior with him, just in case.

They rode into the hills, exchanging flankers every hour to keep in touch with the advanced riders. They paused for luncheon on a hummock, looking back down at the track and the train, almost a toy behind and below them as it crawled up the escarpment.

'It really is a joy to be alive,' Murdoch said, looking up at the perfect blue of the sky only occasionally dotted with hovering white cloud. 'Even the heat is just about perfect.'

'This has got to be the best defensive country in the world,' Holt observed. 'Very like the North-West Frontier, in fact. Let's hope the Boers don't shoot any more straight than the Afghans.'

'What's it like?' Murdoch asked without thinking, immediately wishing he had kept quiet.

But Holt showed no embarrassment, either personally or for the innocence revealed by the question. 'It's like nothing,' he said. 'Right now, if you knew those hills were filled with Boers, and that you were the party sent out to draw their fire, your throat would be dry and you'd have wind.'

'Yes,' Murdoch agreed, because that exactly described his physical state at that moment, and he had to suppose the hills were empty.

'But as soon as your first shot is fired,' Holt told him, 'all that goes. Then you become a machine, remembering only your training, what needs to be done.'

'Does everyone react that way?'

Holt glanced at him. 'No. Not everyone. There is a sour apple in every barrel. Sometimes two.'

'But no one knows he's a sour apple until the actual moment.'

'I suppose you're right.' He slapped the boy on the shoulder. 'I wouldn't worry about it, Murdoch. Not with your pedigree.' He finished his coffee and handed the cup to the waiting Reynolds. 'Let's move out.'

Two days later, after penetrating the mountains and passing beneath the strangely shaped peak called the Horseshoe, they crossed the Brak River, itself a tributary of the Orange River, and arrived at De Aar junction, to the great relief of the small garrison there. This consisted of four companies of the Lancashire Regiment, unsupported by any cavalry or artillery, and yet obliged to guard not only the vital junction, from whence branch lines ran off to the east, but also a vast quantity of military stores and equipment.

'I tell you, colonel,' said Major Wilmot, 'I am only amazed that the Boers have not come down here and seized the junction and us with it. Or blown us out of existence.'

'Do they have that kind of artillery?' Edmonds asked.

'Oh, indeed. They have some Creusot guns, twenty-four pounders. And of course there is no question but that the population around here is wholly in sympathy with them. The sooner we get Buller's entire force up here the better.'

As there seemed no doubt that the Boers were going to defend the line of the Orange River, Colonel Edmonds determined on a reconnaissance, and out went Captain Rodgers' squadron, with Lieutenants Chapman and Fielder. Murdoch was disappointed at being denied this first opportunity to exchange fire with the enemy. He waited anxiously with the remainder of the regiment for the return of their comrades. especially when they heard the sound of rifle-fire to the north.

The squadron returned the following day with the news that they had encountered a Boer commando, albeit a small one, and exchanged fire; three men had been wounded, and Rodgers claimed that several of the Boers had been hit, but the firing had been at long range and both sides had withdrawn. More important, the captain reported that the track had been torn up in several places, but he suspected this was more likely to have been the work of local, officially British, Boers rather than the enemy.

But they were in touch at last. That night there was high expectation in the British camp, the more so as news arrived via the telegraph from Cape Town that the rest of the army corps had at last arrived in South Africa, and a victorious advance could now surely be anticipated.

Murdoch used the first spare time he had had in a fortnight to write to his mother and sisters. He did his best to describe the vast country over which he had travelled, to give them some idea of the heat, and of the first black people he had encountered. They seemed amazingly docile, and he found their attitude difficult to reconcile with what he had learnt at Sandhurst of the campaigns against the Zulu and the Matabele, hardly a generation before, which had involved some of the hardest fighting in British history; certainly the Africans seemed determined not to become involved in this entirely white war.

He also considered writing to Rosetta Dredge, whom he felt he owed some kind of an explanation. But he had no idea how to begin what would have to be some kind of a love letter, and decided to shelve it for a few days more. Before he got around to it, the entire situation changed; the whole plan had been dissipated. Instead of moving forward up the railway in a vast compact mass of forty thousand men, against which surely the Boers would be unable to stand, Sir Redvers Buller had allowed himself to be distracted by the cries for help from the Government of Natal. Committing the most elementary of military errors, he had divided his forces, taken the bulk of the corps on to Durban to effect the relief of Ladysmith, and left one of his subordinate generals, Lord Methuen, to take command of a single division and move up the railway to the relief of Kimberley and then Mafeking.

'Well, gentlemen,' Colonel Edmonds told his officers, 'we must assume that General Buller knows what he is about, and I personally am confident that Lord Methuen will have ample forces with which to chase these farmers back where they belong.'

Or so we must hope, Murdoch thought. 'What do you think?' he asked Holt, with whom he was now firm friends.

'That Buller has made a mistake,' Holt agreed. 'But at least we are going to see some action at last.'

They saw action sooner than they had expected. Lord Methuen arrived at De Aar a few days later, and even Murdoch, prepared to be sceptical about any commanding officer after Buller's flagrant disregard of the rules of war, had to be impressed by the tall, powerful-looking, soldierly figure. The general was a champion fencer and boxer as well as a superb horseman, and had seen much service in India. He summoned his colonels, for he now had command of some ten thousand men, even if the main bodies had not yet arrived, and listened to Edmonds' report on the situation.

'Very good, colonel,' he said. 'It would appear from what you say that the Boers have wholly committed themselves to their campaign in Natal, or there would surely have been more activity in this theatre. Our first task must be to take advantage of this weakness in their dispositions, and as soon as the whole division is concentrated, I propose to push up to and seize the line of the Orange River, from which a march on Kimberley should be feasible. However, from everything I have heard about these Dutch gentlemen, it would seem that they are capable guerilla fighters and may well be hoping to surprise us.

'We will therefore begin with a reconaissance in force. Brigade strength will be necessary, I think, and as you are already acquainted with the situation here, I wish you to command it. You will take two squadrons of your regiment, two companies of mounted infantry, and three guns. An armoured train will support you, and will contain engineers, as I wish the line repaired wherever necessary. Your objectives will be any sizeable Boer force, or failing that, the Orange River and then the Modder. Once we are across the Modder, Kimberley is only twelve miles away. Should you encounter an enemy force considerably stronger than your own, however, you will not engage, but will fall back on the division; when we fight these fellows we want to smash them once and for all. Understood?'

'Yes, sir,' Edmonds acknowledged, delighted at having been given brigadier rank, however temporarily. So was Murdoch; as it had already exchanged fire with the enemy, Rodgers' squadron was the one left behind on this-occasion – and Holt's and Shortland's were taken, together with two companies of the North Lancashires and the half battery.

'Great stuff,' Johnnie Morton declared, also in high spirits at the prospect of the fight. 'We are going to have a few scalps.'

Supposing there were any scalps to be found, Murdoch thought, for the country once again appeared deserted as they moved north; the commando with whom Rodgers and his men had exchanged fire was nowhere to be seen. Even the Orange River crossing was undefended, save by a few sharpshooters, who very rapidly disappeared when they realised the strength of the force approaching them.

Having sent despatches back to De Aar, Colonel Edmonds then, in accordance with his orders, led the brigade across the river and up the line as far as Belmont Station, which had been held since the beginning of the war by a small British garrison. Remarkably, as with De Aar, this had not yet been attacked, although the commander reported considerable Boer activity during the preceding week. But the line was unbroken as far as the station, and not a Boer was to be seen. So the brigade continued its cautious advance. The cavalry preceded the mounted infantry, forming a wide screen, and the artillery and the armoured train travelled in the centre.

That night they bivouacked at Fincham's Farm, a little to the north of Belmont itself. It was a superb evening, and as Murdoch walked the pickets with Tom Holt, he felt a tremendous glow of anticipated elation. But there was not a sound to break the silence of the starlit night. 'You wouldn't believe there could be an enemy within a hundred miles,' he said. 'Perhaps there isn't.'

'They're around,' Holt said. 'I hope it is occurring to Colonel Edmonds, and will also occur to General Methuen, that there has to be a reason for the Boers not to have seized Belmont and De Aar when they could have done so with a few hundred men. I have an idea they want us to keep on coming until we reach the position they have already chosen to fight us. The point is that, unlike them, we can't live off the country and therefore have to follow the railway. That means they know exactly the route we have to take — and the country, which we don't.'

The next day they reconnoitred in every direction about Belmont, again without finding any trace of the enemy, and so Colonel Edmonds decided to carry out the final part of his instructions and move up as far as the Modder River itself, sending another despatch rider back to De Aar to inform Lord Methuen that the country appeared clear at least as far as Belmont. The brigade then set out as before, B Troop of Holt's command taking the left advanced guard, D Troop of Shortland's the right, while the train pulled along behind with the mounted infantry to either side. Murdoch realised that Holt could very well be right in his somewhat sinister prediction; quite apart from the railway line, the noise of the train would certainly warn the Boers of the approach of their force long before they would be able to see their enemies.

As usual, Holt rode out to accompany Murdoch, and they studied the undulating country through their glasses. 'Damned good defensive country,' Holt remarked again. 'See those kopjes?' He pointed to the low hills immediately in front of them. 'One could conceal an entire brigade up there and we'd not know a thing about it. Murdoch, I'm going to have to ask you to take a squad up there and have a look amongst those rocks. I'll hold the troop here until you signal they're clear.'

'Yes, sir,' Murdoch said, and summoned Sergeant Bishop. Corporal Yeald was signalled forward, and with a dozen men Murdoch cantered towards the undulating ground, discovering Trooper Reynolds at his elbow. 'What the devil are you doing here?' he inquired.

'You might want a brew-up, Mr Mackinder,' Reynolds pointed out.

Murdoch was actually glad of his company. He felt more exposed than at any moment in his very brief career, the more so because, while he and his dozen men were now a good way out in front of the rest of the brigade, he was at the same time overlooked by them all, and he had no doubt that Johnnie Morton and Hobbs and Craufurd, as well as Colonel Edmonds and Tommy Holt, were all watching him through their glasses. Of course, he told himself, the chances of there actually being Boers concealed amidst the rocks ahead was remote in the extreme, judging by their scarcity during the preceding week. But still it was an uncanny feeling to be riding right up to the kopjes, the only sound the clip-clopping of the horses' hooves.

The morning was shattered by a single shot from in front of them. No one was hit, but the patrol drew rein as one man, and Murdoch gazed at the tumbled natural ruin in front of him. There was so little evidence of where the shot had come from that he was almost wondering if it had been their imagination.

'Boers,' said Corporal Yeald, very definitely.

'Or a single Boer,' Murdoch commented.

'Where there are. . . .' Yeald hesitated. He had fought in India and his officer had not.

'If there is only one, or even two,' Murdoch said, 'we might be able to nab the blighters; I am sure Colonel Edmonds would appreciate some positive information. Corporal Yeald, you will take four men and skirt to the left. Trooper Williams, you will advance into the centre of those rocks with four men. You others will come with me to the right. We'll rejoin here in ten minutes. And remember, we want prisoners.'

He wheeled his horse and cantered off to the right, Trooper Reynolds riding behind him, and the other four men immediately behind Reynolds. The rocks became even more tumbled, and they soon had to slow to a walk, picking their way through the outcroppings. Murdoch noted that Holt had been entirely right and this was indeed superb defensive country; the brigade was now lost to sight behind the rocks beneath them.

He was so keyed up he did not even feel surprise when the fire came. What he had not expected was the amazing accuracy. The first Mauser bullet shattered the brains of his horse. Edward IV fell like a stone, his blood flying up over Murdoch's face and shoulders. Undoubtedly this saved his life, because the second bullet whipped the topee off his head, and if he had not dropped so abruptly he would certainly have been shot as dead as the horse.

He found himself on his hands and knees, for a moment totally uncertain as to where he was or what had just happened. Dimly he heard the drumming of hooves, and looking over his shoulder, discovered that the four men who had accompanied him were hastily withdrawing behind the rocks, chased by Boer bullets. Only Reynolds remained close by, holding his horse under control, an expression of horror on his face as he supposed that his officer had been killed.

Murdoch shook his head to clear his brain and waved to the batman to get out of the line of fire, at the same time scrambling to his feet and drawing his revolver. Up to then he had not seen an enemy, but now he discovered several men galloping towards them. They were certainly Boers, judging by their full beards and their scraggy ponies – but it was hard to consider them soldiers, for they wore very rough civilian clothes and slouch hats; only the rifles and the bandoliers across their chests gave any indication of a military purpose.

'Surrender,' one of them called in English. 'Surrender.'

Murdoch levelled his revolver and fired. He was still shaken by his fall and missed his target, but the riders veered off and dismounted, unslinging their rifles as they did so.

'Here, sir,' Reynolds shouted, trotting up to Murdoch's side and extending his arm. 'Up behind me.'

Murdoch grabbed the arm and was swung into the saddle behind the batman. As he did so a swarm of angry bees seemed to be whirring about his head, but remarkably none hit; the Boers had clearly fired too soon after throwing themselves from their saddles. Then Reynolds was galloping down the slope, joined now by Corporal Yeald and Trooper Williams and their men, and hurrying back towards the brigade, which, having heard the shots, had already begun to deploy.

'By God, Reynolds,' Murdoch gasped. 'But I think you saved my life.'

'Oh, they wanted to make you prisoner, Mr Mackinder,' the batman said. 'But if I may say so, sir, by God, but you're a chip off the old block.'

Murdoch looked down at his hand; it still held his revolver. As he thrust it into his holster, it touched each side of the leather, he was shaking so.

'Indeed, Murdoch, Trooper Reynolds shall be recommended for the Military Medal,' Colonel Edmonds said. 'And I would like you to know that I think you came through your baptism of fire admirably. But I must point out that you endangered the lives of Trooper Reynolds, your patrol and yourself, and lost a good horse, quite unnecessarily. It is quite remarkable that no one was killed.'

'With respect, sir,' Captain Holt said. 'If Lieutenant Mackinder had not ridden into the kopje, he would have been able to tell us nothing more than that there were people in there. They could have been civilians.'

'That was all he was required to tell us, captain,' Edmonds said. 'Once a shot was fired, then the brigade would have carried out its primary task of reconnoitring the kopjes. Remember that for the future, Murdoch. However. . . .' He smiled. 'I would rather have an officer who went too close to the enemy than one who would not approach them at all. Dismissed.'

Holt punched him on the shoulder when they got outside the tent. 'That was well done. Now tell me, what was your reaction to the first shot?'

'To shoot back. Thank God I didn't hit anyone.'

'Don't be absurd. Next time you'll bring your man down. But now you don't have to worry about your reactions any more.'

His fellow subalterns were less pleased with him. 'Trying to be a hero, are you?' Morton inquired coldly. 'It's the regiment you want to think about, young Mackinder. Not your own bloody glory.'

Murdoch as usual ignored him, and was delighted with the reception he received from his troop, who all wanted to congratulate him, having been regaled with stories of his coolness from Reynolds and Yeald. He did not recall being particularly cool. In fact, he was aware of a strange mixture of emotions: elation at having survived his baptism of fire without letting either himself or his name down, mingled with an understanding that he *had* endangered his entire little force – and lost Edward IV.

But more than anything he was anxious to get back at the Boers who had ambushed him, and he was up at dawn the next morning exercising the remounts. Sergeant Bishop and Reynolds were with him to help him make a choice; they finally settled on a grey named Lucifer, with some reason, for he was considerably more lively a mount than Edward had been.

After breakfast the brigade advanced on the kopjes in

61

force. But this was mainly an infantry operation, and the dragoons were kept in reserve, a squadron on each wing. Soon the entire force was surprised by the bursting of several shells over their heads, whining out of the broken country in front of them. Colonel Edmonds immediately called a halt to the advance and brought up his own artillery to smother the kopjes with fire. This went on for some time, and Murdoch, standing his horse beside Holt and Morton and watching through field glasses, found it difficult to believe that anyone could survive such a holocaust of exploding iron. Certainly the Boer fire diminished and then ended altogether, and the British moved forward, expecting to find a shambles.

They found nothing at all. There were one or two stains on the ground which could have been blood, but not a single body, and certainly no abandoned weapons, although there were spent cartridge cases in abundance. In the distance they could make out the Boer wagons trundling to the north. Clearly, if they had suffered any casualties, they had taken both their dead and their wounded with them, and far from being driven out of their defensive position, had equally clearly withdrawn in perfect order.

The only positive gain was the return of Murdoch's sword and scabbard, still hanging from the saddle of the now decomposing Edward IV. 'Pongs a bit,' said Lieutenant Fielder, who brought it in. 'But I expect you can find a use for it.'

'Just shows what contempt the Boers have for our weapons,' Morton remarked.

'Good defensive country,' Holt mused, stroking his chin as he gazed at the rocks. 'And good defensive fighters, who engage when *they* want to, and disengage in perfect order when they don't feel like fighting. I'm beginning to understand what Sir George White found himself up against, especially where they have artillery as well. Let's hope Lord Methuen has thought out how to cope with them.'

Next day a reconnaissance made by Fielder's troop reported that the Boers dislodged from the kopjes had united with a considerable force just south of the Modder River; he thought there might be several thousand of them. Colonel Edmonds therefore determined to fall back to the Orange River and await the arrival of the division. This was galling to the men who had fought for the kopjes, but they had now carried out their orders and ascertained where the main Boer body was. As the enemy lay across the line of the advance to Kimberley, there could be no doubt that they would have to be defeated before any relief of the beleaguered town could be attempted.

Colonel Edmonds therefore waited at the river, sending despatch riders back to report on what he had found. A couple of days later Lord Methuen caught them up again and the rest of his division arrived soon after. This was the first time that Murdoch, for all his military background and the number of times he had attended reviews and tattoos, became truly aware of the feeling of strength that went with being part of a division; he felt enormously proud standing with his troop to form a guard of honour as the men came in.

The division was headed by the Guards Brigade, compromising the 2nd Grenadiers, the 1st and 2nd Coldstreams, and the 1st Scots Guards, probably the three most famous regiments in the British Army; they were commanded by Brigadier-General Sir Henry Colville. The Second Brigade, commanded by Brigadier-General Fetherstonhaugh, consisted of the 1st Northumberland Fusiliers, the 2nd Northamptons, the 2nd King's Own Yorkshire Light Infantry, half a battalion of the 1st Loyal North Lancashires – burning for a fight as the other four companies of the regiment were part of the besieged garrison in Kimberley – and two companies of the Munster Fusiliers. Supporting them was a small naval detachment – looking very odd in khaki instead of blue, and wearing enormous straw hats – who were principally intended to man the two huge four-point-seven-inch guns which had been brought up from the coast, but there were in addition three batteries of field artillery, giving a total of twenty guns in all. For cavalry, there were some volunteer companies, together with the 9th Lancers and of course, the Dragoons.

In all the force numbered a good ten thousand men, and there was much toing and froing, blowing of bugle calls, officers' conferences, daily parades and training sessions. A good deal of hospital drill was ordered for the men who had not yet become acclimatised after being rushed out from an English autumn. They had not been allowed the breaking-in period the Westerns had enjoyed outside Cape Town. The Westerns themselves looked on with some condescension, as they now regarded themselves as veterans.

Meanwhile, Lord Methuen and his officers studied their maps, listened to Colonel Edmonds' reports and considered their strategy. Which was, obviously, to force the passage of the Modder River, thus opening the road to Kimberley, a few miles further on. It was, however, necessary to fight their way even to the river, as by now the Boers had advanced again and reinforced their position above Belmont, which Lord Methuen determined to carry by frontal assault.

To Murdoch's surprise and concern – his head being filled with all he had studied of Napoleon and Frederick, Marlborough and Wellington – the general made his dispositions without undertaking any personal inspection of the ground to be covered, relying entirely on what he was told by Colonel Edmonds and the commander of the Belmont garrison. The dragoons were not involved in this battle and could only watch from a distance, chafing, as the infantry went forward following a tremendous bombardment. Yet it all seemed to work. The advance began at three in the morning, dawn on the high veldt in summer coming about three quarters of an hour later. By six the kopjes had all been secured and the Boers had withdrawn, as usual in a most orderly fashion. Their wagon laager could be seen trekking across the plain to the north, and Murdoch could not understand why the cavalry, which had not so far been committed, were not loosed against them.

'Because we'd be cut down by their bullets,' Morton

said scornfully. 'Cavalry can't charge repeating rifles, young Mackinder.'

'Cavalry can always have an impact on retreating troops,' Murdoch argued stubbornly.

But Methuen seemed content with the limited victory he had achieved. He delighted in taking the war correspondents who had accompanied the division up from the coast over the battlefield, and explaining to them how the Boer morale was undoubtedly shattered. He could not play down the cost of the operation – fifty-one men had been killed and two hundred and thirty-eight wounded during the brief battle – amongst the dead being both Brigadier-General Fetherstonhaugh and Lieutenant-Colonel Crabbe, commanding the Grenadiers. But he explained that casualties were always high in a frontal assault, and he had opted for that form of attack in order to establish moral supremacy over the Boers, which he had no doubt he had achieved.

The army was left in an unsettled state by all this, as again there was little concrete evidence of the Boers having suffered any casualties; all the dead and wounded as usual had been taken away, together with every gun. The men were becoming aware that, however it was presented to the correspondents, the victory, like those trumpeted by Sir George White in Natal the previous month, was actually nothing more than a tactical withdrawal on the part of the Boers, who were happy to fight for as long as it suited them, and then equally happy, unconstrained by military manuals or regimental traditions, to steal away and leave their enemies to occupy barren ground. It was also becoming apparent that the British rank and file no longer possessed absolute confidence in their officers, who, while displaying a great deal of rather absurd gallantry – which was what had led to the high casualty rate amongst the brass – were revealing no matching tactical ability.

From this, happily, the dragoons were for the moment exempt, being well pleased with the leadership of Colonel Edmonds and his subordinates. And there was no doubt that they would be given their chance when it came to forcing the Modder River.

*

There was another sharp encounter at Graspan before the Boers retreated again and the army came in sight of the river at last. From a distance it appeared as surprisingly small, winding its way through low bluffs and backed by high purple mountains to the north. However, it was only twelve miles from Kimberley, and spirits immediately rose; by heliograph they could now communicate with the garrison, who were apparently eagerly awaiting their arrival.

More important yet, it did not, after all, appear to be heavily defended. Lord Methuen and his staff, with an escort of B Troop, the Royal Western Dragoons, rode forward to reconnoitre the crossing, while the rest of the army bivouacked some miles to the rear. The men were really exhausted, having marched a considerable distance and fought two fair-sized battles in five days, and not all of them were in as good physical condition as B Troop of Holt's squadron. Now Murdoch sat his horse to the rear of the staff as he surveyed the river through his binoculars, as indeed did every officer. There was no sign of movement, either on the banks of the river itself or in the kopjes behind it. The railway bridge had been blown up by the Boers at the commencement of the war, but not very successfully, and presented an odd picture of tangled girders drooping over the fast-moving water.

The river itself appeared to pose little obstacle to a successful crossing. It was about thirty feet wide and unattractively brown – its name, the Modder, or Muddy, was aptly descriptive. Apart from the stony bluffs at the riverside itself, the country to either side was flat and sandy, with only occasional thorn bushes as vegetation. Immediately beside the railway station, however, on the far side of the river, quite a little village had grown up, built around some farms and an imposing-looking hotel, in the garden of which were to be seen swings and slides and tree arbours.

'They say this village is quite a holiday resort for the people of Kimberley, in more peaceful times,' Tom Holt observed; he had as usual accompanied Murdoch's troop.

'There doesn't seem to be anyone there now,' Murdoch said, continuing to study the apparently deserted buildings.

But even as he spoke there was a shot, followed by several others, and spurts of dust flew from around them, causing the horses to move restlessly.

'Mr Mackinder,' called one of the staff officers with the general.

Murdoch rode forward. 'Sir.'

'Mr Mackinder.' Methuen gazed at him for a moment. 'I knew your father.'

'Yes, sir.'

'And I'm told you're quite a chip off the old block when it comes to drawing enemy fire. Would you then be so good as to approach the river with your troop, wheel to your left and proceed at a canter for the space of five minutes.' He pointed. 'As far as that bluff over there. You may take shelter behind that rise.'

Murdoch saluted, and returned to his troops. 'We're to let the general count guns.'

'Then I will come with you,' Holt said, and they led out their men past the general, who saluted them, and then down to the bluffs overlooking the river. Immediately there was a burst of fire from the vicinity of the hotel, and one of the troopers grunted in pain.

'Fall out,' Murdoch told him, 'and return to camp for attention. Troop will wheel left and canter.'

They swung to their left and proceeded along the bank, maintaining a brisk speed, while the firing from the other side became more general. Despite their pace, two other men were hit, although not seriously, and it was intensely frustrating to be under fire and not able to reply. As they approached the low hill behind which they would be sheltered the bullets started to come from behind them. 'What do you think?' Murdoch asked Holt, who rode beside him.

'Doesn't appear to be more than a few hundred men,' the captain replied. 'But you never can tell with the Boers. It could be a. . . .' He gave a little gasp, and fell forward over his horse's neck.

Instinctively Murdoch leaned across and grasped his bridle, reining his own horse as he did so.

'Maintain your order,' snapped Sergeant Bishop at the men behind him. 'Maintain your order.'

Holt was bleeding very badly from a wound in the back of his right shoulder, and Murdoch had to grit his teeth to proceed to the bluff, still leading the captain's horse. There he reined his men out of sight of the enemy, who continued to fire in a desultory manner, and looked over the troop. Seven men were wounded, one or two barely able to sit their saddles.

'Corporal Yeald,' he said. 'Take ten men and escort the wounded back to camp. Take Captain Holt immediately to the surgeon. Sergeant Bishop, maintain the troop here until I return.' He left the bluff and galloped back to the staff, who were slowly withdrawing out of range, then drew rein and saluted.

'That was well done, Mr Mackinder,' Methuen said. 'Kindly congratulate your men for me and give them my thanks. The enemy have revealed their dispositions, and now we know what needs to be done. Were any of your people hit?'

'I have suffered seven men wounded, sir.'

Methuen nodded. 'Those people are fine shots, you must give them that.'

'And Captain Holt.'

'Holt?' The general frowned. 'He had no business to be with you. That was careless of him. You'll bring me a report on his condition, Mr Mackinder. Dismissed.'

Seething with anger, Murdoch saluted and galloped back to the bluff to collect the troop, then returned to camp. After dismissing them, he hurried over to Surgeon Major Deardon's field hospital to see to the wounded. And to find that Tom Holt was dead.

3

The Orange Free State, 1900

Captain Holt was buried that evening, and General Methuen himself attended the funeral, together with several of his staff, and of course all the officers of the regiment. 'Brave man,' the general remarked after the padre had finished the service. 'But he should not have been there.'

Colonel Edmonds escorted the general to his horse, then returned to where Morton and Murdoch waited.

'Mr Morton,' he said, 'General Methuen has approved your promotion to brevet captain in command of the squadron. I'm afraid you will have to double as troop lieutenant until a replacement is received.'

'Yes, sir,' Morton said, saluting. Plainly delighted, he looked at Murdoch, who remained staring at the grave as it was filled in and the captain's sword was stuck into the soft ground at the head, his topee placed over the haft. He was realising that he had never thought deeply enough about the business of soldiering before. That it might be a dangerous career, or that it might involve the taking of life, had always appeared as an abstract – one would hardly know the man one was killing; and one never truly considered the possibility of one's friends being killed any more than one considered the possibility of dying oneself – to do so would have made it impossible ever to advance against an enemy.

His instinctive reaction, as a human being, on that first day amidst the kopjes north of Belmont, was thankfulness that he had not actually killed any of the Boers who sought to take him prisoner, because he had seen their faces. But poor Tom Holt had not seen the face of the man who shot him. He had not even been advancing against him.

'What a waste,' he said. 'What a God-damned waste.'

69

'He was in the wrong place at the wrong time,' Morton said.

'And you are in the right place at the right time,' Murdoch said bitterly.

'Why, my dear fellow, that is the key to success. Beats spit and polish or physical jerks, eh?'

Murdoch did not sleep; he walked to and fro outside his tent while the camp glowed with light, especially from the direction of the headquarters tent, where Lord Methuen and his staff were examining their maps with Colonel Edmonds and all the other regimental commanders.

Murdoch could not get the waste of it out of his mind. Holt had been his friend. His only friend – apart from Trooper Reynolds, who was waiting patiently in the door of the tent, with a cup of tea. Murdoch's sole aim in life at that moment was to get a bearded Boer face in his sights and shoot it down. He would not hope to miss this time.

Apparently Holt's death *had* served a purpose. Edmonds returned to the regiment just after midnight and called an officers' conference.

'It is General Methuen's opinion,' he said, 'based on the information we gained for him this afternoon when poor Holt bought it, that the river bank is not held in any strength. We know there are Boers in the village, but there is no evidence of them anywhere else, and the general estimates that there can hardly be more than a thousand so concealed. They have been caught napping, it would appear, by the rapidity of our advance.'

Murdoch pulled his ear; he had observed nothing particularly rapid about the advance.

'On the other hand, there can be no doubt that there are still considerable forces between us and Kimberley, and that these will be concentrated in the near future, once their commanders are aware that we have brought the division up to the Modder. It is therefore the general's intention to force the river crossing immediately. We march off at three o'clock.' He looked at his watch. 'In two hours from now.'

'With respect, sir,' Murdoch said, 'that will hardly give the men time to breakfast.'

'There will be no breakfast,' Edmonds told him. 'Quiet and stealth are essential. The men may have a cup of coffee. The river will be in our hands by six, and they can breakfast then. Now, gentlemen, the 2nd Brigade will assault by the railway bridge, the 1st to their left, flanking the village and the Boer position. The lancers will force a crossing below the bridge. We have been given the task of crossing the river on the left of the guards. I'm afraid I can promise you little glory, as obviously there will be no Boers to oppose us, but his lordship's plan is to make the crossing with as few casualties as possible. We will therefore establish ourselves on the north bank, whence we will enfilade the entire Boer position and simply roll them up from the west. Once we are in position it is doubtful they will attempt to maintain themselves. However, our assigned task is essential to the victory of the division, and I am sure all officers and men will carry it out with diligence and determination, remembering the death of Captain Holt. Now, the men must be awakened with as little noise as possible. We will walk our horses to our position, in case we need them to pursue the fleeing enemy. The actual crossing of the river will be made on foot. Mr Mackinder, B Troop will remain in reserve to guard the animals until they are required. The other five troops will form the assault force.'

Murdoch opened his mouth, and then closed it again.

'Very good, gentlemen. I wish the men fallen in by two thirty. You have one hour and a half.'

'Colonel's boy,' Fielder grunted as they walked back to their tents.

'Oh, I suspect the old man is afraid poor Mackinder may still be affected by Tommy Holt's death,' Morton said, not unkindly. 'You'll be able to tell us where we go wrong, Mackinder.'

Murdoch summoned Sergeant Bishop and gave his orders. The troop was awakened by a touch on each shoulder rather than a bugle call, the horses were unpicketed and brought into line.

'Don't we breakfast, sir?' Reynolds asked, as he gave his lieutenant a cup of coffee.

'We breakfast,' Murdoch said savagely, 'on the other side of the river.'

With a huge, stealthy rustle, the division got on the move. Despite the instructions for absolute silence to be maintained, there was a steady clanking of equipment and muttered curses as stones were kicked and men stumbled. The guards brigade and the 2nd moved up towards the river, and the lancers and volunteer cavalry trotted off to the east. The artillery was wheeled into position with squeaking limbers, and the dragoons walked their horses away to the west. It was impossible to doubt that the Boers were awakened by all this, but if there were only a thousand or so of them in the village there was very little they could do about it.

But they certainly meant to try. The regiment hadn't gone very far when there was a rifle shot, and then another, and then the whole river seemed to burst into flame, continuous fire being poured across the water at the advancing British, who taken by surprise at the reception – which indicated several thousand rather than a few hundred men – they immediately went to ground and replied as best they could, although without any idea of where to aim their shots, supported by the artillery, who concentrated on the hotel. The dragoons kept silently on their march, ignoring the cacophony to their right and rear, until Edmonds decided they had reached their allotted position. By now it was obvious that the river was indeed held in far greater strength than General Methuen, with his extremely abortive reconnaissance, had considered possible; Boer artillery was replying to the British, hardly suggesting that they had left only a rearguard to contest the crossing. Neither the 1st nor the 2nd Brigade had got near the river as yet; they were pinned down by the blanket fire which was coming from the far side. As the sun rose, they were left in a very exposed position, while they still lacked targets at which to aim, the Boers being concealed amongst the kopjes and rocks of the far side. Edmonds therefore gave his men the command to

72

advance on the double, as clearly their turning movement would now be vital to the success of the entire battle.

Murdoch was left with his troop in charge of the several hundred horses, watching in impotent fury as the dragoons, playing their part as riflemen now, hurried forward towards the river bank – to be met by a sudden wall of fire. Gazing through his binoculars, Murdoch saw Fielder fall, and Major Craufurd, and several men. The regiment recoiled from the shock and tried to advance again, only to be sent to ground by the continuing fire from the Boers, who did not indulge in volley fire as such, and yet, with each man loading and firing as fast as he could, *seemed* to be delivering volley after volley. What was far more serious, Murdoch observed, was that the main part of the enemy fire came from the south, or *near* bank of the river; the Boers were actually entrenched down there, as it now became apparent they were right along the battle front, preventing the British from getting near the water at all. And they must have been there all the time, although they had resisted the temptation to fire upon B Troop as it cantered by above them yesterday morning. So much for Methuen's reconnaissance, he thought angrily, which had discovered nothing except what the Boers meant them to discover, and had cost the life of one of the few competent officers in the entire army, in his opinion.

The wounded were brought back; Craufurd was shot through the leg. Fielder had apparently died instantly. Hobbs, who as paymaster had remained with Murdoch, was walking up and down and slapping his leg with his cane in agitation. The sun was swinging high into the sky now, and the day was growing intensely hot – and the men's bellies were rumbling. They had been going to breakfast on the far side of the river. If they were really going to wait for that, Murdoch thought bitterly, they would all starve to death.

But there seemed nothing to be done. With his glasses he could look to his right along the sweep of the British army, and see that every brigade was pinned down by the Boer fire; the artillery roared ceaselessly, huge plumes of dust and earth rose from the far bank, the hotel disintegrated into shattered timbers, swings and arbours thrown left and right – but still the Boers replied, and still the British could not move, while almost every minute someone fell and had to be taken to the rear. There seemed a total lack of direction about the whole thing. No movement could be seen amongst the British, save where someone was hit. There was no adjustment to the plan, presumably because there was no alternative plan. The men just lay and fired, and the Boers fired back. It was impossible to believe that this was a battle being conducted by the product of twenty years' professional soldiering and learning about soldiering; it appeared an entirely senseless exercise, lying in the sun and shooting off one's rifle at an invisible target – save that one was being killed while doing it.

And he could not even take part in it, while he watched his comrades being shot down, one after the other. It was the longest and most terrible day of Murdoch's life, and at last in the afternoon he could stand it no longer. 'I want forty volunteers,' he said.

The troop stepped forward as a man.

'I'm afraid you will have to remain here with the horses, Sergeant Bishop,' he said. 'And I want you here as well, Reynolds. Corporal Yeald, Corporal Compton, you'll accompany me.'

'You have no orders,' Hobbs objected. 'You'll be cashiered.'

'Not if I can get across the river,' Murdoch told him, and led his men away from the protecting hillock, veering to the left of the regiment's position. They were seen immediately and fired upon, but they advanced slowly from cover to cover until they actually reached a bluff which looked down on the river. Below them the bank appeared to be empty, and the river itself, which was obviously quite deep in places, here tumbled over some shallows.

'Do you suppose we could get across there, Yeald?' he asked.

'Nothing to stop us, sir,' Yeald replied.

'Because if we can, and enfilade their position along the south bank. . . .'

'Just to get across, sir, would be a tonic to the army.'

'You're right. Let's go.'

They crept down the far side of the bluff and there paused to check their position. There was no means of letting the rest of the regiment know what they were intending, which suited Murdoch, as he rather felt he might be forbidden to try it. The remarkable thing was that, like the commanding general, Colonel Edmonds was apparently so concerned with dislodging the men in front of him at whatever cost, that he was not paying any attention to the possibility of outflanking them. It was therefore a case of taking his career in his hands, as Hobbs had warned; but Murdoch reckoned he had nothing to lose – he had already disobeyed orders by leaving the horses.

'This has got to be on the double, Yeald,' he said. 'We will approach the bank, volley fire along it against any Boers who may be visible on this side, cross the river and take up our position in that nearest kopje, immediately enfilading the Boer position. We will maintain ourselves there until the regiment crosses to our support. Understood?' He looked from one corporal to the other.

'Yes, sir,' they answered enthusiastically.

'Then, at the count of ten.' He counted slowly, while the men checked their rifles. 'Ten!' he snapped, leapt to his feet and ran down the slope; he had left his sword with Lucifer and carried only his revolver.

Instantly the Boers spotted them again, and discerning their intention, directed a heavy fire on them. He heard a cry from behind him, but there was no time to stop. He reached the embankment, slid down and turned to look along it. Several Boer riflemen were perhaps a hundred yards away to his right, only now turning to face him. But most of his troopers had come down the slope behind him and they opened fire: three of the Boers fell, and the remainder withdrew behind the next bluff.

'Across,' Murdoch panted, and plunged into the brown water. It was deeper than he had supposed, and he was

75

immediately immersed to his waist, while splashes rose all around as the Boers fired at him. He heard shouts from behind him, but never looked back as he strode through the water, once or twice dipping to his shoulders, having to brace all his strength to resist being swept away by the current, which was also faster than he had supposed. Only moments later he was splashing up the far side and throwing himself down amidst the rocks to reload his revolver.

There he was joined by thirty-two men; two were drifting down the river, either shot or drowned, and several more had fallen on the south bank. But they were in position, and they commenced firing as fast as they could reload – they could now see the Boers quite clearly on the south bank, sheltering amidst the bluffs and bushes as they fired at the British army.

The troop's success brought the full wrath of the Boers upon them, however. Although they certainly killed or wounded several men and sent the remainder huddling further down the bank – thus opening an even wider exposed area to a British crossing – the rest of the regiment was apparently too exhausted, after several hours of lying in the sun with neither food nor water, to take advantage of the situation, while the Boer command reacted both vigorously and violently. Within seconds one of their guns, which had been shelling the British position south of the river, was re-aimed and its first shot struck the water, causing a huge splash which soaked them all over again. The next shell was even closer, and Murdoch realised that he must advance or retreat, or be blown out of the water. All his instincts called on him to advance, but at that moment he heard the notes of a bugle from the south bank, signalling recall. This was a direct order. Again he looked back at the regiment, but although they were firing as vigorously as ever, there was no indication of any movement to their aid.

'We've no choice, Corporal Yeald,' he said. 'We will have to retire.'

'But sir, we've established ourselves across the river,' the corporal protested.

'We can't take on the whole Boer army,' Murdoch

pointed out. 'Nor can we disobey orders quite so flagrantly as to try. Back over, boys. We've proved it could be done.'

Muttering curses, the dragoons returned into the water. Three more fell before they regained the south bank.

The firing died down with the coming of darkness; the men were at last able to rise from their improvised shelters and have something to eat and drink, and count the cost. Murdoch accompanied Colonel Edmonds to divisional headquarters, where Methuen and his other general officers were waiting for them. Morton, as squadron captain, came along too.

'I should have thought that you, Lieutenant Mackinder, would have been the last man in this army to act without orders. In disobedience of orders, in fact.'

Murdoch stood rigidly to attention. 'I felt it was a justifiable act, sir,' he said. 'I had received no orders at all for several hours. I had no knowledge of whether or not Colonel Edmonds or Acting Captain Morton might have been hit. I only knew that the regiment was pinned down and unable to move, and it appeared to me that I might be able to turn the enemy's flank or at least divert him sufficiently for an advance to be made, in accordance with our original orders.'

'I would like your opinion on that, Colonel Edmonds,' Methuen said.

'I believe Lieutenant Mackinder acted in good faith, sir,' Edmonds said. 'And perhaps to good purpose. His error was in not sending a messenger to inform me of his intention in time to enable me to make something of it. As it is. . . .'

'Quite,' Methuen said. 'We have another six men to add to our considerable casualty list, and a generally bloody nose to report. Thank you, gentlemen. I am sure you are all as weary as I am of these insidious Boer tactics. Second Lieutenant Mackinder, I intend to indicate my disapproval of your action in my despatch, and this will of course have to be entered on your record. Perhaps, in future. . . .' He turned his head at the sound of hooves. 'Who is that?' he snapped.

One of his staff officers stepped outside into the darkness

and returned a moment later. 'Captain Lindop, sir, returning from reconnaissance.'

'Bring him in. Well, captain?'

Lindop, of the lancers, looked excited, panting as he saluted. 'I have to report, sir, that the Boers have evacuated their positions both on the river and in the town.'

'Are you sure?'

'I am certain, sir. I rode with my men right down to the water without being fired upon, and then crossed the river and went right up to the hotel, without encountering anyone. I saw the canvas of their laager in the distance as the wagons withdrew. It is my opinion that they have evacuated the entire position.'

'By heaven,' Methuen said. 'Now there is a stroke of fortune.'

'Ahem,' Colonel Edmonds remarked.

Methuen looked at him.

'May I suggest, sir,' Edmonds said, 'that the Boer withdrawal may have been caused, at least in part, by the realisation that if some of our people could cross the river even under their very heavy fire, then the whole army might well manage to do likewise, tomorrow?'

'Hm,' Methuen said. 'Hm.' He snapped his fingers. 'We have beaten the bastards, by sheer grit and determination. By God, this'll please the newspapers. I thank you, gentlemen. I thank you all,' he said, looking at Murdoch. 'Now you must attend to your wounded and get some rest.'

'You were damned lucky,' Morton pointed out as they rode back to their cantonment. 'If the Boers hadn't had enough. . . .'

'Do you really think they have had enough?' Murdoch asked, adding 'sir' as an afterthought. 'A victory, by God. To please the newspapers. This army is being led by the nose, and God knows where they are going to take us yet.'

'I would keep that opinion to myself, if I were you,' Morton recommended. 'Or you could wind up being one of the newspaper johnnies the general is so anxious to please.'

*

At least he had won the hearts of his men, Murdoch realised, as they crowded round him to congratulate him on the boldness of his action. Even the wounded members of B Troop expressed their pride in their officer when he visited the field hospital. The rest of the regiment, like indeed the rest of the army, was less happy about the events of the day. Casualties had been severe: four officers and sixty-eight men killed, and nineteen officers and three hundred and seventy-seven men wounded. Fielder was buried next to Holt the next morning, while Major Craufurd's wound was so severe he had to be sent back down the line. Hobbs was given brevet rank of captain and made adjutant; the regiment was now becoming seriously short of officers, and there were no sign of any replacements from the depot at Bath. Troop strength too was down to an average of sixty, which meant that regimental strength had been almost halved since leaving Cape Town.

Murdoch was holding his normal morning inspection the following day, still awaiting orders from Lord Methuen to cross the river in force, when he was greeted by a horseman in civilian dress, although his breeches and jacket were very well cut and he wore a topee. 'Hi there, mind if I have a word?'

'In a moment.' Murdoch dismissed the troop, while the stranger dismounted and held out his hand.

'Name's Harry Caspar, New York *Globe*. I just got here in time for the battle.'

'Oh, yes,' Murdoch remarked. He was not in the mood to discuss the failure with an American.

'Quite an experience,' Caspar said. 'Say, aren't you the lieutenant' – he pronounced the word 'lootenant', which made Murdoch wince – 'who got across the river?'

'Yes, I am,' Murdoch said.

'Then allow me to shake your hand,' Caspar said, and did so. 'I've been learning one or two things about you, Mr Mackinder. Would you object if I did a little piece on you? The fact is, the folks back home don't know too much about this war or the people who are fighting it. If I'm going to get it across to them, I have to give them names, personalities, they can latch on to. Get the idea? And I think you just fill the bill. How about it?'

Murdoch shrugged. 'If you think I could possibly interest them.'

'Sure you will. Son, grandson, great-grandson of famous soldiers . . . that's always interesting.' He grinned. /You might even be able to tell me who won this darned battle.'

Murdoch looked him in the eye. 'Why, Mr Caspar, we did. Haven't you observed that the Boers have withdrawn?'

The orders were given at last, and the army crossed the Modder River the next day – and there rested for twelve days. There were sound reasons for this, to the casual observer. The men were exhausted after their day-long exposure to sun and hunger and thirst and Boer gunfire, and they had expended so much ammunition during the battle that supplies were short. Even so, with Kimberley only twelve miles away, and daily heliograph messages being flashed to and from the defenders and the relieving force, it seemed absurd just to sit in camp. Murdoch was convinced that by a dash the two cavalry regiments might catch the Boers napping and gain the beleaguered town. Certainly, as he surveyed the country between the Modder and the diamond city, it seemed to him that a detachment should be thrown forward immediately to seize the large kopje known as Magersfontein, half a dozen miles north of their position and overlooking the railway line along which their precious line of communication had to run.

The orders remained to rest and recuperate, however, and there was an informal truce arranged between the two sides in order to exchange wounded prisoners. The Boer general, Cronje, even came down to speak to the British padres. Like all of his compatriots, he wore a heavy beard and was dressed in civilian clothes; a short, stocky man, he carried no weapons and indeed gave no suggestion of being engaged in military activities at all, save for the binoculars slung on his shoulder.

The British staff affected to regard him with contempt, but they later realised how wrong they were when a reconnaissance in force was sent out, preparatory to a general advance upon Kimberley. It was then discovered that General Cronje had not neglected to observe the potential of the Magersfontein Ridge, and had occupied it in strength; the reconnoitring party, consisting of the lancers and some horse artillery, were forced to return in a hurry.

General Methuen fumed when this was reported, but he had to accept the fact that he had been outmanoeuvred by his own carelessness. He could not attempt to march on Kimberley, with a Boer force of some six thousand men sitting on his immediate flank. The only course, other than another frontal assault to clear the way, would have been to attempt to outflank the Boers in turn, but this was impossible, not only because Cronje looked down on his every move, but because he dared not leave the line of the railway, without which his army would have starved in a few days.

Murdoch, thinking of all he had read of Sherman's march on Georgia – and some of Bonaparte's campaigns – when lines of communication had been abandoned to achieve certain objectives, regardless of hardship, was once again deeply disappointed in the quality of British leadership.

Harry Caspar, who had become a regular visitor to B Troop, took a somewhat wider view.

'Sherman lived off Georgia, sure,' he agreed. 'But I suspect Georgia had more to offer than the veldt around here. And Sherman was driving at the back of an already beaten enemy. You guys haven't won a single real victory so far. Seems to me your Lord Methuen has a problem.'

One it appeared he intended to solve in the only way left to him. He had now been reinforced, not only by the arrival of ample supplies of munitions, but by one of the most famous brigades in the British Army, the Highland, commanded by Brigadier-General Wauchope and comprising the Gordons, the Seaforths, and the Argyll and Sutherlands. The kilted warriors marched into camp behind the skirl of their pipes and amidst the cheers of the rest of the division; here were fresh troops with a formidable fighting reputation, which greatly increased the strength of the army.

'I have no doubt that we now outnumber the Boers by two to one,' Methuen told an officers' conference. 'I therefore intend to destroy General Cronje's command, once and for all. He holds Magersfontein, and will, I suspect, feel obliged to do so as long as possible; it is his last natural defensive position between ourselves and Kimberley. In thus committing himself, I would say he has played into our hands.'

He paused to look over the faces, and Caspar passed a scribbled note to Murdoch: *Do you think he meant Cronje to occupy the Mag?*

Murdoch scribbled back: *If we could only believe that.*

'Gentlemen,' General Methuen continued, 'it is my intention to seize Magersfontein by a *coup de main*. It will be a bloody business, but we will succeed. I can now tell you that some weeks ago I sent to Cape Town for a supply of lyddite shells, and these have now arrived. I need hardly remind you that these are the most terrible weapons of destruction yet invented by man. You may think I am taking a sledgehammer to crush a nut, but that is precisely what I intend to do. The artillery will smother that hillside with lyddite. When they have done their work, the army will advance, led' – he looked at Brigadier Wauchope – 'by the Highland Brigade. Supposing there are any Boers left alive in their defences, they will be killed or captured. The 1st Brigade will move forward on the left, the 2nd on the right, so that the enemy position will be entirely overrun. The cavalry brigade will prepare to move on immediately the enemy has been driven from his position, and I estimate that we will be in Kimberley in twenty-four hours. Now to detail. The bombardment will commence at midnight tonight, and will last for three hours. At three ack emma the troops will move out. That will give them the benefit of the last hour of darkness in which to approach the Boer position. Now . . .'

He prodded the large sketch plan – it could hardly be called a map – erected on a blackboard behind him and gave his orders. Murdoch listened in consternation, not daring to look at Caspar. There had been absolutely no reconnaissance of the lower slopes of the hill, the ground over which the three infantry brigades would have to cross in the darkness, simply because the Boers had fired at anyone who had attempted to approach their position. There had not even been any reconnaissance to ascertain the exact size of the force opposing them. General Methuen, relying on a map drawn up entirely on information supplied by various locals and natives, was simply pointing his sword and saying Forward. This might well have worked against ill-armed and totally undisciplined African or Indian tribesmen, but surely the general realised, after his experience just a fortnight ago at the Modder River, that it would never succeed against such born defensive fighters as the Boers?

For the first time Murdoch felt relieved that the regiment was not to be involved. They, with the lancers, were simply to make ready to commence their march on Kimberley the moment the Union Jack flew from the top of Magersfontein Ridge. He, as well as his men, therefore had a distant view of the catastrophe that now took place. For three hours the artillery roared, and with his glasses he could make out the shell-bursts on the hill-side. Certainly the entire Boer position appeared smothered with fire – but Murdoch could not help remembering those kopjes outside Belmont, when the Boers had appeared to be exposed to a fire they could not withstand, yet suffered almost no casualties at all.

At three o'clock sharp the guns fell silent and the three infantry brigades began their advance, each led by their brigadier-general. They disappeared into the darkness, and the rest of the army waited, anxiously watching the slowly lightening sky to the east. But the sun had not yet risen when there was a sudden tremendous fusillade from far lower down the hill than any Boers were supposed to be. An almost unbroken wall of red fire spread across the darkness.

'By Christ, but they've walked straight into it,' muttered Sergeant Bishop, at Murdoch's elbow.

The firing became general along the whole front, and when the sun rose the true situation could be discovered. As was only to be expected on a night march over unfamiliar ground, the three brigades had not advanced at the same speed. The Highlanders in the centre had progressed much faster than those to either side, and had thus been the first to encounter the enemy. At the tremendous outburst of firing, all three brigades had gone to ground, but whereas the 1st and 2nd had done so in reasonably sheltered terrain, the Highlanders could be seen, easily identified by the green of their kilts beneath the khaki tunics, well up on the lower slopes of the Boer position, but pinned down in the open by the accurate fire of the enemy Mausers, much as the entire army had been at the Modder.

Once again, there was a total lack of direction; the Scots lay and fired up the slope, at invisible enemies who did not appear to have been the least affected by the bombardment, and the Boers fired back from their concealed vantage points. It later transpired that Brigadier-General Wauchope had been killed in almost the first Boer volley, and that no other officer felt sufficiently in command of the situation to take any initiative. What was disturbing was the way Methuen, as at the Modder, merely sat and watched what was going on. No doubt he was again waiting for darkness, and perhaps for another Boer withdrawal, Murdoch thought. But this was not to be.

All morning and into the afternoon the Highlanders sat it out, steadily losing men, being able to advance only a few feet at a time before falling back again . . . and then the unthinkable happened. Watching through his binoculars, Murdoch saw one or two men filtering back from their advanced positions. He assumed at first that they were wounded dropping out for attention. And then realised they were not, as whole clusters of men rose and began to retire down the hill. If retire was the right word. Soon the panic spread through the entire brigade, and men could be seen unashamedly running away from the deadly Mauser fire of their enemies.

Within half an hour, the Highland Brigade was in head-long retreat, streaming back to the shelter of the rest of the army. Lacking leadership, they had been routed.

'I wonder how his lordship is going to represent *this* to the newspaper johnnies,' Murdoch remarked to Morton, as they stood their men down and had a cup of tea. 'They were actually looking on. Has anything like this ever happened before? Yes, in India once, didn't it?'

'Did it?' Morton asked. Even his contemptuous ebullience had faded. 'It won't be represented at all, young Mackinder. The general will simply slap down a censorship order on all reports until we have retrieved the situation.'

'Oh, yes?' Murdoch queried. 'And how do you suppose we are going to do that?'

But Morton was absolutely right. Caspar came over that evening. 'Would you believe that we have been *told* what we must send back to our papers?' he demanded. 'Hell, I thought you were a free people.'

'What have you been told to say?' Murdoch asked.

'That the assault on the Magersfontein position was not as successful as had been hoped. Jesus Christ!'

Murdoch had to grin at his frustration. 'Well, I suppose that is a perfectly true statement.'

'Yeah? So what do you reckon is going to happen now?'

'If I knew that,' Murdoch told him, 'then presumably I would be the general?'

'Yeah?' Caspar commented again. 'Well, in my opinion, he doesn't have a clue.'

Because the British army remained on the plain, and the Boers remained in command of Magersfontein, the battle might never have been fought – save for the loss of nearly a thousand casualties, including over two hundred dead, amongst them several senior officers apart from General Wauchope, who was buried with full military honours that evening.

And save too for a general collapse of morale, a feeling that under commanders who could think of nothing better than frontal assaults on impregnable positions, there was no hope of ever winning a decisive victory. That, Murdoch realised, was not going to be put right in a hurry, even as the Highland Brigade, under a new commander, Brigadier-General Hector MacDonald, painfully began to pull itself together.

No doubt General Methuen was as stunned as everyone else by his defeat. But before he could consider what to do, even more disastrous news arrived – first of all from the south-east, where General Gateacre had also attempted an assault on the Boer position at Stormberg and been heavily defeated, and then, worst of all, from Natal. General Buller, determining to relieve Ladysmith, had attempted to force a crossing of the Tugela River south of the town, which the Boers had taken as their line of furthest advance. His attack – undertaken, Murdoch guessed, with the same lack of adequate reconnaissance as Methuen's – had been utterly repelled, with heavy casualties. To compound the disaster, two batteries of guns, which had been prematurely advanced, had been lost. Two pieces had been gallantly retrieved by several officers, amongst them Field Marshal Lord Roberts' only son, a lieutenant, who had been mortally wounded in the process. The loss of ten guns made Colenso, the name of the village where the crossing had been attempted, just about the worst defeat in British military history since the surrender of Lord Cornwallis at Yorktown in 1781. And neither Colenso nor Stormberg nor Magersfontein could really be concealed by censorship. 'Do you know what they're calling the last seven days back in England?' Harry Caspar asked, having been busy on the telegraph. ' "Black week"! I would say that just about sums it up.'

Buller, indeed, was so shaken by his repulse that he heliographed Sir George White in Ladysmith, advising him to surrender as there was no hope of relieving him in time. To his credit, Sir George declined to obey the suggestion. When the news of Buller's action reached England there was a storm of protest, and instant action by the Government – action which should have been taken at the very outset of the war.

'Gentlemen,' Colonel Edmonds told his officers. 'Sir Redvers Buller has been relieved of the general command of Her Majesty's forces in South Africa, although he retains command of the Natal front. We have a new commander-in-chief, who is already on his way to join us.' He paused and looked from face to face, savouring the news he was about to impart. 'Field Marshal Lord Roberts is now general-officer-commanding, South Africa.'

There was a murmur of delighted consternation. Bobs, the greatest living British soldier, was coming to them. Bobs, Murdoch thought, with whom Father had marched on Kandahar, and at whose orders the dragoons had charged and routed the Afghans outside Kabul. Bobs, who had once patted him on the head – so he had been told; he did not remember the incident himself, as he had been in his pram at the time.

'Nor is that all,' Edmonds went on, clearly as pleased as they were. 'Field Marshal Roberts is bringing with him, as chief of staff, General Lord Kitchener.'

Again consternation. Kitchener was generally agreed to be the most formidable of all the British generals, the man who, with determined efficiency, had reconquered the Sudan for England and Egypt, whose reputation for thoroughness and ruthlessness was fearsome.

'Now, gentlemen,' Edmonds concluded, 'I suspect that we are going to fight a *war*.'

The division's spirits had been so crushed by the defeat at Magersfontein that Methuen had felt quite unable to make any fresh move against the Boer citadel. He was clearly relieved that the responsibility of deciding what should be done next was in mightier hands than his own. But it was none the less galling for the men to remain in their cantonments, in sight of the enemy but only exchanging occasional shots with them for several weeks, including Christmas. Meanwhile the daily heliograph exchanges with Kimberley told of dwindling morale as the town was being subjected to continued bombardments by one of the Boer heavy guns. The small pieces which were all the garrison possessed could make no adequate reply.

'I am sure it could be done, if we just had the will,' Murdoch grumbled.

'If the general had the will, you mean,' Morton corrected him. For once they were entirely in agreement. With inactivity there came disciplinary problems, and then health problems. Men fell out sick because they were bored. Only the prospect of the arrival of Roberts and Kitchener kept the division in being, Murdoch sometimes thought.

In the new year he received a letter from Rosetta. It had been written some time before, soon after his departure from Cape Town, in fact, but had taken all this time to catch up with him. In it she gave vent to some of the feelings he suspected she was about to reveal when the regiment left Cape Town. It was the first love letter he had ever received, and he might have enjoyed it more had it not given a definite impression that she now regarded herself as engaged. He sat down to write a reply, attempting to disabuse her of that idea without appearing ungallant, but had made little headway when, to the great excitement of the camp, Lord Roberts arrived at the Modder River.

'Now, say,' Harry Caspar said when the news that the field marshal was at hand was received, 'just what is so big about this guy, anyway?'

'Well. . . .' Murdoch assembled his memory. 'He's getting on for seventy now – '

'Seventy? And commanding an army in the field?'

'Why not? Marshal Bluecher was older than that at Waterloo. And Bobs has been a fighting soldier since the Indian Mutiny forty years ago. He won the Victoria Cross at Khudaganj, took part in the capture of Delhi, the relief of Lucknow and Cawnpore. He's fought in Abyssinia, and all over India, and of course on the North-West Frontier. He beat the Afghans in '79, when he made the forced march from Kabul to the relief of Kandahar. He's never been beaten.'

'Maybe. But it doesn't sound to me as if he ever really met any organised opposition,' Caspar objected.

'Maybe. He's still regarded as the greatest soldier in the army. And more than that. His men have always worshipped him. They'd follow him anywhere. As will we. He'll show us how to lick the Boers, you'll see.'

'I'm looking forward to it,' Caspar said. 'I didn't come to Africa to spend the rest of my life here.'

The entire division was turned out for the field marshal's inspection. The little man with the white moustache and the twinkling eyes was quite dwarfed by the huge, stern-featured figure of General Kitchener behind him. Roberts smiled and made a point of stopping and speaking with as many men as possible. Including Murdoch. 'Mr Mackinder,' he said. 'Your father was with me in India. One of the finest soldiers I ever knew. I am sure you will always remember his example.'

He passed on, and Morton muttered, 'Teacher's pet.' But Murdoch was left wondering if in some way he had just been given a reprimand, and if Methuen had after all reported adversely on his conduct in the Battle of the Modder.

Murdoch was sure that Roberts had already formed a plan of how to beat the Boers – and he particularly remembered that his hero's watch-word had always been mobility. But troops, artillery and munitions were poured into the Modder River camp, in full view of the Boers, and it appeared obvious to everyone that the famous general was contemplating another frontal assault on Magersfontein to open the way to Kimberley, where conditions were now apparently becoming desperate.

'And he is Britain's greatest soldier?' Morton sneered. 'It's going to be just another old-fashioned slogging match.'

Murdoch could not believe that, and he felt a surge of optimism when they were informed that they were to be brigaded, with all the other cavalry regiments, into a cavalry division – something which had never been known in the British Army before. General Sir John French, reputedly Britain's finest cavalry leader, who had spent the past few months operating on his own with a small mounted force away to the east, arrived to take command. He was accompanied by his adjutant, Colonel Douglas Haig, another cavalryman with a widespread reputation as horseman and swordsman. He also had the reputation of being the best-dressed officer in the army, and this Murdoch could believe as he gazed at the perfectly creased breeches, the flawlessly cut tunic and the handsome, wide-moustached face.

The three cavalry brigades were placed under the commands of Major-General Porter, who had the First, Brigadier-General Broadwood, the Second, and Brigadier-General Gordon, who commanded the Third, in which were the Westerns. In addition, the division was to have, they were told, seven batteries of the Royal Horse Artillery and two small brigades of mounted infantry. But none of these were as yet at the Modder River, and although it seemed clear that when they did arrive French would have a very powerful and very mobile force at his disposition, there was still no inkling that they were intended for anything more than a march on Kimberley, once Magersfontein had been taken, until the evening of 10 February, when Lord Roberts visited the cavalry cantonments, accompanied by General French and Colonel Haig. They spent some time with each regiment, finally arriving at the Westerns, where Colonel Edmonds assembled his officers to hear what the field marshal had to say.

The little man looked over the faces in front of him; if he grieved for his dead son – who had also been awarded the Victoria Cross, posthumously – there was no sign of it in his demeanour, which was at once calm and purposeful. 'I am sorry to have kept you inactive for so long, gentlemen,' he said, 'when we all know the desperate condition of the garrison in Kimberley, and when I know how anxious you are to regain the initiative from the enemy, but it has been necessary to make some careful preparations before I could act. We now have available some forty thousand men in northern Cape Colony. This may sound a formidable force; however, we are opposed here by some twelve thousand Boers, well entrenched in that mountain of theirs, appearing indeed to control our every option. It is up to us to prove the enemy wrong, but not by sacrificing lives in another senseless assault on so strong a position.' He paused, and the officers looked at each other. 'No,' he went on, 'our task must be to winkle him out, and very rapidly, if we are to relieve Kimberley in time. I therefore propose to turn the Magersfontein position.'

There was a moment of utter silence, while Murdoch was tempted to scream with joy. This was what he had wanted to do from the beginning.

'This too is a difficult task,' Roberts went on, 'for it means abandoning what has hitherto been our sole line of communication: the railway. Indeed, it is because the Boers are so certain we must depend on the railway that they have concentrated such a strong body of men immediately in front of us here, leaving the rest of the country weakly held. This I propose to take advantage of, and I can now tell you that a few miles back down the track there has been assembled a wagon train of two hundred vehicles, ready to carry all the munitions of war wherever we want to go.'

Another pause, this time rewarded with a gasp; the field marshal had only been in South Africa a few weeks, and had already achieved what no other general had even considered attempting.

'The possession of this wagon train gives us more mobility than before,' Roberts told them. 'But the main part of our army must still move on foot, which is necessarily slower than the Boers. This is where you cavalrymen come in, and indeed you are the lynchpin of our plan. General French?'

French stepped forward. 'Obviously, the moment Cronje discovers that we are no longer contemplating a frontal assault upon Magersfontein, but are attempting to flank him, he will pull out the main body of his men to oppose our advance. We shall, of course, endeavour to deceive him as to our purpose for as long as possible, but we do not know for how long that will succeed. We must therefore pay attention to the places where the Boers might success-fully oppose our march. There are, fortunately, no other naturally impregnable positions such as Magersfontein. That leaves him with only the rivers.' He turned to the blackboard, where Haig had just pinned up a huge map of the area. 'There are only two fords which will admit the passage of a large army and wagon train. These are De Kiel's Drift over the Riet River, here.' He placed his hand some thirty miles to the south-east of the Modder camp. 'And Klip Drift across the Modder, here.' He indicated a position some twenty miles due east of Magersfontein. 'Once we can get the army across those two fords, the way to Kimberley is open, and indeed, Magersfontein can be surrounded. On the other hand, if the enemy reaches either of those fords before us and entrenches himself there, we will be faced with another almost impregnable position to storm. This must be avoided at all costs. It will therefore be the responsibility of the cavalry division to seize each of those river crossings in turn, before the Boers can do so.'

Now it was his turn to pause and survey the faces in front of him. 'I want every officer to be very clear what this is going to entail. It will mean very hard riding, and it will mean from time to time cutting ourselves off from the main body of the army and from the support wagons. On such occasions it will not be possible to carry fodder for the horses, and only the minimum rations for ourselves. We will therefore travel as light as possible. All greatcoats for example will be left here. Only weapons, munitions and canteens will be carried. I am relying upon each of you to impress this on your men. Is that understood?'

They gazed at him, and he nodded. 'Very good. Now prepare your men. I am sorry to have had to delay until this last moment to give you your orders, but of course it has been, and remains, essential that the Boers should not know what we are planning to do in advance. In fact' – he glanced at Lord Roberts and smiled – 'I did not know myself until last night. Now I must tell you that the division leaves here at three o'clock tomorrow morning. Good riding, gentlemen.'

Murdoch and Morton gazed at each other. 'At last,' Murdoch said. 'We are going to carry the fight to *them*.'

'Mobility,' Morton agreed. 'Why else have we been given horses?' His mouth twisted. 'Even if we are about to ride them to death, it seems.'

4

The Transvaal, 1901

Murdoch summoned Sergeant Bishop and had him alert the men. He had no intention of limiting their stamina by repeating the mistake of the Modder River, and ordered them to breakfast at one o'clock in the morning. By then rations and ammunition were being doled out, and each man was allowed to fill three canteens with water. Haversacks, canteens and bandoliers apart, they carried nothing but the uniforms they were wearing and their weapons.

Murdoch was supervising the final equipment of every man when he heard hooves crunching in the darkness, and Caspar dismounted beside him. 'Hi, there, Lieutenant Mackinder,' he said, pronouncing the word 'lootenant' as usual. 'Mind if I ride along with you?'

Murdoch raised his eyebrows. 'Do you have any idea where we're going?'

'I haven't been told,' Caspar admitted. 'But I reckon I can guess.'

'You'll have to obtain permission from the general officer commanding.'

'I've done that. He told me it was my funeral. But I guess he'd like to have me along to let the folks back home know something about how this war is going to be won.'

'Well. . . .' Murdoch held out his hand. 'You'll have to bring your own rations.'

Caspar squeezed his fingers. 'I have them right here.'

The division paraded in utter silence at two on that Sunday morning. Even now the rank and file had not been told where they were going, and they were astounded when they moved off, walking their horses to avoid making a noise, in a south-easterly direction, leaving all their tents and remount picket lines exactly as they had been for the past two months, gradually diverging from the railway line and apparently turning their backs on both Magersfontein and Kimberley.

'Well, hell,' Caspar remarked. 'Seems like I guessed wrong. Do *you* have any idea where we're going?' He rode beside Murdoch at the head of B Troop.

'I've an idea,' Murdoch said enigmatically.

'Well, I sure hope it ain't straight back to Cape Town,' the American remarked.

By sunrise Magersfontein was out of sight and they were nearly at Graspan. As Lord Methuen had remained at the Modder River with the better part of a division to blow bugles and move around between the deserted tents and exercise the remounts, there was no way the Boers could have any idea that the entire cavalry force had been withdrawn from in front of them, or that the three divisions of infantry coming up the railway line were also about to diverge to the east.

Now the pace was quickened, as they were definitely within the boundaries of the Free State itself, and by midday they were at Ramdan Farm. Here was the rendezvous for the remainder of the division, and as their manoeuvre was still regarded as secret from the enemy, and to give time for the infantry and the wagon train to catch up; the men and horses were allowed to rest all evening and into the first hours of the night. Meanwhile their comrades arrived in a steady flow, until by dusk the full ten thousand, together with the artillery batteries, were assembled.

At three in the morning the division set off again, this time marching due east. By now the men began to have some inkling that they were at least making an extended raid into Boer territory, and spirits rose accordingly.

'Now this is just like carrying the fight to the Indians,' Caspar said enthusiastically. 'But I'll tell you something, lieutenant – I have never ridden with so large a body of men before.'

'I don't think anyone in the division, from General French down, has done that,' Murdoch said.

Their goal now was Waterval Drift, beyond which was

the first practical river crossing of the Riet – which branched off from the Modder just below the railway bridge – at De Kiel's Drift, a couple of miles further on. Progress was slow at first because of the intense darkness, and more than once French called a halt to regain his bearings. But with sunrise the rapid walk was continued, until they came in sight of the kopjes surrounding Waterval. Instantly flanking parties were thrown out and preparations were made to go into action should the drift be defended, and just in time, for a few minutes later a gun exploded and then fired again, the second shot bursting close to the general and his staff.

'Colonel Eustace,' French told the officer commanding the horse artillery, 'wheel your batteries and blast that fellow.'

Clearly the hills were defended by a considerable Boer force, but French determined to ignore them – except for a brief bombardment – and continued to lead his men past the kopjes in their march for the ford. The rapidity of his dispositions, the total confidence with which the British proceeded – in contrast to the ponderous and uncertain movements of earlier days – and the absence of any baggage train, all had their effect in confusing the Boers. Realising that they could not now stop the division from reaching the drift, they soon withdrew from the hills and hurried north themselves; the British found the ford undefended.

Thus far all had gone very much according to plan. The Boers were obviously still unaware of the real objective of the expedition, or even of the enormous strength of the invading force, and at present seemed to regard it as merely a large-scale cavalry raid. The British had gained their first objective, and were now well to the east of Magersfontein, with only the Modder left between themselves and Kimberley.

Now, however, it was necessary to wait, holding the ford, until the first of the infantry came up – and the supply train as well, for both men and horses were out of food. It had been hoped that these would arrive on that Monday afternoon, but they did not reach the drift until dusk. Then distributing food and fodder took longer than had been anticipated. Thus it was not until early the following morning that French, having seen that the infantry brigade was firmly in control of the ford and would be able to hold it until Roberts and the main body came up, led his men on to reach Klip Ford on the Modder, if possible by nightfall.

Now they were very definitely in enemy country; every farm that they approached had been abandoned. It was also a tremendously hot day, and must have been hot and dry in this area for some time: there was no water in any of the various pools they came across, and as French insisted on maintaining a fast pace, it was on this day that the horses began to die. Soon they were all so exhausted that even the staff officers were walking and leading their mounts, while the field artillery were having a terrible time of it. Just before noon they at last came to a pool of good water, but the order was passed back that no one was to stop; the water was to be left for the infantry toiling behind them, who would be suffering even more.

Worst of all, the intense heat caused the bush several times to burst into flames, and their parched throats and nostrils were assaulted by clouds of smoke. A despatch rider came up to inform them that the fires had burned out the telegraph line the sappers had been laying behind them, and they were thus cut off from any communication with Lord Roberts.

That afternoon mounted Boers were seen on the north-eastern horizon. General Gordon's brigade was now forming the advance guard, and he called on the dragoons to move towards the Boers and disperse them before the main body of the division came up – and also to make sure they did not retreat to the west towards Cronje and the main Boer army, which with luck was still waiting to be attacked on Magersfontein.

'Action at last,' Morton shouted, kicking his horse forward as the regiment moved out, the three squadrons abreast.

'Are you sure you want to be involved in this, Caspar?' Murdoch asked.

'I wouldn't miss it for the world,' the correspondent told

him, although, as he was also wearing khaki, no Boer would be able to tell the difference between him and any of the troopers.

They rode forward at a steady trot – their horses were too tired to go much faster – and the Boers, after exchanging some shots at long range, rode off towards the kopjes now coming into sight. Colonel Edmonds led the regiment in pursuit, but as they approached the treacherous broken ground called a halt to make some tactical dispositions. Rodgers' squadron was sent to the west, in an enveloping movement; Shortland's was held in reserve, and Edmonds himself led Morton's directly into the hills.

'Some country,' Caspar remarked, as they began to file between the hillocks of the rising ground. 'What the Sioux would make of this. . . .'

The Boers were apparently just as adept as the Sioux, and a volley came from their left. Several men were hit, and the bugler blared the command to dismount and take cover. Murdoch hurled himself from the saddle, Sergeant Bishop to one side, Caspar and Reynolds to the other, while the rest of the troop followed their example, lying behind the rocks and thrusting their Lee-Metfords forward as they sought some sign of the enemy. Behind them Morton's troop faced the other way, and they listened anxiously for some indication that Rodgers' squadron was coming up from behind the Boer position. But the next burst of firing came from a good way away, and was accompanied by the heavier *crump* of a field gun. They realised that they had stumbled on to a much stronger Boer force than envisaged, and that Rodgers could be in deeper trouble than themselves.

'Sound the recall to Captain Rodgers,' Edmonds told the bugler. 'Captain Morton, prepare to take your men out of here and rejoin Captain Shortland. Send a rider back to General Gordon to tell him that we need reinforcements and artillery.'

'Yes, sir,' Morton acknowledged. 'Squadron will prepare to mount.'

The men scrambled amidst the rocks to regain their horses.

'Mount,' Morton shouted, and everyone got into the saddle as quickly as possible. 'Squadron will withdraw,' Morton bellowed, an order which was obeyed with alacrity, as the Boer bullets were again humming about them.

Murdoch hung behind while his men gained the partial shelter of the next line of kopjes, then looked back to check that all the wounded had been taken out, and thus saw Colonel Edmonds fall. The colonel had waited further behind him, to make sure the entire squadron had got out; now, as Murdoch watched in dismay, it appeared that both he and his horse were hit simultaneously, because both went down with a thump.

'Take command, Sergeant Bishop,' he shouted, and spurred Lucifer back to where his commander lay. Shots buzzed around his head, but he presumed he was the luckiest man alive because none touched him. Dimly he heard Morton shouting behind him, but he ignored the captain and rode up to the colonel, who was trying to push himself up, but with great difficulty – blood was pouring from the wound in his leg.

Murdoch dismounted. 'Here, sir,' he said, thrusting his left arm round Edmonds' shoulder, as he remembered Reynolds doing for him at Belmont. He raised him up and tried to get him on to Lucifer's back.

'Mackinder,' the colonel gasped. 'Mackinder!' he shouted.

Still holding the wounded man, Murdoch swung round and saw several Boers approaching him, confident that the dragoons would not fire for fear of hitting their own officers. 'You surrender, eh?' one called.

Their rifles were pointing at him, but Murdoch reacted without hesitation. This was the first time he was actually face to face with the men who had shot Tommy Holt. He reached for his revolver and was firing as he brought it up from the holster. The first shot missed; the second cut down the leading Boer, the man who had summoned him to surrender. The third hit the man behind, and he dropped another before his hammer clicked on an empty chamber. By then the other three had thrown themselves behind the nearest rocks, returning fire but with no accuracy, taken by surprise at Murdoch's unexpected assault.

Murdoch pushed Edmonds behind some rocks and fumbled for his cartridge pouch as he heard the Boers shouting from all around him. Lucifer had prudently trotted some distance away and was regarding him with a quizzical expression, but Murdoch knew he would never be able to carry the wounded man without them both being hit.

'Mine,' gasped Edmonds, faint now with loss of blood. 'Use mine.' He pressed his revolver into Murdoch's hand.

A bullet crashed into the earth beside him, and Murdoch looked up to see several Boers on the rocks above him, aiming their rifles. He fired, and dropped one, then felt a weird sense of shock as a bullet slashed into his leg. There was no pain from this, but a moment later he felt a sharp stab in his chest from another shot cutting through his jacket. Now the colonel's revolver too was empty. Murdoch rose to his good leg, reached across to the colonel's dead horse and drew the sword from the scabbard attached to the saddle.

The Boers stared at Murdoch in amazement as he faced their Mausers with only steel in his hand, but then there was a fusillade of shots from behind them, and Morton appeared over the rise, leading B Troop back to the rescue of their lieutenant, while at the same time Rodgers' and Shortland's squadrons came spurring up the defile. The Boers hurriedly withdrew to the protection of their field pieces, and Murdoch dropped to his knees, then, as his right leg gave way, rolled over on to his side, still holding the sword.

Johnnie Morton stood above him, Caspar beside him. 'You're the best material for a hero I've ever had,' the journalist said.

'Yes,' Morton agreed, for the first time allowing genuine admiration to enter his voice. 'I think we had better do something about getting you a medal.'

*

The regiment withdrew to a defensive position, artillery was brought up from the brigade and the Boers were dispersed. But now there could be no doubt that Cronje knew what was happening and had sent this force to try to check the British advance until he could reorganise his defences. The cavalry thus pushed on even more rapidly than before to gain Klip Drift before it could be fortified.

Klip Drift was the real goal of the entire manoeuvre, for it was not only due east of the Magersfontein position, but only a dozen miles from Kimberley itself. Their continuing rapid advance surprised a considerable Boer force, who fled before them, abandoning their camp and even several of their wagons – one of which, to the great joy of the parched troopers, was filled with fresh fruit.

They reached Klip Drift by dusk. French halted again to wait for the main body to come up to them, but that night General Kitchener himself rode into the bivouac, having hurried ahead of the infantry to tell them that the remainder of the army were only now at De Kiel's Drift, there was a possibility that Cronje might abandon Magersfontein and withdraw to in front of the diamond city itself. So Roberts' orders were for the cavalry again to move on as rapidly as possible, making a dash to reach the besieged town before the Boers could make up their minds.

This French accomplished the following afternoon, although at a terribly heavy cost to the already exhausted horses; very nearly two thousand had died in the march from the Modder. But Kimberley had been relieved with hardly fifty human casualties, and the British had at last gained a substantial success.

Better was to follow soon afterwards, as Cronje and five thousand men found themselves bottled up at Paardeberg. Another of those suicidal frontal assaults on their position – commanded by Kitchener in the temporary absence of Roberts, who was ill – was repulsed with heavy losses. But on the field marshal's return to command, Cronje was surrounded and made to realise that he would be starved into surrender, whereupon he accepted the inevitable and laid down his arms. The Orange Free State was won, and so, in effect, was the war.

In these triumphant events Murdoch played no part, except as an observer. He had been very fortunate that the bullet which cut his tunic no more than tore a furrow in his flesh and cracked a rib; the shot in his leg was more serious, but the bullet was extracted easily enough, and as no bones were broken it was estimated, correctly, that he would be back in the saddle within a few weeks. He was thus spared the long journey back to the general hospital in Cape Town, whence poor Colonel Edmonds had been sent to join Craufurd.

The regiment was left without any of its senior officers. Rodgers was appointed brevet lieutenant-colonel, with the permanent rank of major, Chapman was promoted captain and Morton confirmed in his rank; everyone got a bump up, Murdoch receiving his second star, or pip, to become a full lieutenant, from the hands of General French himself.

'We need you on your feet, Mackinder,' he said. 'We have a lot left to do.'

Indeed there was, even if the victory of Paardeberg and the destruction of Cronje's army meant the beginning of the end for the Boers. A fortnight after the relief of Kimberley, Buller at last forced his way across the Tugela and reached Ladysmith. In mid-March, Roberts entered Bloemfontein, the capital of the Free State, and two months later a flying column of cavalry and mounted infantry relieved Mafeking, where the heroic Colonel Baden-Powell had withstood a siege of seven months. On 24 May 1900, the Orange Free State was annexed to the British Empire.

Murdoch was pronounced fit to rejoin the regiment the following day, in time to take part in the invasion of the Transvaal. He now was the senior lieutenant, A troop being under the command of Peter Prendergast, one of the replacements out from England to bring the regiment almost back up to strength. Murdoch was welcomed back with three rousing cheers by his veterans, and was present when Lord

Roberts invested Trooper Reynolds with the Military Medal for his gallantry in saving Murdoch outside Belmont.

The invasion of the Transvaal was no more than a formality as the Boer forces were melting away on every side before the now overwhelming British strength. Johannesburg was taken after only a week on 31 May, and Pretoria, the capital, five days later. Roberts' army and Buller's army finally met at Vlakfontein on 4 July. By then President Kruger had fled to Holland, and on 3 September 1900 the annexation of the Transvaal was announced. As this officially ended the war, Field Marshal Lord Roberts returned home, handing over the command to General Kitchener to clean up the few pockets of Boer resistance which remained.

But these few pockets contained all the hard-core fighting men in the Boer armies who resolutely refused to surrender either their arms or themselves. The British soldiers, who had anticipated an early return to a heroes' welcome in England, received a rude shock as Generals de Wet, de la Rey, Botha and Smuts carried out extensive guerilla raids, sometimes deep into Cape Colony. Attacking isolated outposts, tearing up railway track, fighting a war entirely of movement, unencumbered now by the requirement to defend any fixed positions or to carry out sieges, they once again asserted their vast superiority in mobility.

Nor could they be caught. Weary days were spent in the saddle by the dragoons, or by forces of mounted infantry, following Boer tracks which always eventually petered out. Sometimes they felt they were on the verge of success as they chased a commando right into a hamlet of farms. But by the time they got there, the rifles had disappeared and so had all evidence that any male inhabitant of the settlement had ever left his farm; they were all to be found hard at work with their livestock or sitting by their fireside smoking their pipes, attended by their devoted womenfolk.

General Kitchener's first reaction to this unexpected huge-scale guerilla warfare was wholly defensive. The railway lines had to be protected, and this he did by building blockhouses at regular intervals and stretching miles of barbed wire to deter the Boer cavalry. But these measures seemed to have no effect at all in checking the commando raids.

Murdoch had no idea how they were ever going to be coped with; he could only envisage a huge British army having to be maintained in South Africa for the next fifty years. He much missed the shrewd observations of Harry Caspar, but the American journalist, supposing like everyone else that the war was over, had returned home. Towards the end of the year Colonel Edmonds was able to resume command of the regiment, and Major Craufurd also returned to duty. But they still mourned the loss of Fielder and many other good men, all it seemed to very little purpose. They all yearned to be able to return home, having been out of England for nearly two years.

In these circumstances, supporting morale became an all important and increasingly difficult task. During their first month in Africa, outside Cape Town, the regiment had been filled with enthusiasm for the coming struggle, and all problems had been incidental to that goal. During the hard campaigning between October 1899 and the summer of 1900, the troopers had been mostly in a state of exhaustion when they were not actually fighting. But throughout the second half of the year they stagnated, or engaged in fruitless pursuit missions. More seriously, they were in a permanent cantonment on the outskirts of Joahnnesburg, and they were separated by a great distance from their wives and families.

The officers could seek the company of those Boer women whose husbands had surrendered, or of the Uitlanders, the expatriate population whose determination to share in the gold of the Transvaal had caused the war in the first place. The men, unfortunately, had to look elsewhere. Liaisons between white soldiers and black girls had to be discouraged as much as possible, not only because it would present a considerable problem were the regiment to return to England with a company of black wives in tow, but because of the high incidence of venereal disease.

Yet the men had to have some outlet for their energies, and organising football or cricket matches did not always serve this purpose. The numbers of both sick and men up for punishment grew with every day, and commanding the troop became more difficult and less rewarding with every day as well, however much both officers and men understood the other's problem. When, at the end of January 1901, Queen Victoria died, they began to feel they were forgotten men. There was not a man in the regiment who had been alive when the Queen had come to the throne, more than sixty years before, and it was difficult for most of them to envisage any other situation than 'serving the Queen'.

No doubt this feeling spread right through the army, and even reached headquarters level. In the early summer of 1901, General Kitchener called a conference in Johannesburg, to which every commissioned officer who was not actually on duty was commanded. The general, huge, with massive shoulders and the most military of moustaches, his red shoulder tabs seeming almost like an extra pair of glowing eyes as he stared across their faces, was obviously deeply concerned about the situation.

'The Boer leaders,' he said, 'are behaving in a most irresponsible manner. They are fighting entirely for the sake of fighting; there can be no hope of anything they achieve altering the political situation, of their ever regaining control of the Free State or the Transvaal. They have, in short, become mere bandits, encouraged, I may say, by those who have an interest in snarling at the lion's tail.' He paused, but everyone knew he was referring to Germany and France, who were arming the guerillas and openly singing their praises.

'All our efforts to reach an agreement with these thugs having failed,' Kitchener went on, 'I have determined to put a stop to their activities once and for all, regardless of the methods I have to employ. I have called you all here today because I wish no one of you to be in any doubt that I mean what I say. Thus far, we have endeavoured to deal with the Boers as gallant enemies who fought honourably and met defeat with fortitude. Now I propose to deal with them as what they are – outlaws, who require to be stamped out of existence.' Another pause, while his audience waited patiently, but with little conviction; they had supposed for the past six months they *were* engaged in stamping out the guerillas by every means they could think of, without success.

'Now, gentlemen,' Kitchener continued, 'let us examine the problem with which we are faced. It is simply this: the ability of the Boer commando to melt away when its pursuers come too close, and lose itself amidst the apparently ordinary population. How often have you and your men all but caught up with a commando, chased it into a Boer village and found nothing but apparently innocent civilians? Well, gentlemen, as of this moment, there will be no more innocent civilians.' He looked across their faces. 'Neither men, nor women, nor children. All are equally guilty of resisting us. I wish this to be clearly understood.'

The officers gazed at him. They were not sure they did understand.

'I am not asking any British officer to indulge in indiscriminate massacre,' Kitchener told them. 'But I am commanding you to deal firmly with an intolerable situation. To this end, I have commanded the construction of several large camps, prisoner-of-war camps, if you like, outside all the main Boer centres where we now have complete control. From now on, your procedure during a pursuit mission will be as follows: when you follow a Boer commando, and they disappear into a community of their fellows, however large, or however small, you will surround that community, and you will demand the surrender of all fighting men, or men of fighting age. Should that demand be refused, or not complied with to your satisfaction, or should you meet with any resistance at all, you will arrest the entire population of the settlement, down to the smallest babe in arms, and march them off to the nearest camp. We shall call these camps concentration camps, rather than prison camps, because that is what they are going to be, camps for concentrating the Boer supporters until their menfolk have the sense to surrender.

'To impress upon these villains even more firmly that we intend to put an end to their depredations, once the civil population has been rounded up and placed under arrest their farms and houses will be burned to the ground and their livestock appropriated as army property.' Again he looked across their faces. 'I trust you have all understood exactly what I have said. I will take it as extreme dereliction of duty should any British officer from this moment allow misguided sentiments of generosity or humanity to interfere with his duty as I have outlined it. Now, gentlemen, are there any questions?'

Yes, Murdoch wanted to say. Is there any legal basis for what you are commanding us to do? Will such measures not damn us as Cumberland's butchers were damned in the Highlands of Scotland after the defeat of Prince Charles at Culloden in 1746, for just the same barbarity?

But, like everyone else in the room, he said nothing. Because Cumberland's measures had certainly been successful in ending Scottish resistance, and because he knew that to question Kitchener would be the end of his career.

'God damn you, Englander. God damn you to hell,' shouted the woman. She stood with several others, their children at their sides, tiny hands twined in their mother's skirts. Beside them, teenage boys glared at the dragoons with faces twisted in hate, and old men plucked their beards and shuffled their feet as if, ancient as they were, they wanted to seek weapons and at least go down fighting. Of men between the ages of sixteen and sixty there were none to be found; they had seized their weapons and escaped when the squadron was seen approaching. News of the new British tactics had spread.

So now Murdoch and Prendergast and Morton sat their horses, backed by their men in straight lines, rifles resting on hips rather than in scabbards, to quell the least sign of resistance, while several troopers ran from house to house in the village, setting each on fire. The flames caught quickly in the tinder-dry wood and thatch, and soon leapt high into the air. Other dragoons were rounding up the livestock to take back to camp. The women and children and old men would have to walk there, surrounded by the soldiers.

'I feel like a reincarnation of Attila the Hun,' Prendergast muttered. He had arrived too late to see much actual fighting and was clearly horrified by this aspect of war.

'Or Genghis Khan,' Murdoch agreed. He gazed at the woman who had cursed him – middle-aged, sun-browned and labour-wrinkled, the mother probably of several of the youths and girls who exuded so much hate. Neither she nor her children would ever stop hating the British, he realised. He wondered if Kitchener had considered far enough into the future after he had finally eradicated the guerillas; or if he dismissed that as a matter for the politicians, his business being to end the war.

It took them twenty-four hours to gain the camp, with but two brief stoppages, so that by then the prisoners were nearly dead on their feet. It required a supreme act of will not to dismount and give some of the older ones a ride, or the very young ones for that matter. But that would be interpreted as weakness. Nor would conditions be much improved inside the camp – which was already full – where the food was poor and the hygiene virtually non-existent, where there was already fever and typhus, where the wail and the stench of accumulated misery filled the air. All without the slightest indication that the Boer men were preparing to give in, no matter what happened to their families and their farms.

'They do not believe that we will persist in our policy,' Kitchener wrote in a circular. 'But we must maintain our course, and they will surrender soon enough.'

To the eternal discredit of the British Army, Murdoch thought.

'The troop will fall in at three ack emma tomorrow morning,' Murdoch told Sergeant Bishop. 'A Troop reported seeing a Boer commando in the vicinity of Blockhouse Thirty-Five last evening, and the colonel has instructed us to discover their track and follow it at first light.'

'Yes, sir.' Bishop looked very unhappy and seemed to find it difficult to remain at attention.

'At ease, sergeant,' Murdoch said. 'Tell me what is on your mind.'

'Sir . . . the men don't like it. They're soldiers, sir. Show them an enemy with a gun in his hand and they'll follow you right up to him. You know that, sir. But this making war on women and children. . . .'

'I don't like it any more than you do, sergeant,' Murdoch told him. 'But it is a necessary policy if we are going to end this war before we are all grandfathers.'

'Yes, sir.' Still Bishop hesitated. 'Do you approve of what we are doing, sir?' he asked, with the boldness of intimacy; they had now lived and fought together for nearly two years.

Murdoch looked at him. 'No, sergeant,' he said. 'No, I don't. I also thought I had joined the Army to fight against armed men. But I also joined the Army on the clear understanding that I would carry out the orders of my superiors without question, and took an oath to that effect. As did you, and every man in the troop. So there it is. If we are fortunate, tomorrow we will make contact with the commando before it goes to ground, and have a real fight on our hands. In any event, the troop will move out at three ack emma. Understood?'

'Yes, sir.' Bishop saluted and withdrew, and Murdoch was able to look at his letters again. A whole batch had arrived with the last mail train. Several were from his mother and sisters. They were alarmed to hear that he had been wounded, reassured when he had returned to duty, but were now querulous that he was still in South Africa, carrying out what appeared to them to be police duties – no word of Kitchener's 'concentration camps' had of course been allowed to leak back to England. Rosemary was especially querulous as her engagement had now lasted more than two years and she was still waiting for her Captain Phillips to return. Murdoch had only seen his future brother-in-law on a couple of occasions during the long struggle, but he knew Phillips was as fed up as everyone else, even if, as a guardsman, he was spared the seek-and-destroy missions on which the cavalry were engaged and was instead confined to permanent garrison duty.

Then there was a letter from Harry Caspar, asking if the rumours he was hearing from other correspondents were true, that the British were burning the Boer farms. That was a letter he dared not answer.

And then there were three letters from Rosetta Dredge. She seemed to write him every week, but her letters always arrived in batches, each batch more difficult to accept than the last. While in hospital he had written her and suggested that, in all the circumstances, she should find someone else; her reply to that had been sizzling with accusations of dishonour and ungentlemanly conduct, and he had never dared suggest it again. But as he had no intention of ever finding himself married to Rosetta Dredge, it was a situation which was going to have to be faced one day, and probably soon. Thus the thought of returning to Cape Town was just about as forbidding as the thought of continuing with this dishonourable and ungentlemanly campaigning up in the Transvaal.

He put them all aside. They could wait until he returned from tomorrow's unpleasant duty. He slept soundly, as he always did, was awakened by Reynolds at a quarter to three with a cup of tea, shaved and washed and put on his uniform and stepped outside into the crisp predawn blackness. It was always cool at this height above sea level until about ten in the morning, when the sun would be high.

'B Troop ready for patrol, sir,' reported Sergeant Bishop, who appeared to have regained some of his spirits.

'Thank you, sergeant. We should be back by this evening, Reynolds,' he told the batman.

'I'll have a hot bath waiting, sir,' Reynolds promised.

Murdoch inspected the troop, commanded them to mount and walked them out of camp, saluting the sentries as he passed the pickets. Then they followed the beaten-earth roadway to the blockhouse, some ten miles distant, from where Prendergast had sighted the commando the previous day. Dawn broke just before they got there to see the Union Jack fluttering proudly in the breeze.

'Lieutenant Mackinder,' said Captain Blewitt of the Northamptons, looking down on him from the crenellated roof. 'Thought you'd never arrive. Those fellows came back last night and exchanged fire.'

'Anyone hurt?'

'No. It was long-range stuff. The odd thing was that there weren't many of them – only about twenty, I would estimate. Certainly not enough to have any chance of successfully attacking this fort – I have forty men here, apart from the Maxim gun. It seemed almost a sort of demonstration. Anyway, they abandoned it about two. They'll be well away by now.'

'Those tracks look clear enough,' Murdoch told him. 'We'll take a look.'

Blewitt nodded. 'Good hunting. Hard to decide what they were after, really.'

'Twenty men,' Murdoch said. 'Good day to you.'

The tracks were certainly well marked, leading in a north-easterly direction towards some distant kopjes about twelve miles from the blockhouse.

'We've been out here before, sir,' Sergeant Bishop commented. 'I'm sure just beyond those hills is that village we burned last month.'

'Yes,' Murdoch agreed thoughtfully. Twenty men, demonstrating against a well-fortified position. That was utterly pointless. And now making for a deserted village. 'There may be more to this than meets the eye, sergeant. We'll have an advanced guard and flankers, if you please.'

'Yes, sir,' the sergeant said enthusiastically. He also had been in South Africa long enough to be wary of apparently simple situations. The orders were given and the advance guard of six men under Corporal Yeald moved up, while three flankers went out to either side. But the morning remained quiet as the troop trotted up to the hummocks and rocks. The advance guard disappeared into them and the main body followed a few minutes later. The tracks led right through the first kopje, to emerge into the small valley they knew lay on the farther side, where the burnt-out stumps of the Boer village remained, a scar on the brown earth. Here the advance party drew rein, while Corporal Yeald dismounted to peer at the ground and Murdoch led

110

the rest of the troop up to them, gazing down at the earth as well, and the still clearly visible hoof marks, now greatly increased in number.

'There have been more than twenty horses here, sir,' Corporal Yeald said. He had become quite an expert tracker during the last couple of years. 'And quite recently.'

'Yes,' Murdoch agreed. He raised his head, looked at the kopjes which surrounded the valley and felt his skin crawl. Of course it was only a matter of time before the Boers determined to strike back at the men who were looting their homes. 'We'll withdraw the troop, sergeant,' he said in a quiet voice. 'Take up your position on that high ground over there, call in your flankers and erect the heliograph equipment. Signal the blockhouse to signal the camp that we have made contact with a large Boer commando and need reinforcements. At least another troop out here, on the double, and a battery of artillery.'

'Yes, sir,' Bishop agreed. 'Follow me, lads,' he said. 'Easy, now.'

The troop wheeled to the left, the advance guard falling back into line. Murdoch waited as they passed him. His hair still seemed to be standing on end. He knew he was in the presence of a large number of men, but where they were he could not tell. Until the first bullet flew, followed by a hail of others, as the Boers realised that the troop was not, after all, going to ride into their trap.

Several men were hit, but all managed to keep their saddles. 'Ride,' Murdoch shouted, and the rest galloped for the high ground he had chosen as a defensive position. He turned Lucifer to follow them, and felt the deadening thump he had known once before, when Edward IV was shot from under him. The horse dropped like a stone, but he was more prepared for it this time; he landed on his feet and kept on running, drawing his revolver as he did so and glancing to his left, where the troop was disappearing, and then to his right, where several mounted men were riding at him. He brought up the revolver, fired and saw one of the Boers tumble backwards out of the saddle. Then the rest were upon him, clearly intent upon taking him prisoner, as they held their fire. The shoulder of a horse cannoned into him and he was thrown headlong, the revolver flying from his grasp. He sat up, gasping for breath, searching from left to right for the gun, then found himself looking into several rifle muzzles.

'Easy, now, lieutenant,' said one of the men. 'Easy. Make a wrong move and you're a dead man.'

Murdoch hesitated, then heard another voice. 'By God,' it said. 'Murdoch Mackinder, by God.'

He raised his head in consternation, gazed at Paul Reger.

5

The Transvaal, 1901

Murdoch was taken utterly by surprise. He had inquired after Reger when the British occupied Johannesburg, and was told the young German had gone away – and presumed he had returned to Germany. Now he gave him an astonished look, then glanced at the kopje, but his men had retired out of sight, on his orders. And there were a very large number of Boer riflemen close at hand and on the rocks above him.

'You are our prisoner,' Reger said. He then spoke in Dutch, and a horse was brought forward. Murdoch accepted the inevitable and had his wrists tied to the reins, which were then secured with a loose line to the bridle of Reger's horse. 'Mount up,' Reger commanded.

Murdoch swung into the saddle. 'What do you hope to achieve?' he asked. 'The war is lost for you. You can only get yourself killed.'

'We can take some of your British with us,' Reger said. 'Let's go.' He swung the horses, and the riflemen formed an escort around them.

'With *us?*' Murdoch demanded. 'You're not even a Boer.'

'I have chosen to fight with them,' Reger said. 'They have found my military training very useful. I am deputy field cornet of our commando.'

The horsemen were now filing out of the western side of the valley, leaving the regiment behind. 'And what do you mean to do with me?' Murdoch asked.

'Why, as you are the first officer we have captured, we intend to exchange you for some of our womenfolk who were taken when you burned our village a fortnight ago and have been locked up in those death camps of yours. I will confess that I am delighted; we had of course hoped to capture a British officer by luring you into our little trap, but I never dreamed it would be *you*.'

'What difference does it make who it is? Kitchener will never agree to an exchange.'

Reger grinned. 'Then you will spend a long time in our company, Murdoch. We must hope that your General Kitchener is a sensible man. I think he will be, where you are concerned.'

They were now on the plain beyond the kopjes, and looking back, could see the flashes of light in the sky. 'They are sending for reinforcements,' Reger said. Murdoch nodded. 'On my orders.'

'But when they get here, there will be nobody to find.'

The horses were kicked into a canter, and the commando, which numbered nearly a hundred men – as opposed to the twenty who had demonstrated against the blockhouse – made off to the north-west. Murdoch was aware of feeling more angry than alarmed at his situation. He had, after all, ridden into a trap. He had even known instinctively it was a trap, and had yet reacted too slowly. At least he was the only positive casualty. But he had lost another good horse, and he was a prisoner. For the sake of his reputation and his honour, and his peace of mind, he had to escape. But that was not practical at the moment, with his horse secured to Reger's, and surrounded by Boer sharpshooters. He would have to practise patience for a while.

Three hours of hard riding brought them to the laager, two dozen wagons tucked away out of sight in a ravine, where anyone might have ridden by a dozen times and never known they were there, save for the wisps of smoke from the cooking pots; but the place was surrounded by sentries on the high ground.

Murdoch realised that the war had taken on yet another new dimension, one as yet unknown to Kitchener; now that their homes could no longer be used for shelter, the Boers had reverted to the social structure that obtained in the days of the Great Trek, and were moving as a tribe, with their cattle and their families. Here there were women and children as well as men, and they surrounded Murdoch's horse, reaching up to drag him from the saddle. With his hands bound and secured to the reins, he could not defend himself; he had to submit to being manhandled while people spat and cursed at him in Dutch. For a moment he thought he was about to be lynched, but Reger and the other men drove the angry women away and released him from the reins, although his wrists were left bound. He managed to straighten his tunic, which had been torn open by the clawing fingers of the women.

'You'll observe that you are not very popular here,' Reger said.

'Yes,' Murdoch gasped, reaching for breath.

'Can you blame them, when they hear of what is going on in those camps?' He pushed Murdoch through the throng, to face a tall, thickset and heavily bearded man. 'Cornet Voorlandt speaks English.'

'You have secured an officer,' Voorlandt remarked. 'That is good. How many of the bastards did you kill?'

'Only a couple were hit; I do not think any were killed. We did not fight a battle. It was the officer I wanted,' Reger told him. 'I know this man. He comes from a famous family and is very well thought of in his regiment. They will be anxious to have him back.'

Murdoch opened his mouth to correct Reger's mistaken impression of the situation, based obviously on having known him as a friend of Holt's, and overvaluing the Mackinder name – at least as applied to this last member of the family, who had already blotted his copy-book too often – but then changed his mind. It was no part of his business to point out his enemy's misapprehensions, and Reger had to be considered an enemy, now.

'You will arrange for a flag of truce,' Voorlandt said. 'Meanwhile, tie him to a wagon wheel and let him stew a while.'

'No,' Reger objected. 'With respect, cornet, he was my friend – and he is too valuable to be ill treated. I will place him in our wagon. Margriet can feed him. And guard him, too.'

115

'English scum,' Voorlandt growled. 'How could you make a friend of such a man?'

'That was before the war,' Reger reminded him, and escorted Murdoch to one of the wagons.

'I suppose I should thank you for that,' Murdoch said.

'Indeed you should,' Reger agreed. 'Were you confined in the open, those women would have your eyes – if they did not leave you an eunuch.' There were steps at the rear of the wagon and he helped Murdoch up. 'If you were to give me your word as an officer and a gentleman that you would not try to attempt to escape, I would untie you.'

'Well, I'm afraid I cannot do that,' Murdoch said.

Reger shrugged. 'Then you will have to be uncomfortable. But the choice is yours. Sit.'

Murdoch sat on the floor of the wagon. Here there were mattresses and cooking pots and stores of grain and sides of beef, as well as a large assortment of weapons and ammunition – and three women, who came closer to stare at him. One of them was quite elderly, and he assumed she was the wife of the cornet. The other was younger, although still much older than himself, Murdoch estimated, and looked very like her companion. The third was only a girl, not yet twenty, Murdoch decided, very Dutch in appearance, with her long, thick yellow hair, and large, solemn features – but it was a handsome face. She was taller than the other two, very nearly as tall as Reger, in fact, and he suspected she would have a decidedly athletic body beneath her somewhat shapeless gown.

Reger spoke to them in Dutch, and then beckoned the girl forward. 'This is Margriet Voorlandt,' he explained. 'Field Cornet Voorlandt's daughter. She speaks English.'

'Juffrouw,' Murdoch said. 'I wish I could say it is a pleasure to meet you.'

Margriet Voorlandt gazed at him. She had large pale blue eyes. 'You are an English scum,' she said. But he had the feeling she didn't really mean it and might even feel sorry for him.

Reger grinned. 'Margriet is my fiancée,' he said, and Murdoch saw the ring on her finger. 'Another reason for

116

identifying with these people, eh? You will take care of Lieutenant Mackinder,' he told the girl. 'I wish him to be well fed and not ill treated in any way.'

'Well fed,' Margriet Voorlandt remarked. She sat opposite Murdoch, still gazing at him. 'It is not dinner time yet.'

Reger grinned again, picked up a rifle and handed it to her; she placed it across her knees. 'She can use it, too,' he told Murdoch. 'But as long as you behave yourself, she will not harm you.' He spoke again to the other women and then swung himself from the back of the wagon and returned to where the field cornet and the other senior members of the commando were waiting for him.

Margriet's mother and aunt, as Murdoch presumed them to be, also came back to sit and stare at him, and talk to each other – about him, he supposed, but he knew very little Dutch. After Reger's remarks about what the Boer women might wish to do to him, he felt distinctly uneasy at the thought of being at the mercy of these three harpies with his hands bound together – even if to call the girl Margriet a harpy was hardly to do her justice. But she was an enemy, and he had to remember that. On the other hand, if she was to be his gaoler, she was also his only hope of escape.

The thought came quite suddenly, partly because of that earlier feeling that she might not hate him quite as much as she pretended, and partly because it was apparent that the other women knew no English. Thus Reger might well have made a mistake, because in his absence, Murdoch and the girl would enjoy a very private world. Of course, he would have to be careful. If he offended her in any way, or said anything that she might choose to repeat to her fiancé, he might find himself in even greater discomfort. But she was his only prospect, and he could not help remembering how Rosetta Dredge had found him more attractive than Reger.

The realisation made his heartbeat quicken. It was a very long time since he had had any dealings with a woman at all, much less a very pretty girl. He would have to act the cad in every way, of course – she was Reger's betrothed, and she was an innocent young girl ... and Reger had protected him from the full wrath of the Boers. But she was an enemy, and so was Reger now. Seducing her would be a duty as well as a pleasure, if it could be done.

If he was going to attempt it, the sooner he started the better. 'I am very thirsty,' he said.

She considered for a moment, then reached out of the back of the wagon, where there was a barrel of water, dipped in a long-handled ladle and held it to his lips. Some spilt down the front of his opened tunic to soak his shirt, but enough went down his throat to take away a little of the dust-parched discomfort. 'Thank you,' he said. 'You are very kind.'

Once again a long stare, then she sat down again. Before he could continue the conversation there was a great deal of bustle as the laager prepared to move out; they knew they could probably be tracked when the reinforcements Murdoch had sent for reached the troop. But he observed half a dozen riders heading back the way they had come, carrying a pole to which a torn sheet had been attached. They were going to negotiate. He wondered what Kitchener's reaction *would* be? To write him off as a thorough nuisance, he suspected.

Mevrouw Voorlandt herself drove the wagon, with her sister beside her. Murdoch observed that all the wagons were being driven by women, while their husbands mounted up, some forming an escort, others riding ahead to find a new camping ground and to make sure there was no risk of encountering an unsuspected British patrol; still others formed a rear guard – the whole manoeuvre was very military.

Margriet remained seated in the rear of the Voorlandt wagon, her rifle across her knees. But as Reger had ridden off with the advance guard, Murdoch realised he would never have a better opportunity than now to break the ice.

'When are you and Paul to be married?' he asked.

'Soon,' she replied.

'And will he then take you to live in Germany? On his uncle's estates?'

A faint frown creased her forehead. 'We will live here,' she said.

'As fugitives, outlaws, for the rest of your life?' he persisted. 'That would be a pity. And a waste. You would love Berlin. And Berlin would love you.'

This time the frown was deeper. 'You have been to Berlin?' she asked.

'Of course,' he lied.

'Captain Reger will not speak of it. I should like to go to Berlin. But . . . it is all the fault of you British that I cannot,' she said.

'Perhaps he will also take you to London, one day,' Murdoch suggested.

Her nostrils flared. 'You talk too much, Englander,' she said. 'Be quiet.'

Murdoch obeyed, He thought he might have made some progress.

The laager found another gully in which there was a spring of good water, and camped there for the night. Murdoch was taken out of the wagon, marched under the guard of two men into the bushes to perform his necessaries, and then fed, along with everyone else, around a roaring camp fire. The camaraderie was impressive, with small cups of geneva being passed around, solemn toasts – which he gathered were mainly to the damnation of the British – and then some deep-throated songs in which the women and children joined with enormous feeling.

'They do not regard themselves as defeated,' Paul told him. 'They know they have been deserted by those, like Kruger, who led them into this war and then fled the moment the going got rough. But now they are determined never to submit to Kitchener's yoke. They are a proud people. And I am proud to be one of them.'

Murdoch's wrists had been released to allow him to eat, and he worked his fingers gratefully as the pins and needles filled his hands. 'I still say there is a time when a man must know that he cannot surmount the odds facing him. Eventually this laager will be surrounded by British troops. Then you will either surrender or be killed – with your women and children, who in the meantime will have been exposed to continuing hardships. There is no alternative for you. So why not end it now by submitting, and then endeavour to get on with your lives?'

'This is these people's lives,' Paul told him. 'They would rather die than have it end.'

Next day the laager remained where it was, waiting, Murdoch surmised, for its messengers to return. But a considerable body of men, led by Reger, rode off – presumably to raid one of the railway lines; those who remained went up into the hills above the gully to watch. The women performed the daily tasks of milking the cows, cleaning the wagons and cooking the food, aided by the older children. Several remained interested in Murdoch, but Margriet Voorlandt sent them away. He had spent the night sleeping in the open, a Boer to either side of him, but now she allowed him to sit in the wagon, his hands again bound together in front of him, where she could watch him while she performed her chores. She scraped the family washing up and down her ridged board, every so often glancing at him. Her rifle leaned against the wagon wheel within reach, while one of the camp dogs lay at her feet.

'It is a shame to see a beautiful woman like yourself labouring over a washtub,' Murdoch remarked.

Her head came up for a moment, then she resumed her labour.

'Because you are, a beautiful woman,' Murdoch said. 'You should be dressed in satin and ride in a carriage. Paul should take you away from here to some place where you would enjoy those things. You should not be buried in this wasteland, with only a bullet or a concentration camp at the end of it.'

Margriet emptied out the tub, muscles rippling in her sun-browned arms. 'Are you married?' she asked.

'No.'

'Why not?'

He decided against confessing that he was too young. 'I have never met anyone I could fall in love with. Until now.'

Her head started to turn, sharply, then she checked it. 'You are in love?'

'I could easily be,' Murdoch told her. 'In fact, I think I am, yes.'

And realised that, although he *was* behaving like the most utter cad, he could very well mean it. He watched her strong body as she hefted the clothes to the line she had erected and began hanging them out.

'You are an English swine,' she said over her shoulder, but rather, he thought, to remind herself of that fact than from conviction.

'I would like to show you London,' he said.

Once again her head turned. 'You? I am betrothed to Captain Reger.'

Captain Reger, he observed for the second time. Never Paul. 'Do you love him?'

'I am going to marry him.'

'But you do not love him.'

'A wife must love her husband.'

'Must she? You will never love him if you do not love him now.'

'He is the man my father has chosen as my husband,' she said. 'Now be quiet. You speak too much, Englander.'

The men returned that evening, apparently well satisfied with their day's work – Murdoch could not discover what that had been – but concerned that their negotiating party had not yet come back. 'We will remain here for one more day.' Paul told Murdoch. 'You had better hope that your General Kitchener has not abused a flag of truce, or it could go hard with you.'

'You mean you'd hand me over to the women?'

Paul grinned. 'They would tear you limb from limb if I let them. I would not like that to happen, Murdoch. I like you. I liked you from the moment of our first meeting. Tell me, whatever happened to that plump little girl we flirted with?'

'We are by way of being engaged,' Murdoch said.

'Ha ha. I thought she was quite fond of me. But I knew she was out to snare one of us. Well, well. I will wish you every happiness. But if Kitchener has taken our envoys, you may never be able to achieve it. You had best pray.'

Or work even harder, Murdoch decided.

'Do you think it might be possible to have a bath and a shave?' he asked Margriet the next morning after the men had left. 'I feel absolutely filthy.'

'It is not possible until Captain Reger returns,' she said.

'Why? You could take me to the creek along there and keep guard over me with your rifle. I would even give you my parole that I would not attempt to escape – without you.'

He wasn't sure she had noticed his addition. Her cheeks were pink with embarrassment. 'How could I watch you bathing?' she asked.

'Would it concern you if we were lovers?'

'We are not lovers, and your conversation is indecent, Englander.'

'I would like to be your lover,' he said. 'I would like to take you to England, to London, to walk with you down the Strand and show you off. I would very much like to do those things. If you would come with me to England, you would have servants and carriages and fine clothes, and you would live in the most magnificent house.' And you would save me from Rosetta Dredge, he thought.

She tossed her head. 'As your lover?'

'As my wife.'

'How can you say such things?' she demanded, cheeks pinker yet. 'When you have only known me for three days, and I am betrothed to another man? Your friend,' she added.

'Once he was my friend,' Murdoch said. 'Now he is my enemy. Worse, he is the enemy of your people, for encouraging them to continue this senseless war. As for my feelings for you, what are three days when a man sees the woman with whom he is going to fall in love? Those things are decided by fate and the stars, not by days and weeks and months.'

She came close to him, standing above him, her thick

122

yellow hair fluttering in the breeze. 'You are a dishonourable liar and a cheat who is trying to take advantage of an innocent girl,' she told him.

'I will give you all of those things. I swear it on the grave of my father.'

She stared at him, then dropped to her knees beside him. 'That is a terrible lie to tell,' she said.

'It is not a lie.' He placed his bound hands on top of hers, then slowly moved them up her arm. She caught her breath as she turned her head from side to side to make sure no one was looking, and he watched the bodice of her gown heaving. But she did not pull away. He wanted to hold his own breath, and for more reasons than that he felt success might be coming closer. She *was* a lovely girl, in every sense, and he *would* be proud to walk down the Strand with her on his arm, and to take her back to Broad Acres to show her off to Mother and the girls. He even thought they might love her too. But in addition, to think of possessing all of that strong beauty . . . he felt himself flushing as well as he gazed into her eyes. He had never thought of a woman quite so physically before.

As she could tell. But then she said, 'You are a bastard,' and got up and walked away.

At least, he thought, she had not said he was an *English* bastard.

When the commando returned that evening, it was accompanied by one of the five men sent to the British camp. There was a great deal of noise and bustle and excited shouting.

Paul came over to Murdoch. 'Well,' he said, 'your General Kitchener has acted the fool. He has refused to recognise our flag of truce and has placed four of our comrades under arrest. Do you know the message he has sent back to us? That if you are not returned unharmed within forty-eight hours, he will have them shot.'

Murdoch kept his face impassive with an effort. 'I warned you that he would never deal with you. I think he means what he says.'

'That will be bad for you,' Paul said. 'Cornet Voorlandt has decided that if our people are shot, you will be executed in turn, before the eyes of one of your blockhouses.'

'Will that solve anything?'

'It will avenge our comrades,' Paul told him. 'And you would have your own general to thank for it.'

Murdoch found it difficult to sleep that night. He had no doubt at all that Kitchener did mean what he had said; he was that sort of man. It was therefore very necessary either to compose himself for death, or finally to break down Margriet Voorlandt's reserve tomorrow – and now he had absolutely nothing to lose. He could hardly wait for daylight, for the men to depart as usual and for the work of the encampment to commence. And for her to come and feed him at midday.

'They are going to kill you,' she said. 'Father has resolved on it. Did you know that?'

'I knew it was likely. Will you be happy to see me dead?'

'I would not like you to die,' she said.

'Well, you are the only one who can prevent it. Margriet . . . I do love you. I will love you forever, if you will let me. I will take you to places you have never dreamed of. I will make you the happiest woman on earth. I swear it.'

She gazed at him. 'Will you beat me?' she asked.

'Beat you? Good lord, no. Why should I do that?'

'Father beats Mother,' she said thoughtfully. 'And he beats me. He says it is good for a woman to be beaten regularly. And Captain Reger has told me that he will beat me too.' She gave a little shudder. 'I do not like being beaten.'

Murdoch held her hands. 'I will never beat you, Margriet. I will never let any harm whatsoever come to you.'

Again she made no attempt to free herself, but sat in silence for some time. Then she said, 'If I try to help you and am found out, they will beat me worse than ever. And they will kill you.'

'But they are going to kill me anyway,' he reminded her.

'And they are going to beat you anyway, too. Reger has told you this. So neither of us has anything to lose.'

She freed herself and got up. 'You are asking me to desert my family and my people. To betray my fiancé,' she said.

'I am asking you to come with me to a better life than you have ever known. And in doing that you may even be able to help your family. They can only be helped by ending this senseless war. Once that is done, you will see, the British will be magnanimous, and your father will soon be a prosperous farmer again.' He could only hope he was right about that.

She considered him for some moments, then said, 'And Captain Reger?'

'You do not love Captain Reger, Margriet. Nor will you ever. Can you tie yourself to a man you do not love, for the rest of your life?'

'And will I love you?' she asked.

'I think you already do,' he suggested.

'I have work to do,' she told him, her cheeks flaming.

He knew he was making progress, but it was now a race against time, and to make matters worse, that night he was shackled to the wheel of the wagon, with one of the men sleeping near him; clearly he was, as Margriet had said, already a condemned man. Tomorrow the forty-eight hours would be up, and Kitchener would undoubtedly carry out his threat – as Voorlandt and Reger expected. They rode out with the main body of the commando to seek news, leaving Murdoch still shackled, and today under the guard of a man.

'When the commando returns tonight, I will be executed,' Murdoch told Margriet as she fed him breakfast.

'I could not help you last night,' she said.

'Then you must help me now.'

'Now? In broad daylight? With men in the hills, watching us?'

'They are not watching us,' he told her. 'They are watching the veldt. Release me and take me into the bushes, as if I needed to go to the toilet. You will cover me with your rifle. From there it is only a few yards to the horses.'

'The men on watch will certainly look at us when they see two horses being taken,' she insisted. 'We cannot succeed.'

'We will succeed because, like you, they will not suppose we will try it in broad daylight.'

She chewed her lip. 'I cannot take you into the bushes,' she said. 'That would be indecent. Nor do I have a key to your shackle. That man has it.'

'Then tell him that I need to go. And you follow.'

Once more she hesitated, then she went to the guard and asked him to release Murdoch from the wagon. There was some discussion, but he finally agreed, unlocked the shackle and then nudged Murdoch towards the bushes with the muzzle of his rifle. Murdoch took a long breath as he realised he was being given the opportunity he sought, by a young girl who was abandoning family, friends and fiancé to come with him. Undoubtedly she was motivated by her hatred of the life she was being forced to lead, by the apparently pointless beatings which her father inflicted whenever he was in the mood, by the dream of living the life of a lady of fashion which he had suggested could be hers – as much as by any affection for him. Yet having made that promise, he would be honour bound to keep it. Just as he was honour bound to succeed now, for her sake as much as his own.

The man said something, and Murdoch gathered he was considered to have gone far enough; certainly he was out of sight of the laager. He half turned, and the man gestured with his rifle, telling him to get on with it. He was unaware that Margriet had followed them and was only a few feet away, also carrying a rifle. Now he heard her footfall, and turned to remonstrate at her indecency in wishing to follow the men when they sought privacy. For that moment he was off guard, and Murdoch, bringing his hands together to use as a club, struck him across the back of the neck with all his strength.

The Boer fell as if poleaxed. 'You have killed him,' Margriet gasped.

'Just laid him out.' Murdoch knelt and took the man's hat, bandolier and Mauser. 'Let's go.'

'We are going to die,' she said dolefully, but followed him through the bushes, bending double until they reached the far end of the thicket, where they were within a few yards of the picketed horses. As usual there was one man in charge, but he was at the far side. 'Can you ride bareback?' Murdoch asked.

'Of course. I have done so since I was a child.'

'Me too. Come on.' He crept forward, knelt down and released the picket line. There was no time to select their mounts. He simply grasped the manes of the two nearest, and Margriet vaulted on to the first, hitching up her skirts to her thighs to ride astride, long white legs flashing in the sun. Murdoch was beside her a moment later, left hand still twined in the horses' manes as he guided them through the rest of the animals, who were milling about aimlessly.

The guard gave a shout, and then another. Murdoch pointed the Mauser into the air and fired. The shot sent the horses rushing to and fro and started the cattle lowing anxiously, and for a moment there was total pandemonium as women and children shouted and screamed, dogs barked, several other people fired their rifles, and the men on watch in the hills also started calling. Margriet looked back at her father's wagon, where her mother and aunt stood together, obviously recognising her. For a moment she hesitated, then Murdoch slapped the rump of her horse and sent it down the defile that led to the open veldt, following on his own mount.

A bearded man on a horse appeared in front of them, calling on them to stop. Murdoch released the mane to unsling his rifle, and the man's gun came up. But he hesitated to shoot because of Margriet, and Murdoch fired past her and sent him tumbling back out of the saddle.

'My God, but you have killed *him*,' Margriet cried.

'Or he would have killed us.' Murdoch leaned across to seize the horse's bridle and lead it behind them, controlling his own mount only by his knees. They were going to need all the transport they could find. He would have liked the dead man's rifle and bandolier, but there was no time to stop and pick them up. So they continued on their way down the defile and found themselves on the open veldt.

'East,' he shouted. He had only the vaguest of ideas of their whereabouts, but he knew the laager had travelled west two days previously, and that the railway line was to the east; there and he would be able to reach a blockhouse.

They galloped across the undulating ground, very aware of the sun beating down on them. Soon the horses were blown and they had to slow. Murdoch looked back and saw four men behind them, perhaps a mile away, showing for the moment on the top of each rise, and then disappearing into the dips.

'We must stop them coming,' he said.

'I cannot kill my own people,' Margriet protested.

'You have already killed one of your people, Margriet, in their eyes. If we do not stop them, they will kill us. I am your people now, Margriet. You have no one else.'

She bit her lip, as if she hadn't entirely weighed the consequences of her action. Murdoch looked left and right, and found a gully a few hundred yards away. He rode towards it and was delighted to find that it contained a pool of what appeared to be good water; they could stand something of a siege here. He rode on down and slipped from the saddle. The third horse was still with them, and in the saddlebags he found some dried meat, biscuit and, best of all, a water bottle. Margriet dismounted beside him and he gave her a drink and something to eat, then refilled the bottle.

'They will know we have gone to ground,' she said.

He nodded. 'But not where, exactly. We have the advantage.'

He lay down on the upper slope, only his head showing, and even that he reckoned would be invisible at any distance. He was fighting like a Boer now; it would be interesting to see if they had any instant answer to their own tactics.

After a moment, Margriet lay beside him. 'I have never killed a man,' she said. 'Not even an Englander.'

'You won't have to, unless they get close enough to rush us, and I don't mean to allow that,' he said.

She gazed across the veldt for a moment and saw the four men appear then disappear again. In a few minutes they would be within accurate range. 'Are you afraid?' she asked.

He turned his head to look at her. 'I have not thought about that. It is better not to.'

'Because you are a soldier. Killing people is your business. I am afraid.'

He supposed she was right – about him, at least. He had never considered being afraid, only doing his duty and not letting down the regiment, or the troop, or himself. And now, not letting down Margriet. He doubted she was as frightened as she thought. She lay on her stomach beside him, rifle thrust forward, hair falling falling to either side of her head, body nestling on the warm earth, legs spread as wide as her skirt would permit. He kept thinking of those legs as he had seen them while she was riding – suspended, exposed, on either side of her mount, muscles ridged as she had clasped the animal's sides.

He leaned towards her and kissed her mouth. Her eyes widened, but she made no effort to withdraw, even when his tongue parted her lips to seek hers.

'Have you never been kissed before?' he asked.

'No,' she said. 'No.'

'I am sorry about the beard.'

She smiled. 'I like you better with a beard.' She had only ever known men with beards.

There was so much more he wanted to do to her. But there were more important matters to be attended to first. He looked back and saw the Boers appearing over the next rise, only a few hundred yards distant now. They were trotting, confident of finding the fugitives, following the tracks rather than worrying about an ambush. Perhaps they did not realise he was armed, Murdoch thought. But he had to destroy them without hesitation.

'It would help if you were to fire too,' he said. 'Not

129

necessarily at them. Just to make them know we are both armed and determined.'

'Yes,' she said.

'So do it now,' he said. When the men reappeared, only three hundred yards away, he took careful aim and fired. The leading Boer threw up his arms and fell backward from the saddle. Beside Murdoch, Margriet also fired, deliberately high, but Murdoch had already swung his rifle to bring down the second man. The other two promptly dropped from their saddles and disappeared from sight, but he could still see their horses. He didn't want to kill the animals; he wanted to make the men abandon their pursuit. He sighted again and fired, aiming just to miss the horses. Once again he squeezed the trigger, then held his fire and waited. Only a few minutes later the horses slowly retreated; obviously they were being led to a more sheltered position by the men crawling or bending very low. Then the other two were also led back. He stared at the vague, shimmering figures, watched the two bodies being placed across the horses' backs. The two unwounded men were easy targets, and his finger caressed the trigger. But he was not in the business of murder. They were doing what he wanted of them. The wounded men secure, the other two mounted up and rode back towards the laager; they knew there was nothing they could do against two concealed and accurate rifles.

'They will return with Father and Captain Reger and every man they can find,' Margriet said. 'They will surround the gully and force us to surrender. Then they will hang us both.'

'If we are still here. They have to find the others first, and then find us.' Murdoch watched the horses out of sight and then rose to his knees. 'We have time.' He gave her the water bottle again, then went down to the spring and refilled it. 'Would you object if I had that bath I wanted? I want it even more now.'

'You said I should not object, if you were my lover.'

They gazed at each other. 'Yes,' he said. 'It will give the horses a chance to rest.' He led them to the water and let them drink, then stripped and splashed water over himself.

He did not know if she was watching him or not; if she was, then she would know how affected he was by her presence.

'What are those scars?' she asked. She had risen and was standing only a few feet away.

'Bullet wounds. From Boer rifles.'

'Were you very badly hurt?'

'Not very badly, no.' He turned to face her and discovered that she had also undressed. He had never seen a naked woman before – and perhaps she had never seen a naked man. From her expression, she might be finding him as beautiful as he found her. Crisp, short black hair; or long golden tresses shrouding the strong face. Gleaming white shoulders; and powerful muscles. Thin blue veins coursing across surprisingly small, upturned breasts with pink nipples: against more muscle, covered in the thick mat of black hair. Both possessed slender bellies, but she had the wider hips; and her pubic hair was almost as pale as the rest of her, where his was dark. There her beauty, and her desire, remained for the moment concealed; his was obvious and impatient, but not, it seemed, frightening. Perhaps she had, after all, seen enough of men – at least her father – in the crowded intimacy of a Boer wagon.

The legs which had so filled his mind were long and straight and strong. Again he matched her, save for the added muscle. He did not know if she was a virgin, although he presumed so, but he was glad that he had waited for someone so lovely.

But he would wait no more, nor did she want him to. She came into the water beside him and said, 'I am your woman now, Murdoch Mackinder.'

'I know that,' he acknowledged, and took her into his arms. It was his first kiss, first embrace, since that night in Cape Town – and the first time he had ever held a naked woman in his arms.

'I do not want to wait,' she said. 'If I am yours, make me yours, now and forever.'

They lay on the ground, their bodies still wet. Their mutual eagerness led them through the barrier of their ignorance. By doing what seemed most natural and most appealing he was inside her in seconds, and she was ready for him, her passion heightened by the enormity of what she had just done and the promise of what lay ahead.

The sun burned their flesh as they lay together and he kissed her hair. 'I shall love you, and honour you, and protect you forever,' he said. 'Forever.'

'As I shall love you,' she promised in turn. 'I pray that I may one day be forgiven by my mother and father.'

'I will pray for that too,' he told her. 'And work to make it happen. Now we must get on, before those men come back with support.'

They dressed themselves, and he set her on the saddled horse, while he took one of the others. It was a strange journey because they could go at no more than a walk, owing to the exhaustion of the animals, and because for all their real peril, their minds were filled only with thoughts of each other. When at about five in the afternoon the two ponies could clearly go no further, they put the saddle on the third, which had faithfully followed them, and then abandoned the others, hoping they would be found by the commando coming behind them. Then they rode together, Margriet sitting behind him with her arms round his waist, her body moving against his as they proceeded on their way.

By nightfall this horse too could carry them no longer, but by then they were in sight of the railway track.

'Murdoch,' Colonel Edmonds said, shaking his hand. 'My God, Murdoch! It is so good to see you. We had supposed you lost, especially when we received that Boer ultimatum. You understand that we could not possibly agree to any exchange, or every British officer would have been at risk.'

'Of course I understand that, sir,' Murdoch said. 'Which was why I determined to escape.'

'And escape you did, by God,' Major Craufurd said, also shaking his hand.

'With the aid of a young lady, sir,' Murdoch reminded him.

132

'Quite a looker, too, if I may say so,' said Johnnie Morton, taking over the handshaking from Craufurd.

'Where is she?' Edmonds asked.

'Waiting in my office, sir,' Hobbs told him, having also hurried in to join the welcoming party.

'I would very much like you to meet her, sir,' Murdoch said. 'She and I. . . .'

Edmonds held up his hand and winked. 'I don't think I had better know about that, Murdoch. Captain Hobbs, will you attend to the young lady?'

'Of course, sir.'

'She, I. . . .' Murdoch was not sure how to continue without involving her reputation.

'Of course, my dear boy, of course,' Edmonds said. 'I know exactly how you feel. But Hobbs will look after it.'

Hobbs was already at the door. Murdoch hurried behind him. 'I'll come with you.'

'Lieutenant Mackinder,' Craufurd said. 'You have not yet been dismissed.'

'Leave it with me, old man,' Hobbs said. 'No need for you to be involved. Better not to be, in fact.'

Morton punched Murdoch on the arm. 'You are a sly old devil, after all, eh?'

The door opened and Murdoch gazed at Margriet, seated in the straight chair in front of Hobbs' desk, obviously anxious. 'Murdoch,' she said, getting up. 'Is it all right?'

'Of course,' he said. 'Of course. I. . . .' He glanced at Edmonds and Craufurd, who were obviously waiting to continue the discussion. 'I'll be with you in a little while. But right now, this gentleman will take you somewhere to have a bath and something to eat, and perhaps a change of clothing?' He glanced at Hobbs.

'Oh, I am sure that can be arranged,' Hobbs said.

'I do not wish to be separated from you,' she protested.

'Lieutenant Mackinder,' Craufurd said again.

'It will only be for a little while,' Murdoch repeated. 'Do take good care of her, Captain Hobbs.'

'Oh, I shall,' Hobbs promised, and closed the door.

133

Murdoch turned back to the room. 'I am sorry, sir,' he said. 'But I do owe her my life, and we. . . .'

'Murdoch,' Colonel Edmonds interrupted. 'I have the most marvellous news for you.'

'Have you, sir?' Murdoch had no idea what he was talking about.

'Indeed. The powers that be have at last decided to recognise your gallantry in saving my life before Klip Drift last year.'

Murdoch had almost forgotten the incident. 'Why, sir,' he said, 'any member of the regiment would have acted as I did. I merely happened to be the closest.'

'I would like to think that you are right. But as it happened, you were the man who did it. My report and recommendation were supported by those of Captain Morton and the American journalist Casper, both of whom were present, you may remember. Well, the upshot of it is that His Majesty has graciously consented to award you the Victoria Cross.'

'The. . . .' Murdoch was struck dumb. Britain's highest award for valour? Not one of his famous forebears had achieved that.

'My most hearty congratulations,' Edmonds said, coming round his desk to shake his hand again.

'And mine,' Craufurd agreed. 'It is too long since the regiment had a VC.'

'It's an honour for the entire squadron,' Morton put in.

Murdoch still didn't know what to say. But it seemed that everything was falling into his lap; as a VC his determination to marry Margriet Voorlandt would surely be the easier to achieve.

'Now, my dear boy,' Edmonds said, 'I know you will wish to have a bath and get rid of that ghastly stubble on your chin, and then General Kitchener himself wishes to see you, both to pick your brains and to congratulate you himself, I should think.'

'Yes, sir. Thank you, sir. May I ask what accommodation is being made available for Miss Voorlandt?'

134

Edmonds frowned at him. 'Accommodation? Why, she will be accommodated in the camp, of course.'

'The camp? You mean . . . ?' Murdoch half turned to look at the closed door. 'You have sent Margriet to a concentration camp?'

'My dear boy, she is a Boer.'

'Who helped me to escape,' Murdoch almost shouted. 'To whom I am betrothed. To. . . .'

'Betrothed?' Edmonds demanded. 'You cannot be serious.'

'I am, sir, We. . . .' he bit his lip.

'Ah,' Edmonds said. 'Of course I understand. You found it necessary to seduce the young lady in order to escape.'

'No, I. . . .' Murdoch checked himself, because wasn't that exactly what he had done?

'Well,' Edmonds remarked, 'they say that all is fair in love and war. Eh, Harry?' He glanced at Craufurd and Morton.

'And this seems to be a case of both combined,' Morton grinned. 'You are quite a rascal, Mackinder, behind that dedicated exterior. But then, ruthlessness is a very desirable quality in a soldier.'

'Ruthlessness? You don't understand,' Murdoch said. 'When I asked Miss Voorlandt to marry me, I was serious. I love her. I. . . .'

Edmonds glanced at the other two officers. 'I think perhaps I should see Mackinder alone,' he said.

'Of course,' Craufurd agreed, and left the office, followed by Morton.

'Sit down, Murdoch,' the colonel invited.

Murdoch hesitated, then obeyed. The colonel returned behind his desk and also sat down. 'I hate to sound like a father,' he said, 'but I am very conscious of the fact that you do not have a father. How old are you?'

'I will be twenty-one next year, sir.'

'Twenty-one. You are of course aware that no officer in the British Army can marry under the age of thirty without the permission of his commanding officer?'

'Yes, sir. But I would have hoped that in all the

135

circumstances. . . .' He didn't really know how to go on, so finished lamely, 'Miss Voorlandt undoubtedly saved my life.'

'Perhaps she did. And very honourably you wish to do the right thing by her. But has it occurred to you that she was more concerned with leaving her own people, and the living death to which she was condemned, and saw in you a possible passport to safety?'

'Can you honestly say that incarceration in a concentration camp is not a living death, sir? And if the people in there discovered she helped a British officer . . . my God, sir, you cannot do it.'

'I did not make the rules, Murdoch. And neither did you. As soldiers, we obey orders. This young woman is an enemy.'

'Who has served our cause. Who has surrendered.'

'We do not know her motives. She may even be a spy. She is an enemy. That is unquestionable. And until the Boer commandos cease their depredations, General Kitchener's orders are inflexible and must be obeyed: any member of the family of any of these marauders must be placed in a camp until the entire commando surrenders.'

'You are condemning her to life imprisonment.'

'I doubt that. I think her people will give in, soon enough.'

'But she cannot go back to them.' Again Murdoch wanted to shout in despair.

'That is a matter between her and her family.'

'And you would be making me break my sacred oath.'

'I am endeavouring to prevent you making a colossal fool of yourself. My dear boy, believe me, I understand the circumstances entirely. You found it necessary to undertake certain actions, make certain promises, in order to persuade this woman to help you. Do you really suppose that makes her a fit consort for a man who has an enormously bright military future, a great family tradition to uphold? Have you thought of your mother and the girls? Has it not occurred to you that a girl who could give herself to a man she can only have known a couple of days can hardly be better than a whore? I'm afraid I must not only refuse to consider any

136

proposal you may have made to her, but I must forbid you to attempt to see her again.'

Murdoch stood up and came to attention. 'Then sir, I must request to be relieved of my commission.'

'You *what?*'

'I cannot remain in the army, sir, if I am forced to abandon that girl. I will not abandon her. I will do everything in my power to obtain her release, and then I will marry her.'

Edmonds leaned back in his chair. 'You must have a touch of the sun. A Mackinder, resigning his commission? I have never heard such nonsense. In any event, I refuse to accept your resignation.'

'Then I will walk out,' Murdoch declared.

'You really are ill,' Edmonds said. He stood up himself. 'Lieutenant Mackinder, as of this moment you are confined to your quarters until further notice. I will have Dr Grahame examine you, and I have no doubt he will prescribe rest and a sedative. When you have recovered your senses, you may return here and we will attempt to have a reasonable discussion.'

'I refuse to place myself under arrest, sir,' Murdoch said. 'I am going to leave the Army.'

Edmonds stared at him. 'If I do not have you placed under close arrest this minute,' he said evenly, 'it is because I admired and respected your father, as up to this moment I have admired and respected you, almost as a son. I am also aware that you saved my life above Klip Drift and that you are a hero. But you are also a soldier. Now listen to me, boy. Nothing that has happened or been said in this room need go on your record. If you will now obey me and return to your quarters and have a rest – and put this girl out of your mind – not a soul on this earth will ever even suspect what has happened here today. I most earnestly beg and entreat you to do as I ask.'

Murdoch remained at attention. His heart was pounding so hard he thought it might find its way out of his chest. He knew he was adopting an indefensible position in the eyes of any soldier. But he also knew what he had promised

Margriet Voorlandt, what he had felt as he had lain with her in his arms. 'I am afraid I cannot do that, sir,' he said, just as evenly as his commander. 'I feel that I am bound to Miss Voorlandt by honour and by gratitude, and by sheer humanity. And by love. You are condemning her virtually to death. I would never be able to look myself in the face again were I to accept that decision.'

Edmonds sighed. 'Then I am afraid you leave me no choice.' He went to the door and opened it. 'Captain Morton,' he said. 'I order you to place First Lieutenant Murdoch Mackinder under arrest, escort him to his quarters, using force if you have to, and see that he remains there until further orders.'

Part Two

THE CAPTAIN

6

Bath, 1902–06

The band played 'Here the Conquering Hero Comes', and the crowd on the quayside at Southampton cheered and became almost hysterical as the liner slid into the dock. Murdoch gathered from the ship's officers that this was the reception every troopship received on returning from South Africa, but it was none the less impressive and stimulating. The crowds, the band, Mother and Rosemary and Philippa standing with the other officers' wives and families . . . these were all meant to make those returning from the battlefields believe that it had all been worthwhile, that whatever the rest of the world might say, these were men who had upheld the integrity and the glory of the Empire – and suffered in doing so.

The *SS Union Castle* was indeed very much a hospital ship. She was filled with rank and file who had contracted various fevers, mainly enteric, and had therefore to be invalided home, accompanied by those who had actually taken a serious bullet wound in a conflict with the guerillas, or those who had succumbed to the venereal complaints which were rife in Africa – also described as suffering from enteric fever. And then there were those who had fallen victim to the pressures of living and fighting in South Africa, and waging a remorseless war against apparently defenceless women and children. Such men were described as suffering from exhaustion – and possibly enteric fever – and were to be pitied even more than the actual casualties. And amongst them Murdoch numbered himself.

'Well, sir, there's no place like England, even if it is raining,' remarked Trooper Reynolds.

Murdoch was not sure whether Reynolds had volunteered to accompany him to escape further service in Africa, or

141

had been appointed some kind of watchdog, or most likely, simply sent off because as batman he knew the inside story of Murdoch's 'illness'. Reynolds had never once trespassed on that taboo ground, and had indeed been his unfailing cheerful and faithful self throughout the voyage.

He was right, Murdoch thought. Even the sight of the Isle of Wight, appearing mistily green through the wintry murk of a December morning – indeed, the blast of cold air which solidified their breaths, the slate grey of both the heavens and the sea – testified that they were home, far away from bullets and Boers, brilliant sunshine and scorching heat. With not a spot of African dust left on them. For Murdoch, a glittering future lay ahead; a visit to Buckingham Palace, no less, for an investiture with his country's highest military award. Unless he turned his back on the whole thing and returned to South Africa . . . to nothing. He would not be able to see her, to reclaim her. He did not even know if she was still alive. Certainly she would not have forgiven him for his betrayal. English scum, she had once called him, and she had been proved right. There had been too many factors involved; family and tradition and glittering prizes were only a part. It was his own weakness that he would never be able to come to terms with. His life had been left with a hideous scar slashed across it.

At first he had seriously considered mutiny. He had even considered attacking Johnnie Morton and Billy Hobbs as they escorted him to his quarters . . . but breaking free would have accomplished nothing. There had been no way to gain access to Margriet, no way to avoid being retaken and tried as a mutineer.

Everyone had been so very helpful. Even General Kitchener. He had wanted to know about the Boer commando, about conditions in the laager – questions which Murdoch had answered as best he could: his only hope of ever seeing Margriet again was a speedy end to the war. Kitchener had listened and made notes, the eyes above the flat moustache as cold as ice. Then he had said, 'And now you are to be invalided home. You are fortunate, Lieutenant Mackinder.

142

Many a man would have come out of an experience such as yours with far less a reward than that.'

Which was as far as Kitchener would go in censure. Apparently the announcement that he was to receive the Victoria Cross had already been released to the newspapers. To have such a hero charged with insubordination and cashiered, and possibly even shot for collaboration with the enemy, had been unthinkable. Clearly he had been ill. Dr Grahame and the padre had whole-heartedly supported that theory. Here was a man who in a moment of heat-exhausted, fever-ridden madness might have refused to accept the diktat of his superior officer – but he had also stood across the shattered body of that same officer and defied the Boers, and had then escaped from captivity . . . why, there was a young journalist named Winston Churchill who had also been captured by the Boers, while with Buller's command in Natal, and had gallantly escaped, and was now commencing to build a political career upon that very feat. Of course, Mr Churchill had been more fortunate, or more thoughtful of the future: he had made his escape without the aid of a Boer maiden. But even there, a young officer could be forgiven for having lost his head when exposed to the wiles of such a siren. Certainly he was more to be pitied than condemned.

So he had taken the coward's way out and written Margriet a letter, which Hobbs had promised would be delivered. In it he endeavoured to explain both his horror and disgust at what had happened to her, and his total helplessness: he tried to suggest that a future might still be possible for them if they could both practise patience. There had been no reply. But had he really expected one? To Margriet Voorlandt he had to be a betrayer of her love and faith, and of the sacrifice she had made for him; no matter what kind of a hero the world might call him. *That* was what he had to live with for the rest of his life.

The only good thing about the whole disastrous episode was that he had been shipped out quickly and secretly – escorted straight from the train to the ship without spending

143

more than half an hour in Cape Town itself. He wondered if Rosetta would endeavour to contact him in England.

But after Margriet, behaving dishonourably to Rosetta in telling her that he could not and would not ever marry her, and had never considered himself engaged to her, would present no difficulty at all.

Mother was in his arms, Philippa was clinging to his shoulder, Rosemary and her Major Phillips were shaking his hand. Phillips had been returned on an earlier ship; Murdoch wondered what had been his particular brand of sickness.

'We were so worried,' Mother said, 'when we heard you had been wounded, and then had got sick . . . but you look quite well.'

'There's nothing like a sea voyage,' Murdoch told her. 'Besides, I had Trooper Reynolds to look after me.'

Reynolds beamed contentedly.

There was a great deal to be done. There were photographs to be posed for, and newspaper reporters seeking interviews – at which nothing could be said which might be the least derogatory to the Army or to the famous soldier who was directing its fortunes in South Africa. Then there was a call to be made, at his request, on Lord Roberts and his wife at their home in the Isle of Wight, again to be congratulated.

'How sad that you will not receive your medal from the hands of the Queen,' said Lady Roberts. 'Do you know, she came to see me herself when poor Fred was killed. She drove over from Osborne to hold my hand and tell me how sorry she was. It was so very nice of her. Then, just before she left, she gave me a little parcel and said, "I have this present for you, but I do not wish you to open it until after I have gone." So I didn't, and when she had left, I untied it, and there was the box, and inside the box was the Victoria Cross. I cried and cried. It was so very sweet of her.'

Lord Roberts took Murdoch into the study. 'How are things in South Africa?' he asked.

'I think we are winning, sir,' Murdoch said. 'Slowly.'

'Are the rumours one hears true?'

'I do not know what the rumours are, sir.'

Roberts gazed at him for several seconds, the old eyes bright and lively as ever. Then he said, 'You have old eyes, Murdoch. Do you know, all soldiers who have seen combat come home with old eyes. I suppose living with death does that to a man. But I have noticed that those coming home from this war have older eyes than any I have seen before. And you . . . you did not return to England when you were wounded. You stayed, and returned to your regiment as soon as you could, and have now been invalided out over a year later. There are many officers like you. War is always a beastly business, but sometimes it is more beastly than others, depending on who is controlling affairs.'

Murdoch was well aware that there was no love lost between Britain's two greatest soldiers; but Lord Roberts had retired, whereas *he* had surrendered to Lord Kitchener. So he merely said, 'Yes, sir.'

Roberts smiled. 'You are a good and faithful officer, Murdoch. Your father would be proud of you. You will not leave the Army?'

'I have nowhere else to go, sir,' Murdoch told him. And that was the plain truth.

But he had a month's convalescent leave, and could accompany his mother and Philippa and Rosemary – and Major Phillips – down to Broad Acres. There the talk was entirely about the wedding, which would be taking place at Easter. Invitations were being prepared, as were gowns; Philippa was of course to be maid of honour, and two other friends would be bridesmaids. Murdoch was thankful Phillips had arranged for one of his brother guards' officers to be best man, but Murdoch would of course have to give his sister away.

He just wanted to enjoy the peace and the prosperity of his home. 'By the Lord, sir,' Reynolds remarked, 'what would some of the lads in B Troop give to be here with us.'

Reynolds made a strange sight in a brown tweed jacket

and a flat cap; but then, Murdoch supposed, his hunting pink and silk hat must look equally strange to the batman. In fact, everything had felt strange to Murdoch himself – abandoning khaki for sky blue on the voyage home, then abandoning uniform altogether for the clothes of a country gentleman; riding across fields, here green despite the chill, there black earth, with not a speck of red dust or a vulture to be seen. But both he and Reynolds instinctively drew rein whenever they saw a low, tree-covered hill or a rocky outcrop, half expecting to hear the crack of a Mauser rifle and have to dive for shelter.

'Yes,' he agreed. 'How I wish they *could* be here.' Because that had been another concomitant of his secret – he had not even been allowed to bid farewell to his troop.

In the new year the family went up to London for the investiture. There were several soldiers there, as well as civic dignitaries who were to receive awards, but as the only Victoria Cross recipient Murdoch went in first. He shook hands with the portly, bearded man in the brilliant red uniform jacket with the pale blue sash of the Garter across his chest, who was now King of England, and beside him, his small, dainty Danish wife.

'You are a soldier's soldier, by all accounts, Lieutenant Mackinder,' King Edward said. 'A proud upholder of a proud tradition. We salute you.'

Clearly the Army had secrets which it hid even from the monarch.

'Thank you, sir,' Murdoch said, stepping back and saluting in turn, looking down at the crimson ribbon which showed bright against the sky blue of his jacket, at the dull gun metal of the cross beneath it, with the simple inscription *For Valour*. Then he was being shown out to receive the congratulations of his family, before taking them off to a champagne lunch at the Café Royal. How proud Margriet would have been to stand here and be a part of his glory, he thought. He dreamed of her every night and deliberately relived in his mind every second of that unforgettable sun-scorched day when they had escaped the laager. Her image remained as bright in his mind as if he had seen her yesterday, and had still the power to provoke despair – more than ever on such an occasion.

The next day he answered a summons to the Horse Guards, to meet Sir John French, who had also returned from South Africa.

'Sit down, Mackinder,' French said. 'That ribbon sits very nicely on your chest. My congratulations.'

'Thank you, sir.'

'I imagine it is good to be home.'

'It is, sir. But I look forward to rejoining the regiment.'

'In South Africa? I don't think that would be a wise move. In any event, I imagine the regiment will soon be coming home. We have heard that Botha has been making overtures and may well be prepared to lay down his arms. Well, it is about time. They have fought hard and long, and in the main honourably, but the stringency of Lord Kitchener's measures have forced them to their knees at last.'

Murdoch saw no reason to keep secrets from French, who undoubtedly knew them anyway. 'You are aware of what those measures consisted, sir?'

French looked into his eyes. 'Yes,' he said. 'Whether I would have had the determination to impose them I would not like to say. But in war, it is winning that counts. You should never forget that, Mackinder.'

'I shall endeavour not to, sir,' Murdoch agreed, wondering just how much French knew about him.

'And looking over one's shoulder never does any good,' French went on, 'except as a means of correcting one's course.' The General had spent four years in the Navy as a boy before transferring to the Army. 'In this regard, we have a good deal of course-correcting to do, in my opinion, if we are going to guarantee the future security of this country. Do you know how many men the Boers had under arms at any one time? Hardly more than forty thousand. We had five hundred thousand in South Africa when Lord Roberts handed over his command, and there are not far short of that number now. So we won in the end. We had to, with such a preponderance of men and matériel. That does not alter the fact that our army was caught lacking in a great many respects. A century of fighting colonial wars is no adequate preparation for facing a determined, skilful and well-armed enemy. God alone knows what would have happened had we found ourselves in the middle of a European war. Or were to do so, now. This is something that must be put right, and quickly – and it is men like yourself who have to do that. You will be returning to Bath next week, as your leave is now up, and there you will take command of the training squadron.'

Murdoch sat up. 'The squadron, sir?'

French gave a brief smile. 'Why, yes, Captain Mackinder.'

'Why, sir . . . thank you. I am deeply honoured.'

'You mean you are deeply experienced and, I believe, have the intelligence and the military mind to make the changes that are necessary. What I want you to do is train your cavalrymen to fight a modern war; to learn from your experiences in South Africa and pass those experiences on to your men. Always remember that you are a VC, and therefore will be an object of great respect to those less fortunate than yourself.

'Now there were three things above all else in which the Boers were undoubtedly our superiors, and they were the things which have kept this war going for far too many months after it should have been won. The first is mobility. This above all else is a cavalryman's business in modern warfare. It should be the business of the entire army. The Boer army was composed only of cavalrymen, but they nearly always fought on foot; their horses were used to convey them rapidly from one place to another.

'We should have known, had we studied sufficiently the American Civil War or even more the Franco-Prussian War, that in these days of long-range rifle-power and machine guns the concept of advancing en masse to the attack is suicidal. Even more suicidal are cavalry charges. I am not suggesting you discard your swords; it may still be possible to use cavalry in the old-fashioned sense against a totally broken enemy. But in the main it is movement which matters. Positions which cannot easily be surprised and overrun must be turned. You must teach your men to move suddenly and if necessary over vast distances, in order to get the better of their enemies. Understood?'

'Yes, sir,' Murdoch said enthusiastically. Those were Roberts' precepts.

'The second lesson we have to learn from the Boers is that of concealment, of camouflage, as some people are calling it. Wearing khaki uniforms as opposed to red or sky-blue tunics is obviously a step in the right direction. It is my hope that khaki will be adopted universally, even for service in Europe, instead of just for colonial wars. But merely wearing khaki is not enough. We need to learn to use the ground the way the Boers did. How many times did you go into action without the slightest idea of where your enemies were? Good camouflage can double the size and hitting power of a defensive force, but it can also be used effectively in an advancing army.

'The third lesson, and perhaps the most important, is proper use of fire-power. The old concept of firing by volley and word of command was all very well when the enemy was doing the same thing, arrayed in line opposite us, and when the range of our muskets was perhaps two hundred yards. Now that our enemies are likely to be concealed and able to kill us at a distance of nearly a mile, such an idea is absurd. You must train your men, once the order to open fire has been given, to fire at will – and at targets they can see rather than at lumps of rocks which may or may not conceal a man. There again, one man who knows how to use his rifle is worth ten men who perform their actions by rote and have no accuracy. These are things which you, as a squadron commander, can attend to. There are other deficiencies in our armed services, heaven knows. But those are governmental concerns. I wish you fortune.'

'Thank you, sir. But . . . do you expect Great Britain ever to become involved in a European war? After a hundred years?'

French leaned back in his chair. 'When we were embroiled in South Africa, Mackinder, we discovered just who were our friends in this world. They appeared to

149

amount to precisely none, outside our own empire. This is again something that is up to the Government to remedy, but should they neglect to do so, or should they fail in their attempts to do so, why, yes, I would expect Great Britain to take part in a European war within our lifetimes. I would very much like to think that we will be capable of winning that war, and we cannot rely on the Navy alone. There is a great deal to be done, Captain Mackinder.'

It was an almost eerie feeling to return to Bath, to pass through those gates again, in such very different circum-stances. It was less his promotion or his decoration than that he had never known the regiment other than on a war footing. Technically, of course, it was still on a war footing, but no one doubted that the Boer commandos were seeking peace at last, as they were increasingly hounded and their families were dying in great numbers in the concentration camps.

The war had meant a heavy and continuing drain on the depot. Apart from Major Bowen, who because of a badly broken leg, sustained in a fall from his horse several years ago, was unfit for active service, and a handful of NCOs who acted as drill masters, there was not a familiar face to be seen; even Morag the mascot had died and been replaced by another pony, Brigitte, who was decidedly more skittish. Bowen himself was delighted to have Murdoch back, and introduced him to the newly promoted squadron sergeant-major, Hanley, whom Murdoch remembered as a newly promoted sergeant two years before. Both men were clearly overawed by the crimson ribbon on the young captain's breast, and equally neither of them had the faintest idea as to exactly why he had been pronounced unfit for further service in South Africa – for which Murdoch was profoundly thankful.

He had also to make the acquaintance of a new horse, a black gelding named Hengist, a magnificent beast which seemed to take to him immediately. As he cantered across the training field and took a couple of low jumps, Murdoch found himself thinking of poor old Edward IV, and then

Lucifer. But surely he and Hengist, in time of peace, would survive longer as a pair.

Then there was the squadron, one hundred and eighty-five of the rawest recruits Murdoch had ever seen. There was only one sergeant available, and no corporals; they would have to come from the ranks of the recruits themselves, once he had got to know them. Nor were there any troop lieutenants when he first arrived, but they came along a few days later, straight from Sandhurst – Peter Ramage and Tom Knox. It was incredible, Murdoch thought as he shook hands and gazed at their brand new sky-blue tunics, that they were only two years younger than himself – indeed, that only two years before he had been equally raw. But they were good horsemen, which was more than could be said for the majority of the recruits, and like everyone else, they were prepared to worship a man who had won the Victoria Cross. That he preferred not to talk about South Africa seemed quite reasonable – everyone knew it must have been grim.

The Treaty of Vereeniging was signed in May, and then everyone looked forward to the regiment coming home. Except perhaps for Murdoch himself. He had to consider the matter of coming to terms with his fellow officers. But here again, possession of that crimson ribbon was an admirable prop to his confidence, while he was determined that the reserve squadron should be fully capable of matching any of the veterans who would be returning with such grim stories of their experiences. He worked them twelve hours a day, and having got them looking like soldiers and riding like them too, began to devote a great deal of time to rifle drill and camouflage; he could do nothing about their uniforms, which remained the traditional blue, but he could put into practice French's other two precepts. Sergeant-Major Hanley looked somewhat askance at these new-fangled ideas, but he remained willing to cooperate – even when Murdoch abandoned the traditional volley firing by numbers, and instead made his men pick out specific targets and then fire at will as rapidly as possible, until the object was hit. 'Is that how they did it in South Africa, sir?' he asked his captain.

'That is how the Boers did it, sergeant-major,' Murdoch told him. 'And how we *should* have done it. If we had, there'd have been less good fellows lost.'

Of social life he allowed himself practically none. He had, of course, to take part in the festivities surrounding Rosemary's marriage. In his sky-blue tunic and dark blue breeches, with his sunburnt complexion and that precious ribbon, he was as much the centre of attraction as the bride herself. Invitations followed in great numbers from all the matriarchs of Somerset, Gloucestershire and Wiltshire, who perceived in the handsome young captain a possible future husband of one of their daughters. But he declined them all, through pressure of work. The thought of waltzing with a girl in his arms, when Margriet Voorlandt's face was ineradicably in his mind, was not something he could contemplate. Soon the invitations stopped coming.

The regiment disembarked in Plymouth and marched up to Bath beind the band. Captain Mackinder's squadron provided the guard of honour, naturally, his men sitting their horses rigidly to attention, burnished helmets with the drooping plumes gleaming in the late spring sunshine, while the sky-blue tunics filed through the gate in column of twos. A sadly depleted regiment, even with the constant flow of replacements – the total establishment returning was only three hundred and forty-seven men. With Shortland also invalided home with a shattered leg, the three squadrons had been amalgamated into two, under Rodgers and Morton, with a clutch of still raw young lieutenants below them.

Murdoch had a lump in his throat as Colonel Edmonds gave the command, 'Eyes right!' to pass the reviewing stand, where Sir John French had himself come down to take the salute, and he looked at the faces of Bishop and Yeald, and several others he recognised – but not Corporal Compton, who had been killed in a skirmish with a laager. The number of his original troop had shrunk to twenty-eight. But the

152

lump almost became tears when those twenty-eight, headed by Bishop and Yeald, came round to shake his hand the moment the parade was dismissed, and to tell him how much they had missed him, and how happy they were that he was obviously fully recovered. And how proud they were of him, too.

There were also handshakes all round and drinks in the mess as soon as the visiting bigwigs had left.

'All well?' Johnnie Morton asked, taking Murdoch aside, and gazing into his eyes. Morton had perhaps been the most upset of anyone when he had to place Murdoch under arrest.

'All well,' Murdoch lied. He knew he could never involve any of his fellow officers in his nightmares, or anyone else. They had to be private to himself alone, and his only course was to go along with the charade that he had indeed been suffering from heat stroke. But he could not stop himself from asking, 'I don't suppose there is any news of her?'

'As a matter of fact, there is,' Morton said. 'She was returned to her family the moment the camps were opened following the surrender.'

'You mean she survived?'

'Oh, very much so.'

'Thank God for that.'

'But you'll not do anything stupid,' Morton begged. 'In any event, I understand that she was to marry one of the commandos, a German named Reger . . . my God, Reger! Not that fellow who used to hang about the camp outside Cape Town?'

'The same,' Murdoch said.

'What a small world it is. I always said he was a bad 'un.' Morton frowned at him. 'That upset you?'

'I'm just relieved that she came out of it all right,' Murdoch said. Married to Reger, after all. To be beaten whenever he felt like it. And what else would she have to suffer, after the way she had betrayed him for an English lover? But whatever had happened, she was beyond his reach, now. Surely he could forget about her – and as she was another man's wife, *should* forget about her.

Edmonds, obviously also concerned about his frame of mind, invited him into the office the next morning. 'By Jove, but it is good to be back,' he remarked. 'And yet, damned strange. The whole country seems strange. One expects to see Boers lurking behind every tree.'

'That's exactly how I felt for the first month or so,' Murdoch agreed.

'You look very fit.'

'I am.'

'And been working hard, I gather from Major Bowen. That looked a fine body of men you have turned out.'

'Thank you, sir.'

'We were delighted to hear of your promotion, of course. Twenty is a very young age to become a captain. I'm afraid you can hardly expect to rise quite that fast in the immediate future. Unless we have to fight another war, perhaps.'

'I appreciate that, sir.'

'But Sir John French has the highest regard for you. And I may say that he is in possession of your entire record.'

'Yes, sir.' Well, he had guessed that.

'All he needs is to be convinced that you are fully recovered.' Edmonds paused, to peer at him.

'Yes, sir. I believe I am.'

'Good, good. I shall be interested to hear some of these new ideas the general tells me he is trying to get adopted by the whole army, but by the cavalry in particular, and which I believe you have already begun to put into practice.'

'Yes, sir. I should be pleased to show them to you.'

Edmonds nodded. 'We shall have to have a field day as soon as we are settled in.' He held out his hand. 'Welcome back, Murdoch. I don't believe you ever truly went away, but I would like to know that there is no ill feeling between us.'

Murdoch took the proffered fingers, noting as he did so how thin and weak they were, as he had already noted the pallor beneath the colonel's sunburnt cheeks, the hollowness of the eyes, the thinness of the always spare figure. 'I am grateful to you for your forbearance, sir,' he said. There was nothing more he could say; they were all damned with the same crime – and the colonel seemed to have come out of it with an even heavier burden.

Morton was less happy with the changes Murdoch had instituted. 'Hiding behind bushes, or *in* bushes, firing at will – things like that have got to be bad for discipline,' he complained. 'I mean, it was all very well for the Boers, but they didn't have any discipline anyway. The whole tradition of the British Army is that we fight, advance or retreat shoulder to shoulder. What about the charge of the Light Brigade, or the thin red line? Neither would have worked had they been little red clumps scattered about the place.'

'Not a man of the Light Brigade, or of that thin red line, would have survived against accurate magazine rifle fire, much less a machine gun,' Murdoch pointed out.

'We beat the Boers, didn't we?' Morton demanded.

'It cost us something like ten to one. What do you suppose would have happened if we had had to fight the Prussians?'

'Who on earth wants to fight the Prussians, except the French?'

Actually, Morton respected the advances in techniques, even if he didn't really care for them, just as he respected Murdoch all the more for his South African 'escapade', which had proved that he was as dab a hand with the ladies as with a horse or a sword or a pistol. That was what made a *man*, in his opinion; his only criticism now was that Murdoch neither smoked nor would grow a moustache like any proper cavalryman should.

But Morton, like everyone else, was for the moment more concerned about the changes which were taking place in the regiment itself. Colonel Edmonds was indeed not a fit man, his wounds having caused a general debilitation of his health, and by the end of the year he was retired. Major Craufurd also retired, another long-term victim of a Boer bullet.

This naturally aroused much speculation amongst the officers, and it seemed that Rodgers was an obvious heir to the lieutenant-colonelcy. But it was not to be. Gordon Rodgers was regarded as just a little young – he was only thirty and had been the junior captain when the regiment had left for South Africa – to be made lieutenant-colonel. This was explained to him by General French, who as colonel-in-chief continued to make the Westerns his own special interest; his disappointment was somewhat mitigated by the confirmation of his rank as major, and he became adjutant, while a new colonel was introduced to them.

Colonel Martin Walters had been with the lancers and had served in South Africa with distinction, just like his new command. He had also shared the burden of the guerilla struggle against the commandos. A small, slight man with a fair moustache, he looked over his three captains – Chapman had been promoted to take over Rodgers' squadron – and shook hands with each of them in turn, and with Hobbs, who had also been confirmed in his rank.

'Well, gentlemen,' he said.. 'The Royal Westerns have always been one of my favourite regiments, and I am proud indeed to be wearing this uniform. I am sure you all have a lot to teach me about dragoon tactics, and I look forward to learning. Captain Mackinder, this is the first time I have had a VC under my command. I hope you will not find peacetime soldiering a bore.'

'I find any soldiering fascinating, sir,' Murdoch said. But his heart sank; there could be no doubt that Colonel Walters had read the full report.

In fact, Walters turned out to be an able officer, quite lacking in prejudices, and as proud as anyone else to have a VC serving with his regiment. The tiresome daily routine consisted of kit inspection, drill, punishment and hospital parades, veterinary conferences, and what were called father-and-son chats, when the squadron commander, assisted by the relevant troop lieutenant and, in extreme cases, by the padre, had to listen to the domestic problems of the men under his command and endeavour to solve them.

However, peacetime soldiering proved to be utterly fasci-

156

nating, over the next few years, for General French's prediction that the whole military establishment would have to be shaken up proved to be correct. Also, as he had predicted, the main impetus for reform had to come from the Government, and Mr Haldane was appointed Minister of War in 1904. Under the encouragement of his progressive mind, all the ideas and lessons learned in South Africa became part of the regular army procedure, much to the disgust of the traditionalists, who argued that if there should be a European war, it would be fought in the traditional style between traditional armies. They pointed to the examples of the Franco-Prussian and Austro-Prussian wars of a generation before, when early machine guns had been in use, as well as breech-loading rifles, and nobody had worried about camouflage – to them, the Boer War had been an aberration. The change from scarlet to khaki was the worst of all the innovations in their eyes, even if it was only as the service dress of each regiment. Flat caps instead of helmets, puttees wrapped around the trouser legs, cloth webbing and cartridge pouches, all represented the last word in ugly anonymity.

'Quite disgusting,' Morton remarked, after a day of manoeuvres with several other cavalry regiments on Salisbury Plain. 'Couldn't tell my own men, half the time – found myself riding at the head of a bunch of bloody hussars.'

There were other changes as well which seemed to be entirely dismantling the accepted structure of warfare and replacing it with something even more hideous. Each squadron now had to have a field telephone instead of a heliograph section, the men being specially trained to lay the lines and use the newfangled machines; observation balloons, which had first been used in South Africa, became commonplace; new grenades were issued to the infantry, who also sprouted an entirely new variety of machine gun – the old water-cooled Maxim, so prone to jamming, being replaced by a French invention, the gas-cooled Hotchkiss.

This was a very heavy mitrailleuse, but capable of firing an enormous number of bullets every minute, once it was erected. A Hotchkiss gun was provided for each squadron of the dragoons, and the men had to apply themselves to this new art, as did Murdoch. Machine guns upset even him, for they were so strictly defensive, and yet, because of their awesome power, brutally offensive as well. They were also complicated. The gun was carried in dismantled sections as part of the horse furniture, and the squad in charge of it, under a corporal, had to become adept at leaping from their mounts after a simulated retreat, assembling their weapon and taking up their position as rapidly as possible while the squadron formed around them, and then dissembling the gun again in seconds when the word to advance was given. As Morton put it, 'What are we become? Cavalrymen, or bloody mechanics?'

But there were those enthusiastic about this latest and most proficient means of killing. 'By heaven, Captain Mackinder,' remarked Sergeant Yeald, who had, to his undisguised pleasure, been reassigned to Murdoch's command, during the reconstitution of the regiment, in which Murdoch's recruits were divided up amongst the veterans to restore the full establishment of three squadrons, 'if we'd had these in South Africa, eh, instead of those old Maxims?'

'I doubt it would have made all that much difference, sergeant,' Murdoch told him, 'since we were always doing the attacking. Even a Hotchkiss gun has to be aimed at something the gunner can see.'

'We'd have blown off a few more heads, though,' Yeald said stubbornly.

There was no means of knowing how much the rank and file were aware of what had happened out there on the veldt, or in Edmonds' office afterwards. Murdoch had been arrested by Morton and Hobbs, and having accepted the inevitable, had merely been escorted to his quarters. That one of the pair had remained with him until the ship had sailed for England could have been friendship rather than duty. Obviously, even if Reynolds had been totally loyal, there must have been rumours, if only spread by Hobbs' office staff, who would have seen Margriet and were bound to have gathered some idea of what was going on. But once again, the crimson ribbon wiped away all of that, and even more important to the survivors of the old B Troop, they had no doubt at all that he had sacrificed himself to the Boers to enable them to withdraw in comparative safety. He was the regiment's own private hero, and whatever he might have done, or considered doing, was irrelevant.

But even Yeald was aghast when, at the next manoeuvres, an officer in an infantry regiment commandeered an open touring motor car, mounted one of the Hotchkiss guns in the back seat and drove up and down and through the outraged cavalry, claiming to have destroyed them all. 'Whatever will they think of next?' he asked.

It was indeed time to look to the future, a future in which the possibilities of that European war they had all half feared and yet, as professional soldiers, half wanted, seemed to be coming nearer and nearer. That there had been no European war, in a general sense, since the Battle of Waterloo, had been entirely because of Great Britain's refusal to involve herself in any continental squabble, or to ally herself with any other power; splendid isolation, the newspapers called it.

But the Boer War had taught some harsh lessons there too, as General French had told Murdoch in 1902. Britain had become the pariah of the world for hounding the hapless farmers. The Kaiser, Wilhelm II, long regarded as the traditional friend of England, had gone so far as to send a telegram of congratulations to President Kruger after the catastrophic 'black week' of October 1899. If the Boers had also been at least tacitly supported by most other European nations, that single incident had most incensed the British. The result had been perhaps the greatest upheaval in European politics since Catholic France had allied herself with Protestant Sweden to defeat Catholic Austria in the Thirty Years War: Great Britain had concluded an 'entente' with France, her oldest and most implacable enemy. The word 'alliance' was carefully avoided for public consumption, but no soldier could doubt that the new arrangement meant they would one day be fighting side by side with the poilus.

Britain had already allied herself with Japan, causing an earlier diplomatic furore – the idea of the Brigade of Guards and a Japanese regiment advancing into battle shoulder to shoulder was disconcerting even to British soldiers. But Japan was clearly the emergent power in Asia, with a fleet and an army trained and equipped in the best European style, a sure bulwark, it was felt, as Britain's ally, against foreign encroachment on India, and a safeguard for Australia and New Zealand as well. However, the treaty was defensive in character, and although it required support by one power for the other should either of them be attacked by *two* adversaries, no one could imagine how the Japanese would be able to lend any military support to a British campaign in Europe, at least in time to affect the outcome. Thus it had become a toss-up between Germany and France, and the fact of that famous telegram rankled. There were other, more sensible reasons for choosing France, of course; Germany was seeking an overseas empire of her own, and was openly attempting to match Britain in building warships to protect it. This was unacceptable to the British Government, who regarded themselves as custodians of the seas, not to be challenged. The accession of the strong French fleet to the British side meant that the Mediterranean could be left in French hands, and the entire British naval might could be concentrated on the North Sea, Germany's only exit to the oceans.

But it was none the less a remarkable sensation to have to carry out manoeuvres watched by officers in blue tunics and red breeches and wearing kepis, and discuss with them not only new and secret weapons, but the manner in which the next war, to which the French – presuming it was to be with Germany – were eagerly looking forward, should be fought.

From the start, apart from the language difficulties, there was a total difference of opinion on the probable character of the coming struggle. The Boer War had taught the British generals the value of the defensive, and of manoeuvre on a grand scale; but then Wellington had always been a defensive general, preferring to let the French armies, even when commanded by Napoleon himself, dash themselves to pieces against his carefully chosen positions. Obviously it would have been tactless to remind their new allies of this, nor would it have done any good. The French regarded a defensive strategy with contempt, and had deduced that their defeat by Germany in the war of 1870 had been entirely caused by their being forced too often to fight on the defensive, due to bad staff work. The offensive, the arme blanche, was the only form of tactical manoeuvre they would consider; they dreamed of, and had no doubt of the success of, endless lines of blue-coated and red-trousered poilus marching behind bayoneted rifles, sweeping the fearsome Boche to left and right. Machine guns did not frighten them; they had invented the mitrailleuse, and were not about to be taught its value by any British general who had never fought a continental war.

Nor were they impressed by anything else the British had to offer. In numbers, of course, there could be no comparison between the two armies. The British, depending entirely upon voluntary service, talked in terms of a few divisions; the French, with their conscripted recruits, spoke of *scores* of divisions. As regards skill, the British again were wholly devoted to accurate rifle fire, a defensive concept; they doubted they would, under modern conditions, ever get close enough to an enemy to use their bayonets – they had seldom succeeded in doing so with the Boers. The French were wholly committed to cold steel. As for the British cavalry, the French regarded them as a joke, and seemed unable to decide what the dragoons actually were. Nor could Murdoch altogether blame them, as their only impressions of what the British might be like in a war were gathered from watching the annual manoeuvres, which even he found an appalling muddle of uncertain and often countermanded orders, obscure objectives and confused thinking, exacerbated by the mental division which existed in the British Army between the traditionalists and the modernists, and even more between those, like himself, who regarded soldiering as an important and indeed vitally serious profession, and those, like Johnnie Morton, who persisted in seeing it as a great game, in which flourish and style mattered more than determination and vigour.

161

The catastrophe which had been waiting to happen for some time finally overtook them during manoeuvres on the White Horse downs in Berkshire in the spring of 1906.

As was the custom, the final action of the 'battle' was to take place in front of the assembled generals and military attachés of foreign countries who had been invited to look at Britain's growing military might, together with several members of royal houses, including the British. This great accumulation of brass hats was situated on Weathercock Hill, beneath a purple observation balloon, which seemed to typify the seriousness of the occasion.

The 'battle' had from start to finish been a shambles of misdirected orders and lost opportunities, culminating when the dragoons, with the hussars with whom they had been brigaded for the occasion, were commanded to charge the retreating 'enemy'. This they had done with great panache, led by Gordon Rodgers, who was temporarily in command as Lieutenant-Colonel Walters was one of the judges. However, there then arose a wrangle as to whether they had sent the opposing infantry flying in rout, or whether they would have been cut to pieces by the machine guns brought to bear on them. While this argument was being resolved, the brigade was stood down.

They gathered in a hollow just below the natural grandstand, out of sight of the rest of army, and the men were dismounted to have a stand-easy and a smoke; the hollow became a huge khaki-clad ants' nest. Murdoch, who heartily agreed with the infantry point of view that their machine guns would have carried the day, was very aware that, as the 'battle' was not yet officially over, they were behaving in a most unsoldier-like fashion – a single shell from one of the Boer heavy Creusots would have just about destroyed the entire brigade.

No further orders had been received when they heard the drumming of a very large number of hooves from the other side of the hill, together with a ripple of cheering and applause from the spectators, and the blast of bugle calls. Murdoch and Morton remounted their horses and rode up to the crest to see what was going on, and gazed at a mass

162

of cavalry galloping towards them, past the dignitaries on Weathercock Hill; the newcomers were wearing, not khaki, but the blue service dress of the Household Cavalry. Their appearance was absurd, not only because their uniforms were distinguishable at a distance of well over a mile, but also because they were advancing in parade order, in vast ranks, which could equally have been cut to pieces by a well-placed machine gun. But from the bugle calls and flying ensigns they were decidedly pleased with themselves.

'By Jove,' Morton said. 'Aren't those fellows on the other side?'

'They were,' Murdoch agreed.

'Well, we haven't been given the all-clear yet. And with us hidden down here, those blighters seem to think they've won the bloody war. I think we should do something about them.' He trotted back down to where Rodgers was chatting with the major commanding the hussars, and explained the situation.

'You're right,' Rodgers agreed; his instinct for the offensive was as pronounced as that of any Frenchman. 'If we could take them in the flank, we'd win no matter how they looked at it.'

'I rather feel they think the battle is over, and are parading,' Murdoch suggested.

'As if they had won the bloody thing,' Morton declared. 'Can't have that. Must make a show, old man.'

As Rodgers was of the same mind, there was nothing for it; Murdoch was the junior captain. Orders were given, the men were mounted, and the whole mass of khaki-clad horsemen cantered up to the top of the rise – to find that the blues were much closer than they had expected, and indeed were almost upon them. Nor were they now capable of stopping, as they charged along behind their blaring bugles, while the applause of the watchers slowly turned to gasps of horror as they realised what was about to happen.

'Wheel left,' Murdoch bellowed at his men, but it was too late. A mass of blue-clad riders smashed into his squadron, which could only twist this way and that in an attempt to avoid disaster. Without success. Horses and riders tumbled in every direction, khaki and blue inextricably mixed. High-ranking officers left their places and hurried down to the chaos of neighing and shouting, ambulances were sent for, foreign observers scratched their heads and attempted not to smile while making polite remarks about British sang froid . . . and Murdoch lay beneath his horse. When they found him he was unconscious.

7

The Transvaal, 1906

Returning consciousness was accompanied by pain, far more severe than any he recalled in South Africa when he had been shot; but by then the shock had worn off, physically. He did not suppose he would ever forget the awful feeling of impotence as that wall of cavalry had come at him.

Mother and Philippa spent much time with him, and Rosemary wrote from Caterham to wish him a speedy recovery – as did Lord Roberts from the Isle of Wight and Sir John French from Aldershot. He was visited regularly by the padre and by his fellow officers, who had been more fortunate than he. In fact, he was the most seriously injured of any of those knocked down in the 'clash of titans', as the newspapers called it. Colonel Walters came too, endeavouring to discover who had been responsible for the disaster. It appeared some heads had to roll – it was a miracle no one had actually been killed – and poor Rodgers' was one of them. Major Bowen having retired, Rodgers was appointed permanent head of the depot outside Bath, with all thoughts of further promotion dashed.

But the fault had lain equally with the commanders of the blues, who had not taken evading action in time. 'If it leads to a general tightening-up of the system it can be no bad thing,' Walters said. 'Morton has told me that you opposed leading your men over the ridge.'

Murdoch said nothing; he had no wish to play the good boy at the expense of his fellow officers.

'And all you have got out of it is . . . what exactly have you got?' He surveyed the array of bandages, the suspended leg and arm.

'One broken leg, one broken collar-bone and seven

broken ribs,' Murdoch told him. 'Together with various minor fractures.'

'My God! I'm afraid we have had to have Hengist put down; he broke both his forelegs.'

Murdoch couldn't nod; it was too painful. 'Yes, sir. I'm afraid I have a bad record with horses; I have now lost three.'

'None of which could have been considered your fault,' the colonel pointed out. 'What you have to do now is get well, just as soon as possible.'

'Yes, sir,' Murdoch agreed. But getting well was a slow progress. Dr Williams told him he was very lucky to be alive, and not even permanently crippled.

The main trouble with lying on his back, hardly able to move for day after day – and night after night – was that it gave a man too much time to think. He had cut down on his thinking since his return from South Africa by burying himself in his work and endeavouring to make sure that he collapsed into bed every night utterly exhausted – as his men were no doubt doing too. But now thought was inescapable. He thought a good deal about his profession, and his part in it, which had little to do with the military manuals he had consumed since boyhood, or the biographies of Wellington's generals and Napoleon's marshals he had always preferred to penny dreadfuls.

He had never contemplated any other career than that of a soldier; he had never been allowed to do so. But then, he had never been allowed to think of the British Army as anything less than the finest fighting force on earth, officered by men who were always gentlemen and, even when they were not brilliant, were always decisive, determined and inevitably victorious. Nor would anyone argue with that appraisal he knew, even after the Boer War.

On the ground and at the time, it had been too easy to see the warts and appreciate the way the Army seemed to stumble from blunder to blunder in its quest for victory. Presumably other armies made the same mistakes. Even the Boer generals had made mistakes. They had fought, after their initial assaults, too much on the defensive, had enjoyed defeating the British forces dashed against their impregnable kopjes, but had at the same time allowed an enormous army to be concentrated against them, where a systematic destruction of the railway line would have made that impossible. And they had been slow to react to the altered situation.

But would he make any less mistakes than anyone else? As an independent commander, on a very small scale, to be sure, he had led his men into a trap, entirely through overconfidence. That he had sent them back in time might have made them the more proud of him; it did not exonerate the original error.

And one day in the future he would have to face the responsibilities of higher rank; Colonel Walters had all but told him that day might not be all that distant. Here again, as a boy, he had never doubted that he would make his way steadily up the ladder, supposing he stayed alive, and would become at least a major-general, as had Grandfather Murdoch – and as no one doubted Father would have achieved had he lived. Then he would have to play with hundreds, perhaps thousands of lives. He would have to direct a troop of horse to ride in front of the enemy to ascertain their strength. He would have to order infantry brigades to assault enemy positions, see them pinned down, and then have to decide whether to admit defeat and withdraw them, before a small army of foreign correspondents, or leave them to slog it out in the hopes that sheer guts and determination might win the day – and risk the disintegration of a magnificent body of men like the Highland Brigade. If he felt he might have been prepared to carry out a more thorough reconnaissance before sending his men into action, he did not envy Lord Methuen his problems before Magersfontein. Nor, supposing, as would have been the case, that his reconnaissance had proved Magersfontein to be impregnable, did he have any idea how he would have coped with them, save that he might have tried to turn the position earlier. But without the resources Roberts had been given, that might have been a disaster which could have cost his entire force.

Then there was the even harder business of winning a

won war. Kitchener had triumphed. His name might be anathema to the Boers for the rest of time, but he had been given a job of work to do, and he had done it. Nothing more could be asked of any soldier. And if the newspapers, having finally got hold of the story, were claiming that some twenty thousand women and children had died of disease and malnutrition in the concentration camps – whereas only four thousand Boers had actually died in battle – he could claim that in murdering that number of civilians he had perhaps saved the lives of a large number of British soldiers.

It had still been an enormous decision to have to take, to believe that British control of the Boer republics was worth that number of innocent lives. And having taken it, it must have been even harder to enforce, day after day, knowing that to start something like that and then not succeed in the announced objective would be to bring down the wrath of the entire nation on his head. Would *he* ever have the determination to carry through a policy like that, much less to think of it in the first place? It was a daunting thought that he probably would not.

Murdoch dreamed of Margriet less often now, and never on purpose; it seemed dishonourable to dream of another man's wife. And yet . . . he did not actually know that she was married to Reger; Morton had only said that he had been told she was *going* to marry the German, not that she actually had. He knew that was something he had to find out, because if she was not, was existing in some kind of mental and physical wasteland . . . the old enmity, at least on the British side, was over and done with. Now the Boers were being invited to form part of the government of South Africa. If he doubted he would ever be given permission to marry her, he was yet twenty-four, and approaching that magic age when he could do so without permission; in any event, he would be able to bring her to England. He had no doubt Mother would support him in that, once he had explained the situation.

But finding out came first, if only to save himself from slowly going mad. When Dr Williams told him that even after leaving hospital he would have to take at least three

168

months' convalescent leave before he would again be fit for duty, the idea of returning to South Africa began to form in his mind.

His resolution was actually crystallised by an event which took place in the autumn of 1906, only a fortnight before he was due to be released. He was sitting on the hospital verandah, in his dressing gown, having had his afternoon walk up and down the corridors to help in rebuilding the strength in his wasted muscles, when Sister Anderson told him there were visitors to see him. 'An American gentleman and lady,' she explained.

'American? I don't know any Americans. . . .' Murdoch snapped his fingers. 'Harry Caspar!'

'The same,' Caspar said, coming through the doorway with arms outstretched. 'My dear Murdoch, what in the name of God have they done to you?'

'My horse rolled on me,' Murdoch told him. 'Poor fellow, he broke both forelegs and had to be shot.'

'You sure do live an exciting life. You going to be all right?'

'I'm nearly all right now. And all the better for seeing you.'

'Snap! Say, do you mind if I have you meet someone?'

'It'll be a pleasure.'

A girl was hesitating in the doorway. As she came into the open air, Murdoch took in the small, slight body, the dark hair – worn short rather than in the huge pompadour which was the current style in England – the somewhat sharp but certainly attractive features, the lively green eyes.

'Marylee,' Caspar said. 'This is the man himself.'

She came closer, still hesitantly, and held out her hand. 'Captain Mackinder! I've so looked forward to meeting you. Harry has told me so much about you.'

Murdoch took the softly strong fingers. 'But never a word about you, Mrs Caspar.'

'Not Mrs Caspar,' Caspar grinned. 'Marylee is my sister. Thought it was time she saw how the other half lives.'

Murdoch realised he was still holding her hand, and

hastily released it. 'Well, you never mentioned that you had a sister, either.'

'I guess it's not something he wants to talk about,' Marylee Caspar said. 'But he sure has talked about you. Told me, told all America, I guess, how you won the Medal of Honour—'

'Not the Medal of Honour, honey,' Caspar corrected. 'The British equivalent: the Victoria Cross. That's even better, because it's given only for valour in the field.'

'Isn't that something,' Marylee Caspar said, gazing at Murdoch, cheeks pink.

'It was an accident,' Murdoch told her, feeling equally embarrassed. 'It always is an accident.'

'And even more an accident that you stayed alive to get it,' Caspar said. 'That's what makes you so special.'

Their enthusiasm, so typical of their countrymen, was overwhelming. As was their unaffected admiration for what he had done. Obviously they knew nothing of Murdoch's 'illness'.

Caspar's concern was only for the scanty knowledge he had of the camps. He had the somewhat pragmatic point of view, being an Anglophile, that the war had had to be won. 'Don't seem all that different to what we had to do to the Sioux or the Apache,' he remarked. 'When you're fighting whole peoples, as opposed to professional armies, boy, it sure can be tough.'

'Maybe too tough,' Murdoch suggested.

'Well . . . it's winning that counts, right?'

Which was what General French had said, Murdoch remembered.

They had brought him flowers, in a big way, and in return he gave them a letter of introduction to his mother and sent them down to Broad Acres – and also one to Colonel Walters, so that they could visit Bath and see how the regiment worked in its peacetime establishment, which was really what Caspar wanted to do.

They obviously took advantage of the opportunity immediately, because when Mother came to see him the following Sunday, she remarked, 'Such a nice girl, that Miss

170

Caspar. And she fell in love with Broad Acres. I saw Martin Walters yesterday, and do you know, he liked her too.'

A decidedly pointed remark, Murdoch thought, and could not help but wonder if, after all, Mother knew what had happened in South Africa. What really alarmed him, however, was a return visit Marylee paid to the hospital, the day before he was due to be released.

'I just wanted to thank you for putting us in touch with your folks and your friends,' she said. 'I have never enjoyed a visit with anyone so much as with your mother and sister. They were so kind. And that place, Broad Acres ... it's just a heaven.'

'It's been in the family just over a hundred years,' he said modestly.

'A hundred years! Gee. Do you know, that's about as far back as we *go!* And it's yours?'

'Well ... I suppose it is. But Mother will live there for the rest of her life.'

'But you'll live there when you're through soldiering?'

'Why, I suppose I will.'

'That must be a very comforting thought,' she said seriously.

He hadn't considered it in that light before, but he supposed it was a very comforting thought. It was a part of the background to which he had surrendered, probably the more important part, he thought. And yet Broad Acres and the Army were inextricably mixed. Margriet would have adorned Broad Acres, but only as the wife of an army officer, not as the wife of a disgraced member of society. Otherwise, with every memento in the house one of the regiment, he would have driven them both mad. 'I suppose it is,' he agreed.

They sat in silence for a few minutes. Then she said, 'The sister told me you'll be discharged tomorrow.'

'About time. There's been nothing wrong with me for weeks. They seem to think I am going to walk straight out of here, jump on a horse and gallop twenty miles across country.'

'It must have been a bore, not doing any of the things you wanted to. Will you be going back to the regiment?'

He shook his head. 'That scares them too. No, I'm to have three months' convalescent leave.'

'Now that sounds pretty civilised. Will you be spending them at Broad Acres?'

He gazed at her, and she flushed. 'Harry and I are going across to Paris, France, next weekend. And then Berlin, and Vienna, and Rome. Maybe Madrid on the way home. It's some kind of grand tour he's taking me on, I guess you could call it.'

Murdoch realised that Harry Caspar was either a very successful journalist or, like himself, came from a moneyed background. He rather felt the latter. This girl had all the obvious trappings of wealth and position, even if to a British officer it was difficult to associate Americans with anything more than wealth. But she dressed superbly, in an advanced style which suited the way she wore her hair; she did not, for instance, indulge in the bustle, and her skirts were an inch shorter than normal, allowing a good deal of boot to be revealed. Her pearls were glowing white against her throat as her matching earrings gleamed against the dark hair, and she exuded a softly seductive perfume. But more than any of those physical attributes, she was possessed of that indefinable quality of knowing what she was and to what she belonged. Something that he thought he possessed himself, if perhaps for different reasons.

'But we'll be coming back to England to catch the ship to America,' she added shyly.

'Oh, that is a shame,' he said. 'I won't be here.'

'Oh.' She was taken aback. 'But you said you had to convalesce.' She was very direct. 'We'll be back in a couple of months.'

'I'm sure Mother and Philippa would love to see you again,' he said. 'And do please go down to Broad Acres to stay.'

'But you won't be there?'

'No,' he said. 'The doctor says I have to take a sea voyage

172

to get myself really fit again. I'm to sail to South Africa and back.'

The final decision had been taken on the spur of the moment, in the very midst of their conversation, because Marylee Caspar was very definitely developing a crush on him – or perhaps she had had a crush on him long before she ever met him, thanks to her brother's purple prose. And she was a girl on whom it would be very easy to develop a crush in return, especially with both Mother and Colonel Walters nodding approval in the background. But there was no possibility of Murdoch Mackinder ever falling in love with any woman while Margriet Voorlandt dominated his thoughts. He simply had to go, and see, and *know*, whether he could begin to love again.

And Marylee Caspar? He might never meet another like her.

But she did not seem especially put off by his decision, although she was certainly disappointed. 'Well, then,' she said, 'I guess I'll have to take a rain-check. But I do hope we'll meet again, some day.'

'So do I,' he said. And he meant it.

Mother was no less surprised by his decision to return to South Africa. She was somewhat perturbed when he told her he wanted no word of his intention breathed to a soul, especially anyone from the regiment, or indeed the Army at all. 'Tell them I've gone to Italy,' he said.

'But . . .' she pursed her lips, as she had done when he was a little boy and she felt he had misbehaved, but could not put her finger on what he had done. 'Why South Africa?'

He shrugged. 'I suppose it's because I spent two years there, killing people. I would like to have a look at it again, now the killing has stopped.'

'Yes,' she said. 'Yes, I think I can understand that.' She considered for a moment, and he knew then beyond doubt that she had been told about Margriet, and was now wrestling with her conscience, whether or not to betray that confidence – and wondering if it would accomplish anything to do so. 'Would you like me to come with you?'

'No,' he said. 'I think you should stay here. I promise I'll come back with nothing on my mind.'

That was as far as he could go in telling her he was aware of her concern.

'But are you sure you are strong enough,' she said.

'I'll get strong enough, on the voyage. Anyway, I'll be taking Reynolds; he's had a long enough holiday while I've been in hospital.'

Reynolds was also somewhat taken aback at the idea. 'South Africa, sir?' he asked. 'Cape Town?'

Reynolds could not help but be aware of the existence of Rosetta Dredge – who was a risk that had to be run, even if Murdoch had not heard from her for three years.

'Briefly, Reynolds.'

'You'll be going up to the Free State, then, sir? And the Transvaal?'

'Why, yes. Revisiting old haunts, you might say. You don't have to come if you don't want to.'

'Oh, sir, wherever you go, I'll be there,' Reynolds protested. 'But . . . are you sure it's the right thing to do?'

'It's something I *have* to do, George,' Murdoch told him. 'If I am ever going to get a good night's sleep again. Savvy?'

'Yes, *sir*,' Reynolds said. 'I'm looking forward to it.'

Perhaps he was. He was the best of company on the voyage out, and the voyage itself completely restored Murdoch to health. Only the weakness of too long in bed remained, and that could be combated simply by good food and fresh air, and time.

He arranged with the ship's captain to wireless ahead and reserve them berths on the first available train to Johannesburg – or at any rate out of Cape Town – after they had docked. He discovered his haste was unnecessary when he learned from the customs officer at Table Bay that Rosetta Dredge was married and a mother. Yet however relieving that thought was, it was also alarming, and made him the more anxious to get to the north.

The railway line was the same – it might have been the same locomotive as had towed the regiment's armoured carriages six years before. Now there was more comfort, certainly, but only for a favoured few; if he sat in a first-class compartment and enjoyed cooling drinks supplied by the steward, the black people confined in the third-class carriages looked as hemmed in, and as uncomfortable, as the troopers had been on that unforgettable journey.

Within a couple of days they were back at other places which he supposed would remain forever imprinted on his mind: De Aar, then Belmont, where he had seen his first action, and where Reynolds had saved him from capture. He glanced at the batman, who was also staring at the tumbled kopjes, clearly also remembering; Murdoch knew that Reynolds never went anywhere without his Military Medal in his pocket – but he had left his Victoria Cross at home.

The train rumbled across the Orange River, and then came to the Modder. The bridge had long been rebuilt, of course, and the village around the station was larger than he remembered it, but the brown water still flowed between those high bluffs which had concealed the Boer riflemen, and he could remember it soaking him to the neck as he had floundered across it, bullets splashing all about him. He had thought he was untouchable and immortal, then. Now he carried more scars than he cared to count.

But he was still alive. As the train made a lengthy stop at Modder, he walked back across the foot bridge, and after a few minutes spent in regaining his bearings, found the graves of Holt and Fielder. At least, he presumed they were the graves; both the helmets and the swords had long been removed. He stood there for some time, gazing at them; it was a sobering thought that Holt, but for that utterly sense-less episode, would probably now be colonel of the regiment.

He rejoined the train, and watched Magersfontein looming, huge and formidable even in peace, on their right, and then they were back at Kimberley, before heading north for the great city of gold. Here he was truly amazed at the way Johannesburg had quadrupled in size in the four years since he had been here, the architecture of the buildings, the obvious prosperity of the inhabitants – if they happened to be white – the way heavy-bearded Boers and thin-moustached Englishmen walked the streets and were to be seen talking together, while the Union Jack waved lazily above all of their heads.

They put up at the Union Hotel, had a hot bath and a good dinner, and the next morning Murdoch began making inquiries. 'Voorlandt,' said the clerk at the town hall. 'Voorlandt.' He checked various lists. 'You say he was field cornet of a commando in the closing days of the war?'

'Yes.'

'Man of about sixty, would he have been?'

'I would say so.'

'Would he have been a farmer before the war?'

'That sounds like the man.'

'Yes. Well, I'm sorry, Mr Davis, but he died two years ago. Heart attack.'

'Oh. Did he not have any family?'

'Yes. He had a wife, who survived him, and a daughter. I imagine the wife now lives with the daughter.'

'That seems probable,' Murdoch said, trying to ignore the pounding of his heart. 'Well, perhaps you could give me their address? I would very much like to pay my respects to Mrs Voorlandt.'

'Friends of yours, were they?' The clerk was interested.

'Ah, acquaintances. I was in South Africa before the war and met them then,' Murdoch lied easily.

'Yes. Hm.' He flicked through more files. 'Well, I would say your best bet is to try Reger's Farm. It's not far from here, maybe twenty miles. There's no railway, but you should be able to hire a horse, I should think.'

'Reger's Farm,' Murdoch said, his heart slowing and seeming to sink. 'That is where they live?'

'I should think they do. According to my records, Juffrouw Voorlandt married Meneer Paul Reger on 1 July 1902.'

Barely a month after she would have been released from the concentration camp. So there it was. Now he had found

176

out for certain that she was another man's wife, he knew he should get back on the train and hurry back to England as quickly as possible, and try to start living his life over again.

Except that he wasn't going to do that, after having come all this way to see her. But the next morning he left Reynolds behind; he had no idea what he was going to find, and did not wish to involve the good fellow in anything which might turn out very unpleasant. Reynolds protested, aghast at Murdoch taking a long ride by himself, but Murdoch knew he was now as strong as ever, and insisted.

He hired a horse from the livery stable next door to the hotel and made his way down the track out of the city, riding slowly across the veldt as the scars of the gold mines were left behind, and the Negro shanty town which had grown up around and beyond them. Those mines had been the real cause of the war, and the real prize that Great Britain had sought and secured. He hoped their possession would bring her joy.

He rode slowly, not wishing to tire either the horse or himself, and besides, every hoofbeat was pregnant with memory. When, about fifteen miles west of the railway line, he came across a gully with a spring of clear water and stopped to eat the sandwiches with which the hotel had provided him, he was sure he was on personally hallowed ground.

Then in the early afternoon he approached the kopjes into which he had led the troop that other afternoon, and had to check his horse, waiting for the rifle shot that would mean he had been discovered. There was none, and he walked the animal through the rocks and bushes, and looked down from the low rise into the shallow valley beyond.

When last he stood here he had gazed at a shambles of burned timbers and ruined crops. Now, though the village had not been rebuilt, there were several farms fairly close together. There were men to be seen in the fields on the next rise, and there were some children playing closer at hand, but the only members of the community who showed any interest in him as he walked his horse down the slope were a couple of barking dogs.

He drew rein above three lads who were playing marbles on the track. 'Good afternoon,' he said. 'Can you direct me to Meneer Reger's farm?'

'It's the far end of the valley,' said one of the boys, hardly looking up.

'You won't find him in,' said another. 'You want to go over the rise to the new ground.'

'Then I'll do that,' Murdoch agreed, and surveyed them for a few moments longer. 'You don't care for strangers around here,' he remarked.

'Not Englanders,' one of the boys said.

Murdoch realised that they would have been amongst the children, hardly more than babes in arms, who had stared at him when he was brought into the laager as a prisoner; fortunately, none of them appeared to remember him, probably because he was not in uniform. He touched his horse with his heel and walked on, passing the driveways to several farms before, about three miles further on, he came to the one at the end. This was clearly a communal settlement, and equally clearly it was composed of the survivors of that last commando, pooling their resources, continuing to live in each others' pockets, as they had always lived.

And doing well at it, he estimated. Apart from the cattle pasturage – and the sizeable herd which occupied it – and the pig pens and the chicken runs, over the hill there was an extensive acreage, presumably under corn or wheat. The houses themselves were well built and freshly painted, and most had smart traps standing outside their doors, while black servants tended the neat lawns and black nursemaids walked white babies in their prams beneath huge parasols. The village he had burned had not been as prosperous as this.

The house at the end of the valley was the finest of the lot, with a second storey which, from the number of windows – all with jalousies thrown wide – he surmised might contain several bedrooms. The ground floor was surrounded by a

178

wide verandah, and as he approached a huge ridgebacked hound rose up and gave a low growl.

'He ain't going hurt you, lessen you rile him up,' said a young black man, emerging from round the side of the house carrying a bucket. 'You looking for Captain Reger? He's out over the ridge, where they's clearing that new acreage.'

'So I've been told.' Murdoch eyed the hound and slowly dismounted. Having been shot by the Boers and crushed by his own horse, he was in no mood to be mangled by this creature. 'Would Mevrouw Reger be in?'

'She would be,' the man agreed, standing by the steps.

'Well, perhaps you would tell her I'm here.'

'She'll be resting now,' the man said.

'Tell her. . . .' Murdoch checked himself, because even as he spoke he knew she was there. He looked above the verandah at the upstairs windows, where the blinds were drawn to keep out the afternoon sun. But one blind had opened, just a little. 'Ask her if I may have a word,' he said.

The servant had caught the movement of his eyes and guessed what had caused it. He went up the steps, gave the dog a pat and opened the front door. A few moments later he was back. 'She says to come in,' he invited.

Murdoch climbed the short flight of steps, and the hound growled again.

'He does not like Englanders,' the black man said.

'He probably fought against them during the war,' Murdoch agreed, stepping carefully past the dog and into the cool interior of the house, blinking in the sudden gloom. He made out the staircase, which lay across the polished wooden floor, beyond the very comfortably furnished living area containing a grand piano and innumerable silver-framed photographs. And at the head of the stairs, looking down on him, was Margriet.

She wore a dressing gown, and had changed, slightly; he thought she might have put on a little weight. But the face, the body, the hair, and above all, the scent, were the same.

'Thank you, Dick,' she said to the servant, who gave a half-bow and withdrew to the verandah, closing the door behind him. 'I recognised your voice,' she said. 'You must be mad, coming here.'

She did not move, so he advanced to the foot of the stairs, still looking up. 'I had to know. At least that you were alive.'

'Reger will kill you if he finds you here. You must leave.'

'Is he that jealous?'

'Jealous?' She inhaled, and bit her lip. 'I had to survive.' She hesitated, but as he said nothing, went on. 'I had to say that you forced me, at gun point. Both to leave here, and to . . . to submit to you.'

'And they believed you? The guard . . . ?'

'I said I followed you into the bushes because I was suspicious of your intentions. Oh, they believed me. Reger could not accept that I might have run off with another man in preference to him.'

Murdoch put his foot on the bottom step. 'Has it been very hard?'

She looked down at him. 'It has been as I expected.'

'You mean he has beaten you?'

'Of course. It is his way.'

He took another step; she had not yet commanded him to stop. 'Margriet . . . I wrote you a letter.'

'I received your letter.'

'But you did not reply to it. Do you hate me that much?'

'I do not hate you at all, Murdoch. I . . . I had to destroy your letter, pretend I hated you. I had to survive.'

'But did you believe what I had written?'

'I believed it. I think I believed it before we ever left the laager. I knew then what had to happen, to us both.'

'Then why did you come?'

'Because I loved you. I wanted to save your life.'

'And now?'

'Now I am married to Reger.'

'Do you love him?'

'Love *that*?'

He reached the top of the stairs and took her in his arms, quite forgetting that her mother was probably only feet away. 'Then come with me. Now. We can be on the train tonight, and in Cape Town long before he can catch up with us — and take a boat to England.'

'And then?'

'Then . . . now, we are not at war. I might not be able to marry you for a few years, but it would probably take that long to obtain a divorce anyway. But I would care for you, and love you . . . and you would be away from Reger.'

'Do you really believe that could happen?'

'Do you really believe I came back, this far, just to look at you?' He kissed her lips. Where was family honour now? He was proposing adultery, the seduction of another man's wife. Because she was the only woman he could ever love and he could not fight that. For her, he knew, now, he would sacrifice everything.

She stayed against him for a few moments, then pulled away.

'Will you do it?' he asked.

She stared at him, then moved his hands and walked away from him, along the corridor. 'Come.'

He followed, heart pounding, but frowning too, as he feared what he was going to be shown.

Margriet opened a door. 'Be quiet,' she whispered.

He gazed at the sleeping child.

'He is our son,' she said, and closed the door.

'*Our* son?'

'He was born in the concentration camp.'

'But . . . my God . . .' He turned to the door again, but she checked him.

'He thinks Reger is his father.'

'But Reger. . . .'

'Come,' she said again, and opened another door. Again Murdoch hesitated, this time hating what he was about to see.

'Our daughter,' she said. 'Reger's and mine.'

The hatred grew. Not so much of the baby girl, but of the acts, the constantly recurring acts, which had created her. Yet the love remained there, as well. And only feet away was his son. 'Bring her with you,' he said.

'I cannot.'

'She is yours.'

'She is Paul's as well,' she pointed out. 'And they are both mine.'

She gazed at him as she spoke, and he frowned, but knew he could not challenge that; she had borne the boy in the concentration camp, alone and friendless, concerned only with survival. While he had been receiving the Victoria Cross.

'You said you hated him,' he reminded her.

'Paul? Yes, I do, often enough. I can never love him as I loved you. But I cannot rob him of his child, his children, either.'

'*His* children?'

'They are his,' she insisted. 'I do not know if he truly believed my story. Certainly there are those who did not, who would have made it very hard for me. So he *chose* to believe me, to stand between me and my detractors. Without him it would have been impossible for me, I think; I do not think I would be alive today. Then he adopted little Paul as his own, and has treated him as his own. They are his children. I cannot steal them away from him.'

Little Paul, Murdoch thought bitterly. But the boy was *her* child. 'Then you wish me to go.'

'You must,' she said.

He turned away from her and went to the stairs.

'At least until I have had an opportunity to think,' she added.

He turned back to her, heart pounding all over again.

'I would like to see you again,' she said. 'When I have thought.'

This was madness, he knew. Yet it was a madness he could not withstand. Because she had not, after all, said no.

'Will you permit me to do that?' she asked, coming to the stairhead herself.

He was aware of the strangest mixture of emotions. If she wanted to see him again, then she must wish to go with him . . . if only he could now be certain that *he* still wanted that to happen. A married woman, twice a mother . . . but one of her children was his.

'Where are you staying?' she asked, taking his silence for acquiescence.

'At the Union.'

'Can you remain there another three days? I am coming into town the day after tomorrow to see my mother.'

'My God, your mother! I was told she was here with you.'

'No, Paul would not permit that for more than a few weeks after Father died. She has an apartment in town, and I visit her once a week. If I told her I could not stay long, I would be able to see you as well.'

'At the Union Hotel?' He frowned at her. 'Will they not recognise you?'

She shrugged. 'I am not that well known in Johannesburg. I think it can be managed.'

Madness, he thought again. But if she was taking that sort of risk, she must mean to go with him. 'Will you bring the boy . . . the children, with you?'

'If I can.'

He looked into her eyes. It is going to happen, he thought. It is going to happen. 'I will remain there another three days,' he promised.

He hardly remembered the ride back across the veldt, and it was late evening when he regained the hotel.

'Thought those rascals had assaulted you, Captain,' a very worried Reynolds confessed.

'Those rascals have just about done better out of losing the war than we did by winning it,' Murdoch told him.

'So do we go home now, sir?'

Murdoch shook his head. 'I think I'll stay on in Jo'burg for a day or two longer. There's no boat out of Cape Town for another fortnight, in any event. We'll be back in plenty of time for that. And this climate will be just what the doctor ordered.'

Next day he took the batman exploring, keeping on the go all day, so that the following morning he could reasonably claim to be tired as he was not yet back to his full strength. 'I'll just rest today,' he said. 'But there's no need for you to hang about the hotel. Go off and enjoy yourself. Oh, and

I tell you what you can do: make reservations on the train leaving tomorrow, for Cape Town. Reserve an entire compartment for our use.'

'Sir?'

'I feel like travelling in style,' Murdoch told him, wondering if it was true that no man could lie to his valet.

Reynolds gave him an old-fashioned look but obeyed, and Murdoch was left alone in his room, standing at the window to look down on the busy thoroughfare beneath him, feeling more nervous than at any time before going into battle. He was about to commit a crime – if she came. But of course she was going to come, and what a glorious crime. He didn't know about afterwards. Getting her back to England would present no problem. Having her accepted by Mother . . . but it would be Mother's first grandson; she would hardly be able to resist that.

Of course what had happened would leak out. He might be blighting his career. But did that matter, if he would have Margriet, and . . . Paul. He supposed he would have to accept the name.

Would she be worth his career? He had to believe that, had to be certain of it. For a moment he almost hoped she wouldn't come, after all. But he leapt to his feet at the sound of the soft knock, and a moment later she was in his arms.

She had indeed prospered, he thought, as he kissed her mouth and felt her against him. Yesterday he had taken her by surprise. Today she was dressed for a visit to the city. She wore silk and satin, and smelt of expensive perfume; her golden hair was gathered in a pompadour beneath a broad-brimmed straw hat, which was slowly slipping from her head and then struck the floor with a plop. With it went the veil which, as a white woman exposed to the tropical sun, she had been able to wear without exciting comment, but which had kept her identity concealed. Perhaps.

She moved her head back to stare at him. 'I have dreamed of this moment. For four years. I never thought it would ever happen. But . . . you have left the Army?'

184

He shook his head. 'I am on leave. Where are the children?'

'It was not possible to bring them. Tell me about what has happened to you since 1901.'

He sat beside her on the bed, trying to work out what her plan might be, as she had not been able to bring the children, and told her something of the years since he had been forced to abandon her. 'Very boring,' he said, longing to touch her. As she understood. She took his hand and placed it on her breast, and then kissed him again. 'The children . . .' he said.

'I said it was not possible,' she repeated with a touch of brusqueness. 'Would you like to hear about me?'

'Yes,' he said. He didn't really, but obviously she wanted to tell him.

She got up and began to undress, while he watched her in fascination. She had indeed put on weight, just enough to make her breasts larger, her hips appear a little wider. There were stretch marks on her belly. And on her back? 'If you would care to look,' she said, 'you will see the weals.'

She stood before him, and then turned around. He found himself kissing the soft flesh of her buttocks before he could stop himself; the weals were easier to find by touch than to see, as they had almost faded. 'Reger did that to you?'

'No,' she said. 'Father. When I went home, he made me strip and lie on his bed, and he beat me with his sjambok until I bled and he was exhausted. I had borne a child for an Englander, you see.'

'Reger allowed this?'

'Reger was there, watching.'

'My God! And he did not interfere?'

'I think he enjoyed it. I did not know then he still wished to marry me. But I think he enjoyed thinking I had been raped, as I claimed.'

'And your father did not believe you?'

'I don't know if he believed me or not. He still wanted to punish me for having had the child.' She turned, rubbing her pubic hair against his face.

'Do you hate him?' he asked.

185

'He is dead,' she said simply.

'But you went to Reger.'

'Where else was I to go?' She moved from in front of him, and lay down on the bed. 'Will you not come to me?'

He undressed himself, knelt beside her on the bed, his mind clouded by a jumble of emotions, of which mounting passion was the greatest. 'Then I think you must hate me, for having exposed you to so much misery.'

'I did hate you, Murdoch,' she said. 'Even as I believed what you wrote in that letter, I hated you for having given me the child, but even more for being British, for being responsible for what was happening all around me, and to me. You can have no conception of what life was like in that camp. There was not enough food, there was no proper sanitation, there were no adequate medical supplies. And far too few doctors. We just fended for ourselves, and if we were lucky we lived. If not, we died. The children suffered most. How could you people do such a thing?'

'I don't know,' he said.

She took him in her hands for a few seconds, then slid her fingers up to his shoulders and brought him down on her. 'I believe that too.'

She was as lovely to hold and to touch and to watch and to experience as his memory of her, as his dreams of her, too. She was tall and strong and soft, all at the same time; to feel her body against his was to reach the extreme of passion.

'What will you do now?' she asked, when his head rested on her shoulder.

'You mean if you were not to come with me? Why, go home, I suppose.'

'Back to the Army?'

'Yes.'

'If I came with you, would you leave the Army?'

'I don't know,' he said.

Her head turned; her chin brushed his forehead.

'If you wanted it, I would leave,' he explained. 'But I really have nothing else to do with my life. I know that now. Without the Army I would be only half a man.'

186

She was silent for a few minutes. Then she said, 'Will you become a famous general?'

'I doubt that,' he said. 'I don't think I have the will, the guts, if you like, to become a famous general. Perhaps it would be better for me to leave.' He sat up. 'Margriet, I have a compartment booked on the train to Cape Town tomorrow morning. If you could bring the children to town tonight, we would be away by eight. Or I could meet you on the veldt.'

'I cannot,' she said, and sat up in turn.

He frowned at her. 'You mean you are *not* coming?'

'I cannot,' she said again.

'Because of the Army?'

'That is part of it. I would always be an outsider, an outcast, in fact. Then there are my children. They too would be fish out of water, away from Africa. And I would be abandoning my home, my dog, my horses ... my wealth. Reger may beat me, but he also buys me everything I wish, everything I require for the children.'

'Do you not think I could do that as well?'

'He is a very wealthy man,' she said seriously. 'Or he will be, one day. His uncle is a Prussian junker. Perhaps you did not know that.'

'Perhaps I did not,' Murdoch agreed, balls of lead seeming to form in his stomach. But they were balls of anger as well.

'This uncle is childless, and Paul is his favourite nephew,' Margriet went on. 'It is possible – probable, even – that Paul will be returning to Prussia to inherit all of that wealth, thousands of acres of land, in a few years' time. And I will be his wife.' She smiled. 'You once told me he should take me to Berlin. Well, he is going to do so.'

'And that is why you wish to stay with him? Not the children?'

She gave a little shrug; ten minutes ago the sight of that movement, while she was lying naked on his pillows, would have aroused him all over again. 'Life, decisions about life, are made up from many things.'

'Then tell me something. Your mind was made up before you came here today?'

'There was never any question of making up my mind,' she said, and rested her hand on his arm. 'I told you that, at the house two days ago. I told you I could not come.'

'And I did not believe you. Not when you agreed to meet me.'

She made a moue. 'I thought that was what you wanted, more than anything else. I thought that was what you came all this distance for.'

'And you were prepared to jeopardise all this happiness, this prosperity you claim to enjoy, just for an outside fuck?' He got up and started to dress.

She sat up. 'Now you are angry with me.'

Now I could strangle you, he thought. But he said, 'Just surprised.' And also disappointed, and crushed – but those were very private thoughts.

'I do love you, Murdoch,' she said. 'When I think what I risked for you, I am amazed. But I was only a girl then. And you did turn my head with your talk.'

'You mean you would not risk that much again now?'

'You *are* angry.' She got out of bed, uncoiling her legs, and stood against him, her arms round his neck. 'Because I have been honest with you?'

He sighed. 'Because I have dreamed of you, and feared for you, every night for four and a half years.'

'And now you have possessed me again, in a way no man has ever had me before or ever will again. Does that not please you?'

'No,' he said. 'Not if I cannot have you again, or have my son.'

She said nothing, until she had finished dressing, rearranged her pompadour as best she could and adjusted her veil. Then she said, 'You had best forget me. Forget both of us.'

'Yes,' he said. 'I had best do that.'

She smiled at him. 'But I will not forget you, my dear Murdoch.' She blew him a kiss, opened the door, and was gone.

8

Somalia, 1907

'Welcome back, my dear fellow,' said Lieutenant-Colonel Walters. 'How was Italy?'

'Italy? Oh ... ah ... very interesting,' Murdoch said.

'And the Italians?'

'Oh, indeed,' Murdoch agreed. 'Very interesting people. Sort of ... exciting.'

'Good. Good. And you're quite fit again? I must say, you look very fit.'

'I feel absolutely in the pink, sir,' Murdoch said. Physically, that was no lie. And mentally? It was over. He had to be determined about that, allow himself no more dreams. He had fallen in love with a mirage, a woman who had never really existed, except in his imagination. The woman who had come to his hotel in Johannesburg had been a totally selfish, totally sensuous creature. How Colonel Edmonds' words came back to him – once so hotly rejected – that she could be nothing better than a whore to have yielded to him so quickly.

That she was the mother of his son was irrelevant. He did not even know if that was true. She had been in the camp for more than ten months. And she could have been pregnant when she escaped with him: which might have been part of the reason for that so ready acceptance of his proposal.

What really made him boil was the way he had considered, once again, abandoning his career and his position and his future for her. And he was a soldier who might possibly one day become a general.

There had been a letter waiting for him from Marylee Caspar, telling him of Harry's and her adventures on the continent, a witty, chatty, informative letter, the letter of one friend to another; as a well-brought-up Baltimore young lady she could hardly write in any other way. And she wanted him to tell her about South Africa in turn, how it had changed. But he had no desire to write to her at all, or risk anything further developing between them. He had no desire ever to become involved with any woman again.

'That's splendid news,' Walters said. 'Are you in the mood for some active service?'

'Yes, *sir*,' Murdoch said with genuine enthusiasm. He certainly wanted to fight somebody. 'India? The North-West Frontier?'

'As a matter of fact, the regiment is being sent to India, yes.'

'Oh, that is splendid,' Murdoch said.

'Of course, it was where your father earned his reputation. But . . . I'm afraid I have been instructed to second a squadron for other duties first.'

Murdoch frowned. 'Sir?'

'Somalia.'

'Somalia? Somaliland?'

'That's what they call it, yes. Do you know where it is?'

'Well . . . on the Red Sea, isn't it?'

'The coastal strip is on the Red Sea, yes. It actually is quite a large area east of Abyssinia, so far as I have been able to make out, and next door to Italian Somaliland. That's one of the reasons why I am sending you, as you have been to Italy and know the people. I imagine you even speak something of the language. eh?'

Murdoch opened his mouth and then closed it again. Then opened it again. 'You are sending me to Somaliland, sir?'

'With one squadron of the regiment, yes. It appears there has been some bother there for the past ten years or so. Oh, the Italians stirred it up. They had designs on Abyssinia itself. You must remember that dreadful business at Adowa in ninety-six. Or was it ninety-four? No matter. An entire Italian army got chopped up by the fuzzy-wuzzies. Really nasty. Now, of course, we don't wish to get involved in any war with Abyssinia. But the Italians have also stirred up

190

some Somali holy man, chap called'—he glanced at the notes on his desk—'Muhammad Ibn Abd Allah, who regards himself as some sort of offshoot of the Mahdi, you know, and has been making life difficult for everyone for some time now. Well, we may not agree with the Italian point of view, but British Somaliland is, well, British, and we can't have some local lunatic causing trouble. He *is* a lunatic, you know. The newspapers call him the Mad Mullah. Perhaps you've heard something of him.'

'Yes, sir,' Murdoch said, his mind still reeling at what his deception had got him into.

'Well, he's becoming more obstreperous all the time, raiding villages and caravans and generally trying to stir the people up against us. So we are going to take a somewhat more offensive stance against him, and it is felt that a squadron of dragoons, especially with the South African experience of the Westerns, will be just the chaps to seek and destroy these brigands.'

'Yes, sir,' Murdoch agreed unhappily.

Walters could see he was disappointed at not going to India, and hurried on. 'Once you have captured this Mullah, why, then you will be sent on to India to join us.'

'Thank you, sir.'

'I didn't only choose you for this job because you speak Italian, you know,' Walters said. 'It was necessary to give one of my captains an almost independent command.' He paused, gazing at Murdoch. 'And I have selected you. I would regard that as a compliment, if I were you.'

'Yes, sir,' Murdoch said. 'I do.'

'It will be a great opportunity for you to prove your skill as a leader of men. You will, of course, be under the overall direction of Brigadier-General Hardie, who is in command out there. But he has always been an infantryman, and I imagine he will leave you very much to yourselves. He has a battalion of the Lancashires and another of the King's African Rifles, together with a contingent of armed police and a battery of artillery, but what he has always lacked is cavalry, and the mobility which cavalry will provide. You will supply that want.'

'Yes, sir,' Murdoch said, somewhat more enthusiastically. If it had always been his dream to serve in India, the thought that he had been singled out, ahead of either Morton or Chapman, as the man most likely to succeed, was exciting. And if the campaign could be settled quickly enough, he would be in India before very long.

'However,' Walters went on, 'I must warn you that according to the report I have been given'—he flicked the folder on his desk—'this is an unpleasant place and an unpleasant business you are becoming involved with. The country sounds like somewhere God forgot – it's very close to the Equator – and these Somalis appear to be the most unpleasant people on earth to fight against. Some of the things mentioned in that report are quite blood-curdling if they are true, which I must confess I take leave to doubt. However, you must study it and circulate its more relevant details to every man under your command, so that no one is in any doubt what he is up against. On the other hand, it must be treated as absolutely confidential. If a word of it was ever leaked to the newspapers, it would be very unfortunate.' He held out the folder. 'Understood?'

Murdoch took the stiff cardboard. 'Yes, sir.'

'Good. Well, there is little time to lose. The regiment sails immediately after Christmas. You'll want to acquaint your men with their destination.'

Murdoch saluted.

'Oh, dear, Murdoch,' Mother complained. 'Just back, and now you are off again.'

'Well, the regiment has been posted, and it will be active service at last, after five years of these pointless manoeuvres,' Murdoch pointed out. 'And an independent command. If I don't come out of it a major, I'll eat my hat.'

'In Somaliland?' Philippa demanded. 'I don't even know where it is.'

'The Horn of Africa,' Murdoch explained, although clearly that did not make her greatly the wiser.

'Who on earth are you going to fight in the Horn of Africa?'

192

'The Mad Mullah. Chap called Mohammad something. You must have heard of him. He's really just an outlaw chieftain, so far as I can gather. My brief is to capture him. Should be a piece of cake.' He didn't want them to start asking too many questions; he had only just had the time to dip into Colonel Walters' confidential report on conditions in Somalia, and he did not like what he had been reading.

Fortunately, Mother was more interested in the past than the immediate future. She came into the study after dinner. 'Murdoch . . . you haven't really talked about South Africa.'

'Well, there isn't much to talk about, really.' Only that you are now a grandmother, he thought; but I could not tell you that, even if I knew for sure it were true. 'They seem to have recovered remarkably well. With our assistance, of course.'

'And you . . . enjoyed yourself?'

'Very much,' he said. 'But I don't think I shall ever return there again.'

Which seemed to satisfy her.

'Somaliland, sir?' Sergeant-Major Hanley frowned. 'Sounds hot.'

'It is hot,' Murdoch agreed. 'And beastly, from all accounts. I want this report typed up in quadruplicate and circulated throughout the squadron the moment we sail. Until then it is top secret, but before we reach Berbera every man must have read it. It seems these people have a different concept of warfare to us. Understood?'

'Yes, sir,' Hanley acknowledged, more doubtfully yet, and took the folder as if it had been one of the new Mills bombs – grenades – they had all been issued with.

'My God,' remarked Peter Ramage, turning the pages of the report. 'Have you read this, sir?'

'Of course I have,' Murdoch said.

'Do you suppose it's true?'

'I should think there must be some truth to it. It is based on eye-witness accounts.'

'You mean British soldiers have actually been, well, muti-lated by these people?'

'Apparently.'

'So we must tell our men to commit suicide rather than allow themselves to be captured?' Tom Knox asked.

'I think we must tell our men not to get themselves captured under any circumstances,' Murdoch said.

'And this bit about the women being worse than the men, and to be shot on sight. Have you ever shot a woman, sir?'

'No,' Murdoch told him.

'Are those going to be orders?'

'I'll issue orders when I see exactly what the situation is on the ground,' Murdoch decided. 'But if I have to give orders to that effect, I will.'

He hoped he meant what he said. In his present mood, he thought he could very well be that ruthless – certainly as regards the women.

The regiment sailed together on board the *SS Columbo* from Plymouth across the Bay of Biscay, in freezing conditions and heavy seas which made coping with the horses a continuing problem, then down the Portuguese coast to Gibraltar, as it had done in 1899 on its way to South Africa. But from Gibraltar it this time turned into the Mediterranean.

Murdoch had actually spent far more time studying the Mediterranean, and especially Italy, and endeavouring to master some words of Italian from a phrase book, than he had Somaliland. But his heart sank when he discovered that it was a toss-up whether the troopship called at Naples or Valetta. To his great relief Valetta was chosen, because the winter gales were making Naples roadstead untenable.

'Now there is a disappointment,' Walters remarked. 'I was hoping you would be able to act as our guide in Naples, Murdoch.'

'Well, actually, sir,' Murdoch confessed, 'I have never been to Naples.'

'What, spent three months in Italy and not seen Naples?'

'See Naples and die,' Billy Hobbs remarked.

'That's what worried me,' Murdoch told him. 'I was more interested in Venice. Spent most of my holiday there.' There was no possibility of the troopship being diverted to Venice, or of any British soldier ever finding himself there, he was sure.

'Ah, Venice,' Colonel Walters said, to his alarm. 'I was supposed to go there on my honeymoon, do you know. But the confounded Boer War started and I had to abandon the idea.'

'Not to mention Mrs Walters, sir,' Hobbs put in; he regarded himself as the regimental wit.

'Oh, indeed. I may say that she was not at all amused.' He paused reflectively, while his officers waited, also reflecting that Judith Walters had not appeared to have been amused since, either. 'Tell me, Murdoch, is it as romantic as they say?'

'Oh, indeed it is,' Murdoch said enthusiastically, deciding that the outbreak of the Boer War had not after all been such a catastrophe.

From Malta, they made their way east, into warmer but no less boisterous weather as they approached Suez. With Italy behind them, Murdoch could get down to the real business of considering what he and his squadron were undertaking. Returning from furlough so soon before their departure, he had not had an opportunity to give the men any idea of what they might expect – he did not really know himself, apart from the horrendous details contained in the report.

He had not even had the time to become properly acquainted with his new horse, a grey gelding named Buccaneer. Buccaneer appeared a powerful and well-trained mount, so far as he could gather from the few occasions he had been able to put him through his paces; but they did not know each other well enough to embark on a campaign which suggested that a good horse might be a lifesaver. So he spent much of every day in the hold, which had been converted into a stable, talking to the animal, while keeping an eye on the other mounts as well.

'I thought we were done with Africa,' Corporal Reynolds

grumbled; Murdoch had secured his promotion as a reward for his faithful service in South Africa, although he remained his batman.

'I think you'll find Somalia isn't the least like South Africa,' Murdoch told him. 'Unfortunately.'

'That's what's bothering me, sir,' Reynolds agreed. 'Is it true those Somali women like to chop off a fellow's dingdong?'

'If they can get hold of it,' Murdoch said. 'Do bear that in mind, George.'

After a brief stop in Port Said, where they had their first glimpse of the sort of people they were going to fight – although the fellaheen looked peaceful enough – the troopship proceeded down the Suez Canal and into the Red Sea. It was intensely hot, especially after the chill of the Mediterranean, and Murdoch began to worry for the horses. But after only a few more days they dropped anchor off the seaport of Berbera, which was the capital of British Somaliland.

There was not sufficient water for the *Columbo* to get alongside, and there were in any event no port facilities, so the squadron had to be transferred ashore by lighter. All the rest of the regiment was paraded on deck to bid them farewell, and Colonel Walters shook hands with Murdoch and the two lieutenants, as well as Sergeant-Major Hanley and Squadron Sergeant Yeald. 'Just lock up that madman as quickly as you can,' he told them.

'We'll expect you in Peshawar within three months,' Hobbs remarked.

'And don't forget to have fun with those Somali bints.' Johnnie Morton winked. 'I'll want a blow-by-blow description. Unless you pick the wrong one, and join us singing falsetto, of course.'

Murdoch grinned at the quips as his men were loaded into the waiting dhows, which were manned by Somalis whom he presumed could well be followers of this Mad Mullah. But it was difficult to associate these tall, dignified men with murder and mayhem.

He sent Knox ashore with the first load to supervise the landing and remained until the last man and horse had been lowered, then took his own place. The regimental band, arrayed on the foredeck of the troopship, struck up the march from *Aida* as the lateen sail was hoisted and the dhow pulled away from the liner's side. Murdoch saluted Colonel Walters, feeling quite odd to be leaving the umbrella of the regiment so completely – in South Africa, when sent on patrol, one always knew one would be back in a few days. Now the entire squadron of two hundred and twelve officers and men – for he had with him farriers and medical orderlies, as well as his troopers – was his responsibility alone.

A large crowd gathered to watch the dragoons land was pointing at their weapons and their horses, especially interested in the dismantled machine gun. Waiting for Murdoch was an infantry officer, Captain Halstead of the Lancashires.

'Good to see you, Mackinder,' he said. 'By Jove, you've a fine-looking body of men there. Now we should be able to show those devils a thing or two. Our trouble is that we've been kept too much on the defensive. Now, old man, the brigadier is waiting to review you.'

He mounted his horse and rode on ahead to inform the brigadier that the cavalry were on their way, and Murdoch formed up his squadron, Knox and Ramage at the head of their troops, himself, with Sergeant-Major Hanley, Sergeant Yeald, Corporal Reynolds and Bugler Andrews – a lad of seventeen – at the front of the entire squadron. Andrews sounded the command, and they walked their horses through the town in a column of twos, the street lined with people of every colour, sex and description, amongst them several obvious Europeans, while the cavalcade was followed and surrounded by cheering Arab and Somali children, as well as innumerable half-starved dogs.

Murdoch felt the sun scorching down on his pith helmet and seeming to burn its way right through his khaki tunic, and although he kept his gaze rigidly to the fore, he could not help noticing with growing concern the decrepit houses, so oddly juxtaposed with several ornate mosques, the veiled women, the bearded, grinning men. He inhaled the many odours, few of them pleasant, as he watched the dogs and chickens, goats and jackasses scattering before the approaching horses – he had not campaigned in so totally alien a society before; in South Africa, probably because they had been sent there to fight the Boers rather than the Africans themselves, one had at least had the comforting feeling that one's enemies were likely to be more Christian than oneselves. Even if the report had not already made up his mind for him, he was coming to the conclusion that he did not like Somaliland.

'Things improve in the wet season, which starts in March,' the brigadier told him over whiskies in the mess that evening. 'Or at least you can say they change. A lot of the natives migrate to the Ogo Highlands during the hot season, now, and return when it cools off. Mind you, the monsoon does not always actually get here. When it doesn't, it gets hotter than ever, there's a drought, and all manner of unpleasantnesses, cattle dying, and God knows what else.'

'Wouldn't that make things easier for us, sir?' Murdoch asked. 'Wipe out the rebels' livestock?'

'Quite the contrary,' said Colonel Killick of the King's African Rifles. 'All the Mullah does then is increase his terrorism of the local sheikhs, poor chaps.'

'Mohammad Ibn Abd Allah has been up in those mountains'—Brigadier-General Hardie pointed at the serrated peaks, blue in the distance, but in the clear, still air perfectly visible from the mess verandah—'for eight years, would you believe it. I would give ten years' pay to nab the beggar.'

'What exactly are our measures against him, sir?' Murdoch asked.

'In the main, retaliatory expeditions. But of course we can never bring him to battle.'

'If he raids the outlying villages, cannot we organise a defence amongst the sheikhs?'

'Ah, now, there's the rub. At least half of them are in league with him, think they are fighting a holy war to drive out the infidel. Trouble is, we don't know which half. They pay the Mullah tribute, you see; or so they say. When a village is burned, it is always a result of failure to pay this blackmail. When a village is never touched, the sheikh claims it is because he makes his payments regularly. We may think he is lying, but there is no way we can prove it.' He held up his finger as Murdoch would have spoken. 'Don't tell me: Lord Kitchener would soon have settled that. The misfortune is, Mackinder, that Lord Kitchener's methods in South Africa, successful as they were, have had their repercussions. If I were to start rounding up Somali women and children and placing them in camps until their menfolk surrendered, I suspect I would be on the next boat home with nothing accomplished. Nor have blockhouses proved very effective; I simply do not have the men. I erected some up in the foothills, but when one was overrun and the garrison massacred long before a relief expedition could get there, I decided to pull them out. That's another thing we lack, you see – railroads, or roads of any sort, for quick communication. We must hope that the Mullah makes a mistake and gives us the opportunity to force him to stand and fight. I believe it's possible; he seems to be growing more confident, and arrogant, with every raid. And of course, now that you and your cavalry are here. . . .' He allowed his gaze to drift to the crimson ribbon on Murdoch's breast; it had now been joined by the orange and blue of the Queen's South Africa Medal. 'Yes, what I propose is this: you will maintain your men in camp for a couple of weeks, acclimatising them to conditions here and perhaps doing some training in desert warfare – for it is just a bleeding desert out there – and then we will mount a serious reconnaissance into the Togdheer and see if we can smoke him out.'

'Do we have any cooperation from the Italians, sir?'

'By Jove,' remarked Colonel Norton of the Lancashires, 'do we just. They're as keen as mustard, bless their hearts. But not worth a tinker's damn as fighting soldiers. We're better off on our own.'

Getting down to serious training outside Berbera was

difficult, because the arrival of the squadron, commanded by three unattached and handsome young men, stirred the social life of the small British community into violent action. Murdoch and the two lieutenants were bombarded with invitations to supper parties and luncheon parties and garden parties and beach parties.

Murdoch would have declined most of these, but was dissuaded by Halstead. 'Really must try to accept them, old man,' his brother captain pointed out; he had apparently been told to mother the new arrivals. 'Must keep the memsahibs happy, eh? Just don't get hooked on any of the daughters. When you want a woman, just give me a wink.'

'Will I want a woman?' Murdoch asked.

'Well . . . everyone does. And the local bints can be absolute charmers.'

'When they're not chopping bits off their prisoners, you mean.'

'Oh, well, those are the women in the mountains. Mind you,' he said thoughtfully, 'I'm bloody sure quite a few of them down here are the same breed. But they know their places in Berbera, and besides . . . no harm in getting to know the enemy, eh?'

Murdoch surmised, correctly, as it turned out, that he was about to be confronted with a whole new set of venereal problems. But in fact these were only aspects of the health question. Even if there was little malaria in the dry season – that was apparently something to look forward to when the monsoon arrived – there were other tropical ailments enough. These varied from chiggers – little insects which would burrow into the men's toes and lay their eggs, which, if not completely removed, would fester and cause debilitating sores – to plain heatstroke, which, despite such required kit as spine pads and cloth covers for their necks, constantly had ten per cent of his strength on sick parade.

The question of coping with the heat was compounded by the very necessary training in desert campaigning, an aspect of soldiering which neither he nor his men had ever encountered before. In South Africa it had been considered a fact of life that an army, or a division, or a brigade, or a regiment, or even a squadron, moved in close proximity to its supply line, be it by road or train, or, in the case of Lord Roberts' famous turning movement, wagon train, and that it was suicidal to cut loose from that essential source of food and water. In Somalia this was apparently necessary for several days at a time, and it was therefore important for every man to learn how to survive under these conditions.

According to the veterans from the Lancashires, this was much easier than might have been supposed. There was, for instance – so they claimed – always water to be found in even the desert, if one knew where to look and was prepared to dig; the old rivers were sometimes as deep as ten feet below the surface, but they were usually there, wherever any positive vegetation showed itself. Murdoch equipped a section in each troop with spades.

Then it was necessary to relearn the technique of the heliograph, as telephone wires were impractical over the huge distances they would be covering; and to make the acquaintance of Hassan, the somewhat supercilious Somali, tall, dignified, oval faced, who was to be the squadron guide and indeed mentor, once they left civilisation behind.

It was not all work, however. Murdoch endeavoured to keep his men's minds off women as much as possible by organising cricket matches for their leisure hours. He himself was introduced by Halstead into the pleasures of hunting, for there were lions in the vicinity, driven closer to the town by the scarcity of game in the dry season. One evening they actually bagged two, although Murdoch felt like a murderer when he gazed at the proud, tranquil features, the enormous power and agility he had so carelessly destroyed.

Halstead also felt that Murdoch should be entertained in other ways, despite his patent lack of interest. Only a week after the squadron's arrival, Murdoch returned home from a supper party one evening, with Tom Knox, to find Reynolds in a very agitated state. 'Captain Halstead was here, sir,' he explained, 'and . . . well, there's this person to see you.'

Murdoch frowned at him. 'Person?' He opened the door

of his quarters – this was a permanent encampment with wooden barracks and offices – and, followed by Knox, looked around his small lounge, nostrils twitching as he inhaled an unfamiliar and not unattractive scent. Then he opened the bedroom door, and by the light of the lantern hanging from one of the joists above his head – for the sake of coolness there was no ceiling – saw that his bed was occupied by a woman.

'Good Lord,' Knox commented. 'Shall I go?'

Murdoch opened his mouth and then closed it again, because she was a very attractive woman indeed, really hardly more than a girl, he supposed, with light brown skin, hair black as midnight, matching her eyes, nose somewhat large and definitely hooked, but sitting well over the thin mouth and the pointed chin. And beneath, as she threw back the covers and revealed herself, entrancingly firm breasts and seductive thighs, with short, but muscularly slender legs.

'You like?' she asked, looking from one officer to the other.

Murdoch took off the forage cap that was regulation wear with his undress blues, and scratched his head. 'Who the devil are you?' he inquired.

'I am Mulein,' she replied. 'I speak English, all good.'

'And who sent you here?'

'Jimmy Halstead.' She stretched, then nestled into the bedclothes, spreading her legs and bringing them back together, slowly and seductively. 'You come feel Mulein?' she invited.

She was certainly a temptation. But even if he had not been quite off the female sex, he had come here to fight these people, not sleep with them. 'No,' he said.

Mulein frowned and sat up. 'You no like?'

'I am sure you are absolutely charming,' Murdoch told her. 'But I am very tired. Corporal Reynolds?'

'Sir!' Reynolds had been hovering outside the door.

'Would you be good enough to escort this young lady from the premises? I suppose she should be escorted from

202

the camp. It would help, Mulein, if you were to put some clothes on.'

She glared at him, her nostrils flaring, her lips drawing back from her fine white teeth almost in a snarl. Then she got out of bed and draped her hair around her shoulders, in an instant totally concealing herself; like most Somali women, as opposed to the Arabs, she did not wear the yashmak, although presumably she was a Muslim.

'Thank you,' Murdoch said. 'Now go with the corporal.'

'You are sheet,' Mulein remarked.

'Take her away, Reynolds.'

Reynolds approached her cautiously. 'No scratching now,' he warned.

'When I scratch you, white man, you *die*,' Mulein hissed at him. She stared at Tom Knox for a moment, then went through the doorway.

'Out of the camp, George,' Murdoch reminded Reynolds.

He undressed and got into the bed himself. But sleep was difficult. The sheet was warm from her body, and the pillows smelt of her perfume.

Next morning he intended to remonstrate with Halstead, but to his surprise, Halstead remonstrated first.

'Really, old man, Mulein is quite a catch. I got her for you specially. She's no common bint, you know. Her father is a sheikh, out in the desert, close to the mountains.'

'And the daughter of a sheikh is a whore?'

'Well . . . I gather she fell out with the old man when he wanted her to marry someone she didn't like, and she refused. She's not cheap, you know. She cost me one pound three shillings for the night.'

Murdoch felt in his pocket and handed over the money.

'Well, thanks,' Halstead acknowledged. 'But the fact is, I'm afraid you will have upset her. She's, well . . . she's very useful. She goes out into the desert, into the mountains, in fact, quite regularly, and brings back some quite useful information.'

'You mean she's a spy.'

'You could say so.'

'For us, or for the Mullah?'

'Why, for us, of course.'

'Let's hope you're right.'

'I say, old man, I *have* been here somewhat longer than you. If she is annoyed, well, there could go a useful contact. And she's certain to ruin your reputation in the bazaars,' he added.

'So I'll keep out of the bazaars,' Murdoch agreed. 'But Halstead, if you don't mind, old man, I'll select my own bedmates from now on.'

Ten days later the brigadier decided to make his move; reports had come in from the native police of several villages being raided and looted only fifty miles in the interior, and he wanted to carry out his campaign and be back in Berbera before the rains started in earnest – it was already the first week of February.

He assembled all his officers in the mess for a chat. 'Now, gentlemen,' he said, 'we know that the Mullah is in the field, and at last reports not far away. Of course we also know that he moves quickly and may have withdrawn some distance, and we also know, those of us who have been here for some time, that it is nearly impossible to bring him to battle, because of his superior mobility. But I think we may at last have a factor which will enable us to force the issue. I refer of course to the arrival of the Royal Western Dragoons.' He paused to give Murdoch an encouraging smile.

'Now, gentlemen, the format will be the same as last autumn. We are turning out in response to attacks upon friendly villages. It is important that we behave in our usual manner, so as not to arouse the Mullah's suspicions. We will therefore pick up the trail wherever it can be found, and follow it. Odds are one to a hundred it will lead to Sheikh Rahman's village, as it always does, and that Sheikh Rahman will tell us he has not been attacked because he always pays his tribute regularly.'

'Sheikh Rahman is Mulein's father,' Halstead whispered to Murdoch. 'A right bastard.'

204

'I'd give a month's pay to be able to prove *he* was working for the Mullah,' Brigadier-General Hardie went on. 'But . . . we shall see. Now, gentlemen, once we have picked up the trail, the dragoons will push on ahead of the main body. This will seem a natural enough move to the enemy. I think you could let yourself get up to twenty-four hours ahead of us, Captain Mackinder. No further, and you must always have in mind a suitable defensive position, with water, where you can make a stand. You will be, in effect, the bait of a trap.

'You should be able to travel fast enough to keep up with the Mullah's force. My hope, and my belief, is that when he discovers he cannot throw you off his trail or leave you far behind, as he invariably does with foot soldiers, he will turn back and seek to annihilate you. You will then, keeping in constant heliographic communication with the brigade, select a suitable defensive position and hold it until we arrive. I realise that the Mullah will have the option of breaking off the engagement as he becomes aware of our approach, but if we can get within striking distance of him we may be able to accomplish something. And of course, the more you can involve him in attacking you, the more difficult it will become for him to disengage. I know that I am asking a great deal of your men, captain. Are they up to it?'

'They will be flattered, sir,' Murdoch said.

'Good. Good. Now there are one or two points I must make very clear. You may be separated from the brigade for up to three days at a time. It is therefore essential that food and water be rationed at all times, and that fodder be found for your horses. Your guide, Hassan, will be invaluable here. The second point is a grave but necessary one. You have all read the report I had issued on the nature of the enemy you are going to encounter?'

He looked from Murdoch to Knox to Ramage.

'Yes, sir,' Murdoch answered for the three of them.

'Well, what I am about to say may be taken as an order. That report was no exaggeration. Therefore at no time will any surrender to the enemy be contemplated. No matter how desperate the situation, fight to the last man and save the last bullet for yourselves. I am here depicting a situation which I do not for one moment suppose will arise, but if it should, remember my words. More importantly, and sadly, should you engage the enemy, and be forced to withdraw from an established position you *must not* allow any wounded to fall into their hands. They must be taken with you. And if that proves impossible' – he gazed at their faces – 'they must be killed before the enemy can obtain possession of them. And finally, and most sadly of all, should any member of your squadron be taken, through any mishap, there will be no heroic attempts at rescue.' This time he gazed directly at Murdoch. 'However hard it may be to bear, you will not send good men after dead men, under any circumstances. Is this clearly understood?'

Murdoch glanced at the two lieutenants, whose faces were tense. Then he nodded. 'Yes, sir.'

Hardie nodded in turn. 'Then I suggest we get a good night's sleep, gentlemen. The brigade will move out at dawn tomorrow.'

9

Somalia, 1907

Four companies of the Lancashires, as well as the artillery, were left in garrison; supported by the paramilitary police force, they composed something like a thousand men, sufficient to hold Berbera should the Mullah attempt to come in behind the brigade – although that was something he had never yet attempted.

Murdoch felt it was a mistake to leave the artillery, and said so, but the brigadier pointed out that shelling made very little impression on desert wadis, and besides, it had never been taken before on account of the difficulty of moving the guns across such country. 'It is your chaps who are going to do the damage,' he announced.

Murdoch hoped he was right. The brigadier had obviously built all his plans upon the coming of the squadron. Murdoch had no objection to being used as bait – as he had said, he was flattered, and so were his men – he was not at all sure it was a trap into which the Mullah, however mad, would fall. However, the brigade made an imposing spectacle as it moved out of its cantonment. There were eight companies of the King's African Rifles, tall, imposing black men, who wore red fezzes, although the rest of their uniform was khaki, and equally incongruous, bare feet, although they wore regulation puttees; Halstead claimed they could travel very nearly as fast, across the roughest country as mounted infantry.

'But the rebels will see those fezzes coming for miles,' Murdoch suggested.

Halstead merely shrugged. 'Fortunately, the Mullah's people don't shoot very straight.'

Then there were three companies of the Lancashires, who were mounted on mules, the usual hospital wagon and his squadron of cavalry, which undertook the advance guard duties – at least so far as the casual observer could detect.

Murdoch in fact thoroughly enjoyed his role of appearing so enthusiastic that he gradually pulled ahead of the main body. He suspected it might have been suggested to Brigadier-General Hardie by those who had studied his South African record.

He followed the South African principle of alternating each troop each day; he himself always rode with the forward party. Unfortunately, he still found the pace of the advance painfully slow, as he had to maintain contact with the brigade; it was going to take some determined prodding and baiting to make the Mullah accept battle.

'Some bloody country,' Tom Knox remarked, as they walked their horses over the sandy soil. Hardly a tree was to be seen save for an occasional thorny acacia, but the apparently flat surface was actually a mass of shallow ravines and wadis, any one of which could have concealed a hundred armed men. Luckily, the Somalis were not actually attempting to defend their country against the British – as the Boers had been – so much as trying to stir up a large-scale revolt against the foreigners, and there was no evidence of any ambush. However, there were enemies enough in the snakes and scorpions which were invisible until one actually stepped on them; they could do little damage to stout boots, but were a menace to the horses – how the KAR were faring Murdoch did not like to consider, but presumably they had campaigned in this country before.

The Mullah's raiders had recently been in the district; that was painfully obvious when they came across their first village. They smelt it long before they actually saw it. Murdoch made the squadron draw rein some distance off, while he went forward with Hassan to inspect the scene of destruction. The village had been burned – after some resistance, he supposed. The hideous red-headed vultures which flapped lazily away from the blackened timbers had been feasting on several dead bodies, and the spring which was the reason for the village's existence was also choked with dead bodies, including those of women and children, nearly all savagely mutilated, and now being further reduced by flies and maggots. Close at hand the stench was quite sickening.

'Where would the rest of the inhabitants have gone?' Murdoch asked.

'The Mullah will have taken them off as slaves or recruits, effendi.'

'And he really believes these people will one day rise up and fight for him, when he treats them like this?'

'Oh, indeed, effendi. His reasoning is simple, that in time the people will rather fight for him than be killed by him, and that then they will all rise up together and drive the infidels into the sea.'

Murdoch glanced at him. 'Do you believe this, Hassan?'

Hassan gave one of his rare smiles. 'I do not believe the infidels, or at least the British, will ever be driven into the sea, effendi.'

Which was at least a diplomatic answer.

Murdoch determined the squadron should clean up the mess, instead of leaving it for the brigade, for two reasons: most importantly, he wanted the use of the water from the spring to refill his men's canteens, but he also wanted to let the troopers have a look at the reality of what they were up against. So he summoned both troops forward for Knox and Ramage to detail burial parties, while he and Hassan examined the hoofmarks leading to the south-west.

'These were many men, effendi,' the guide said. 'Perhaps six, seven hundred horsemen.'

'Would that be the Mullah's total force?'

'No, no, effendi, the lord Muhammad ibn Abd Allah commands many men. But this is still a large force.' He looked anxious, as he had not, of course, been told the general's plan of campaign. Murdoch inspected the country before them through his binoculars; they were within a few miles of the foothills of the Togdheer, the high land which lay due south of Berbera.

'How long ago were these men here?' he asked.

'Oh, not long, effendi. Two, three days.'

Murdoch frowned. 'That police report was a week old.'

'That was further to the south, effendi.'

'But you brought us here,' Murdoch pointed out.

Hassan gave another of his smiles. 'It is pure fortune that you have discovered traces of the Mullah's work on our path. I was leading you to the village of Sheikh Rahman ibn Ali, which lies fifty miles to the west, in the foothills.'

'You think this Sheikh Rahman may also have been attacked?'

Hassan's lip curled. 'No, effendi, I do not think he will have been attacked.'

Of course, Murdoch remembered; Mulein's father.

'But now I think it is best for us to wait for the foot soldiers,' Hassan went on.

'Because you think this harka may have gone to visit the sheikh? I think that is a reason for pressing on, Hassan.'

Hassan looked at the tracks. 'They are many men,' he said. 'Many more men than you command, effendi.'

'I still think we should have a look,' Murdoch said.

Sergeant Yeald set up the heliograph and flashed a message back to brigade that they were in contact with the enemy and were following them. By then the spring was beginning to issue clean water again and the squadron was able to replenish their water bottles. The men neither joked nor grumbled now; their faces were pale beneath their recently acquired suntan; and several had vomited. Murdoch did not doubt they would fight the harder for that.

They moved on again and camped for the night several miles beyond the destroyed village. Next day the march was resumed, and in mid afternoon they came in sight of another sprawling village, but this one intact, an oasis of mud-brick houses, painted white and pale yellow and blue and pink, above which waved a cluster of palm trees, although even those were dominated by the tall tower of the minaret which rose from beside the mosque. The land around the houses was cultivated and green, in striking contrast to the aridity over which the squadron had marched for the previous twenty-four hours.

The trail of hooves certainly led up to the village, although there was no sign of any large number of men or horses in the vicinity. Murdoch ordered all precautions to be taken. He halted A Troop, until Ramage had come up, then reconnoitred the position, watched with interest but no hostility by a group of Somali men, and selected a defensive position on the edge of the fields where he was sure there would be water. He then dismounted his men and assembled the Hotchkiss gun. These military preparations were carried out inside a kind of laager of the horses, so that they would not be readily evident to the villagers. When all was prepared to stand a siege if need be, he took Bugler Andrews, Squadron Sergeant Yeald, Corporal Reynolds and six men, and walked his horse into the village; neither Knox nor Ramage had actually seen action before, and he reckoned they would need the solid support of Sergeant-Major Hanley, should there be trouble.

But the people of the village seemed pleased enough to see them, and the sheikh came out to bow to them, watched by several women from the porch of his house – veiled, Murdoch observed with interest, which suggested that he was a very orthodox Muslim. Hassan interpreted, and they were apparently made welcome. Yes, they had been visited by a large body of horsemen on their way to rejoin the Mullah's main force, which Sheikh Rahman suggested was not all that far off. They had, as usual, demanded tribute, and this the sheikh had paid, he explained, complaining at the same time of his total impoverishment. He then invited Murdoch and his officers to a meal.

Murdoch had no doubt at all that the scoundrel was one of the Mullah's men; there was no other reason for his village to be so undamaged, no matter how much tribute he might have paid – not a crop had been trampled, in such strong contrast to the tragic scene of yesterday. But equally he saw no reason not to enjoy the offered hospitality, especially as Hassan told him it was traditional – and he could hope to obtain some additional information about the Mullah's whereabouts.

Yet he would not relax his caution. He had water and food taken out to his men, insisted that the carriers eat and

211

drink some of it before he would let any trooper have a mouthful, and then revealed his full strength, the machine gun trained on the houses, the hundred and seventy riflemen also ready for action. Then he took the two lieutenants back for the meal. The heliograph equipment remained packed on two of the horses; he had no doubt that the brigade was following him as rapidly as it could, but he did not wish the sheikh to understand that.

The meal itself was more interesting than attractive. They were served couscous, which consisted of very stringy mutton on a bed of undercooked semolina, and various local delicacies such as sheep's eyeballs and goat's testicles, which they had to swallow whole as there was no way they could bring themselves to chew them. They were required to eat with their fingers, of course, all dipping into the same pot with the sheikh and his elders, their inexperience causing some amusement amongst the women who were serving them. The women were actually more interesting than the meal itself, for they remained veiled and, indeed, so totally concealed by the combination of haik and yashmak that only their eyes and a very brief portion of forehead were visible, apart from their hands, which were invariably covered in flies. But Murdoch was only half-way through his couscous when he felt a most peculiar prickling sensation on the back of his neck, such as he had not experienced since just before the Boer ambush which had resulted in his captivity.

He raised his head sharply and looked at one of the women, who was at that moment kneeling beside Tom Knox to offer him another fingerful of meat, but whose eyes, dark as midnight, had flickered up to meet his own. For a moment he could not believe his senses, yet he was sure as anything in his life that she was Mulein. Hastily he looked away as nonchalantly as he could, so that she would not understand that she had been recognised. But his brain was racing. Halstead had told him Mulein had quarrelled with her father and fled his house. Yet here she was. . . .

'Can you ask the sheikh,' he said in a low aside to Hassan, 'if all the ladies who are serving us are his wives?'

'It would be impolite to ask him that, effendi,' Hassan

212

replied. 'One does not discuss women, especially our host's women. But I can tell you that they will all most certainly be his wives or daughters.'

Murdoch saw Mulein serving Ramage, while ideas swirled through his mind. Their objective was to bring the Mullah to battle, if it could be done. But once the holy man realised the whole brigade was moving in his direction he would undoubtedly take his men to the south to war on the Italians until the British had gone home again. He would have to be tempted to stay. And Mulein understood English. In fact, that she was a spy for the Mullah and not for Halstead could hardly be doubted. At least he could find out – and perhaps manage to incriminate Sheikh Rahman at the same time, as the general so obviously wanted.

The meal was nearly over. 'Now, what I want you to do, Hassan,' he said, speaking just a little more loudly than usual, 'is see if you can obtain any information from the sheikh regarding the exact whereabouts of the Mullah and his men. I'll tell you frankly, it's all very well for the general to send me and my men out on a reconnaissance by ourselves and tell us we must penetrate the mountains of the Togdheer, but I don't much like the idea of confronting several thousand fuzzy-wuzzies, what?'

Ramage and Knox both stared at him in surprise, never having heard him speak like that before. Hassan looked equally bemused. But Knox then understood what he was trying to do, even if not the reason for it. 'But do we have to go on, sir?' he asked.

'Oh, we must, at least for a while,' Murdoch told him. 'I mean to say, there are those tracks, eh? Must put up a show, what?' He was giving his best possible imitation of Johnnie Morton, but only the two lieutenants had ever met Morton.

The bowl of couscous was offered at his elbow. As he dipped into it, he saw Mulein slipping out of the room.

There was little information to be gained from Sheikh Rahman, who had not of course understood the English conversation and merely kept saying there were many men in the hills. But Murdoch was no longer interested in the sheikh. He could hardly wait for the meal to finish.

'Sergeant-major,' he said when he regained the camp, 'while we were lunching with the sheikh, did anyone leave the village? Fairly recently.'

'Why, yes, sir. A horseman left about half an hour ago.'

'I thought she was a woman,' Sergeant Yeald objected.

Hanley gave him a dirty look, but Murdoch nodded. 'Very good, Yeald. She *was* a woman. Sergeant-major, prepare to move out at dusk.'

'At dusk, sir?' Hanley was aghast.

'Can you follow that horse's tracks in the darkness, Hassan?'

'Yes, effendi. But moving in the dark, it is not good.' He looked up at the hills. 'And there are many men up there. It would be better to wait for the foot soldiers.'

'We are going to let the foot soldiers come to us,' Murdoch told him, 'when we have found the Mullah. And I have an idea that we are going to be escorted to his doorstep. Lieutenant Ramage, as soon as it is dark and we move, you will send a despatch rider back to brigade with a message I will write out for him. Now let's prepare to march.'

They hurried about their duties, but Tom Knox, who by now considered himself a friend – as indeed he was – hesitated. 'What's up?'

'Didn't you recognise the bint who was serving you?'

'Can't say I really looked at her.'

'She was our old friend Mulein.'

'Mulein? Good God! Are you sure?'

'Sure enough. And as far as I'm concerned, she's proved it. The moment she heard what we were saying in English, that we were on reconnaissance on our own and heading into the hills, she took off.'

'To warn the Mullah?'

'To tell him we're coming, anyway. The general said the Mullah was becoming more aggressive, more arrogant, if you like. I doubt he'll refuse the opportunity to annihilate an entire squadron of cavalry, especially when that course will be recommended by someone who loves us both so dearly.'

'But surely this Sheikh Rahman character will see the brigade passing this way.'

'Only after we are already in contact with the Mullah's main force. If we can keep him occupied for just twenty-four hours, we may give Hardie the opportunity he has been waiting for. At the very least, if we can catch up with Miss Mulein, we should be able to turn up proof that her daddy is one of the Mullah's men, and that will be a step in the right direction.' He clapped Knox on the shoulder. 'We came here to get this job done as quickly as possible. So let's get to it, and then on to India.'

They broke camp at dusk and moved out. Of course Sheikh Rahman saw what they were doing, but that was not important; the noise of the cavalry setting off hid the despatch of the rider back to the brigade – he had been instructed to walk his horse for the first two miles then to go hell for leather – and the squadron was almost immediately between the sheikh and anyone to whom he might wish to send a message.

Having taken the risk of advancing in the darkness, however, Murdoch was not taking any more chances that night. He sent up an advance guard of twelve men, under Squadron Sergeant Yeald, who was about the most experienced and reliable man he had. With them went Hassan to do the tracking. A quarter of a mile behind them was A Troop, guided by the shaded lantern Yeald carried; Murdoch himself was with Knox. Another quarter of a mile back was an intermediate party, again of twelve men, commanded by Squadron Sergeant-Major Hanley. A similar distance back was Peter Ramage's B Troop, and then there was a rearguard of a last twelve men, commanded by Troop Sergeant Withers. Each group was in contact with the one behind them by the lanterns, which shone only in that one direction. And while between them they covered more than a mile of country, they were still close enough to lend instant support to all the others should it become necessary.

In fact they encountered no one during the night, although the tracks of Mulein's horse, which had now joined those of the main body, were simple to follow. At dawn they were approaching higher ground, and Murdoch called a halt for breakfast. The squadron closed up, sentries were posted, and the machine gun mounted, while Murdoch inspected the hills in front of them through his binoculars.

'Rather like South Africa, sir,' Yeald remarked.

'Oh, those are definitely kopjes,' Murdoch agreed. 'How far do you think we are ahead of the brigade now, sergeant?'

'Oh, must be forty miles, sir. Maybe more. They wouldn't have marched through the night.'

'Hm,' Murdoch said. To march throughout the night, following the tracks from the attacked village, was exactly what he had requested Brigadier-General Hardie to do. But he had no means of knowing if the general had accepted his recommendation, or had dismissed it as impractically over-enthusiastic. Nor had he any means of finding out; if the brigade had *not* marched, they were now too far away to be contacted; if they *had* marched, he had specifically requested them not to attempt to contact him by heliograph until he sent the first message – he had no wish to alert the Mullah as to what he was doing.

But as yet he had seen no sign of the Mullah's army. Only the tracks, leading onwards into the maze of kopjes he remembered, and feared, so well, indicated that there was a large body of men in front of him. He could not halt now.

'We'll continue, gentlemen,' he told the lieutenants and NCOs. 'Mulein can't be far ahead of us now. But, same order as before.'

The squadron remounted and went on its way. Within an hour Yeald and his men had disappeared into a ravine between two of the hills, and Murdoch felt his heartbeat quicken. But no shots were heard, and a little while later A Troop debouched from the same ravine to find themselves in a long, wide valley, hemmed in by hills to either side, but open to the south-west for perhaps four miles. Yeald's advance guard could easily be seen, proceeding slowly as

Hassan followed the tracks. A Troop followed them, and within another half an hour, both the centre guard, B Troop, and the rearguard had all entered the valley.

'Real Charge of the Light Brigade country,' Tom Knox muttered. He was as keen a student of military history as Murdoch himself.

'Ah, but we're heavy cavalry,' Murdoch said as cheerfully as he could. 'And *their* charge at Balaclava was successful. Anyway,' he added as an afterthought, 'so far as I am aware the Mullah doesn't have any cannon.'

'Something's up,' Knox commented, reining his horse and holding up his arm to signal the troop to do the same. The jingling of harness ceased, and they watched a trooper from the advance party spurring back towards them.

'Sergeant Yeald says to tell you, sir,' he panted, 'that the tracks we have been following break off and lead over there.' He pointed due north, at the hills which rose rather sharply to their right, but were traversed by sufficient gullies and ravines to conceal a regiment of cavalry.

'Hm,' Murdoch said, and cantered forward to join Yeald and Hassan. 'What about the main body?'

'They have scattered every way, effendi,' Hassan said. 'I do not like it. It is my opinion that we should withdraw and wait for the brigade.'

'Hm,' Murdoch said again, and listened to three rifle shots. That was the agreed signal for trouble. He turned in his saddle; the shots had come from behind him, and now he watched the rearguard galloping towards B Troop, while behind them, the entry to the valley had become filled with mounted men.

'Good God,' Knox muttered. 'There must be five hundred of them.'

'Sound recall, bugler,' Murdoch said.

The boy put his trumpet to his lips, and spluttered.

'Spit, boy, spit,' Yeald commanded.

A moment later the notes echoed across the valley, and B Troop broke into a canter.

'Now,' Murdoch said. 'We'll have to. . . .'

'With respect, sir,' Yeald said, the faintest of tremors in his voice.

Murdoch turned back to face west. The exit from the valley was also filled with several hundred men.

'Oh, Christ,' Knox said. He was looking neither east nor west, but north, where another good five hundred horsemen were descending from the high ground.

'We've uncovered the Mullah's whole bloody army, sir,' Yeald said.

Murdoch knew what he would see as he turned to the south: more horsemen descending from the hills.

B Troop had now come up, as well as the centre guard. 'Do we form a perimeter, sir?' Sergeant-Major Hanley asked. 'Unlimber the Hotchkiss?'

'This is bloody *Custer* country now,' Knox growled.

'No, sergeant-major, I don't think that would do,' Murdoch said. 'We can probably hold them back until the brigade comes up, but they would have the option of withdrawing whenever they felt like it.' He did not tell them he had no idea if the brigade *was* coming up.

'Then what do we do?' Ramage asked, his voice also beginning to tremble; there could be no doubt that they were outnumbered by more than ten to one.

Murdoch used his glasses, first of all to inspect the slowly advancing horsemen, who seemed to be waiting to see what the white men were going to do, and then to inspect the hills and especially the western exit to the valley. Strangely, he was not afraid, although he was aware of the vigorous pumping of the blood through his arteries; he was more interested in the problem which faced him – how to hold the Mullah here until the brigade arrived.

'There,' he said.

The western exit to the valley appeared to be somewhat narrower than the eastern. And half-way up the northern slope which bordered the exit, he picked out a cluster of trees and bushes emerging from what seemed to be a slight dip in the hillside. There would be water, he was certain – according to what he had been taught since arriving in Somalia – even if they had to dig for it. And it suggested a sound defensive position, which could be held; if the Mullah wished to leave, he would have to take his army beneath the muzzles of the squadron's rifles and machine gun, while if he chose to leave by the eastern exit, he would be marching in the direction of the approaching brigade. In other words, far from having followed Mulein into the trap she had laid, he had the opportunity to entrap the Mullah and force him into that pitched battle he so urgently needed to avoid – always supposing the brigade was actually marching with all speed in this direction.

'We'll make for that gully,' he said. 'And form a defensive perimeter up there.'

'With respect, sir,' Hanley protested, 'there must be a thousand of those devils between us and the pass.'

Murdoch levelled his glasses at the mass of horsemen who were blocking the western exit, and were now walking their horses slowly forward. 'At least a thousand,' he agreed.

'They won't let us pass.'

'They will, you know, if we charge them. There were fifteen thousand Baluchis outside Hyderabad in 1843, and only four hundred troopers. We have much better odds here.'

They gazed at him.

'We'd be going the wrong way, sir,' Tom Knox ventured to point out. 'If we're going to charge anywhere, shouldn't it be back towards the Brigade?'

'That is exactly where we do not wish to go, Mr Knox,' Murdoch reminded him. 'We want the brigade to come to us. Signal the men to close up,' he commanded.

The troops came closer, until they formed a cluster in the centre of the valley – still watched by the Somalis, who had now ceased advancing altogether, although the men to each side were inclining towards the rear, to join those blocking the eastern exit; they had no inkling that the British might go the other way.

'Join me,' Murdoch shouted. He drew his sword and pointed it at the sky; with an enormous rasp, the other hundred and seventy swords left their scabbards. ' "May the great God of battle, who has guided the fate of this famous regiment on many a hard-fought field, and never failed to lead it to distinction, grant that on this day, faced as we are with a host of enemies of our King and our country, every man will do his duty, so that should we fail in our ordained task, it will yet be said of us, they were the Royal Western Dragoon Guards, who fought and died according to the ancient valour of their regiment and their blood." '

The words, spoken by every man of the squadron, rippled across the valley like a growl of thunder, and when Murdoch had finished, the Amen seemed to hang on the still air.

Murdoch wheeled his horse to face his men. 'Mr Knox, Mr Ramage, command your men to form two lines. Mr Knox, A Troop will compose the first line, Mr Ramage, B Troop will follow. Bugler Andrews, Corporal Reynolds, you will ride behind me. Sergeant-Major Hanley, Sergeant Yeald, you will flank Reynolds and Andrews. Should I fail, Mr Knox will take command. Hassan, you ride between Andrews and Reynolds.'

The guide was shivering with fright.

The horses milled about and dust rose into the air, partially concealing their intention. As it cleared, it could be seen that the two troops had formed a double rank, each presenting a solid mass of some eighty horsemen. Now the Somalis realised what they were about to attempt; behind them the kettle drums started to beat and the cymbals to clash.

Murdoch rose in his stirrups and looked over his command. 'Squadron will use swords,' he ordered. 'Our objective is that tree-lined gully behind and to the left of those people over there.' He settled himself in his saddle, checked the chinstrap for his topee, made sure the sword cord was looped round his wrist, then pointed at the Somali horsemen. ' "Gentlemen," ' he called, ' "there is your enemy." ' He lowered his voice. 'Bugler,' he commanded. 'Sound the charge!'

The notes of the bugle spread across the valley and echoed back from the rock walls to either side. The hundred and seventy men of Mackinder's Squadron, Royal Western Dragoon Guards, walked their horses forward, hooves sounding clearly on the sun-dried earth. Then Murdoch touched Buccaneer with his heel and moved into a trot. The squadron followed, harnesses jingling. Murdoch could still feel the blood pounding in his temples as he gazed at the dark mass in front of him, still milling about, still unable to believe that they were to be charged at such great odds; naturally they could know nothing of the history of the Royal Westerns.

He resisted the temptation to turn his head to see what the rest of the Mullah's forces might be attempting; he concentrated on those in front and beyond the gully which would provide him with a natural fortress. The drumming of hooves told him that the squadron was where it should be, at his heels. Now he quickened his pace again, from a trot to a canter; the men in front of him were only about half a mile distant. They had begun to fire – rifles or muskets, he supposed. He could see the puffs of smoke, but they did not appear to be doing any damage. They were also trying to form a line, but were not moving at any speed.

Four hundred yards, and he urged Buccaneer into a gallop. Now the whole valley was filled with sound, the drumming of hooves, the banging of the drums, the clashing of the cymbals and the shrill cries of the Somalis quite overpowering the shouts of the dragoons and the snorting of their horses. Murdoch's sword arm was extended, his wrist turned and locked, his thumb firmly embedded in its grip. The Somalis began to jostle about; some of them urged their horses forward to meet this small khaki-clad wedge, but more were pulling to either side, and some were retreating.

He could see their faces now, hooked noses and flashing teeth beneath their burnouses, shrouded in their beards and moustaches. One of them levelled his musket and fired at close range – directly at him, Murdoch was sure – but he felt and heard nothing. Then he was smashing into their midst. The man who had fired the musket took his sword point in the face. The jar travelled up Murdoch's arm and

221

nearly unseated him, but the man had disappeared, and so had his mount, shoulder-charged by the careering Buccaneer. Murdoch swung the sword to his right and knew from the fresh jar that he had hit someone else, then he was cannoned into from the left and felt a sear of pain across his shoulder, but Buccaneer miraculously kept his footing and hardly lost speed, and the assailant fell behind them. Another muscle-jarring swing of the sword was accompanied by a blow on the head which made him see stars, but then he was through and galloping towards the now exposed exit of the valley, using the rein to incline Buccaneer to the right and up the first of the slope to the gully; the horse gasped and panted, but was still game.

Having gained the slope, Murdoch sheathed his sword, with some difficulty, as his right shoulder was a mass of muscular pain, while his left was still burning, and dragged on the reins with both hands, bringing Buccaneer to a halt, while his men flooded past him, yelling and cheering, waving their bloodstained swords.

'To the gully,' he shouted. 'Sergeant-Major Hanley, as you get there, unlimber the gun. To the gully.'

The squadron surged up the slope, all except for Hassan, who kept on going, straight through the western exit and out on to the plain beyond; he had clearly had enough of the Royal Westerns. Murdoch followed the last of his troopers to safety. The Somalis had scattered to left and right, while the remainder of the Mullah's army, having witnessed the charge in amazement, were only slowly approaching. The dragoons urged their exhausted horses up the now steepening incline, and threw themselves under cover, while the Hotchkiss gun was set up to cover the approach.

'Hold your fire until they come at us,' Murdoch commanded. 'Sergeant-major, I want a squad to dig behind those bushes back there; we may need water. Lieutenant Ramage, form your men to the right. Lieutenant Knox. . . .' He checked. Tom Knox was not to be seen.

The troop sergeants held a roll-call, while he put Hanley

222

in command of A Troop and left the water patrol to Yeald. In fact, casualties had been amazingly light; there were only six men missing, and both Reynolds and Bugler Andrews had followed him through the enemy cavalry without receiving a scratch. Reynolds wanted to fuss over his wounded shoulder, but he shrugged him away – because one of the missing men was Knox.

He could only pray that they had all been killed instantly, but he got out his binoculars and crawled on to the outer escarpment of the gully to study the valley where they had ridden. The actual clash with the Somalis had taken place only about half a mile from their new position, and he could make out the heaps of white cloth, some lying still, some moving painfully and slowly, which denoted dead and wounded Somalis. Now he saw the other horsemen, scattered by the impetuosity of the British charge, returning to the succour of their wounded, the collection of their dead. And the torment of their enemies? He could see two heaps of khaki. Then he picked out a third, trying to move. But as he watched he saw that three of the Arabs had surrounded the fallen man and were dragging him away. The trooper was clearly badly wounded; his tunic was a mass of blood and he was unable to resist them. The temptation to open fire was enormous. But they were at extreme range, and he would almost certainly kill his own man while killing the Somalis. Would that not be better? He chewed his lip in indecision, while sweat trickled down his cheeks, and his shoulders seemed to redouble their pain.

Then he saw Knox. The lieutenant did not appear to have been wounded at all, only unhorsed and dazed by his fall. He was getting up and fumbling for his revolver; he had lost his sword. But he too was now surrounded by Somalis, and after a brief scuffle led away – not very far, Murdoch surmised, for they had gathered on the right-hand side of the valley, where there was some shelter. The main body remained beyond range.

'You're wounded,' Peter Ramage said. 'Your left shoulder is all bloody.'

'A scratch,' Murdoch told him, still looking through his

glasses at the rocks and bushes behind which Knox had been dragged. His belly felt curiously light at the thought of what his friend must be feeling.

'Well, what about your head?'

'My head?' Murdoch released the chinstrap and took off his pith helmet; the top was completely bashed in. 'Good Lord! I never felt that.'

'There's no blood,' Ramage said.

'So there's nothing the matter with me. How about everyone else?'

'We've twenty wounded, but only a couple seriously. And six missing. Have you spotted Tommy?'

'Yes,' Murdoch said grimly. 'He's alive.'

Ramage swallowed and licked his lips as he gazed at his captain.

'Excuse me, sir,' said Sergeant Yeald. 'I think I have contact with the brigade.'

'Have you?' Murdoch scrambled to his feet incredulously. 'How on earth. . . .' He looked at the hills ringing the valley and effectively shutting it off from the plain beyond, he would have thought.

'Through that gap, sir,' Yeald explained, pointing. Murdoch followed the direction indicated, and saw that the hills were not actually a solid mass, but were split up by various valleys and ravines, much lower than the surrounding peaks. And between two of the peaks, to the east, there was definitely a light flashing. If it was the brigadier, then he was letting his nerves get the better of his common sense – but it was still very reassuring to know he was there.

'What is the message?' he asked.

'They just want to know where we are, sir. Or if we are anywhere.'

'Well, set up your equipment and tell them. Tell them we have a large enemy force opposed to us here in the valley, and that we will try to keep them busy until they can get up. But speed is essential.'

'Yes, sir,' Yeald said, and got to work.

Murdoch returned to the perimeter and looked down.

There was a great deal of activity: horsemen galloping to and fro between the advanced party and the main body, tents being pitched and camp fires being lit.

'They think they have us holed up here,' Ramage suggested. 'And all they have to do is wait.'

'Yes,' Murdoch agreed. 'Which seems to indicate they as yet have no idea the brigade is out there. Any joy with that water, sergeant?'

Troop Sergeant Connolly had taken over with the digging squad to free Yeald for the heliograph.

'Not as yet, sir.'

'Perhaps there isn't any,' Ramage said. 'And the Mullah knows that.'

'Perhaps,' Murdoch said, wishing he would shut up. He wasn't really worried about the water situation at the moment, but Ramage's constant pessimistic chattering was indicative of a high degree of tension.

'Begging your pardon, Captain Mackinder.' Hanley had come across to join them. 'What about those chaps?'

Murdoch swung his glasses to look in the direction indicated, east along the high ground beside the gully, where several Somalis could be seen, dismounted and clambering into the hills.

'They mean to enfilade our position,' Ramage said.

'Yes. Well, as soon as they come within range, sergeant-major, give them a burst of machine-gun fire. Lieutenant Ramage, tell the men to go easy with their water bottles; we will have to stay here for a while.' He looked at the sun, which was just climbing noon high. It was very hot. And there would be several hours of this before dusk. His fingers curled into fists. How casually they had joked about the Mullah's women, never for one moment suspecting one of *them* might be captured. Even worse was the realisation that down there somewhere would be Mulein, who considered Tommy Knox to have insulted her.

Ramage was watching him anxiously. 'There is nothing we can do, sir,' he ventured.

Murdoch did not reply but continued to study the Somali camp through his binoculars. The advanced position was just within rifle range, he reckoned, but it would be difficult to be accurate. The main part of the Mullah's army had remained in the valley itself, where they were certainly making themselves comfortable. They were about a mile away, and he estimated there could be five thousand men down there, with their dogs and their camels . . . and their women. And Tommy Knox.

His duty, he knew, was to stay here and make sure they did not go away. Leading another charge to attempt to rescue the six missing troopers would not only be a dereliction of duty, and a direct disobedience of orders, it would also be utterly impractical: the horses were too blown, and he would certainly lose at least another six men.

A shot rang out, and then another. The bullets whined into the gully and ricocheted from rocks, but without hitting anyone.

'I'd say they are within range, sir,' Hanley called.

'Then spray that hillside, sergeant-major,' Murdoch told him.

'Yes, *sir*,' Hanley acknowledged with pleasure, and a moment later the deadly chatter of the Hotchkiss gun filled the morning, one trooper firing while his mate fed the belt of cartridges into the chamber. Pieces of rock and clouds of dust flew from the area where the Somali marksmen had taken shelter, and two men came tumbling out of concealment to go rolling down the slope and lie still.

'Cease fire,' Murdoch commanded, and the remainder of the sniping party could be seen hastily scrambling back out of range.

'That gave the bastards something to think about,' Hanley said with satisfaction.

'I wonder what they'll try next,' Ramage speculated.

As if in reply a scream drifted up the hillside. A piercing, agonised wail . . . and it had been uttered in English. 'Damned bitch!' it shrieked, through all eternity.

The squadron seemed to ripple, and Murdoch licked his lips.

'You'd think they'd take them to the camp,' Ramage muttered.

'They wanted him close enough for us to hear, sir,' Hanley pointed out. 'That's part of their game.'

Another wail mounted the hillside, but this time the words were unintelligible, although they could hear a babble of conversation and shouts of laughter from within the ravine where the advanced party was sheltering.

'Can you see anything?' Ramage asked, his voice trembling.

'No. You have a look.' Murdoch's fingers were clammy with sweat. He turned away from the ledge and slid back down into the gully. That had not been Tom Knox's voice, he was certain. There were two others still unaccounted for.

'Lunch, sir,' Reynolds said, bringing him two slices of tinned corned beef, the army's emergency rations – bully beef, the soldiers called it – and two biscuits, together with a cup of water.

'Do you really think I can eat anything?' Murdoch demanded.

'You have to, sir,' Reynolds said seriously. 'You're in command. You cannot allow yourself to become weak.'

He had already become weak, Murdoch thought, as he made himself chew and swallow, or perhaps he had never been strong – else he would have commanded his men to fire while they had the chance, and kill their comrade as well as a few Somalis. He finished his meal and went to where Yeald was still catching the rays of the sun on his mirrors and sending them bouncing in Morse code across the hills. 'Any reply from brigade, sergeant?'

'Just come through, sir. The mounted infantry, the Lancashires, will be here by dusk, with four machine guns. The KAR will be up by midnight.'

Not much more than six hours, he thought. Soon enough to avenge, but not to save.

'I reckon they've guessed what we're up to, Captain Mackinder,' Hanley called.

Murdoch returned to the perimeter and studied the main Somali camp. They had certainly seen the heliograph flashes; horsemen were being sent to the eastern exit of the

227

valley to discover what was happening on the plain. 'Tell your men to rest, sergeant-major, Mr Ramage,' he said. 'It'll be a little while before they make a move.'

Not until their patrols come back, he thought. So there was nothing to do but wait, and watch the vultures hovering overhead, anxious to get down to where so much feasting awaited them if the human beings would just stop making so much noise ... and listen to that noise, the continued babble of conversation, like a stream running through the valley, and then some more screams, fainter than before. At every whisper of torment the troopers grasped their rifles tighter, and those who had been pretending to sleep opened their eyes, and it seemed that their tunics became more darkly stained with sweat.

Murdoch watched the eastern exit, and about three in the afternoon saw the Somali patrols returning. He followed them right into the camp, where there was immediately a great hubbub.

'Stand to,' he said. 'Quietly. If they are going to chance their arm, they will do it now.'

It appeared the Mullah *was* going to chance his arm; his scouts had obviously made contact with the brigade, and he now knew he had some three thousand disciplined soldiers breathing down his neck. Murdoch watched four rows of horsemen issuing from the camp, about seven hundred men, he estimated. They advanced slowly until they were just within range of the gully, and there paused, while their commander walked his horse, a magnificent white stallion, up and down before them.

'Do you think that's the Mullah, sir?' Ramage whispered.

'I very much doubt it,' Murdoch told him. 'Here they come. Hold your fire,' he bellowed as the men stirred.

The horsemen cantered to the slope, and then urged theeir horses upwards as fast as they could go. At the same time another several hundred men, who had advanced unseen through the rocks and the bushes, opened fire from the side. But their weapons and their cartridges were too poor to do any damage accept at very close quarters. Murdoch ignored them and concentrated on the charging horsemen. He waited until they were within five hundred yards before he gave the command to fire; he had no fears as to the outcome. Quite apart from the machine gun, each Lee-Metford had a magazine of five cartridges. The rifles were not automatic – as each bullet had to be rammed into the chamber – but the magazine could still be emptied in seven seconds.

The entire hillside seemed to explode as the squadron fired as one man, and then went on firing. Each trooper had selected his target, as Murdoch had taught them to do back at Bath, and their aim was gruesomely accurate. Men and horses pitched this way and that, cut to ribbons by the flying lead. The charge lasted barely a minute, and then the remnants of the Somali force were fleeing back down the hillside, leaving at least a hundred of their number, with a similar number of horses, dead or dying amidst the rocks. The screams of the horses was horrifying, but Murdoch could not help but feel a sense of elation, of revenge, even, for the poor devils who had just been tortured to death. The feeling was evidently shared by the entire squadron, as a burst of cheering broke from their ranks.

'They'll not try that again in a hurry,' Sergeant-Major Hanley remarked.

Murdoch agreed with him. 'Stand your men easy, sergeant-major, Lieutenant Ramage,' he commanded. And indeed he stood himself easy for a few minutes; he was exhausted, his shoulders both remained extremely painful, the one dull and the other sharp, and his head was gonging from a combination of the heat and the blow he had received.

Another hour passed, in which he almost fell asleep, and then was awakened by an urgent summons from Peter Ramage. 'Captain Mackinder, sir.'

Murdoch climbed back up on to the escarpment to be beside the lieutenant. Ramage had his binoculars focused on a point at the foot of the slope, and Murdoch did the same, catching his breath. Beneath them was Tommy Knox. He had been forced out of the ravine by four men, and was being held facing his comrades. He had been stripped naked, and his white body gleamed in the sun. There were bruises and even some bloodstains on his chest and shoulders. But he looked whole – at the moment.

'Dragoons!' The voice wailed up the hill. 'Dragoons! Captain Mackinder! Can you hear me?'

'No reply,' Murdoch snapped.

'For God's sake,' Knox shouted. 'The Mullah invites you to surrender. He says there is no hope for you. There is no water where you are. For God's sake, he will give you safe conduct out of the valley. In the name of God, reply to me.'

The squadron lay silent, but the men were stirring restlessly, and more than one hand slapped a rifle butt in anger. Ramage lowered his glasses. He and Knox had been even closer friends than Murdoch.

'Please,' Knox wailed. 'Help me, Murdoch. If you do not, they will cut me up. For God's sake. . . .'

Murdoch watched his friend and the Somalis around him. They were staking Knox out on the ground, driving thick tree branches into the earth, to which his wrists and ankles were secured, reminding Murdoch of pictures he had seen of Aztec sacrificial victims waiting to be slit open and have their living hearts torn out.

'Help me!' Knox screamed. 'For God's sake, help me!'

Murdoch had to swallow hard before he could speak. 'Sergeant-Major Hanley,' he said, quietly.

'Sir!' The sergeant-major knelt beside him.

'What do you think the range is to those men down there?'

Hanley squinted, and Murdoch gave him the glasses. Hanley looked and caught his breath. 'Oh, Jesus Christ,' he muttered.

'The range, sergeant-major.'

'Ah . . . not less than eight hundred yards, sir. Could be more.'

That was about as far as a rifle could possible carry, with any accuracy.

'Who is the best marksman in the squadron?'

'Ah . . . Trooper Matheson, sir.'

'Bring him here.'

Hanley hurried off, and Murdoch continued to watch Knox. His belly was light, and his genitals too, but his brain was clear. Tommy Knox was already dead. If he had succumbed to the terrible threat and attempted to lure his comrades to their destruction, that was neither here nor there. He could at least be spared an agonising and humiliating last hour.

Stones trickled beside him, and Sergeant-Major Hanley returned, accompanied by Trooper Matheson, a young man of only twenty-one, Murdoch remembered – the same age as Ramage and Knox – with no previous experience of action. His face was pale, and his hands were trembling.

'Matheson,' Murdoch said. 'I want you to fire into those men down there.'

Matheson peered at them.

'Now look through the glasses.'

Matheson obeyed. 'Holy Mary Mother of God,' he whispered. 'Oh, sir. . . .'

Murdoch took the glasses back. The men had finished their work and withdrawn some distance, leaving Knox spreadeagled and waiting. And as he watched, three women came out to stand beside him. Women . . . Murdoch's jaw clamped shut like a steel trap. Even at this distance he could recognise Mulein – she was not wearing her yashmak today. 'Can you hit Mr Knox?' he asked. 'And the women as well. Hit them all.'

'Eight hundred yards, boy,' Hanley said. 'That's no distance to you.'

'But, sir. . . . Mr Knox. . . .'

'Is going to die,' Murdoch snapped, his voice harsh. 'Those bitches are going to cut him before our eyes. Hit him, boy, and hit that damned bitch, too, and I swear I will get you a medal.'

Matheson licked his lips and looked at the sergeant-major, who nodded encouragingly. The boy nestled the rifle into his shoulder, peered down into the valley and wrapped his fingers around the trigger guard. Murdoch raised the glasses again and looked. Mulein was standing beside Knox,

talking to him, stroking him, making him respond to her . . .
she was surely a fiend in human form.

There was no sound from beside him, and he turned his
head; Matheson could have been turned to stone.

'What is the matter?' Murdoch asked.

Matheson did not reply for a moment, then he gave a
sob and his head drooped on to his rifle. 'I can't do it, sir,'
he wept. 'I can't shoot Mr Knox.'

Murdoch looked above the boy's head at Hanley. The
sergeant-major's face was a picture of distress. 'Mr Knox's
men are very fond of him, sir,' he explained.

'Is there no one else?'

'No one as good as Matheson, sir. And with respect . . .
I don't think we want too many of the men to see what's
happening down there.'

Murdoch knew he was right; nerves were already strained
to breaking point – his own amongst them. 'All right,
Matheson,' he said. 'You may stand down. Remain here for
a while.' He didn't want him blurting out what he had seen,
or been asked to do.

Matheson slid back down the reverse slope and sat there,
a huddle of shattered nerves.

'You any good with a rifle, Peter?' Murdoch asked.

'Me? Good God . . . shoot Tommy? I . . . I couldn't hit
him, anyway.'

And Murdoch knew *he* couldn't either; he had never
taken rifle shooting seriously enough. Nor dared he ask the
sergeant-major. To have Hanley unable to carry out an
order could mean the disintegration of his entire command.
His head jerked as there was a scream, and he levelled his
binoculars again. She had done something to him, because
his body was jerking to and fro. But the blood was on his
face. He thought she might have cut off the end of his nose.

'Peter,' he said in a low voice.

Ramage had also been watching through his glasses; now
he lowered them. His face was thick with sweat.

'You understand the situation,' Murdoch said. 'Hardie
should have the eastern exit blocked by dusk. The squadron

232

must hold this position until then, blocking the Mullah's escape route at all costs. Understood?'

'Yes, sir,' Ramage said. 'But. . . .'

'Just remember that it has to be done, Peter, by whoever happens to be in command. If I am hit, that command devolves upon you.'

Ramage realised what he had in mind. 'But,' he protested, 'the orders . . . the risk. . . .'

'Damn the orders, and damn the risk. I don't aim to get captured. Buccaneer has had a rest. It will take me no more than a minute to get down that slope, and maybe three back up. You will give me all the cover you can, without actually hitting me. Understood?'

'Yes, sir,' Ramage said. And hesitated. 'Why not let me go?'

Murdoch grinned at him savagely. 'Do you really want to?'

'Well . . . no. Do you?'

'He's my second in command,' Murdoch reminded him.

When Corporal Reynolds was told to bring Buccaneer forward, he appeared with his own mount as well. Murdoch shook his head. 'No, corporal.'

'But, sir. . . .'

'The job only requires one man. Why risk two?' He checked his revolver to make sure it was fully loaded, loosened his sword in its scabbard and mounted. 'All the cover you can give me, Lieutenant Ramage,' he called. 'On the way back up.'

He walked Buccaneer to the edge of the perimeter. Perhaps Knox was already dead, although he doubted that; Mulein, obviously aware that she was just beyond effective rifle range, would be in no hurry. He dared not let himself think about the coming five minutes. It *would* be only five minutes, at the end of which time he would have regained the squadron – or he would be dead; he had no other possibilities in mind.

He drew a long breath, urged Buccaneer through the waiting, silent troopers, and then sent him cantering down the slope. There was a shout and a shot from one of the nearby gullies, where the Somalis had maintained an advanced look-out position, but he was going too fast to be hit, and immediately there was a burst of fire as the squadron gave him cover to either side. Now he was half-way down the slope and amidst the shattered remains of the earlier attack; here a horse kicked or a dying man stirred. But Knox was now clearly visible only a few hundred yards away.

Mulein for the first time realised her danger. She and her two assistants turned to face him, their features twisting in hatred, Mulein's more angrily than the others as she recognised him. Tommy Knox, bleeding from several wounds, writhed and twisted and moaned behind her – but he was still alive, and he was still whole. He could still even be rescued.

Murdoch rushed them at the gallop, now he had gained more level ground, only just aware that several men were approaching him on foot from the gully to his right. His interest was in the four people in front of him.

Now there were only two; the other women had fled with a shriek at his approach. Mulein stared at him for a moment, then she too gave a yell of pure hatred and turned away from him, to drive the long-bladed knife she carried deep into the left side of Knox's groin, twisting it and drawing it across his flesh with all her strength, until she encountered sufficient bone to force the blade back out. She turned to glare at Murdoch again, while Knox gave a long wail of the purest agony and horror.

Murdoch drew his sword instead of his pistol. Mulein ran away from the man she had killed, but she was too late. Murdoch was immediately behind her, reaching down from his saddle to grasp her flying hair. He was tempted to take her prisoner and watch her hang, but she still carried her knife, and as she felt his grasp she twisted back, screaming curses in Somali, and attempted to cut at Buccaneer. Still holding her by the hair, Murdoch drove his sword right through her body until it protruded at the back. She uttered a dying wail almost as agonised as Knox's, and slumped against the horse's flank. Murdoch kicked his left leg from the stirrup, placed the boot on her shoulder and pushed her body down his blade as he might have removed meat from a skewer; she collapsed in a heap on the ground.

The death of Mulein had taken but a moment, and now he turned back to Knox. The lieutenant had literally been disembowelled, intestines and genitals hanging down from his left side suspended by mere slivers of skin, while his blood poured on to the ground. He would not survive such a wound, even if he would want to, but he would still die in agony.

Murdoch sheathed his bloody sword, drew his revolver and, as Knox raised his head in terrible supplication, shot him through the head.

Then it was time to take stock of his situation, which was grim in the extreme. His gallop, and Muelin's attempt to escape, had carried him to the left of the men on foot, but they were all armed with some kind of firearm, and they were blocking his way back up the hill. Even if the squadron was blazing away with everything they had, most of their bullets were falling short. And now the Somali cavalry had gathered their wits, and Buccaneer was blown. He turned back to consider a charge through the men on foot, who oddly were not firing at him. Other mounted men emerged from every direction, rifles and muskets resting on their hips, staring at him. Like their compatriots, they were not shooting, and not shouting or chanting, while the noise of the drums, which had announced his descent from the hill, had also ceased; in their place was the great rustle of large numbers of men and horses.

Murdoch cocked his revolver. He had five bullets left, but he doubted he dared take the chance of shooting four of the Somalis before himself. So he turned the muzzle upwards, pointing at his own head, while he backed the panting Buccaneer away from Knox's body. It was a simple matter of resolve now; at the first move from the Somalis, he would fire and end it all.

Strangely, the Somalis made no move. They remained still, gathered in a semi-circle round him, while the tension grew almost unbearable – and communicated itself up the hill, for the dragoons also ceased firing. Then there was the sound of more hooves, and a fresh party arrived from the camp in the valley, riding beneath the black flag and accompanied by two of the kettledrummers. The party halted behind the ring of warriors and engaged in a fairly hot dispute for several minutes more. Then the rank of men blocking Murdoch's retreat parted and a single horseman came forward, to draw his rein at a distance of about thirty feet. He was fairly tall, Murdoch estimated, and strongly, if slightly, built. His saddle and bridle were richly decorated, as was the hilt of his scimitar, but his breeches and cloak were simple white, like those of his followers, although his boots were kid. His burnous was green, however, and secured with a band of cloth of gold round his forehead.

His face was aquiline, and solemn. There was harshness, in the wide, flat, slightly downturned mouth elongated by the drooping moustache, and in the dark eyes; the chin was hidden behind a straggling beard.

Murdoch felt his heartbeat quicken; he could not doubt who this was.

'You charged at the head of the horsemen,' said Muhammad ibn Abd Allah in surprisingly good English. 'Are you their general?'

'I am not a general,' Murdoch replied. 'But I am their commanding officer.'

'That was a famous feat,' the Mullah remarked. 'My people will speak of it for many years to come. And now you have descended into the midst of my army to kill one of your own men. And one of my women. Have you no fear?'

'I could not have one of my men tortured to death,' Murdoch said. 'It sickens me that your people should do such things, that you permit it. Those are not the acts of warriors, or of men who are guided by God.'

The Mullah stared at him for several seconds. 'Are your people, then, guided by God, when they bring their smallpox and their tuberculosis to destroy my people? When their priests would rob my people of their ancient ways and turn

236

them against the beliefs of their forefathers? Is a child dying of measles any less to be pitied than a man being robbed of his manhood before he dies?' He pointed at Mulein's body. 'My women make sure that none of our enemies may enter heaven; for how may a man enter heaven without his manhood?'

'That is a philosophy that ill becomes a leader of men,' Murdoch told him.

The Mullah stared at him. 'And you? Are you not desirous of entering heaven?'

'In my philosophy, a man enters heaven by virtue of his behaviour towards other men,' Murdoch declared. 'I have no fear of facing that question, regardless of the condition of my body.'

Another long stare. Then the Mullah half-turned his horse to look up the slope. 'Your men wish to block one end of the valley? It is the wrong end. Your home lies that way.' He pointed to the east.

'But yours lies *that* way,' Murdoch said, pointing to the west.

'And your foot soldiers are coming. My scouts have told me this. I must either fight them, or destroy you. Do you not realise this?'

'My men are waiting for you to try,' Murdoch told him. 'Have you counted your dead from the last assault?'

The Mullah's lips parted in a grim smile. 'You are a very brave man. Would they not surrender if I exposed you to them, stripped and about to be destroyed, screaming for mercy?'

'No, they would not,' Murdoch said. 'Nor would I scream for mercy.'

The Mullah nodded. 'I believe you. You are a very brave man. And a gallant one. The two words do not always mean the same. I give you your life, Englishman, at least for the time. Go back to your men and tell them that the Mullah means to destroy them if they attempt to prevent him leaving the valley. But if you will withdraw with them through the pass, we will not molest them. Go now.'

Murdoch hesitated. He was not sure he could believe

237

what he had been told. But he would not escape under false pretences. 'I will tell them to fight to the last man,' he said.

'So be it. Go.'

Still Murdoch hesitated, glancing at the men to either side.

'You have the word of Muhammad ibn Abd Allah,' he said. 'I give it to you in the name of the Great Muhammad, who was my forefather. Go now, and prepare to die like the man you are. Or live, as my friend.'

Slowly Murdoch released the hammer on the revolver and holstered the weapon. He looked down at Knox's body, but he had no desire to take it with him for burial, nor did he have any wish for his men to see it close to. He touched Buccaneer with his heel, saluted the mullah and walked his horse past him. The Somalis parted to let him through, but not all of them agreed with their leader's generosity – that could be discerned by the lowering glances, the clash of their swords as they loosed them in their scabbards, the restless stir of their horses as they kicked them with their heels. Then he was through, and urging Buccaneer up the slope towards the squadron's position. He did not want to think until he had regained the safety of his men.

A burst of cheering rose from the gully as they saw their captain returning. Murdoch raised his arm to them. It was at that moment that a gigantic fist seemed to strike him between the shoulder blades.

10

Bath, 1907

Murdoch's world became one of shadows, uncertain images flickering to and fro; tremendous heat and yet immense cold as well; pain, which seemed to be trying to break its way out of his chest . . . and noise. He recognised rifle fire and machine-gun fire, and he thought he could recognise the drumming of hooves, but could not be sure.

Then hands touched his body, stripping him of his clothing. He had no doubt they were the Mullah's women, and tried to fight them, apparently without success. He gritted his teeth to stop himself from crying out – as he had sworn he would stay silent, no matter what they did to him – but soon there was blessed oblivion.

He awoke to more shadows and more pain, but this time there was absolute quiet, except for the rumbling in his head. And an uneasy motion which made him jerk from left to right, each movement causing fresh agony. He wanted to touch himself, to find out if he was still whole, but could not move his arms. No doubt they had him spreadeagled, like poor Tommy Knox. But strangely, he could not feel the sun beating down on him.

He opened his eyes, and gazed at canvas above him. It seemed odd, as if he were in a tent, except that the tent was shuddering. He wished to turn his head to discover where he was, but could not move. Instead he heard an urgent whisper, and a moment later Dr Grayson was looking down at him. But that was impossible; Grayson had been with the Brigade.

'By God,' the doctor remarked. 'Talk about bloody miracles!'

Murdoch spoke to him, asked him to explain what had

239

happened, but the doctor did not seem to understand. 'Don't attempt to move, old man,' he said. 'Just rest.'

'I am so thirsty,' Murdoch tried to tell him, and this time the doctor might have heard him. An orderly knelt beside him, and something was held to his lips. It tasted foul, but it was wet; and a moment later he was unconscious again.

When he awoke he was being jolted again, and the pain was all but unbearable. The doctor nodded grimly as he watched the expressions on Murdoch's face. 'It's this damned track and the damned wagon,' he agreed. 'I'm afraid there's nothing we can do. We must get you back to the coast as quickly as possible.'

Murdoch licked his lips. 'The squadron...' he whispered.

Grayson smiled. 'The squadron is fine. And the better for knowing you are alive. Now rest.' Another sedative was given to him, and he slept. But the next morning he felt stronger and was fed some broth by the orderly, who even propped his head up so that he could look out of the back of the ambulance wagon... at the entire brigade, plodding across the desert. 'What happened?' he asked.

'You'll have to ask Dr Grayson that, sir,' the orderly said.

The doctor came to see him that afternoon, along with Peter Ramage, Jimmy Halstead, and Brigadier-General Hardie. 'Only five minutes, now,' Grayson warned. 'He is still very weak. And under no circumstances must he become agitated.'

'But he's going to be all right?' Ramage asked anxiously.

'Providing he doesn't contract a fever, yes. The sooner we get him on that boat, the better.'

'Boat?' Murdoch whispered. 'What boat? To India?'

'No, no, old man,' Hardie said. 'Back to England.'

'To England? But...?'

'You really are very badly wounded,' Halstead explained. 'We did not expect you to live.'

'Live? Nonsense. Here I am, right as rain, virtually, after only twenty-four hours....'

240

'Twelve days, old man,' the brigadier told him.

'Twelve *days?* But. . . .'

Ramage took his hand and lifted it, so that he could look at it. It was difficult to grasp that such a collection of skin and bone belonged to him, or that it had ever grasped a sword.

'Now he's getting agitated,' Grayson said. 'I'm sorry, gentlemen, but I must ask you to leave.'

'I'll be more agitated if they don't tell me what happened,' Murdoch protested.

Grayson hesitated, then shrugged. 'Then ask no questions, and listen. And brigadier, do be brief.'

'Well . . . ah, yes. To be very brief, although you were shot through the right shoulder – quite smashed the blade, Grayson says – and nicked a lung into the bargain, not to mention a deep sword cut on the left shoulder and, we suspect, a touch of concussion from a blow on the head, you still managed to get your horse back up the hill to your men, who were soon after charged by the Somalis, but cut down so many of them with their fire that the enemy were forced to withdraw, and although the Lancashires were by then approaching the eastern exit to the valley, the Mullah seems to have decided that was his best chance of getting out. So they rushed us – I was with the Lancashires, and Jimmy, here, of course. Well, we formed square and took their charges.

'It was a damned good show, if I say so myself, but things were getting a little bit tricky, with the KAR still far behind, when blow me, just as the fuzzies were regrouping for another charge, if Ramage here didn't lead your squadron out of the valley in a counter-attack. That quite discomforted them. He'd had to leave you and the other wounded behind, of course, with just a handful of men to protect you, so as soon as the Somalis dispersed, we proceeded into the valley and occupied it. Then they thought they had *us* trapped, and there was a great to-doing and beating of drums, but by dawn the KAR had come up, and that was that. They were again caught between the two forces, and this time they had had enough. We maintained our position for three days, wondering if they'd come back, but they were gone for good.'

'What happened to the Mullah?' Murdoch asked.

'Well, I'm afraid he got away. But we gave him one hell of a bloody nose. He'll not be back for a while.'

'I think he will,' Murdoch said thoughtfully. 'He struck me as being a singularly determined man. And yet . . . for all his barbarity, I put him down as an honourable man, too, according to his principles. But then, to shoot me in the back after having given me safe conduct. . . .'

'Ah, well, he didn't, actually. It was one of his men, who didn't agree with letting you go. In fact, before withdrawing, he sent a message to my camp, under a flag of truce, expressing his regrets for what happened and hoping you would survive. He said the man who had shot you had been executed.'

'Ah,' Murdoch said. He was strangely glad the Mullah had not betrayed him.

'He also referred to your courage and determination,' Hardie went on, 'and in fact Ramage here has been telling me about how you attempted to rescue poor Knox. You do realise that was entirely against orders? In fact, it was a direct dereliction of duty to abandon your men.'

Grayson coughed warningly.

'I had my men under control at all times, sir,' Murdoch said. 'My intention, in descending the hill, was to negotiate with the Mullah. It was a question of wasting as much time as possible, don't you see?'

Hardie gazed at him for several seconds, then smiled. 'Indeed I see. You are to be congratulated, Captain Mackinder. Both your charge, and your decision to seal off the exit of the valley and force the Mullah to accept battle on our terms, were splendid efforts. I intend to give you full credit in my despatches.'

'Now, gentlemen,' Grayson said. 'You simply must leave Captain Mackinder to rest.'

If he found it difficult to grasp that he had apparently lost twelve days out of his life, Murdoch had to accept the fact

242

that he was terribly weak. The sight of himself in a mirror confirmed the evidence of his hand, and he seemed to possess absolutely no strength in any part of his body. It was all he could do to move his fingers, even by the time the brigade regained Berbera. Reynolds, who had been allowed to commence serving him again, had to feed him and wash him and shave him.

Reynolds reassured him that the squadron had lost very few men, that they were enormously proud of their captain, that Buccaneer was fit and well, and that Peter Ramage, brevet captain until a replacement could be obtained from either India or England, was proving excellent at his job. Ramage himself came to the hospital to report every evening, to discuss the various problems which had arisen during the day and to bring him bits of gossip. He was often accompanied by some of the ladies of Berbera, all anxious to see the hero, as it appeared he was once again.

But Dr Grayson was adamant that he should be sent home, together with the other half-dozen seriously wounded men. He would not be fit for duty again for several months, and although he was making a remarkable recovery, thanks to his immensely strong constitution, there was always the risk of his contracting fever while in such a weak state – and the risk was greater now that the monsoon had finally arrived, bringing constant rain, and constant mosquitoes, too.

'I seem to spend half my bloody life in bed,' Murdoch grumbled, but he knew the doctor was right; he was just a liability, lying on his back in hospital in Berbera. Nor did he have any real desire to remain, if he could not command the squadron. Somaliland was a place of too many memories, all of them nightmarish, as he kept seeing poor Knox's body, Mulein's face . . . both of them had been buried in the valley, along with the other dead, the strangest of eternal bedfellows.

In fact, he had only been in hospital a month when a northbound ship was signalled, and he and the others were transferred, together with Reynolds and Buccaneer. Ramage accompanied him on board and took his farewell after he had been carried to his cabin. 'I'll bring the squadron home, sir, safe and sound,' he promised. 'Actually, now that we've smashed the Mullah, it's going to be dead boring out here.'

'We haven't smashed the Mullah, Peter,' Murdoch told him. 'Not in his eyes, and not in the eyes of his people. Keep your eyes open.'

He was right. Before the ship reached England, Muhammad ibn Abd Allah was invading Italian Somaliland and causing all kinds of trouble, and it was obvious that he was going to maintain himself for a long time yet. But by the time the ship docked, the Mullah and Somaliland seemed a very long way away. Wireless messages had been flashed ahead, and there was an ambulance waiting for Murdoch – which was very necessary, for although the sea air had done him a world of good he was still unable to walk; he was by far the most seriously of the wounded. Gordon Rodgers was there to greet him, as well as Mother and Philippa and Rosemary, who was now a mother herself – which made him an uncle, of a pretty little niece he had never seen.

'I'll bet you didn't expect to see me back this soon,' Murdoch told them; it was still only the end of March, and bitterly cold.

'Oh, Murdoch,' Mother wept, holding him against her breast and looking past him to clasp Reynolds' hands. 'Oh, corporal, what have they done to him this time?'

'Nothing the captain cannot take, ma'am,' Reynolds declared.

'Even Father never managed to get shot as often as you do,' Philippa said.

But she smiled, and hugged him too, into her large, soft bosom. Like her sister, she was made for motherhood, and Murdoch wondered when she was going to get married, if ever. She was handsome enough. But she was also a very earthy person, more interested in her horses and dogs than in what she should be wearing to Ascot. It was something to think about, he decided, as he had to have something to occupy his mind for the next few months or so.

Lord Roberts, now seventy-five years old and decidedly frail, came up from the Isle of Wight to see him and congratulate him on the handling of the squadron. Briga-dier-General Hardie's full despatches had by now reached London, and had been released to the press, and the public was thrilled with the idea of an old-fashioned cavalry charge again carrying the day.

Sir John French, recently promoted to full general and clearly designated as Lord Kitchener's successor, also came to visit. 'It was a brilliant action,' he remarked. 'And combined with everything else, well, there has been some talk about recommending you for a bar to your VC, for attempting to save poor Knox's life. But frankly, I'm against that. It would set a precedent, for one thing, and for another, it was a most flagrant disobedience of express orders. It would be bad for discipline.'

'Yes, sir,' Murdoch agreed, by now used to French's somewhat direct way of putting things.

'So instead we have recommended you for the Distinguished Service Order, and His Majesty has been pleased to agree. You will attend the first investiture at Buckingham Palace after you are fit to leave this place.' He cocked his head. 'The DSO is the highest award that can be given for behaviour in the field where absolute heroism above and beyond the call of duty cannot be proven. You might at least look pleased.'

'Oh, I am, sir. Pleased and flattered. Although I cannot help but feel that the entire squadron should receive a medal. After all, they followed me in the charge.'

'Don't sell yourself, or any commanding officer, short, Mackinder. It's those in command who take the decisions and lead, and either get shot first or torn to shreds by the critics when they make a mistake. The rank and file follow. It is the quality of leadership that counts: a good officer makes good soldiers behind him; a poor officer makes poor soldiers. Now tell me what is really on your mind. Knox's death?'

'I killed him,' Murdoch said. 'Do you realise that, sir? I rode up to him and shot him. And you are giving me a medal.'

'Everyone who was there, or has read Brigadier-General

Hardie's report, knows that you shot Knox, Murdoch. He was found with his head blown away by a Smith and Wesson bullet. But in killing him, you were obeying orders not to allow any prisoners to fall into Somali hands, even if you were *dis*obeying orders by going back to do so. And if it's any consolation to you, he would have died anyway, according to Dr Grayson, even if you had managed to carry him back to your squadron; his entire crotch was torn out.'

'But . . . the waste of it,' Murdoch said. 'I mean, sir, what were we *doing* there, anyway?'

French frowned at him.

'Perhaps you did not know, sir,' Murdoch went on, 'but I spoke with the Mullah himself.'

'Did you? No, I did not know that. You mean he spoke English?'

'Very well. And I should think one or two other languages as well. Oh, his people are barbaric, nasty fighters, and he does nothing to restrain them. He talked about there being religious reasons for mutilating their prisoners, but I suspect it is mainly motivated by the object of creating terror in the minds of those who would oppose him. It was something else he told me that made me think.'

'Such as?'

'Well, sir, it is his land, as he sees it. We have taken it from him. Why?'

'Well, we couldn't let the Italians nab the entire Red Sea coast, could we?'

'But what are the Italians doing there, sir? It is just empty desert, most of it. It's not even a coaling station. It's a complete waste of time. And we have introduced ourselves, and our diseases, and our machine guns, just so another little piece of the map can be painted red.'

French gazed at him for several seconds. Then he said, 'You know, Murdoch, for all your background, and your gallantry, and your very real tactical ability as a commander of horse, I don't feel you are cut out to be a soldier. You think too much. Soldiers should never think, except about the immediate task they have been given. Not even generals. Our masters in Whitehall, who change direction with such

246

regularity, tell us what they want done; and we, having accepted the King's shilling, go out and do it – every so often dying in the process. I am quite sure that Mr Campbell-Bannerman and Mr Asquith would both be aghast if they ever saw what could be done to a man by a machine gun or a lyddite shell – or, I should think, a Somali knife. They would be appalled if they awoke any morning and were told there would be no warm water for shaving or, indeed, no water at all; that for their next drink they would have to walk twenty miles through the desert beneath a burning sun with an enemy sniping at them the whole way. But perhaps that is a necessary state of affairs. If we all understood the truth about soldiering instead, as you say, of sitting in a comfortable office and deciding which parts of the map we will draw red this morning, there would never have been any progress at all. Certainly there would never have been a British empire.'

'Should there have been a British empire, sir?' Murdoch asked.

French regarded him for several seconds. Then he said, 'You *are* in an odd mood, young man. I think the best thing you can do is get well again, just as rapidly as possible. You are either going to go very far in the Army, or you are going to wind up being cashiered. But you have to get out of bed to achieve either of those aims.' He stood up and went to the door, then turned to look back. 'Try thinking about something more positive. And remember: you did your duty. No man can be asked to do more than that.'

Murdoch supposed he was right. The strange thing was that he had never, except when in the throes of his desperate passion for Margriet Voorlandt, contemplated not being a soldier; the tradition was too deeply embedded in his being. Besides, now, at the age of twenty-six, he knew no other profession. More important, he enjoyed soldiering. He enjoyed even the dull daily grind of peacetime spit and polish, and as for active service, if he had had more than his share of wounds, he yet believed, every time he went

247

into action, that he would come through unscathed – and he certainly had no doubt that he would survive.

Yet he must now live the rest of his life with the knowledge that he had executed a fellow officer, and a friend, because it had been his duty to do so. He supposed he would grow grey before he expiated that particular guilt.

And the Mullah would be defeated, of course. There was no native power could stand up against the might of the British Empire, not when its forces were led by men like Captain Murdoch Mackinder, VC, he thought with a wry smile, recalling one of the more sensational newspaper headlines.

His shoulder took a long time to heal. In fact, Sister Anderson, in whose care he again found himself, confessed that the medical staff had not been at all sure the shattered bone would ever knit sufficiently for him to manage a horse or fire a revolver or wield a sword, or even salute properly – in effect, for him to resume his career. And for all of the healing process he was confined in the most rigid of splints – which held his arm away from the body and made it impossible for him to move – to prevent the slightest risk of upsetting the delicate knitting process. But it was at least happening, he was told. All he now needed was patience, which was the hardest thing of all to cultivate.

Letters arrived regularly from India, full of congratulations – the regiment was, as usual, inordinately proud that their VC should have added another laurel to their brow, as it were – but also full of tales of what they were up to. Colonel Walters wrote of the difficulties of maintaining a proper showing in the extreme conditions to which they were so often exposed; Chapman related the various actions they were fighting with the Pathans and the Afghans; Billy Hobbs described the heat and the flies of summer, and the cold and the winds of winter; and Johnnie Morton, naturally, detailed the delights of the bazaars of Peshawar, the glories of the 'bints'. 'Shame you were wounded before you had the opportunity to get together with one of those Somali girls,' Morton wrote. 'I had been looking forward to comparing notes.'

Little did he suspect what sort of notes they would have to compare, Murdoch thought.

There was even a letter from Rosetta Morris, for the reports of the charge in the Togdheer had reached the Cape Town newspapers. 'I look forward to following your career with great interest,' she wrote. 'As you may perhaps be interested in my own progress.' Whereupon she proceeded to tell him, at great length, how well her husband was doing, of the beautiful house she had, of her three lovely children . . . whatever her motives in writing, he was merely pleased that she did not appear to bear any ill will for their abortive romance.

From the Transvaal there were of course no letters.

But they came regularly enough from Ramage, sadly recounting the utter boredom which had set in since the battle in the Togdheer. Brigadier-General Hardie had certainly 'given the Mullah a bloody nose', and the Somali leader was apparently continuing to concentrate his efforts against the Italians in the south of the country, with the result that there was very little for the British troops to do except play cricket and polo and get sick. Ramage also dreamed of being with the regiment in India. He was, however, pleased to report that he had been confirmed as captain of the squadron – and granted the Military Cross for his charge in support of the Lancashires – two new replacement lieutenants having been sent out from the depot.

Murdoch hastily wrote back a letter of congratulations, with his left hand, but could not help but wonder, as he lay awake that night counting the throbs from his shoulder, where that left him. Back to the depot to raise a reserve squadron? But as the regiment already had three almost full-strength squadrons on active service, while not actually fighting a war; training duties promised to be just that, with no end in sight.

'Oh, they'll think of something,' Gordon Rodgers told him, on one of his weekly visits. 'They always do. You haven't blotted your copybook, like me. And besides, your name's Mackinder.'

249

Murdoch could not blame him for being bitter.

'In fact,' Rodgers said, 'you can have my job. I'm thinking of getting out. I'm going to be married next year.'

'Are you?' Murdoch asked. 'Congratulations. I had no idea.'

'Well, I only popped the question last Saturday night. Dorinda Hazelton. You must have met her.'

'Of course,' Murdoch agreed, not altogether remembering Miss Hazelton out of the horde of eager young women who had from time to time attended regimental dances.

'Well, her father just about owns a brewery, and is looking for a good man to run his workforce. Sort of adjutant, I suppose you'd call it. Just up my street.'

'You, in a brewery?'

'There are worse places to wind up.'

'But . . . leaving the Army?'

Rodgers shook his head. 'The Army left me, remember, two years ago. I don't owe them a damn thing. So as I say, there'll be a job going spare any day now.'

'Thanks, but no,' Murdoch said. 'Not even if it means promotion to major.' Which was in any event unlikely at his age.

He couldn't really argue against Rodgers' attitude, however much he regretted his decision – and the waste of a good officer. But the fact that changes were taking place made him all the more anxious to regain his health and the regiment, and made the endless waiting all the more wearisome. His only real pleasure lay in the visits of Philippa, who came every other day, and was willing to sit with him for hours, playing chess or two-handed whist. She was a great favourite of Reynolds, who by this time had managed to have himself installed in the hospital so that he could look after his beloved captain – an irregularity which Sister Anderson was pleased to overlook.

But there arrived the day when Philippa did not come alone.

*

'Hi,' said Marylee Caspar. 'I guess you don't remember me.'

'Indeed I do,' Murdoch insisted, rising slowly to his feet and extending his left hand; this had become second nature now, although his right shoulder was nearly mended.

How could I forget? he wondered. She was, if anything, more attractive than the last time he had seen her, two years before. Her figure had filled out, even if she did not appear to have grown any taller and still did not quite reach his chin with the top of her head. She still wore her hair unusually short, and still dressed as if she were preparing to go for a bicycle ride rather than serve tea to the vicar's wife, with a close-fitting felt hat to match her braided green costume – but she was not the less attractive for that.

He was staring at her, and she blushed. 'It seems that I only ever see you in pyjamas,' she remarked.

'You don't want to let the newspapers get hold of that,' Philippa told her. 'Lee is over here on a visit,' she explained; she was given to the *non sequitur*.

'I would never have guessed,' Murdoch teased. 'Lee?'

'That's what my friends call me,' Marylee explained.

And Philippa was very obviously a friend. 'Is Harry with you?'

'Harry has gone off to North Africa,' she said. 'Some place called Algeciras. That's in North Africa, isn't it?'

'It's in Spain, actually.'

'Well, he seems to think there could be a war starting up down there. Between Germany and France.'

'That'll be the day. European wars are *passé*.' Now he discovered he was still holding her hand, which she was making no effort to free. Hastily he released it. 'I'm forgetting my manners. Won't you please sit down?'

She did so, and they chatted, aimlessly enough, about what she had been doing since last they met, and about what he had been doing too, although he soon got them off that subject. Both girls had things on their minds, that was quite obvious; what bothered Murdoch was that it might be the same idea – he had thought of getting Philippa married off; it had not occurred to him that she might have the same idea about him.

It was preposterous, surely. He hardly knew Marylee – or Lee, which he much preferred. Of course, getting to know her would be a pleasure, but was he interested in getting to know any young woman, however pretty and intelligent and attractive – or recommended by his sister? Besides, could he ever dare to *allow* himself to be interested in a woman, now? Apart from the memory of his desperate pursuit of Margriet, of the lingering shock with which he had uncovered her true nature, there was the even more pressing memory of having killed a woman virtually with his bare hands, of the feeling of savage joy he had experienced when he had put his boot on Mulein's shoulder and pressed down to free his sword. More important, he did not know if he could ever hold a woman in his arms again without seeing Tommy Knox's naked body writhing on the ground, hearing his screams drifting up the hillside: the two were synonymous.

But Philippa definitely had matchmaking in prospect. From then on, every visit she made to the hospital was in company with Lee, who was staying at Broad Acres – 'my favourite place in all the world,' she confessed – indefinitely until Harry Caspar came to England to collect her, having either started a war or decided there was no hope of one. And with every visit, Murdoch became more attracted to the American girl and looked forward more to the next. He even found himself dreaming of her, which was not altogether surprising – it was a very long time since he had had sex.

The situation was not lost on Sister Anderson. 'Next week is der Tag,' she announced with her usual brightness; she would have made a marvellous latterday Florence Nightingale, Murdoch thought. 'You'll be pleased to be getting home, Captain Mackinder.'

'Um,' Murdoch replied. He wasn't sure about that, because what he had most feared had actually happened. Gordon Rodgers had resigned and the War Office had

252

appointed him as officer commanding the depot – pending the return of the regiment from India.

This was a blow, especially as he had learned that Tony Chapman had been shot through the head and killed by a Pathan sniper, and a new commander was required for his squadron. The fact of Tony's death came as quite a shock, but while desperately sorry about it, Murdoch could not help but feel that it had happened at a most opportune moment for him, as he had been pronounced fit.

He wrote to the War Office to remind them of this fact, and to his consternation was informed that the vacancy had already been filled – from another regiment. Furiously he wrote a letter of protest to Sir John French, who as usual took the trouble to reply, pointing out that while he had been pronounced fit for duty, no one had said anything about active service, and medical opinion was it would be at least another year before he would be up to that, certainly in such an inhospitable clime as that of the North-West Frontier. French reminded him that he had to be patient – and assured him that he was not being forgotten.

Murdoch had no alternative but to return to Broad Acres for two weeks' convalescent leave before taking up his new duties. This was actually a great pleasure, as apart from the joy of being once again in his own home, with the dogs and cats and horses and servants, he could also renew his acquaintance with Buccaneer, who had served him so well in Somalia. The horse had been stabled at the house rather than the depot during his spell in hospital.

And of course, at Broad Acres there was Lee, now so much a part of the establishment that he lowered his mental guard. When, after a week, Philippa dropped out of their morning ride with a headache, he did not even raise an eyebrow. By now he was strong enough to raise Buccaneer into a gentle canter, and the moors were there to be enjoyed, with Lee at his shoulder, sitting astride in a divided skirt which was really shockingly indecent because it rode up from her boots and revealed her legs.

'Oh, this is just the most heavenly country on earth,' she cried, when he drew rein on a low brow looking down on a shallow valley through which there bubbled a stream. 'I don't see how you can bear to leave it.'

'Well,' he said, 'it doesn't appear as if I am going to leave it for some time.'

'And that burns you up, right?'

'That's one way of putting it, yes. I just have the feeling life is passing me by.'

'You don't think you have seen enough of life to satisfy most men for a lifetime?'

'Not really.'

'So where you'd really like to be is India.'

'Well, that's where the regiment is, isn't it? India is the traditional battleground of the British Army. Certainly of the Western Dragoons. And they are there now, while I have never set foot on the place.'

'Well,' she said seriously, 'I wouldn't count yourself too unlucky. Harry is convinced that the next real war is going to be right here in Europe.'

'I can't believe that.' They were walking their horses down the slope into the valley, over springy turf. 'Everyone is working like mad to preserve the peace, from the King downwards.'

'You reckon so? Even the Kaiser?'

'Oh, he's a pompous ass. But he really has very little to do with it. It's governments that make war nowadays, not kings. And governments are in the main composed of businessmen who have a vested interest in preserving the peace. Oh, they are predatory monsters; I'll not deny that. They'll snatch a piece of territory here or there, if getting it won't cost them any profit. But there can't be any profit in a major European war. That's what this enormous system of alliances is all about. If we are really going to ally ourselves with Russia as well as France, as the newspapers are suggesting – and that will be a turn-up for the history book, if you like – then, with Germany allied to Austria-Hungary and Italy, the whole of Europe will be divided into two virtually equal camps. It'll be a permanent stand-off. People only go to war when they reckon they can smash someone.

There is no hope of either side smashing the other in the present European situation.'

'Harry thinks that dividing Europe into two camps – two armed camps, he calls it – is the surest way to guarantee an eventual war,' Lee persisted.

Murdoch drew rein to look at her. 'I hope he's wrong. In fact, I am sure he must be. Has he any idea what a war between European armies would be like? Have you? Has Harry studied the reports of what it was like in Manchuria, when the Japanese and the Russians were fighting there three years ago? Searchlights, barbed wire, mines, high explosive shells . . . we had a taste of that in South Africa, and no one could describe the Boers as a modern industrial power.'

'It was horrendous,' she agreed. 'As a matter of fact, Harry was in Manchuria.'

'Oh. I didn't know that. Well, then, can he really imagine anything like that happening in Europe, between civilised people?'

'Yes,' she said, more seriously than ever. 'He can. He reckons our so-called civilisation is only skin deep.' She hesitated, and then said, 'And you'll be in the middle of it.'

He gazed at her, and she gazed back, cheeks pink – but that could have been the fresh autumnal breeze. Yet he was aware of an odd emotion, a feeling of intimacy with her, that he had never experienced before, but he was also aware that it was an emotion which had been struggling to make itself felt for some time. . . . And with the mental rapprochement there was a good deal more. Physical attraction had been there from the beginning. He had been restrained by other factors, and if his own experiences had been the principal part of those factors, fear, or distrust, of woman as such had been the principal part of his experiences. But to suppose that this girl could have the slightest inclination towards deception or promiscuity or viciousness was utterly unacceptable. Of course she had thrown herself at him, was still doing so, in fact. But only at him, so far as he knew. And he was loving every moment of it. He could quite easily love her, too.

But then, what *of* the past, which came back to haunt him every night? Was not marriage to a girl like Lee Caspar the only way of exorcising that nightmare? Perhaps, but was it fair on her? Was it fair, indeed, to involve her in his career at all, with its inevitable long separations, its constant alarms, its high tension. . . .

'Anything I can do to help?' she asked.

He forced a smile. 'Do you think I need help?'

'Sure I do.' She dismounted, let the reins trail and walked to the banks of the stream to look down at the bubbling water. 'Everybody needs help,' she said over her shoulder. 'Some more than most.'

'And I qualify in the second bracket?' He dismounted as well, still moving slowly and carefully, still aware of the odd twinges, still not sure when some of the carefully patched-up parts of his body were not going to give way with a snap.

She turned to face him. 'I think so. You served in Somaliland. Saw action there. Harry has told me what it can be like.'

He frowned at her. 'Young ladies don't think about things like that.'

'Why in the name of hell not? Do you suppose we can't take it? My great-grandparents were massacred by Indians. Shall I tell you what they did to my grandmother? And she survived!'

'You're talking about history,' he reminded her. 'Somaliland is today.'

'So people don't really change. I told you, that's what Harry thinks, too. Just as he reckons the people in Europe haven't really changed either, and a European war, with modern weapons, would be the Thirty Years War, with all of its horrors, all over again.'

'You are a very erudite young lady,' Murdoch observed.

'Oh, I can darn socks too,' she said. 'I can even cook.'

'All of which will help me?'

'No,' she said. 'Although they sure can make a man comfortable. But sharing would help you. Everybody has to share with somebody. Or they go nuts.'

Once again they gazed at each other. She had just

256

proposed marriage, as they both knew. As perhaps they had both known she was going to, eventually. Now she gave a twisted smile. 'I've always been told I shoot my mouth off too often. Harry'll be back in another week. I'm to meet him in London next Friday, in fact. So you won't have me around any more to annoy you.'

'I go up to London next week, too,' he said. 'For the investiture.'

'You mean they're giving you another medal?'

'Well, they have to give them to somebody. Mother and Philippa will be coming up with me. Why don't you come with us too, if you can stand it. Then we can all meet Harry, and have a celebration.'

'You mean you don't intend to throw me out on my ear, or have me strung up and flogged, or whatever it is you do to one of your troopers when he's insubordinate?'

'Flogging is *passé*. The modern punishment is CB.'

'What's that?'

'It's a period of time, depending on the severity of the offence, during which you would be confined to barracks. So, as you have certainly been guilty of insubordination, Trooper Caspar, I think I should certainly confine you to barracks.'

She stared at him, pink spots in her cheeks. 'For how long?'

'How about . . . a lifetime?'

Her mouth opened, and then closed again. Then she was in his arms. Her lips were wet, her tongue was eager. But not less so than his own. It had been too long, and where a girl like Lee Caspar was concerned, it had been forever. The feel of her in his arms, the knowledge that she was preparing to give herself into his keeping, was the most heady he had ever known.

After she had kissed him a few times, she paused to look at him. 'Say,' she said. 'If I come up to London as your fiancée, do I get to shake hands with the King?'

Part Three

THE MAJOR

11

Bath, 1908

Suddenly there was a great deal to be done. Mother and Philippa had to be told, to begin with, and much champagne to be drunk.

'I always knew you and Lee would end up together,' Philippa said enthusiastically. 'Now you won't have to go home, Lee.'

'I guess not,' Lee agreed thoughtfully, as if she hadn't considered that.

But there was also the matter of permission; Murdoch might have been pitchforked into the position of senior officer commanding at the Bath depot, but he was still not yet twenty-seven. He promptly took Lee along to meet Judith Walters, who in her husband's absence reigned over the depot like a somewhat forbidding queen. Lee had been carefully rehearsed, both by himself and by Philippa, and to make matters easier, Mother accompanied them, to leave no doubt that she approved of the match. Even Judith Walters, who regarded herself as the regiment's most important person, had to bow to Mrs Fergus Mackinder, who had ruled Bath only briefly, but as the wife of one of the more famous lieutenant-colonels, and she was graciously pleased to welcome Lee into the fold, on Florence's recommendation.

All the same, she remained a stickler for protocol. 'You'll be writing to Martin, of course,' she remarked to Murdoch.

'This evening,' he assured her. 'I just wanted you to meet Lee first.'

'Oh, quite,' Mrs Walters agreed. 'I shall add a letter to yours,' she said meaningfully.

Which meant endorsement.

261

'Home and dry,' he told Lee, as they drove home in the family trap.

'It seems so God-awful old-fashioned,' Lee remarked, still smarting. 'I mean, here you are, a grown man, one of Great Britain's most famous soldiers, a medal of honour winner—'

'Victoria Cross,' Murdoch reminded her.

'Well, anyway, here you are, and if this Walters character says no, you mean you can't marry me?'

'Well. . . .' Murdoch looked to his mother for support.

'It's all part of what makes the British world tick, my dear,' Florence Mackinder explained. 'What makes Britain Great, if you like. It's what made Murdoch rescue Colonel Edmonds from the fuzzy-wuzzies—'

'Boers,' Murdoch murmured.

'And lead that charge in Egypt.'

Murdoch sighed and did not bother to correct her this time; vagueness had always been one of his mother's most endearing characteristics – but the tendency was getting worse.

'It's part of our tradition, the Army's tradition, of duty and honour and obedience,' Florence went on, and gave Lee a very hard look. 'You are going to have to take your place in that tradition, my dear. And bring your sons up in it, too.'

'Oh,' Lee said. Murdoch wasn't sure if that meant she hadn't really considered what she was marrying before, or that she was taken aback by such an abrupt, and early, reference to children. He squeezed her hand, reassuringly.

But both were aspects of the situation which he realised *he* had not properly considered. Lee had clearly intended to marry him from almost the moment of their first meeting. But of course Lee knew nothing about Margriet Voorlandt, or the son Margriet claimed was his. What her reaction would be to that earthy and unromantic piece of news he could not decide. She seemed so broadminded and unstuffy, and had obviously been told things by Harry which he would never have dreamed of confiding to either of his sisters . . .

262

but there was no way of knowing what she really felt about the seamy side of life, and whether she had any intention of ever letting it intrude upon the essential sunshine she had been brought up from birth to enjoy.

He decided that Margriet Voorlandt was a secret to be kept firmly locked away in his breast, however dishonest it made him feel to have to do so.

But there was also the sheer physical business of being engaged to be married to a girl who was actually living in the same house as himself. Here again, she appeared to be totally modern and broadminded, and apparently not in the least concerned about being left alone with him, as she invariably was. Mother regarded Philippa as a built-in chaperon, and Philippa, who so far as Murdoch knew had never been kissed passionately in her life, could find nothing the least wrong in an engaged couple being alone together as much as they liked, especially when the man concerned was her own adored baby brother.

That Lee might be aware of desire, or even passion, was another question he found it difficult to assess. In addition to being something of a tomboy, she presented a very business-like appearance to the world, and to him. It came as something of a shock when he realised that neither of them had actually said, 'I love you', to the other. It had just happened that they agreed to get married, almost as if it was something decided by their parents, as in the old days, which they had at last decided to implement. Now, her interests seemed to lie mainly in the sort of life she would have to live as Mrs Murdoch Mackinder – some aspects of which clearly did not attract her at all. At first, having to live in the married officers' quarters at the depot sounded fairly exciting – until she actually saw the quarters, which were small, poky, and cheek by jowl with those occupied by the other married officers, with whose wives she was apparently required to spend large portions of each day drinking coffee or tea, or playing whist, or just gossiping. And over the majority of these happy get-togethers, Judith Walters would be presiding.

'Golly,' Lee remarked. 'If you were to get sent out to

India now, leaving me here on my lonesome, I think I would go nuts.'

'Well, my dear, there seems absolutely no chance of me being sent to India,' Murdoch reminded her. 'So that's not something to worry about. As for living here, it'll only be for a little while. As I move up, we'll be able to take a house in Bath itself, or even to live at Broad Acres, if you prefer.' The estate was only three miles from the depot.

'Move up, how far?' Lee asked.

'Well, lieutenant-colonel, certainly. Perhaps even major.'

'How come Mrs Walters doesn't have a house in Bath? She's the wife of a lieutenant-colonel, isn't she?'

'Well, she prefers to live in the depot, I suppose.'

'Where she can bully all of us juniors,' Lee remarked.

'I'm sure you'll find her an absolute brick, when you get to know her better,' Murdoch said, uttering a silent prayer that such a miracle could happen; Judith Walters had never endeared herself to any member of the regiment that he was aware of – or their wives.

'Of course I will,' she agreed, with one of her ready smiles. 'Now come and look at this list of things we will have to buy – or persuade people to give to us.'

Their shoulders touched as he stood beside her over the table, and she glanced at him, and then was in his arms. She did like being in his arms and kissing him, and there was passion in the kiss. For him it was considerable mental agony as he felt her against him, and kept thinking of Margriet's long, muscular, naked body, and felt surges of tremendous passion building inside himself . . . as she could of course tell, for after a few seconds she very gently released herself.

'Sets of twelve, I think,' she said, returning to her linen list. Her ears glowed and her cheeks were pink, and he could not tell whether he had embarrassed her or if she was herself fighting back a desire to do more; he could have laid her across the table there and then.

There was also the very important question of where the wedding was going to take place. Letters were of course sent hurrying across the Atlantic, and naturally Lee's parents – while appearing to be delighted that their daughter was going to marry a soldier who had been made quite famous in America by Harry's articles – wanted the wedding to be in Baltimore, where they lived. This would present difficulties, however, as regards securing the necessary leave; Murdoch had already been off duty for very nearly a year and did not really feel he could apply for another furlough so soon, which Lee entirely understood. She was also rather taken with the idea of a wedding in Bath Abbey, draping it with the regimental colours and having a guard of honour of raised swords for them to pass beneath after the ceremony. That too was obviously going to present a difficulty, as the officers would have to come from other regiments, unless they waited for the return of the dragoons from India. But Geoffrey Phillips promised to organise everything.

Yet it all was academic until a reply was obtained from Colonel Walters, and meanwhile there was the trip to London and the meeting with Harry, who clasped his hand most warmly.

'That charge,' he said. 'How I wish I had been there. And now you're getting to marry Sis. I couldn't have wished anything better than that.'

'Are you sure?' Murdoch asked. 'The life of an Army wife isn't all beer and skittles.'

'I think she'll be able to take it,' Harry said.

He accompanied the family to Buckingham Palace for the investiture, where Murdoch was taken aback to discover how the King had changed in the six years since he had last come face to face with him. This was an old man, and behind the beard the eyes were dull with utter exhaustion. Yet he exuded his usual ebullience. 'That's the trouble with beginning your military career at the very top, Mackinder,' he remarked. 'From then on it's all downhill.'

To Lee's great pleasure, as Murdoch's fiancée she was presented to His Majesty, who gave her one of his most appraising glances. 'I would say you are fortunate in more than just military matters, Mackinder,' he observed. 'I have always rated the American beauty very highly.'

'Gosh, but he gave me goose bumps,' Lee confided as they went outside to have the curved white cross, with its red and blue ribbon, admired by the others. 'Does that one go next to the Victoria Cross?' she wanted to know.

'Oh, indeed. One wears one's medals in order of seniority.'

'I'm so glad. The crimson of the VC does rather clash with the orange of that South African thing. Now they'll be neatly separated.'

He could never be sure whether she was joking or was actually worried about things like that. But the champagne luncheon at the Café Royal was even more enjoyable than last time, because Lee and Harry were able to share it with the family.

Then it was time to make serious plans. Harry was on his way back to the States, and it was necessary for Lee to go with him to make all the arrangements. The date for the wedding was fixed for the following March, only a few months away now, at which time the entire Caspar clan was apparently going to descend on Bath. 'Always supposing your funny old colonel gives you permission,' Lee pointed out, again with that half bantering, half deadly serious are-you-or-aren't-you-a-grown-man tone in her voice.

But saying goodbye to her was totally reassuring. They did it alone in her hotel room, with the cab already waiting to take her and Harry to the station, and for the first time, as she kissed him, he felt she was totally absorbed with *him*. 'It's not going to be long,' she breathed. 'Oh, it's not going to be long.'

'Just three or four months,' he said, as reassuringly as he could.

'Three or four months. That's a lifetime! And over Christmas, too.'

'We have a lifetime ahead of us. And lots of Christmasses.' He kissed her again and held her very close. 'I shall miss you terribly.'

'You better,' she said, beginning to banter again.

He escorted her downstairs in an euphoric mood, but was somewhat taken aback an hour later, when he and Mother and Philippa were on their train down to Bath, and Mother remarked, 'I do hope she's going to turn out all right.'

'Mother! What a thing to say,' Philippa rebuked. 'She's going to be just perfect.'

'She's an American,' Florence Mackinder pointed out, the first time she had raised that subject. 'They're such an undisciplined people. Why, do you know, Barnwell told me that Lee made her bed every morning.' She gazed at her children with arched eyebrows.

'I should think Barnwell would be pleased about that,' Philippa said. 'Americans are brought up differently from us, that's all. And all the best people marry them,' she pointed out. 'Mr Churchill's father did.' She was a great supporter of the ruling Liberal Party, and especially of the dashing young MP who had shared her brother's adventures in Africa – even if several hundred miles had separated the two men – and who was now rising very fast in the government.

'Yes, but *she* doesn't have to be an Army wife,' Mother persisted.

'Murdoch will soon lick her into shape,' Philippa asserted confidently. 'Won't you, Murdoch?'

Murdoch wasn't at all sure about that; he had never made a bed in his life.

The next few months were fairly tense, because the mails to and from India, and then from Bombay to Peshawar and back, were very slow, but just after Christmas the long-awaited letter arrived.

'I must apologise for not having replied before,' Martin Walters wrote, 'but things here have been fairly busy. However, having heard from Judith what a dear girl your Miss Caspar appears to be, so quiet and docile and determined to become one of *us*, it gives me the greatest pleasure to grant my permission for your forthcoming nuptials. I may

267

say that any young officer who aspires to make his way in the Army needs, in my opinion, a good wife behind him, and I only regret that I shall not be there for the ceremony. My feelings on this are shared by your brother officers.'

This was tremendous news, but Murdoch became less happy as he read on.

'I need hardly tell you that I wish you could be here with us, especially right at this minute, when there can be no doubt that something big is about to happen. We could be facing a general uprising among the Pathans and we are preparing ourselves for a hot time. You may rest assured that the regiment will give a good account of itself, even lacking the assistance of its most famous member.'

The thought that there might be a war brewing on the frontier in which he would take no part Murdoch found very galling, especially as there was also a letter from Johnnie Morton.

'You young devil,' Morton wrote. 'I hope your Marylee is a ravishing beauty with the biggest tits in America, and that you flog yourself to death on your honeymoon. If you do not, I truly look forward to making Mrs Mackinder's acquaintance, whenever we are finally relieved from this beastly place. However, while you are bouncing up and down on your Yankee charmer's belly, we are apparently going to have to win some medals of our own. The talk in the bazaars is of nothing but war!'

Murdoch could not help but smile. There was absolutely no point in getting annoyed by Johnnie Morton's vulgarity. But how, wedding or no wedding, he wished he could be in Peshawar with his friends.

Walters' letter meant that preparations could now go ahead in earnest. Murdoch had returned to duty at the depot, and was working his recruits as hard as he had ever done, assisted by a new sergeant, Tomlinson – the strength of the reserve squadron was not yet sufficient to warrant an SSM. Nor did he propose to let the forthcoming ceremony interfere with the requirements of his duty, but Mother and Philippa and Rosemary – who took up residence at Broad Acres, together with little Harriet Phillips – were in their elements, penning invitations, arranging flowers and times of arrivals and departures . . . and confronting Murdoch with the necessity of naming a best man. There was only one possible answer to that: Harry Caspar. He was delighted, and came over early, to arrange such things as stag parties and to acquaint himself with British custom and etiquette.

Lee herself arrived at the beginning of March, together with her mother and father and several uncles and aunts and cousins. These new American relatives-to-be all stayed at Broad Acres, of course, and there was a great round of parties and get-togethers to sort out protocol, thus Lee had been in England for four days before she virtually seized Murdoch by the arm and pushed him out into the rose garden.

'I thought we'd never get alone together,' she said. 'I do like your uniform.'

He was wearing the new service dress of dark khaki tunic, paler khaki breeches, brown boots, and of course Sam Browne belt, with a dark khaki peaked cap.

'Very smart.'

He took her in his arms. 'As you are more beautiful than ever.'

She looked up at him. 'Do you really think so? Have you missed me?'

'Every hour of every day.'

'But what about the minutes and seconds?'

'Some of them too.'

She kissed him. 'And old fuddy-duddy Walters came through.'

'I don't think there was ever any doubt about that. He's not really an old fuddy-duddy, you know.'

'I guess a man can't help his wife,' she said, and grinned. 'Although he sure ought to, given the trouble he has to get one in your army.'

'You can always change your mind,' he said, not altogether jokingly.

'You think I can't take it?'

'I think you can take anything. If you want to.'

'I want to, Murdoch Mackinder,' she said. 'Oh, how I want to.'

But he still wasn't sure that she *did* want to, that she was not having second thoughts.

He realised his mother was having second thoughts about the Caspars. From their clothes and their jewellery and their talk, they were obviously well-to-do people – Jim Caspar was in the liquor trade in Baltimore – but they obviously had no idea of how upper-middle-class English people behaved. Apart from their language, which was decidedly racy, Jennie Caspar insisted on at least beginning to clear the table after every meal, regardless of the aghast presence of Wilkins the butler and Cooley the downstairs maid; and in sorting her own laundry, to the consternation of Barnwell the upstairs maid, who was in any event affronted by the guests' bed-making activities.

Jim Caspar also had a habit of lighting up somewhat pungent cigars – stogies, he called them – whenever he felt like one, and regardless of where, or in whose company, he happened to be. 'Don't they *have* smoking rooms in America?' Mother asked Philippa and Murdoch.

Murdoch was inclined to try to have a word with him, but Philippa forbade it. 'They're different,' she said. 'And difference in people is what makes the world interesting. I think they're charming.'

They certainly were, but it was the difference that bothered Murdoch.

He was as nervous as a kitten, far more than ever before going into action, when the great day finally dawned. The wedding was to take place at eleven in the morning, and as Lee was naturally using Broad Acres, he remained at the depot. Reynolds had him up at dawn, with his full dress uniform – dark blue breeches, pale blue tunic, black boots, burnished helmet, dress sword, medals – all laid out for him.

Harry was along at nine to share breakfast – not that Murdoch could eat a thing – and during the meal the ushers and the rest of the honour party arrived. There were only two from the regiment itself, the young subalterns whom Murdoch was putting through their paces: Harry O'Dowd, and Clem Pinder. The other ten were from a variety of other regiments, and included several guards officers, friends of Geoffrey Phillips, whose red jackets made a pleasing contrast to the blue of the regiment. At ten o'clock the first bottle of champagne was broken, and from then on the wine flowed pretty freely for half an hour, at which time the horses were waiting for the ride to the abbey.

They made an imposing sight, Murdoch thought, Harry in black alongside his dark blue, then two red-jacketed guardsmen, then the blue-coated subalterns, then some more guardsmen, with a smattering of lancers and hussars to make up the numbers, and the good people of Bath, aware that a military wedding was taking place, lined the streets to cheer them on.

'This pageantry, this colour, is what England is all about,' Harry Caspar said enthusiastically. 'What a pity you don't wear full dress into battle any more.'

The abbey was already filled with guests and music, and flowers, and excitement, as Murdoch and Harry made their way up the centre aisle to where the bishop awaited them. They had already had talks and a rehearsal with him, of course, and he was in any event an old friend of the Mackinder family. Then it was a matter of waiting for the bride, who was actually only a little late. They had not been in their places more than ten minutes before Florence Mackinder and Jennie Caspar arrived, the one tall and slender, the other short and stout. And only five minutes after that the bridal march from Mendelssohn was struck up, and Lee entered the door, followed by two Caspar cousins to carry her train, and then by Philippa and Rosemary. Lee arrived at the altar entirely concealed beneath her voluminous veil, but when she threw it back her face was more solemn and intense than he had ever known it, and she too made her pledges in little more than a whisper.

They were to honeymoon in Cornwall, at an hotel the Mackinders had used often enough in the past, and the last train left Bath at six in the evening, which was only an hour after the last speech had been made, following an immense luncheon at Broad Acres.

The guests had returned to the house by a variety of means, from horseback to motor cars, flooding down the country road like some mammoth, multi-coloured hunt gone berserk. Murdoch and Lee had of course travelled together, in an open tourer Harry had hired for the occasion, but they were not in the least alone, as the car was surrounded throughout the journey by cheering mounted dragoons. They had no more time than to exchange a hasty smile and a squeeze of the hand before they were posing for the camera in the grounds, indulging in the obligatory kiss, and sitting down to luncheon.

Then at five it was a matter of hurrying Lee upstairs to get changed for the journey, and hurrying Murdoch away as well, for he was going to travel in mufti. He emerged in his rarely worn civilian suit at almost the same moment as Lee in her deep crimson going-away outfit, held her gloved hand tightly as they ran the gauntlet of the crowd and the confetti, and scrambled her into the motor car which was to drive them to Bath station.

The military guests accompanied the car, still dressed in their finery, cantering their horses up the streets to the applause of the onlookers, and even walking them along the platform as the train came in. Reynolds had gone on ahead to make sure everything was organised – he had only with difficulty been persuaded from coming on the honeymoon himself, to look after them – and found time to whisper to Murdoch that he had spoken to the conductor and made sure they would not be interrupted until they reached their destination.

Then they were in the compartment and blowing kisses at Mother and Jennie Caspar and the girls, who had come along in another motor car, and at last the train was pulling out of the station, and they were actually alone.

'Whew!' Lee remarked, sitting down with a thump and taking off her hat. 'That was some party.'

He sat opposite her. 'I think they all enjoyed it.'

'They jolly well ought to have,' she agreed. 'I sure did. All those uniforms . . . they say her wedding day should be the high spot of a girl's life, and I can't see that being beaten. It was like something I'd always dreamed of.'

'I thought it was pretty good too,' he said, aware that he was uttering inanities, but this was the moment he had been afraid of, he had no idea what the form was.

She gazed at him. 'What time do we get to Penzance?'

'About midnight.'

'Midnight? God, I don't know if I can survive that long.'

'Have some more champagne.' He opened the huge hamper Reynolds had installed.

'If I drink any more of that stuff I'll drown.' She peered into the basket. 'What on earth is in there?'

'Dinner. There'll be consommé, and cold turkey sandwiches, I should think – he knows they're my favourite – and some jelly, I imagine, and cheese and biscuits, of course, and probably a couple of bottles fo claret to go with the cheese, and then some bonbons. And a thermos of coffee. What would you like to start with?'

'Oh, my God! Show me any more food and I'll die.'

'Well, I think it would be a mistake to stop drinking.' He popped a cork and filled two glasses, setting the bottle on the floor as the train rumbled through the darkness. The lights of Bath were already fading into the distance. He gave her a glass, and raised his own. 'Here's to us, Mrs Mackinder.'

'Mrs Mackinder,' she breathed, and sipped, staring at him as she did so 'This is one hell of a public carriage.'

'Easily mended.' He got up and drew the blind over the door, then the one over the window. 'Voilà!'

'Can't we lock the door?'

'As we are on our honeymoon, I don't see why not.' He managed to wedge it, aware of a pleasant sensation which was creeping over his entire body. He was alone with a most exciting woman who had yielded herself into his keeping, who would be his to have and to hold, as she had recently sworn to the bishop, for the rest of his life. Until death did them part! He turned back to face her, picking

273

up his glass as he did so, and found her watching him with that slightly quizzical expression she wore from time to time; her glass was empty. Hastily he refilled it.

'I'm quite tight already,' she confessed, but she took it.

'Join the club. Maybe that's the best way to start married life.'

'You bet,' she said. 'Only . . . midnight. I'll be asleep long before then.'

He put down his glass, took hers from her hand, and sat beside her. 'This carriage is all but policeman proof, at this moment.' He took her in his arms and kissed her. There was so much more he wanted to do to her, and the most magnificent feeling of all was that now he could; she was his wife. Yet his hands were trembling as he unbuttoned the throat of her blouse and kissed the flesh beneath. 'I have dreamed of this moment for a very long time,' he said.

Her arms were still round him, but now they tightened, crushing his face against her flesh for a moment before releasing him again, while he inhaled her scent. 'I will love you, Murdoch,' she whispered into his hair. 'More than anything else in the world. More than any*one* else in the world. I will love you.'

Almost she sounded as if she were trying to reassure herself. He raised his head. 'I'm glad of that. Because I'm going to love you, too.'

They stared at each other, then very cautiously he let his hand touch her breasts. She gave a little shiver.

'I am being an utter cad,' he said. 'I should be making polite conversation until we get to the hotel.'

'No,' she said fiercely. 'No, I don't want to wait. If I thought we couldn't be interrupted . . .'

'We won't be.'

'What about the guard?'

'He's been squared. But there's a station in ten minutes. After that, there's a long break before the next.'

'Ten minutes,' she breathed, kissing him again. He could taste the champagne in her mouth, but also her essential sweetness. Now he felt confident enough to unbutton the rest of her bodice and gently slip his hand inside, feeling

274

the passion mounting to take control of his entire body. He touched silk, but no corset; she did not need one. Then he was inside the silk, and discovering soft flesh, and then the nipple, rising beneath his hand, while she clung to him, kissing him now with an almost savage intensity.

The train slowed, and stopped with a squeaking of brakes and a hissing of steam. They sprang apart with almost childlike guilt, listening to the doors of the adjacent compartments opening and banging shut again, to people talking right outside their window, almost as if they were inside with them. Feet sounded in the corridor, and someone even tried the door of their compartment; Lee held the blouse across her half-exposed breasts, mouth open in a most beautiful expression of dismay. But the wedge held and the people passed on, and a few minutes later the train was on its way again.

'An hour to the next stop,' he said.

'Boy, that gave me the willies. Quite got me going. Would you like me to do a strip for you?' she asked.

He wasn't sure what she meant for a moment, then understood as she slipped from his grasp and stood up, swaying with the train, taking off her blouse as she did so. Then he was completely taken aback. But that she was apparently not the least nervous or uncertain was reassuring – even if the champagne probably had a lot to do with it – because he was certainly fairly nervous himself. Yet he was sure she was not entirely at ease, and was using this kind of half-seduction to settle her own nerves as well. But he was not going to stop her now. He could only watch in fascination as she laid the blouse on the seat beside her, and then released her skirt, sliding it past her thighs, stepping out of it and daintily laying it beside the blouse. She sat down to release her boots, while he gazed at the wealth of white undergarments – Margriet Voorlandt had worn not a fraction of those in the African heat.

But now the petticoat and the chemise were also being laid on the seat, and she was sitting down again to take off her garters and her stockings, wearing only her drawers. Now there was another world of white, but this was flesh,

275

surprisingly large breasts for so small a woman, crying out
to be held and caressed. She was no longer looking at
him; her cheeks were flushed and she was working with
tremendous anxiety.

He felt he should match her, got up and spread two of
the travelling rugs Reynolds had thoughtfully provided on
the other seat, then undressed himself, but could not help
turning to look at her as she slipped the drawers down as
well, and stood there, slightly shivering, a sprite of glowing
white flesh and black hair. His wife!

'I guess you should inspect my mouth and teeth,' she said
– half joking and half defiant, he decided, as if she expected
him not to appreciate her beauty.

'I shall,' he agreed, and kissed her. When he released
her, she sat on the seat, gazing at him, appearing to see him
for the first time.

'Oh, my,' she said. 'Oh, my.'

'Not an entirely pretty sight.'

'Turn around,' she commanded, and again remarked,
'Oh, my!' She leaned forward to touch the blue mark on
his left shoulder, then even darker blue mark behind his
right shoulder, the older scars on his side and in his leg.
'The battle honours of a warrior,' she said.

'I'm glad you can think of them that way.' He sat beside
her, and she kissed him.

'Touch me,' she said. 'With your fingertips. Touch me,
everywhere.'

He obeyed, and could feel the passion joining them as
his fingers coursed lightly over every inch of her skin, and
she held him, also lightly; when Margriet had done that, she
was already a married woman of several years' experience.

Lee lay down on her back, her arm thrown beneath her
head, in the most natural and yet seductive of poses. 'I am
going to love you, Murdoch Mackinder,' she promised,
staring into his eyes. 'For ever and ever and ever.'

He gazed at her breasts, rising and falling with every
breath, and at her slightly parted legs.

'Kiss me,' she commanded. 'There! Kiss me!'

Not even Margriet had ever asked for that. But was it

276

not something he had always dreamed of doing? Reality surpassed expectation, and a few moments later he was on top of her, while her arms were tight round his neck, urging him on with increasing anxiety. He expected her to cry out or make some kind of noise when he entered her, but she did not, just surged against him, gasping as he held her more tightly than he had intended. Only then, as he rolled off her, did he realise she was weeping.

'Oh, my darling,' he said. 'Was it that painful?'

'It was wonderful. Not painful at all.'

'Oh . . . splendid. That's a relief.' He sat up and retrieved their champagne glasses.

She rose on her elbow to take a sip. 'Do we have to dress right away?'

'Fifteen minutes will do.' He stroked a tear away from her eye with his forefinger.

'I . . .' Colour flared into her cheeks. 'I guess I owe you an explanation.'

'For what?'

'For . . .' She sat up beside him, drawing up her legs. 'Have you been with many girls?'

'As a matter of fact, no.'

'But you weren't . . . ?' She looked positively alarmed.

'No,' he said.

'Thank God! I didn't think you were. I didn't think you could be, I mean, being an Army officer and all, travelling all over the world . . .'

'Doesn't actually follow. Maybe you are mixing up the Army and the Navy. Soldiers generally get stuck in one place for two or three years on end.'

'I hadn't thought of that.' She gave her quick smile. 'I guess I do know navies better than armies.'

Of course, he recalled, Baltimore was a port. He didn't want to appear to pry, so he kissed her instead of asking questions. She responded, then went on, 'Confessions are the most ridiculous things.'

'Agreed. And in the main, quite unnecessary. Believe me.'

'But I have to. Please understand . . . There should have

been blood. Just a little. Where you punctured my hymen. Right?'

'I've never thought about it. I know I was supposed to hurt you.' He refused to accept what she was trying to tell him.

'I was just about engaged once before,' she said, meeting his eyes. 'To a naval officer. He had to make another voyage before he reckoned he'd be senior enough to ask for my hand. Not too different to your set-up, after all, I guess. So off he went to sea.'

'And he never came back?'

'There was a storm, or something . . . she went down with all hands. She was only a little ship. One of those new torpedo boat destroyers. Very narrow, and . . . they thought she must have rolled over.' She gave a little shiver. 'There were no survivors.'

He held her hand. 'Were you very much in love with him?'

She raised her head. 'In love? Well, I . . . I don't know. Not the way I am with you.'

He studied her; he was still not sure he understood, or wanted to understand, what she was telling him. It would have been much simpler if she'd said, yes, the drowned sailor had been her true love.

'The trouble was . . .' she sighed. 'I guess Ma never took enough trouble, looking after me. She was always busy, helping Pa in the business, and she always reckoned I could look after myself. Maybe I can. Could, even. But I thought I *was* looking after myself, don't you see? I thought we were going to get married just as soon as he got back. So . . . well, it just happened, the night before he left. I'm so terribly sorry. I think I was sorry five minutes afterwards. But it's one of those things you can't ever undo, can you?'

'I suppose not.' He was still holding her hand, and he knew he couldn't let it go; not at this moment. 'How long ago was this?'

'Autumn of 1905. When Al got drowned. It was a hurricane.'

'Ah. So when you came to England the following year . . .'

'Harry was trying to get me out of my mood of depression, I guess. Oh, he knew nothing about . . . what happened. Only that I'd been in love with Al, and that I was shattered by his death.' She gazed at him. 'When I saw you . . . it wasn't love at first sight. I didn't want to love anybody, ever again. Oh, I thought you were very attractive. And you were so nice, sending me down to Broad Acres and all . . . that had a much better effect on me than traipsing around Europe looking at nude statues. And then Phil was so absolutely sweet, from the start. It was she began the whole thing.'

'You didn't tell *her?*' Murdoch asked in sudden alarm.

'Only that I'd been engaged. I've never told anybody, until now.'

And did he wish she hadn't? He was too unsure of his emotions to know.

'It was when I returned to Broad Acres, you know, after the European trip. You'd already gone off to . . . Italy, wasn't it? The funny thing was, we'd been in Italy only a couple of weeks before. But I thought you'd said you were going to South Africa.'

He squeezed her hand. Italy, he thought. And South Africa.

'So Phil and I went riding together, and walking together, and we talked, and one day, just before I was due to leave, she said, "I think you should marry Murdoch, when he gets home. He needs a wife, and you are just perfect for him. Besides," she added, "I would so like to have you as a sister-in-law." '

Her shoulders hunched, and he squeezed her fingers again; he didn't know what else to do. But he knew he couldn't stop her, now; this was something she had to get off her chest. Besides, he was interested to learn just how he had been captured.

'So we arranged I would come back to England the following spring, to visit with her. But you were sent off to Somaliland almost as soon as you got home, so I cancelled my trip. But then you were wounded, and I had to arrange it all over again . . .' She gazed at him, her eyes enormous, her mouth slightly open. 'I guess you must think I am just about the most awful person you have ever met.'

'Why?' he asked.

'Well, all that deceit . . . and then kind of pushing you into marrying me . . .'

'I'm not that easy to push, save in the direction I want to go,' he told her.

'But . . . if you'd known about . . . if I'd been honest with you . . . ?'

'Would it have made any difference?' He considered, quite seriously, initial dismay already being replaced with objective common sense. He would have gone away with Margriet Voorlandt in 1906, and she had actually been another man's wife. While this man Al was dead. His knowledge of Lee was lost forever, save between them. And between them now was *their* knowledge of each other. When it was complete. 'I don't think so,' he said. He got up and handed her her clothes. 'We'll be passing through the next station in ten minutes.'

'You hate me.'

'I love you.' He willed her to believe him.

'That's the first time you've ever said that to me.'

'You have never said it to me. You said you *would* love me, just now.'

'I meant, if you'd let me.'

'I want you to.'

She was on her knees now, on the seat, facing him, the most appealing picture he had ever seen. 'And the other thing?'

He stooped and kissed her on the lips. 'I never told you I was a father, either,' he said.

'Welcome home, captain. Welcome home. Welcome home, miss . . . I beg your pardon, Mrs Mackinder.' Corporal Reynolds stood in the doorway of their little apartment rather like a diminutive genie of the lamp, smiling his greetings. 'How was Penzance?'

'Chilly,' Lee told him, walking into the small sitting room. 'Is that a fire? Oh boy.' She stood before it, stripping off her gloves to toast her fingers. 'That was real thoughtful of you.' She looked around. She had bought the furniture before the wedding, and even arranged it herself, so the place was not altogether unfamiliar. Reynolds had brightened it up with vases of flowers – badly arranged but still cheerful enough – and had clearly spent the entire fortnight they were away cleaning and polishing; the room shone. 'Say, you've done us proud.'

'My pleasure, Mrs Mackinder. Now, I have some persons coming to see you tomorrow morning, whom I have taken the liberty of interviewing myself. I can assure you that they are clean and honest – I have obtained references – and if you like the look of them, why, they can start right away.'

'Persons?' Lee asked.

'A cook, madam. And a housemaid. I thought that a lady's maid would be better chosen by you personally.'

'Cook?' she repeated. 'Housemaid? Lady's maid . . . ?' She looked at Murdoch.

He grinned. 'Essentials, all.'

'Oh, my,' she said. 'I have never had a lady's maid. Pa didn't believe in servants. What does she do?'

'Everything you don't wish to do yourself, madam,' Reynolds assured her.

'Corporal,' she told him, 'you are an absolute treasure.'

'You have actually done very well, George,' Murdoch assured him. 'But now . . .'

'Oh, yes, sir,' Reynolds said. 'I was just hurrying off. There's some eggs in the larder, and . . .' He gazed at them, uncertain that they could cope on their own.

'We shall manage, George. And if we can't, there's always the canteen,' Murdoch reminded him.

'Indeed, yes, sir. There's the mail.' He pointed at the pile of letters on the table, saluted and backed out of the door.

'He really is a dear,' Lee said. 'How long have you had him?'

'Reynolds has been with me nine years now, all but. Ever since I joined the regiment.'

'Gee,' she said. 'And all of these servants . . . will they be white people?'

'I'm afraid so.'

'Gee,' she said again. 'Ma did have a cook once, when she wasn't well. A black girl. White people . . . I won't know what to say to them.'

'Just be yourself. It'll come naturally.'

She came close to him. 'Do you think I'm a hick?' She made a moue. 'Apart from everything else?'

It was the first time she had mentioned 'everything else' since the first night of their marriage. That had been by mutual agreement. She had, predictably, reacted in her own way to what Murdoch confessed to her. 'But your son!' she had exclaimed. 'Isn't there some way you can get him back?'

'He's Margriet's son. I only have her word for it that he's mine, although the age is roughly right. No, there is no way to get him back.'

'But . . . don't you want to?'

'I don't think so, really. I think I'd rather start again. I wouldn't have mentioned it, if we hadn't been playing Confessions.'

'Gee, have I broken every rule in the book?'

'Every one,' he had agreed. 'But I think we should begin by making our own rules, anyway. If you knew what a load that is off my mind.' The death of Knox, that was another matter. That was a male secret, not to be shared with any woman, even a wife.

Now he took her in his arms. 'I think you are the loveliest hick I have ever met.'

The door behind him opened. 'I am sure you had enough time for all of that down in Penzance,' announced Judith Walters. 'Welcome home. Now, Marylee, my dear, you are of course both expected for lunch. Can't have you cooking the first day home, eh? I suspect Murdoch hasn't even arranged your servants yet. And then, this afternoon, I want to have a good gossip. I know Murdoch will be anxious to get back to work. And there is a lot to be done. I'm afraid

I haven't really released the news yet. I was waiting for you to return.'

'Oh,' Lee said. 'Well, ah . . . gee, it's awfully nice of you to have us to lunch, Mrs Walters . . .'

'Judith,' Judith Walters told her. 'You must call me Judith. After all, you and I . . .' She frowned at Murdoch. 'You haven't opened your mail, have you?'

'There hasn't been time,' Murdoch confessed. 'What's this about news to be released?'

'You'd better read it.' She seized the pile of letters, sifted through it and selected one. 'This.'

Murdoch took the OHMS envelope with some caution, slit it and took out the sheet of paper inside.

'I know this is both unusual, and will disturb you,' Sir John French had written, 'but life is full of the oddest ups and downs. You will be aware that the sad death of Tony Chapman left you the second most senior captain in the regiment, after Johnnie Morton, who was then promoted brevet major and adjutant. It was anticipated that when the regiment returned home next year, he would be confirmed in that rank, and you would then assume command of a squadron as the senior captain. However, as they say, Man proposes, and God disposes. After the catastrophic news from Peshawar . . .' Murdoch raised his eyes to stare at Judith Walters, who appeared to know exactly where he had reached.

'Cholera,' she said briefly. 'It seems men were dying like flies.'

'My God,' he said. 'Colonel Walters . . . ?'

'Oh, he is all right,' she said. 'Or I wouldn't be quite so calm, would I. But the rest . . .'

Murdoch dropped his gaze to the page again. 'And the way Morton has fallen by the wayside . . .' Again he looked up.

'Oh, he's not dead,' Judith said. 'He's just contracted some hideous disease.' She gazed at him archly. 'You know, in the bazaars.' It was the first time he had ever seen Judith Walters blush. But wasn't Morton always bound to wind up like that? he thought.

He resumed reading. '... the whole situation has changed. It has therefore been decided, in view of your seniority and record, to promote you to major immediately, with the duties of adjutant, and to require you to prepare for the return of the regiment, which – in view of its appalling misfortunes and high death rate – will be relieved this summer, and should be back in England by the autumn, a year ahead of schedule. I know that you are very young for the responsibilities entailed, but I am sure you will carry out your duties to the very best of your considerable abilities, and therefore offer you my congratulations. John French.'

12
Bath, 1908–13

'It really must have been terrible,' Judith told them over luncheon. They were the only guests because the other married quarters were mostly empty; Tony Chapman's widow had already moved out, going back to live with her family, and Billy Hobb's wife had gone to stay with her to make sure she was all right. Judith was left somewhat in the position of a queen with no court to rule over, which was why she was so obviously pleased to see the newly weds back – or, at least, Lee.

'And while the epidemic was raging,' she went on, 'the regiment found itself surrounded by rampaging Pathans. It fought its way out, of course. But there were heavy casualties.'

'Poor old Morton,' Murdoch said. 'Is he going to be all right?'

'Well, I believe they can cure these things nowadays. But frankly, he deserves anything he gets, in my opinion. He should have been with the regiment when the shooting started. However, I suppose that is all a part of Army life.' She leaned across the table to squeeze Lee's hand. 'One simply cannot afford to look over one's shoulder. Eyes front and keep them there, is what Martin always says – and he's right. I think we should drink a toast to the new adjutant. And probably the youngest major this regiment has ever had.' She raised her champagne glass. 'How old are you, anyway, Murdoch?'

'I shall be twenty-seven this year,' Murdoch said.

'Why, if you are not careful, you could be lieutenant-colonel when you are thirty-five. Martin retires in eight years' time, unless he gets a brigade or something. Perhaps he will, after an experience like the one he has just had.'

Not if he managed to get himself surrounded by Pathans, while half his men were on sick parade, Murdoch thought. But he knew Judith was right. However unfortunately things had turned out for Morton and Chapman, he *was* the youngest major the regiment had ever had. And however sorry he was to have missed the fight in India, he could not regret having avoided being in a camp suffering from cholera. Nor could he subdue the rising tide of excitement that he was now actually second-in-command of the Royal Western Dragoon Guards.

'That is why you and I, my dear,' Judith was saying, giving Lee's hand another squeeze, 'as the two senior ladies in the regiment, must be the very best of friends. Life can be so lonely here, when the men are away.'

'I wonder you stick it,' Lee said. 'I mean, here in the depot, when you could surely live anywhere you chose . . .'

'But my dear, Martin is the colonel of the regiment,' Judith explained. 'These people left here, the troopers' wives and their children, are all my responsibility. I could never just wander off and leave them.'

Which brought Lee close to choking on her champagne. 'I know she's being terribly sweet and all that,' she confessed to Murdoch when they regained their own quarters, 'but really . . . her reference to those poor sick men, and the suggestion that we just forget the ones who died or were killed . . . and they were friends of yours. You were pretty callous too,' she added.

'You simply have to be pragmatic in the Army,' he told her. 'You cannot keep worrying about other fellows, however close to you, who may have bought it. Otherwise you simply could not keep going. After all, *I'm* extremely likely to be killed some day.'

'Don't say it,' she shouted. 'Just don't say it. Don't talk like that.' She glared at him. 'Have you ever *seen* a close friend killed?'

'Yes.'

She saw the expression in his eyes, and then she was in his arms. He held her close, and she rapidly recovered her spirits. They were both still feeling their way, and although

286

he had no doubt at all that their mutual confessions had been necessary for creating that special sense of intimacy without which a marriage cannot endure, they were both now terribly aware of how different were their backgrounds, their experiences of life. And it was clear that all the adjusting, at least in the beginning, was going to have to be done by Lee, if she was going to fit into the society in which he lived and, above all, the ethos of the regiment.

But that she was proud of him, and that she loved him, too, he no longer doubted, as he was proud of her, and the effort she was making. But then, he was pretty pleased with himself when Reynolds had replaced the three stars of a captain with the crown of a major on his shoulder straps; at the very bottom of the ladder of field command, he was even entitled to red tabs in various places. His mother and the girls were equally delighted, and letters of congratulation arrived from people as far apart as Lord Roberts and Harry Caspar.

Lee actually found life at the depot just as unspeakable as she had suspected it would be. If in the first instance it was a relief to discover that the quarters to either side were vacant, and that there would therefore be no interminable whist or coffee parties as she had feared, this meant that her society within the regiment consisted entirely of Judith Walters, Amy Hobbs, when she returned, and Maureen Llewellyn, the padre's wife; and none of these was a person she would have selected as a friend, hard as they all tried to make her feel at home.

In addition, she was terrified of the regular visits which Judith expected her, as the adjutant's wife, to make to the married quarters of the rank and file, where the wives of the absentee troopers lived in what she regarded as conditions of extreme squalor, surrounded by their children and their coughs and colds. She had to chat with them, and listen to their complaints, and try to cheer them up. To make matters worse, there was a large crop of new widows caused by the cholera epidemic, who had to be eased out of their quarters amidst wails not only of misery, but that they had nowhere to go, and could not possibly exist on their meagre pensions.

Even more miserable were those wives whose husbands had been reported either as ill with cholera, or wounded in the battle with the Pathans, and who awaited each week's mail delivery in dread. With the mails between England and India so slow, and private soldiers not really warranting the use of the telegraph service, it was possible for a woman to have been a widow for several weeks, her husband long since a mass of worms, before she was informed.

'What an existence,' Lee remarked. 'I'm never sure whether I'm the planter's wife visiting the slave barracoons, or the vicar's wife doing her rounds,' she told Murdoch. 'They're all so lonely, poor things. Who'd be a soldier's wife?'

'You would,' he said jokingly. But whenever possible he accompanied her, just to make things easier.

She also had her escape to Broad Acres, which she took whenever she could – sometimes several times in a week – to be with Philippa, to ride with her friend across the moors, play croquet on the lawn or just laze beneath the trees as summer came in, talking about anything that came into their heads.

To her great delight, there was even an American cricket team in England that summer, the Philadelphians. She didn't know anything about the game. 'In fact,' she confessed, 'I didn't know they played cricket in the States at all,' and was even more delighted when Murdoch told her that the Philadelphians were quite a first-class side, and in Barton King had one of the best bowlers in the world. The touring side had no match with either Somerset or Gloucestershire, but when they played Hampshire, Lee and Philippa went over to Southampton to watch them – Murdoch could not get away. Unfortunately they were soundly beaten but she found it all very exciting.

Murdoch found that he had very little time to spare at all, and hardly got to Broad Acres for more than the odd weekend that summer, because in addition to his duties training the recruits he found that his work as adjutant, even for an absentee regiment, was quite considerable. He was fortunate, however, in finding a brilliant assistant in O'Dowd. As well as being a really top-rate horseman – he came from Northern Ireland – he was also a keen soldier in every sense, and was soon capable of taking the training sessions by himself – with some assistance from Pinder, who gave every evidence of becoming a second Johnnie Morton.

But the summer was really mainly a period of waiting for two great events. In June Lee discovered that she was pregnant, and the regiment was due home in the early autumn.

Lee's pregnancy was a source of great joy to everyone, and especially Mother, who had remained somewhat uneasy about Murdoch's wife, clearly regretting the somewhat excessive enthusiasm she had shown when the engagement had first been announced. But if she was going to be presented with a second grandchild – she had long been concerned that Rosemary and Geoffrey Phillips had not improved on baby Harriet, who was at once noisy and spoiled – she was at last prepared to welcome Lee as a daughter rather than as her son's wife.

Lee herself was in a seventh heaven. Now she not only knew herself to be capable of motherhood, she felt that all of her sins had been expiated, and that she was really Murdoch's at last.

He was the least excited of them all, although he put on a good act. Of course he wanted a son to carry on the family tradition . . . or did he? Did he not already have one? Either way, the thought of a male Mackinder not joining the Army was inconceivable. But the thought of his son experiencing half of the hardships and misfortunes and frustrations that he had undergone in his still brief career was distinctly upsetting – however much he had also prospered. He almost hoped for a daughter.

Then the regiment came home.

This was the second occasion on which Murdoch had found

himself in the position of commanding the welcoming guard of honour rather than a squadron of the returning heroes, even if, as usual, he was the most famous hero in the regiment. As in 1902, the dragoons disembarked at Plymouth and marched up through Devon and Somerset behind their band, their tents being proudly accepted by the farmers on whose land they stopped at night – many of those farmers had sons in the Westerns – and thus the march home, as had been the case on the return from South Africa, was a long triumphal procession. Best of all, Ramage's squadron had been relieved from Somalia, and by arrangement joined the troopship carrying the rest of the dragoons, so it was also a great reunion. As before, Sir John French came down to take the salute at the depot, and in the stand behind the box were Mother and Philippa and Lee, just beginning to show, and of course Judith and Amy and Maureen, while the wives and children of the troopers filled the parade ground beyond and cheered themselves hoarse, even as tears ran down their cheeks.

Murdoch sat on Buccaneer out in front of the reserve squadron, sword at the salute. The men behind him now numbered very nearly two hundred, and would be much needed, he realised, as he gazed at the depleted ranks of the three service squadrons. He felt fairly close to tears himself, and could not wait for the march past to be over to dismiss his men and shake hands with Prendergast and Sergeant-Major Bishop, with Ramage and with Sergeant-Major Hanley, with Billy Hobbs and Sergeant Yeald.

'We missed you, Major Mackinder,' Yeald said simply.

'Remember me, sir?' asked a sun-browned young man with sharp eyes.

'Matheson,' Murdoch said. '*Corporal* Matheson. My congratulations.'

Matheson looked embarrassed. 'I didn't think I'd make a soldier,' he said.

Murdoch shook his hand. 'You were always a soldier, boy. I was proud to have you serving under me.'

Then it was time to seek out Colonel Walters. He had already greeted his wife and the other ladies, and been introduced to Lee. 'An absolute charmer,' he told Murdoch. 'Absolute. And Judith tells me there is a pleasant surprise on the way.'

'So it would appear, sir,' Murdoch said.

Walters took him into the office, looked around at the desk he had not seen for more than two years, the picture of Ian Mackinder behind his chair, sighed and sat down. He looked far older than when Murdoch had last seen him, and indeed, than his forty-one years.

'Rough, was it, sir?' Murdoch asked.

'So many good men,' Walters said. 'Not many from the Pathans. But cholera . . . it turns a man's stomach to watch good fellows falling by the wayside, dying in their own filth. But you, Murdoch . . . you look fitter than ever.'

'I've had nothing to do but get fit, this last year,' Murdoch pointed out. 'God, how I wish I'd been with you.'

'Well, don't. There was precious little glory, and one hell of a lot of sweat. And you've done a magnificent job here, as usual. That's a fine body of men you have there. And to have you as my adjutant . . . I really am pleased about that.'

'Thank you, sir. Do you know what they have for us to do next?'

'We've been promised at least a year's rest and recuperation,' Walters told him. 'For which I am heartily thankful. And then, I had a word with French this afternoon. It seems we may be in England for a good while yet. The Government appears to be quite worried about the situation in Europe.'

'You mean the constant snarling between France and Germany?' Murdoch asked. 'I can't believe either of them really wish to go to war. They loathe each other's guts, there can be no doubt about that. But actually to start fighting again. . . .'

'I hope you're right,' Walters said. 'But I can tell you that French, who after all has to do a lot of liaising with his French opposite number, thinks that they are just boiling for a scrap, to avenge the defeat of 1871. Of course they know they can't lick Germany single-handed. But if there were some way to involve the Russians and ourselves. . . .'

'Can they do that?'

'Well, the alliance, the Entente Cordiale as they call it, apparently works like this: if France fights some other power, the Russians and ourselves look on benevolently, but do not interfere. Should a third power, say Austria-Hungary, come in on the Germans' side, then the Russians are obliged to go to the aid of the French. We are still under no obligation other than benevolent neutrality. However, should a fifth power, for example, Italy, then join the central powers, we are at least morally obliged to come in on the French and Russian side. I have to say that I agree with you that such a contingency is extremely unlikely. But the Government feels obliged to show some muscle, not only be keeping a larger than usual army here in England, but by greatly expanding the territorial units. I'm afraid our next manoeuvres are likely to be cluttered up with a lot of bloody weekend soldiers.'

'Are we seriously going to be allied with the Russians, sir?' Murdoch asked.

'There are high-level talks going on, so it could happen. We'll just do our duty, Murdoch, and let others worry about the implications.' He held out his hand. 'Again, I'm glad you'll be standing at my shoulder, from here on in.'

Murdoch took a day's leave as soon as he could and caught the train up to London, where Morton was in the hospital for Tropical Diseases, having apparently conracted more than one ailment. His friend looked fitter than he had supposed he would; he was sitting up, smoking, reading a sporting newspaper and, of course, flirting with the nurses. But he was also terribly thin and sallow in colour, and his good humour was clearly forced.

'Murdoch!' he shouted, clasping his hand. 'Good to see you. You didn't bring the wife? I'm not contagious, you know. Not unless I were to climb aboard, or something like that, and I imagine you'd object.'

'She's not going out right now,' Murdoch explained.

'You are a sly devil,' Morton commented. 'Left at the post when you joined the regiment, and now charging past us all.' He looked at the medal ribbons on Murdoch's tunic, the crown on his shoulders. 'Past us all,' he said sadly.

'You'll soon be up and about again, surely,' Murdoch suggested.

'So they tell me. But malaria apparently stays with you a while. And then this damned syphilis business . . . oh, they can cure it. I mean, I can screw with the best of them right now. But it too can come back later on, they say. Anyway, it's the stink that surrounds a chap when he gets something like that. I'm going to be thirty-four this November. And not yet confirmed as major. If I'm not, maybe even if I am, that'll be it in a couple of years.'

Murdoch had never considered the implications of retirement; it seemed a very long way away for him. But the Army had no use for thirty-five-year-old officers who had not yet achieved field rank. 'What would you do? Supposing you do have to get out?'

'God knows. Go along to Gordon Rodgers and ask for a job, I should think. Do you know he now has a house in Sloane Square, two kids and a bloody great motor car? Seems the nation is drinking more beer than ever before. Or maybe I should begin at the beginning and marry a rich wife. I assume that was the plan you followed?'

'I've never actually asked,' Murdoch said, surprised, in fact, to realise that he *had* never investigated the Caspars' financial background. Old man Caspar had picked up the bills for the wedding without demur, and even if they did not possess a retinue of servants, he presumed that Philippa was right, and that was because theirs was just a different way of life.

'Of course you haven't,' Morton said. 'It wouldn't interest you. Not with Broad Acres to flog if you ever found yourself hard up. You'd better push off before I get all bitter and twisted.'

If he was not already, Murdoch thought sadly. It was hard not to conclude that he had brought his troubles on himself. And in fact a year later Captain John Morton was gazetted major, and then promptly placed on the retired list because of impaired health.

'Sad, but inevitable,' Colonel Walters commented. 'He was never really officer material.'

And am I officer material? Murdoch wondered. Or am I just the most fortunate man on earth? He had now survived several battles, and several nasty wounds as well, with no more than scars to show for them; he had been awarded the nation's two most prestigious military medals; he had escaped the consequences of his utterly irrational behaviour in South Africa; he was a major at the very early age of twenty-seven; he was popular with the new commander-in-chief designate . . . and he was happily married to a superb woman who even handled childbirth without difficulty. Ian Mackinder the Second emerged into the world in the spring of 1909, followed by Fergus Mackinder the Second in the summer of 1910.

The arrival of Fergus enabled Lee to implement her dearest ambition and move out of the depot; their little flat was too cramped for one baby, much less two, as even Judith Walters could see. Murdoch offered to buy her a house in Bath, but she wanted to move back to Broad Acres, and as that seemed to please Mother and Philippa he was happy to let her do so. Mother rearranged the house so that she and Philippa had a self-contained flat in the garden wing, leaving the whole rest of the house to the new mother. When Lee protested, Florence Mackinder refused to listen. 'The house is yours anyway,' she reminded her. 'I'm only here on sufferance.'

Now Lee really was a totally happy person, her only concern that occasionally Murdoch did not get home from the depot. Reynolds was another totally happy man, as he accompanied Marks, the nanny, on walks with the two babies. 'Two more dragoons, I'll be bound, sir,' he told Murdoch, as proudly as if he had been the father himself. But he was somewhat taken aback when just before Christmas 1912 Helen appeared. 'But if we had a women's army, sir,' he said, 'she'd be in it for certain.'

There was every possibility, in Murdoch's opinion, that

before very much longer there could well be a women's army; plans were already laid for an enormous expansion of the armed services should there ever be a showdown with Germany – and this under a Liberal government dedicated to reducing armies and armaments, not increasing them. But the word 'showdown' was becoming increasingly common as Europe moved very distinctly into two opposing armed camps.

The blame for the apparently unceasing sequence of crises was always, at least in the British press, laid at the door of the Kaiser, who since his telegram to President Kruger had become just about the most unpopular man in the world in British eyes. To the discerning observer, it was clear that all the continental powers, including Great Britain, were restless, nervous of each other's growing strength. The Germans and the Austrians were dismayed at the way their hundred-year-old alliance with Russia had disintegrated, to leave them with a potential enemy both east and west. The Russians were still smarting under the humiliation of their defeat by Japan, the first non-European power ever to get the better of a European army in a regular war, and desperate to regain the prestige lost at Mukden and Port Arthur – that they might have to do it with the aid of a country, Great Britain, which was still allied to Japan, did not appear to strike anyone as incongruous. The French were still bitter about *their* humiliation by Prussia in 1871, and dreaming only of the *revanche*, while the British were becoming more agitated as the German fleet grew in proportion to their own Royal Navy, and the German quest for colonies became more urgent.

Yet there had been many periods of acute tension in European affairs since the downfall of Bonaparte, only a few of which had developed into actual shooting – and then the wars had been strictly limited. However impartial one might wish to be, one had to accept that the spark which was nowadays flitting hither and thither, and could at any moment ignite the powder train, was the restless, arrogant and yet strangely uncertain personality of Kaiser Wilhelm II.

The Kaiser had begun 'throwing his weight around', as the British would have it, as far back as 1895, when he had sided with President Kruger over the Jameson Raid, and then in 1898 when he had travelled to Damascus to proclaim German solidarity with all the Muslim peoples of the world – a disturbing act for a nation which, like Great Britain, happened to rule several hundred millions of those Muslims. Murdoch in fact could not help but wonder if that strange journey and bombastic pronouncement had not inspired the Mullah to take up arms – in a campaign which he still sustained, and might be capable of doing so forever, it seemed.

Then had come the South African War, and Germany's open backing for the Boers. This had led directly to the alliance of Great Britain and France, who only a few years earlier, in 1898, had come to the verge of war themselves over *their* African empires. At that time, in 1904, the idea of a British alliance with Russia had seemed too far-fetched to be possible. Not only had the two countries hated each other ever since the Crimean War of fifty years before, but that very autumn the Russian Baltic fleet, on its way to the Far East to fight the Japanese – and to annihilation in the Straits of Tsushima – fired on a British fishing fleet off the Dogger Bank in the North Sea, under the apparent misapprehension that they were Japanese torpedo boats; how Japanese torpedo boats could have found themselves on the other side of the world from Tokyo had never been satisfactorily explained. That had brought England and Russia to the verge of war, and at the time it had appeared that the Kaiser and the Tsar might renew the alliance enjoyed by their respective fathers. This had fallen through, however. Then, as Britain and Russia patched their differences, the Kaiser's concern at the 'encirclement' of Germany began to grow rapidly. When France and Spain concluded an agreement delineating their respective spheres of influence in Morocco and Algiers, without consulting any other power, the Kaiser had exploded in outrage and himself visited Tangiers. The crisis had bubbled up into the most serious for thirty years – it was as if, just before the start of the Boer War, Wilhelm had visited Johannesburg – had led to the downfall of the French Foreign Minister, Delcassé, and had only been settled with difficulty after the conference at Algeciras.

Things had simmered for a year or two after that, only to be stirred up again by the occupation, sudden and unwarrented, by Austria-Hungary of the provinces of Bosnia and Herzegovina, which technically belonged to Turkey, but which through Ottoman weakness had become almost independent. The Porte – the government of Turkey, so-called from the sultan's habit of receiving envoys in the doorway of his palace – could do nothing more than protest, but the action mortally offended Serbia, which had looked on the provinces as virtually her own, and also created tensions with Russia, which regarded Serbia with special concern.

This crisis was alleviated by an agreement between Austria and Turkey – Austria paying financial compensation for the seized province – but feelings ran high again in October 1908 when the Kaiser gave an interview to a correspondent of the *Daily Telegraph*, in which his growing Anglophobia upset even his own ministers.

For a while it seemed that this latest indiscretion by the German monarch seemed to be having a salutary effect. Prince Bülow, who had been German chancellor since 1900, resigned, and his successor, Theobald von Bethmann-Hollweg, actually instigated talks between the British and German governments in an attempt to resolve their differences. But then in June 1911 the Moroccan crisis flared again, when the French, meeting with opposition from the Moroccans to their 'peaceful penetration', found themselves fighting a small war and being forced to annex more territory than they had originally contemplated. The Kaiser despatched a gunboat – the *Panther* – to the Atlantic seaport of Agadir, ostensibly to protect German citizens in the town, but, as everyone knew, actually to remind the French that he was keeping a watchful eye on their adventures.

This really was a serious event, and with Italy – naturally also interested in what went on in North Africa – Austria and Russia all making aggressive noises, mobilisation was expected daily, all leave being cancelled, and Murdoch was forced to abandon Broad Acres and move back into the depot. The Germans demanded vast territorial concessions from the French in return for allowing them a free hand in Morocco, which the French refused, and while the crisis simmered, the new British Chancellor of the Exchequer, David Lloyd George, a Welshman who had hitherto been regarded as a pacifist, made a violent but obviously carefully considered verbal attack upon the German position in a speech at the Mansion House on 21 July. Since speeches at the Mansion House, the town hall of the City of London, were generally taken to represent the views of the Government, and since this speech was accepted as expressing total support for the French position, war then seemed imminent, and there was great excitement.

The regiment was now back to full strength, with three squadrons, commanded respectively by Captains Ramage, Prendergast and O'Dowd, capable of putting six hundred men immediately into the field. More important, and gratifying to the officers, a large proportion of the troopers were veterans, men who had re-enlisted; in the all-volunteer British Army, enlistment was for a period of seven years, with the option of returning for another seven if desired, but there were regiments which suffered wholesale fall-outs when the enlistment period was completed. The dragoons, on the contrary, still retained men who had enlisted just before the outbreak of the Boer War and were as proficient soldiers as could be found anywhere in the world.

This was appreciated by the Chief of the Imperial General Staff, a new position, as the British had long resisted creating a general staff at all – unlike their European rivals – because of the suggestion of militarism which it conveyed. But the continuing abysmal staff work, which had led to such confusion between divisions and army corps as had punctuated the South African War and caused the disaster on the White Horse Downs, had finally made the War Office realise that a co-ordinated general staff was essential if they were ever going to fight a European war.

As expected, the appointment as chief went to Sir John French, making him the senior serving officer in the Army – although not necessarily the commander-in-chief if the Army ever had to take the field.

But he was responsible for the organisation of the various commands, and when he came down to visit his favourite dragoons, he told Walters and Murdoch that in the event of hostilities he intended to form a cavalry division, as he had done in South Africa, which would be commanded by General Edmond Allenby, who had served with distinction as a cavalry commander against the Boers. The Westerns would be brigaded, as before, with a regiment of lancers and one of hussars, and he expected their commander to be Brigadier General Hubert Gough, who had also earned much credit during the Boer War.

Meanwhile leave remained cancelled, ammunition was issued, and every preparation was made for the march down to Plymouth and embarkation for France, where the British Army would take its place alongside their French comrades to invade Germany and teach the Kaiser his manners.

'This is the big one,' Walters told Murdoch. 'The one we have all expected to happen for so long.'

'And all agreed could never happen,' Murdoch reminded him.

'Yes. What do you feel about it?'

Murdoch wasn't at all sure. On the one hand, tremendous excitement. This would be warfare on a scale not seen since the Battle of Waterloo. The regiment wore Waterloo as one of its battle honours, but there had not been a Mackinder in its ranks then. None of his famous ancestors had ever taken the field against a European adversary – the regiment had been stationed in India throughout the Crimean War. This would be a war which would really bring out military ability – or lack of it.

On the other hand, there was the very real realisation that it was going to be a killing war, too, on a scale never before envisaged. He had read everything he could discover on the Russo-Japanese conflict of a few years earlier, and could add that horrifying example of man's ability to destroy himself to his own experiences in South Africa, where a handful of Boers armed merely with good repeating rifles and some light artillery had been able to do so much damage.

He knew that every regiment in the German army, like their British and French counterparts, was now equipped not only with such rifles, but with several machine guns as well, and that the continental powers, again like the British, had developed field guns and howitzers which made those used in the Boer War seem like peashooters. He remembered the awe with which he had inspected one of the 'huge' four-point-seven-inch naval guns which had been brought ashore and mounted on carriages to combat the Boer Long Toms – then the biggest guns ever used in battle – and now the Royal Navy was arming its battleships with twelve-inch cannon, and were even, under the inspiring direction of Philippa's favourite Mr Churchill, now First Lord of the Admiralty, talking about *fifteen-inch;* his imagination simply could not cope.

Lee was almost hysterical at the thought of it all. 'That's absolute madness,' she cried. 'Civilised people, going to war over some crummy African seaport? It makes no sense at all. And for you to go wandering away to get your head blown off. . . .'

'One thing,' Philippa pointed out, 'he won't be away very long. From what I've been reading, there can only be one battle, because there'll be so many men killed right away with these new weapons, there won't be any armies left, and they'll have to call the whole thing off.'

Which sent Lee to her room in tears.

Happily, none of the countries involved took the ultimate step of provoking an incident which might have led to war, and gradually the tension subsided; the British press took the proud view that Lloyd George's threat of entry on the French side had made the Kaiser stop and think. Whatever the true reasons, the orders for mobilisation were reduced to stand by, and then cancelled altogether. The live ammunition was returned to the armoury, normal leave was restored and a feeling of anti-climax spread over the depot.

'Damned shame, if you don't mind my saying so, sir,' remarked the new Regimental Sergeant-Major, Bert Yeald. 'If these lads don't see some action soon, they'll be good for nothing but garrison duties.'

Not many echoed his sentiments. Lee wept for a whole afternoon, but now they were tears of joy. 'If you knew how I have *prayed*,' she said. 'It's the first time I have really believed there might be Someone up there. Oh, thank God! Now we can just get on with living our own lives.'

It was, for all the crises in the outside world, and in England as well, a peculiarly happy time for the Mackinders. Freed of the restrictions of having to live in the depot, and finding herself mistress of the grandest house in which she had ever lived, Lee truly blossomed into a capable, confident wife, mother and – when she was not pregnant – hostess. The staff liked her no-nonsense attitude and adored the children, while Philippa obviously enjoyed having her around all the time, and even Mother was now totally reconciled to her daughter-in-law.

Florence Mackinder was also doing her best to become reconciled to her daughter-in-law's family. As Lee's constant confinements made it impossible for her to return to Baltimore to visit with her family, the Caspars made a habit of coming to England whenever possible, always staying at Broad Acres. Often they were accompanied by Harry, but his growing reputation as a correspondent was sending him all over the world, and increasing his pessimism as to the future.

'Everywhere I go,' he told Murdoch, 'people are talking about the next war. And when people are talking about something all the time, they get to the stage where they actually will it to happen, without knowing why.'

'Well, for God's sake don't say anything like that to Lee,' Murdoch begged him.

'Man talk,' Harry agreed, and leaned back in his deck chair to soak up the sunshine, watch the ladies playing at croquet and defend himself as best he could from his nephew Ian, who at three years old was already proving himself a master of camouflage and the flanking movement on anyone he suspected might not be looking. 'It sure would be one hell of a shame if *anything* was to mess up this existence you have here. You have got to be the most fortunate people on earth.'

Murdoch was prepared to agree with him. Nor could he see how whatever happened on the continent could possibly affect the family at Broad Acres, except in so far as he might be sent off to fight – European events had never truly affected English domestic life in the past. That, he thought soberly – although he would never say as much to Harry – was only likely to be disrupted by events within the British Isles. And disturbingly, England *was* changing. Indeed, it seemed to Murdoch that the entire pattern of life as he had known it since boyhood was changing, for the worse, and again it was mainly the doing of the fiery little Welsh reformer, Lloyd George, who was taking the Liberal Party, and therefore the country, by storm.

Himself the child of a humble home, who had had to fight his way up to power and prosperity, his aim from the beginning had been the redistribution of English wealth. Appointed Chancellor of the Exchequer by Asquith in 1907, in the following spring he introduced a whole array of new taxes designed to soak the rich. England had used Income Tax on and off, as necessary, for years; now it became a serious item of expense to anyone with an income of any substance, and in addition, the new chancellor proposed to levy a tax on *un*earned income as well.

Florence Mackinder's small fortune, carefully husbanded and invested by successive Mackinders, and handed down from generation to generation so that it now produced a very considerable return indeed, was going to be heavily taxed. She immediately let two of the maids and one of the gardeners go.

Even more serious, however, was Lloyd George's determination to introduce an inheritance tax, which received the evocative name of Death Duties. 'Thank God your father willed Broad Acres directly to you,' Mother said. 'My

God, if he'd left it to me, you could well have to sell up when I die to meet the tax. As for when *you* die. . . .'

Murdoch grinned at her. 'That's not likely to happen for a long time, Mother. And by then, surely, we'll have had a change of government.'

The new measures did not immediately become law, as they were thrown out by the House of Lords. But this in turn provoked a parliamentary crisis, with the Liberals calling for the reduction of the power of the Lords. In the middle of it all, the old King complicated the issue by dying, to be succeeded by his eldest surviving son, George V, which led to another constitutional crisis and two general elections within a few months.

The year of the Agadir crisis was also the year of the most serious and angry industrial disputes the country had ever known. When the entire coal industry, some one and a half million men, went on strike early in 1912, the Government had to call out the troops.

'You won't believe this,' Murdoch declared to the women on receiving his orders. 'Tomorrow I take two squadrons of the regiment, dressed in fatigue overalls, and lead them to the Forest of Dean, to go down the mine there. And cut coal.'

There was a moment's silence, then Philippa burst out laughing.

After a moment Lee joined in. 'At least you won't be killed,' she said.

'Don't you believe it. I shall probably contract psittacosis.'

'I thought only parrots got that!'

'Well, it's some disease like that which miners get. As for actually getting killed, the third squadron is coming too – to protect us from the strikers. I think the world is standing on its head.'

'This I have got to see,' Lee said. 'Do you *know* how to cut coal?'

'Presumably there will be mine officials there to demonstrate.'

'It's going to be a scream,' Philippa said. 'Tell you what, Lee, we'll ride over with them.'

'You will not,' Murdoch told her. 'This could just turn nasty. Anyway, you'd better conserve your strength; wait until you see the laundry you're going to have to handle when I get home.'

As a matter of fact, there was no violence, partly because the pickets, and there were a considerable number, were overawed by the sight of the regiment parading before their mineshafts, and partly because many of the miners were relatives of the troopers. But that there was a good deal of bitterness could not be denied, and it was the first time in their history that the dragoons, marching through a town in their own west country recruiting ground, were booed, which had a profound effect upon the morale of both officers and men.

'I would never have thought to hear that,' Colonel Walters complained when they returned to the depot a fortnight later – the strike, at least in the west country, had collapsed following the Government's introduction of a Minimum Wages Bill. 'Makes me ashamed to be a soldier, indeed it does.' He peered at his adjutant. 'Are you ever going to be clean again?'

'With fortune, and a few hot baths.'

'You weren't intended to go down the mines *with* the men,' the colonel pointed out.

'Well, I didn't see that I could command them to do something I wasn't prepared to do myself,' Murdoch explained.

'You'll kill yourself one of these days,' Walters grumbled. 'But now we have to worry about restoring the men's faith in themselves, and in this crazy government of ours.'

The unrest was far from over. On the very day the regiment returned to barracks, a radical named Tom Mann was arrested for attempting to suborn other troops from their duty, and the wave of strikes continued throughout the summer and into the autumn, affecting principally the docks and the transport system.

To crown the feeling that a new era of uncertainty and even chaos was about to engulf the world, a fortnight after the dragoons resumed their normal training, news was received of the loss of the *Titanic*. The newest and greatest passenger liner in the world, labelled unsinkable by her builders, had gone down after striking an iceberg in the North Atlantic on her maiden voyage. Liners had been lost before, but none so large and so famous, and the death list – well over a thousand – read like a who's who of London and New York society. The world, especially the English-speaking world, was aghast at the disaster: if one thing had always seemed certain, it was that the aristocrats of England and New England died in their beds.

Nor was there any cessation in the steadily mounting international tension. Before the end of the previous year, indeed just about the time Helen Mackinder was born, the Italians, hitherto almost silent observers of the heaving European scene, launched an invasion of Tripoli, another of the Sultan's semi-independent satrapies. There was the usual round of protests and conferences, during which the Italians, while proving themselves unable to beat the Senussi in battle, yet managed to seize a good deal of territory which was not theirs, and set up the colony of Libya. But all of this became irrelevant when the various small Balkan states, Serbia, Rumania, Bulgaria and Greece, having observed the way first Austria and then Italy could get away with taking anything of the Sultan's they felt like, allied themselves together and declared war on the Porte, and turned the entire Balkan Peninsular into a battlefield.

The Great Powers were scandalised, but there was very little they could do about it, unless they acted in concert, and this they were not prepared to do, firstly because they were all interested to discover just how hard the Turks were prepared to fight for the remnants of their once far-flung empire, and secondly because while Austria opposed any extension of the various Balkan sovereignties, and especially Serbia, Russia whole-heartedly supported it, envisaging a series of satellite states guarding its south-western frontier.

In fact, the Turks were so rapidly and comprehensively defeated that the Powers *had* to call a conference and impose a peace settlement to prevent a complete disintegration of the Middle East, which hardly satisfied the victors, who soon fell to fighting amongst themselves. The situation was alarming in that it required only the interference of one of the Powers, unilaterally, to start another major crisis, but by now, in the autumn of 1913, British interest, and concern, was turning in another and in their opinion even more sinister direction.

Just before Christmas, the regiment received one of its periodic visits from the CIGS, who had remained colonel-in-chief. 'Just passing through,' French remarked. 'So I thought I'd drop in and have a chat, and discuss the orders you are about to receive.'

Murdoch and Walters exchanged glances; the general had wished to talk with them alone.

'I appreciate you haven't actually been given them yet,' the general went on, 'however, I can tell you, in confidence, that the Royal Westerns are being transferred from the Bath depot to the Curragh Camp.' He looked from face to face. 'You know where that is?'

'It is in the open country in County Kildare, in Ireland, sir,' Murdoch said.

'Correct. Excellent cavalry country. Indeed, excellent country for an entire army to manoeuvre in. Flat, empty plain, close to Dublin. . . .' He paused. 'Close to Dublin,' he repeated. 'There is going to be quite a concentration of troops there. Almost our entire armed strength. Must take these European fellows seriously, eh? If they want to rattle their sabres, we must rattle ours just as loudly.'

He paused, and the two officers waited. He was clearly talking around the subject, and his phraseology was odd too; as Chief of the Imperial General Staff it was his decision as to where, when and how manoeuvres were held. Yet his words suggested that this concentration at the Curragh had been forced upon him.

'I want you to understand the situation as it really is, however,' French went on. 'The Irish situation. It is becoming very serious. Do you know anything about it?'

Walters and Murdoch again exchanged glances. No one

in England could fail to know something about the Irish situation. 'We try not to, sir,' the colonel said.

'Hm. Yes. Well, I imagine you certainly know that the Liberal Party has had this bee in its bonnet about granting Home Rule to Ireland ever since Gladstone first raised the matter back in the seventies. God alone knows why he did; it has caused nothing but trouble ever since. However, there it is. We've had Home Rule proposals and crises ever since, all invariably thrown out by the Lords. And I'm sure that you do know that the last proposal, made at the beginning of this year, has also twice been rejected by the Lords. However, that is not going to be the end of the matter. I am informed that Mr Asquith is determined to reintroduce the bill early next year, and of course under the new laws curbing the power of the House of Lords, they can no longer reject a bill which has been passed for a third time by the Commons. The bill will be law next summer. Now . . . the people of Ulster are aware of this situation, of course, and they don't like it. They have had mass meetings in protest, and there are people – Edward Carson is one, and he should know better – who are openly saying that the Protestant north will not accept Catholic rule from Dublin, and will resist it by force of arms.

'I'm afraid our intelligence reports indicate that this is no idle threat. It is estimated by the Secret Service that there may be as many as ten thousand Ulster volunteers who are armed and train secretly, and are prepared to take the field should Home Rule become law. Ten thousand men, gentlemen. That is virtually the equivalent of a division. If it is well led it could be a most formidable force, and it would be fighting on its own doorstep, aided and abetted by its womenfolk, able to disappear at will and reform at will . . . very like the situation we faced in South Africa after the main Boer armies had been defeated – and at no time did Louis Botha or Smuts command ten thousand men.'

'With respect, sir,' Murdoch said, unable to believe what he was being told. 'You are speaking of a possible civil war, here in the United Kingdom.'

French stared at him. 'Why, yes, Major Mackinder. That possibility is exactly what I am speaking of.'

'Good God,' Walters said. 'But . . . I mean . . . Good God!'

'Obviously such a situation cannot be permitted to arise,' French told them. 'But yet it is a tricky problem, far more tricky, I may say, than any of the so-called crises we have recently had to face in Europe. The difficulty is that the Ulstermen are convinced that if it came to a crunch, they would have the support of the majority of the people of England. And no one knows whether they would or not. Nor can we afford to find out. Carson and his followers must be headed off by a massive display of strength and determination on the part of the Government. Thus the decision has been taken to send the main part of the Army to take part in prolonged manoeuvres on the Curragh. This is sensible in purely practical terms. We do need to hold largescale manoeuvres, involving every branch of the Army, and the Curragh plain is the perfect place for it. At the same time, it is close to Dublin, not Belfast, so no Ulster hothead can suppose we are sending troops to overawe them. Yet we will have a considerable force in Ireland, within striking distance of the north, and it is hoped that this fact will not escape Sir Edward Carson and his cohorts.'

'And if it does not, sir? And Home Rule does become law?'

'It is sometimes better not to try to anticipate the future too closely, Murdoch,' French told him. 'We are soldiers. We will obey the orders given us by the government of the day. I know that not all your men will care for such a task.'

'To fire upon their own kith and kin?' Walters commented. 'With respect, sir, that is an understatement.'

'Nevertheless, it will be your duty, as officers, to see that your men obey orders. We must all hope and pray that such a day never dawns. Tempers are running hot at this moment; what is required is time for them to cool. That is all we can hope for. However, I wished you to be under no misapprehension as to what is happening, and what could happen, as I said. Everything I have told you here today is in the strictest confidence; it is not even to be discussed with your wives. I want that clearly understood. Your officers and men must be given the impression that they are going to take part in extended war games, nothing more. But you yourselves will appreciate your real reason for being in Ireland, and the possibility that you may be called upon, at a moment's notice, to carry out a very unpleasant task. I know that you will do your duty, and that you will ensure that your men do theirs.'

'Will our families be accompanying us, sir?' Murdoch asked.

'No. It is intended to create conditions of actual campaigning. And besides, if it *did* come to a critical situation, they would be a disastrous hindrance. There is also another problem which you must at all times bear in mind. The British Army is not very popular in southern Ireland. It is not forgotten that we have visited them too often in the past as conquerors, and have had to do some unpleasant things to them, too. In fact, that is something that you are going to have to impress upon your men, right away, that any fraternisation with the Irish could be a risky business. I am sure you would not wish your own families to be exposed to any Fenian anarchists.' He smiled at them. 'No need to look so grim, gentlemen. I hope what I have suggested will never happen. And surely it is better than being sent back to India.'

Lee was aghast. 'You're going off to Ireland?' she demanded. 'For several months? Without me?'

'Well, it could have been India,' Murdoch pointed out. 'You always knew we were bound to be separated, sooner or later. And this way we'll at least get letters more quickly.'

'And there's no risk of him being shot or contracting cholera in Ireland,' Philippa pointed out.

If they only knew, he thought. But it was a wrench to be leaving Broad Acres after three such happy years – as they had been, despite the alarums and excursions in the world outside. He played a last game of hide and seek with the boys, gave Helen a last hug, had a last romp with the dogs, kissed all his womenfolk, and with Corporal Reynolds at his side walked Buccaneer, now a very experienced old friend indeed, down the road to the depot for the departure parade.

'Seems hard, major,' Reynolds commented, 'that we can't take the ladies. It's only just across the Irish Sea.'

'Manoeuvres are manoeuvress, George,' Murdoch reminded him.

There was, however, a curious air of why-are-we-doing-this as the regiment marched to Bristol for embarkation in January 1914, amongst both officers and men. Going to Ireland promised to be amusing, and safe, but it still entailed separation from wives and families, and it entirely lacked the excitement, the scent of battle, the suggestion of deeds of death or glory, that departing for South Africa or India had done.

'I don't suppose we shall win any medals for galloping up and down the Curragh,' Peter Ramage grumbled, staring at Lundy Island as the transport slipped down the Bristol Channel, already rolling to the winter gale.

'Except long-service ones,' quipped Harry O'Dowd. He was the only member of the regiment who was completely happy with their new assignment; his parents lived just outside Belfast, and he could not conceive that he was going to be stationed only a hundred-odd miles south of there and not be able to get up to see them every so often. Murdoch wondered what he would feel were he ever to discover the real reason they were going to the Curragh – and what his reactions would be if it did come to a civil war with the people of Ulster.

They disembarked at Dublin and marched through streets filled with silent watchers, as French had suggested might be the case. 'You'd think we were in a foreign land,' Billy Hobbs complained. 'I don't believe they like us at all.'

'We had a better welcome when we landed in Berbera,' Ramage commented.

'It's all this Home Rule nonsense,' Prendergast explained. He always kept up with the political news. 'They think we're here to overawe them when the Lords tell them they can't have it.'

'Bloody papists,' O'Dowd growled.

'What do you think of it all, Murdoch?' Walters asked, when they had reached their encampment and pitched their tents. There were certainly a large number of men – mostly cavalry – already in the area, and hardly a moment passed without a bugle call or the drumming of hooves. A summons from their brigadier, Hubert Gough, to an officers' conference the following morning had been waiting for them.

'Well, sir,' Murdoch said, 'It is damned noisy. And it is fourteen years since I lived under canvas for any length of time, so I don't think it is going to do my rheumatism any good, and we definitely could be in a hostile country . . . but it is a beautiful land, isn't it?'

'I was talking about the political set-up. This Home Rule business.'

They had studiously avoided discussing it before. Now Murdoch considered. 'Ireland is Irish,' he said. 'If they're hell-bent on looking after their own affairs, they should be allowed to do so. After all, we let the Australians and the New Zealanders manage their own show. My God, even the South Africans, against whom we were fighting a dozen years ago, have home rule. Why not the Irish? With adequate safeguards, of course. I entirely agree that we could never allow Ireland to become allied to a hostile power, or anything like that. But that doesn't appear likely to happen.'

'What about the religious question? As I understand it, there is absolutely no common ground between a Catholic Irishman and a Protestant one. They have hated each other since Cromwell's day.'

'Well, then, perhaps they should try growing up,' Murdoch suggested. 'For God's sake, Martin, Catholics and Protestants live cheek by jowl in the United States, in England, in Germany, without having to shoot at each other all the time.'

'What you are saying is that if there was an uprising in the north rejecting Home Rule, you would be willing to lead the regiment in there to fire upon people who are British citizens.'

'Sir John French told us not to anticipate, sir,' Murdoch

reminded him, 'but to do our duty when required.' And to pray, he thought.

For the time being, at any rate, there was a lull in the tension, as Mr Asquith and his ministers considered the situation and redrafted their latest bill time and again, suggesting that there might yet be room for a compromise. Meanwhile the army encamped on the Curragh got on with their manoeuvres, and thoroughly enjoyed themselves – especially the Westerns, who found in Hubert Gough a potentially brilliant cavalry commander, with an eye for country and opportunity, under whom it was a pleasure to serve.

The only drawback to their situation was the hostility of the Irish themselves, which meant that their social activities were confined very much to themselves. Murdoch was therefore the more surprised when, in early May, he received an invitation to dine in Dublin . . . and quite taken aback when he read the name on the card: Baron Paul von Reger.

13

The Curragh, 1914

Murdoch gazed at the printed piece of cardboard in utter consternation. It was a large visiting card, on which the name of Baron Paul von Reger was printed, together with his address, which appeared to be some schloss in East Prussia. And across it was scrawled, 'We should be delighted to meet you again, after all of these years, Paul.' It was addressed to Major Murdoch Mackinder, VC, DSO, Royal Western Dragoon Guards, Curragh Camp, County Kildare, Ireland. Underneath he had written, 'We are staying at the Royal Dublin, and will expect you for dinner, Thursday 14th.'

Which was the day after tomorrow.

His first instinct was to refuse. But he decided that would be stupid, and besides, he did not want to refuse. It would surely be amusing to see Reger again . . . and he could obviously know nothing of that strange interlude in 1906; while the very fact of the invitation made it apparent that he had recovered from his former hostility.

And then, Margriet herself . . . but did he want to see her again? Of course he did, the more so now that there was no risk of him again falling under her spell. He was married, in the happiest possible way, and as Lee knew all about her, there would be nothing clandestine in having dinner with her. In fact, he would write and tell Lee about it afterwards, and they would have a good laugh.

And he might be able to find out something about little Paul. Little Paul! The boy would be damned near twelve years old by now.

Additionally, the Regers were on his territory, for whatever reason. They would have to accept things as he wanted them to be. Besides, it might be important to discover just what they were doing in Ireland and how they had known where to find him.

He sent an acceptance, and arranged to have the night off; it would be too late after dinner to return to the camp, so Reynolds booked him into another hotel in Dublin. They arrived at five in the afternoon. Murdoch changed into sky-blue shell jacket and dark blue overalls, then took a cab, arriving in the lounge of the Royal Dublin at six o'clock sharp, as invited.

'Murdoch Mackinder!' Reger wore evening dress, and came forward with hand outstretched. He had changed very little in a dozen years; his yellow hair might have receded slightly, and he might have put on a little weight. He looked very fit, although Murdoch knew he could not be all that far short of forty. But his face had definitely coarsened, the curl of the lip more arrogant than Murdoch remembered, the eyes brighter, the smile more brittle. 'You are more handsome than ever,' Reger declared. 'And those medals . . . my dear fellow, I have never shaken hands with a genuine hero before.'

Sarcasm, obviously, but Murdoch reckoned that if that was the worst he had to put up with it would be a successful evening. 'Being a hero is a matter of luck. But you, a baron?'

'Also a matter of luck. But uncles do die, eventually, and nephews then prosper, even wildcap nephews. Now come . . . you remember Margriet, I imagine?'

Murdoch allowed himself to be escorted across the room to where the woman waited. Here was beauty, and wealth, and composure. Margriet von Reger wore a pale blue satin gown, cut square across the bodice to expose her throat and the tops of her breasts, over the left of which was pinned a huge dark blue satin rosette. The gown and bodice were decorated with wide vertical silver bands; the gloves were white kid, she wore a pearl necklace, and there was an aigrette in the upswept golden hair. Murdoch did not care to estimate the value of the rings on her fingers. And even the clothes and the jewellery could not match up to the calm beauty of the face.

Yet his gaze was more taken with the boy standing at her

side, hardly up to her shoulders, dark-haired where both his parents were blond, also wearing evening dress.

'Major Mackinder,' Margriet said softly. 'How good it is to see you again after all of these years. You have not met our eldest son, Paul.'

Murdoch bent over her hand, inhaled her scent – the same scent he remembered from eight years before – and then shook hands with the boy, who gazed at him with solemn eyes. My son, he thought – a fact of which both Reger and Margriet were aware. Perhaps he had, after all, walked into at least a sentimental trap.

'Ha ha,' Reger said at his shoulder. 'He is interested in uniforms. And confused. He thinks all British officers wear red jackets.'

'Most of them do,' Murdoch acknowledged. 'My regiment is an odd one.'

'Unique, one could say,' Reger agreed. 'And do you see that crimson ribbon, Paul? That is the Victoria Cross. It is the equivalent of our Pour le Mérite, eh? Major Mackinder is a true hero.'

He was being almost offensively effusive. But Murdoch smiled, and accepted a drink. He had walked into this with his eyes open, and must now enjoy the evening.

'And the blue and red one?' asked Margriet.

'That is the Distinguished Service Order.'

'Again, an award given only to men who have proved themselves on the field of battle,' Reger said. 'And the orange and blue?'

'That shows that I served in the South African War,' Murdoch told him quietly.

'Ah.'

Murdoch glanced at Paul; the boy's face seemed to have closed.

'He is a fine boy, is he not?' Reger asked, observing the glance. 'We have five others at home.'

'Five?' Murdoch raised his eyebrows.

'Not all of them are boys, of course. Two are girls. Including our baby. But I believe in keeping my wife occupied. Do I not, dear?'

'I am always occupied,' Margriet agreed.

It was difficult to decide whether she had inspired this evening, or was as uncomfortable as himself, Murdoch thought. Her face was certainly serene, but her fingers were nervous.

'But Paul is the only one of them to be born in one of your Lord Kitchener's concentration camps,' Reger said. 'He cannot remember what it was like, of course. But I have told him all about it. I felt it was my duty. What do you think of the way the British treated your mother, Paul?'

'It was hateful,' Paul von Reger said. 'The British are hateful people.' His eyes glowed.

'Paul!' his mother remonstrated. 'You. . . .' She glanced at Murdoch and bit her lip.

'That was unforgivably rude,' his father told him. 'I will speak to you later. Now go to bed. After apologising to Major Mackinder.'

The boy stood up, took his place before Murdoch. 'I apologise for my rudeness, Major Mackinder,' he said, clicking his heels and bowing as he did so. Then he said good night as formally to each of his parents and left the room.

'I hope you will not be hard on him,' Murdoch said. 'After all, you did ask the question.'

'And children have the rare privilege of speaking the truth, without giving offence, one trusts,' Reger observed.

'It is absurd to be offended by a child,' Murdoch agreed.

'Nevertheless, he was rude. But I shall only whip him a little.' Reger grinned at him. 'Now tell me, what are you doing in Ireland with your splendid regiment?'

'Training,' Murdoch said, trying not to think about the boy, because he could not help him now; the pair of them had been equally entrapped. 'That is all we ever do, nowadays.'

'Ha ha. But that is true of all armies. It is becoming too expensive actually to fight, so they train. Even in Germany we train, and send observers to look on at these little wars in the Balkans to see if we can learn anything.'

'We?' Murdoch inquired.

316

'Paul is a colonel in the Uhlans,' Margriet said quietly.

'A colonel? I remember you telling me that you were a reservist . . . my congratulations.'

Reger grinned some more. 'Being a baron helps.'

'But you mean your reservists have been called to the colours?'

'We are called to the colours several times a year. Our reservists are not . . . what do you call yours? Militia?'

'Territorials. That is because they cannot be forced to serve outside England.'

'Of course. Your last line of defence against invasion, eh?'

Murdoch stared at him. 'We prefer to rely upon our first line, the Royal Navy.'

'Oh, indeed. The never-broken shield. Our reservists, having no water frontier behind which we can hide, are required to be as professional as those in the regular army, to be able to join that army at a moment's notice and take their places in the line of battle.'

'That must be very comforting for you,' Murdoch remarked. He turned to Margriet, 'If not for your wives and families.' Having riposted as best he was able, he hurried on. 'But what brings *you* to Ireland?'

'Horses,' Reger told him. 'I am looking for some new blood for my stables, and Ireland, so I am told, has the finest horses in the world. Would you agree with that, old friend?'

Murdoch didn't care much for the term of affection, but he nodded. 'I would say there are some fine horses to be had here.'

'Good. Good. I am looking forward to discovering some. Ah, our table is ready. I took the liberty of ordering. I hope you do not mind?'

'Saves time,' Murdoch agreed.

The food was good, if somewhat heavily weighted in favour of cabbage and sausage, the wine was excellent, and the conversation deliberate.

'It was a wrench, in many ways, giving up the farm, the

whole community, in the Transvaal,' Reger said. 'We had been friends for so long, fought together, worked together, experienced many hardships together, and died together. But of course, you saw something of our life at first hand.'

'I did,' Murdoch agreed. 'And, of course, it was Margriet's home.'

'Oh, I think she was more pleased than I to leave it. Wouldn't you say so, my dear?'

'I would have hated to live all of my life in one place,' Margriet said.

'Exactly. And yet . . . once the war was over and we were allowed to get back to work, we prospered. It is a pity you never saw our little valley after we had rebuilt it, Murdoch.'

My God, Murdoch thought: he knows about our meeting in Johannesburg. He glanced at Margriet, but her expression had not changed.

'However, duty called, so we sold up and came back to Germany, and my estates there. You must visit us in Prussia, Murdoch. You would enjoy it. It takes me a whole day to ride from one end to the other of my property.'

'Sounds gross,' Murdoch said, carefully accenting the word to make it into the German *grosse*, meaning great.

'So I have become a farmer and a part-time soldier, while you have been soldiering and earning more medals,' Reger observed. 'And leading your men in famous cavalry charges, I understand.'

'It seemed the right thing to do at the time.'

'You were badly wounded,' Margriet said.

'That was afterwards. But I recovered. I always do.'

'And now you are a major. Soon to be a colonel?'

'One day, perhaps.'

'So we are both prospering,' Reger said. 'In our own chosen fields. I am glad of that.' His complacency would have been insufferable save that he obviously had no idea that Broad Acres existed – even if Murdoch could ride from one end to the other of *his* property in a couple of hours – and more surprisingly, neither of them seemed aware that he was married. No doubt that news had not been important enough to reach either the Transvaal or Prussia. But now

318

that he realised Reger knew all about his visit to Africa in 1906, he could only wait for the German to show his hand.

Sure enough, when the meal was finished and they adjourned to the lounge, Margriet made ready to leave but her husband shook his head. 'You remain here and entertain our guest for a few minutes. I shall not be long. Unless you would care to accompany me, Murdoch?'

The correct thing would be to say yes, Murdoch knew. But then Reger would just engineer another tête-à-tête, and he was both curious and impatient to arrive at the reason for the evening. 'I'm content, thank you,' he said.

'Of course.' Reger gave one of his cold smiles and left the room, while a waiter hurried forward with a decanter of port, three glasses and a box of cigars on a tray.

'Have you really recovered from all of those wounds?' Margriet asked.

'Yes. I must congratulate you on having realised all your ambitions.'

'My ambitions,' she said. 'Murdoch . . . I must speak to you. In private.'

He gazed at her through a cloud of smoke. 'You believe in living dangerously. Don't you know that's why your husband has left us alone?'

'Oh . . . he suspects nothing of us.'

'You mean you didn't tell him about Johannesburg?'

'My God . . . he would have strangled me, I think.'

'And you think he has forgiven me for "raping" you, back in 1901?'

'It would appear so, or he would hardly have invited you to dinner. But he has not forgiven me for allowing myself to be raped. Murdoch.' She leaned forward. 'My life is hell. It becomes more of a hell with every day.'

'I find it hard to believe that.' He looked at her fingers.

'Oh, these baubles . . . do you think they are mine? They are his, and he decides which ones I shall wear, and when. If I am heavily laden tonight, it is because he wishes to impress you. The same with my clothes . . . my very life. He parades his beautiful wife in public, so that he can take her back to his bedroom and humiliate her afterwards. My

God, if I were to tell you some of the things he does to me. . . .'

'I would prefer if you did not,' Murdoch said. 'What a man and his wife do together is private to them alone. You can always leave him, if he ill-treats you.'

'A wife, leave her husband, in Germany? And that husband a baron? I would be arrested.'

'You could have left him in South Africa,' he reminded her. 'Under the protection of British law.'

'I was so foolish not to. And you have not forgiven me for that.'

'On reflection, I thought you did the right thing. I could never have given you what Reger has, the things you wanted to have. I was angry with you for deceiving me, yes. But I got over it.'

'I will come to you now,' she said, and almost gasped at the boldness of her words.

'Now? With six children?'

'I hate the children. They are his, not mine. I will bring Paul, if you wish. He has been brought up to be a very proper little Prussian, but perhaps we could re-educate him; he is still very young. But *I* will come. Murdoch' – she rested her hand on his arm – 'I have always loved you. I dream of you at night. Murdoch, I would make you the happiest man on earth. I swear it. I will sacrifice everything for you, and keep on doing so. I. . . .'

'As you once said to me, I cannot.'

She stared at him. 'It is cruel to throw my words in my face. I was very young and very foolish then.'

'I cannot,' he said again. 'Because now I have a wife. And children.'

The stare grew in intensity, and then slowly relaxed. She released his arm and leaned back in her chair. 'An English woman?'

'An American.'

'An American?' Her voice was heavy with contempt. 'Do you love her?'

'Very much.'

'As much as you love me?'

'I do not love you, Margriet,' he said. 'I think I did, once, because of what we shared, and you risked and suffered, I shall always think of you with great affection, and if what you tell me is true, with pity. You are also the mother of my eldest son. But as you say, he has been adopted by Reger and brought up as his. To attempt to change that now would be to give the boy an intolerable burden of divided loyalties to carry for the rest of his life. And I am not in love with you now.'

'I would make you love me,' she said. 'I would. . . .' She sat straight, fingers twisted together, then untangled them and sipped her cold coffee.

'Do you know,' Reger said, standing above them. 'I have discovered that it is most remarkably mild outside. Why do we not all take a stroll in the garden? It is very pretty there, and there is nothing like a walk after a good meal to aid the digestion.'

'I am very tired, Paul,' Margriet said. 'I think I will retire.'

'You will enjoy a walk, my dear,' Reger said, his voice laden with authority and menace.

Margriet hesitated, then stood up.

Murdoch stood up also. The next act in the comedy – or the tragedy – was about to begin, and he was more curious than ever to discover what Reger had in mind. They descended the side stairs, the doorman hurriedly producing the baroness's wrap, and then went out into the scented garden, which ran down to the waters of the Liffey.

Reger led the way until they were out of sight of the hotel. They looked down at the river itself and the moored boats gleaming in the dull light of the street lamps, half shrouded in a slowly gathering mist.

'This will be thick by morning,' Reger said. 'But the more beautiful for that. I find Ireland a beautiful place. It is a shame the Irish hate the British so much. But then, so many people do hate the British.'

'I have a feeling that you are amongst them, Paul,' Murdoch said, deciding to force the issue. 'I think I should leave.'

'So soon? I was hoping you would tell me where you and Margriet have decided to meet.'

Margriet caught her breath, while Murdoch frowned; he had provoked more than he had anticipated.

'I observed her hand on your arm, my dear fellow. You were certainly having a very intimate conversation. Or were you merely reminiscing about your last clandestine meeting, at the Union Hotel in Johannesburg?'

Margriet took a step backwards, almost as if she would have fallen. Neither man made any effort to help her, and she regained her balance.

'I had you followed, my dear,' Reger explained. 'I have always had you followed. My wife, spending an hour in another man's bedroom. I would have been within my rights to kill you.'

'But you preferred to beat her instead,' Murdoch suggested.

'Oh, indeed. Without even telling her why I was doing it. She is a dull girl, really. But it is always a pleasure to whip Margriet. She cries so, and begs for mercy.'

'God,' Margriet whispered. 'Oh, God!'

'So I think I am entitled to challenge you to a duel,' Reger said. 'I still have the deposition of my agent in Johannesburg. His description is undoubtedly that of you, Murdoch. So I have the evidence that you are the adulterer, supported by evidence that you were in Johannesburg, using an assumed name, at the time. I am therefore in a position to demand satisfaction.'

They stared at each other, while Margriet looked from one to the other, holding her breath.

'You are in a position to demand what you like, Reger,' Murdoch said. 'And I certainly owe you an apology. When I met Margriet that day I was under the impression she was going to leave you and come away with me. I was wrong. But I have no intention of fighting you.'

'Because, for all of your medals, you are really a coward.'

'Because,' Murdoch said, speaking very quietly, 'duelling is forbidden in the British Army. And because, secondly, I have wronged you sufficiently. I have no wish to kill you into the bargain.'

'You?' Reger sneered. 'Kill me?'

'You have challenged me, baron,' Murdoch reminded him. 'It would hardly be a question of sabres. And I would blow your brains out quite without compunction, but for the reason I have given, and because you once saved my life. I will now bid you good night.'

'You *are* a coward,' Reger said. 'Perhaps I should see if a slap on the face will not put some fire into your belly.'

'Do that,' Murdoch agreed, 'and I shall break your jaw.'

Reger stared at him for a moment, then grinned. 'Then take yourself off.'

'You cannot,' Margriet gasped. 'You cannot leave me here, with him.'

Murdoch hesitated. 'I am sorry, baroness,' he said. 'But I cannot interfere in the domestic affairs of another man and his wife.'

He returned to his hotel, awoke a confused Corporal Reynolds, checked out and rode back down to Curragh that night. British troops were as a rule refused permission to leave the camp after dark except in groups of at least six strong, as there had been incidents where single men, or even pairs, had been set upon and beaten up by Irish Fenians. And indeed, Murdoch and Reynolds had only just left the lights of Dublin behind them when they found themselves confronted by half a dozen men, also mounted.

'Well, if it ain't a couple of Orange lads out for a midnight stroll,' said one of the strangers. 'Now, get down off those horses and bow to your betters.'

Murdoch looked him in the eye. 'If you do not take yourself and your louts out of my way,' he said quietly, 'I am going to break every bone in your damned body.'

The concentrated ferocity in his tone left no doubt that he meant what he said, and the matter was settled by the click of the hammer as Reynolds cocked his revolver. After a moment's hesitation, the Irishmen pulled their mounts aside, and the British pair rode on.

'Are you all right, sir?' Reynolds ventured, when the lights of the camp were in sight; he had never heard his superior speak so viciously before.

'I am fine, George, fine,' Murdoch told him. 'Just mind your own bloody business, would you?'

He hardly slept. His whole being was screaming at him to return to Dublin and accept Reger's challenge and blow the bastard's brains out, even if it meant being cashiered and tried for murder. And then? Take Paul away from his mother? That would be all he could do. And a great deal of water had flowed under the bridge since he and Lee had confessed their past indiscretions and she had offered to accept his son. Now she had two sons of her own.

To leave Paul, and his mother, to the whims of that sinister brute of a man went against the grain. Yet it had to be accepted. Once again that spectre from the past had risen up to haunt him and snatch away whatever dreams of permanent happiness he might have. But was it not his own fault for accepting the invitation?

But only a week later thoughts of even the Regers were swept from his mind when the regiment received a visit from their brigade commander, Brigadier-General Gough, who after reviewing the squadrons asked Colonel Walters and Major Mackinder to accompany him into the colonel's office. 'At ease, gentlemen,' he said. 'Sit down.'

They obeyed, while the brigadier himself sat behind Walters' desk; he obviously had something on his mind. 'I suppose you know that the Home Rule bill is to be introduced into the Commons for the third time within the next month?' he asked.

They nodded.

'And that since the powers of the Lords have been limited, if it is passed a third time by the Commons, as it will be, it will immediately become law?'

Again they nodded.

'I know there have been rumours that the new bill will contain an element of compromise, such as enabling the northern counties to opt out of the union with the south for a period of a few years. To my mind that is meaningless, and indeed, deceitful, if Ulster is in any event going to be coerced into a general Irish dominion at the end of that time. It is my opinion that the Government's course is almost certain to lead to civil war here in Ireland, and such a war could well spread to Great Britain. It is, of course, out of the question to consider such a possibility, even here.' He paused, and looked from one face to the other. 'It seems to me that someone has got to inform Mr Asquith of the feelings of the troops who will be required to carry out such a policy. Those feelings are almost wholly negative, so far as I have been able to ascertain. It is therefore my intention, as of today, to resign my command and my commission.'

They stared at him in consternation. 'Resign, sir?' Walters asked at last. 'Is that necessary?'

'It must be done now, Martin. If I resign *after* I have been given an order to march this brigade upon Belfast, I shall be a mutineer. I may tell you that there has indeed been talk of mutiny, amongst officers of your own ranks. That course I have not permitted anyone to contemplate. However, resignation is an honourable option, if it takes place in cold blood and before the event, as it were. There are several other officers who will be following my example.' He held up a finger. 'The more who do so, the most strongly will our view of the situation be impressed upon the Government. However, I did not come here today in order to persuade or coerce anyone. I am aware that neither of you has the affinity with Ulster that I possess. I wish you only to be guided by your own concept of duty, of patriotism, of right and wrong. I also wanted you to know, in advance, of my decision. And lastly, I would ask you to look kindly upon those of your regiment who might feel as I do.'

'Captain O'Dowd,' Murdoch said.

'Him, certainly,' Gough agreed. He stood up. 'It has been a pleasure serving with you, gentlemen,' he said, and shook hands.

'What a hell of a mess,' Walters commented after the brigadier-general had left. 'Brigadiers resigning? I've never heard of such a thing before.'

'Well, he comes from an Ulster family, of course,' Murdoch said. He was still brooding on O'Dowd.

'Maybe. But he was really appealing for our support, you know. I wonder just how many of the others have agreed to go along with him.'

It turned out that there were quite a few. The news of wholesale resignations by officers spread through the regiment with almost the speed, and the demoralising effect, of the cholera epidemic in India. Nothing like it had ever happened before in the British Army. And as Murdoch expected, Harry O'Dowd requested a private interview with the adjutant.

'Is it true about Brigadier-General Gough?' he asked.

'I'm afraid it is,' Murdoch agreed.

'And all the others?'

Murdoch nodded.

'May I ask, sir, if there *is* any possibility of the regiment being required to march on Ulster?'

'I would hope there is no possibility of that,' Murdoch said, as reassuringly as he could. 'There is talk of a compromise, and I am sure even Sir Edward Carson is a sensible man. After all, he is a prominent member of the Conservative Party, almost certain to hold office the next time they are in power. He knows the true problems facing the Government. I cannot believe he would willingly plunge the country into civil war.'

'You regard the entire onus for such an act to rest on the Ulsterman, sir?'

Murdoch sighed. 'I am sure there are faults on both sides, Harry. However, we are supposed to be living in a democracy. If a government representing the majority of the British people decides that the majority of the Irish people should conduct their own affairs, at least as regards internal matters, while we may not like the decision, we must abide by it – or the entire system breaks down. And when a democratic system breaks down, you have first of all anarchy, and then military tyranny. That is the lesson of history. It has never changed, and it never will.'

'With respect, sir, you are not personally involved,' O'Dowd said.

'With equal respect, Harry, I think every man, woman and child in the United Kingdom is personally involved in this one. Ireland has been a bleeding sore in the side of Great Britain for five hundred years. Is it going to remain that for the rest of time? Or are we going to attempt to solve the problem once and for all?'

'Have you any idea what it will be like, to be a Protestant living under Catholic rule?'

'Harry, this is the twentieth century. There will be safeguards, and the very idea of compromise arises from the desire to allow the northern counties to retain some measure of autonomy.'

'For a period of years,' O'Dowd said bitterly.

'While everyone learns to get on with everyone else. The essential thing, Harry, is that you will all still be part of the United Kingdom, and thus have all the safeguards of the law that such a membership provides. I am sure you will be protected, your family will be protected, and that, given time and goodwill, this antagonism between north and south will dissipate.'

'Easy to say,' O'Dowd commented, staring at the ground. 'I do not think I have any choice, sir, but to resign.'

'I would like you to consider that very seriously,' Murdoch said. 'I think you have a most brilliant career ahead of you. You are a soldier through and through, and what is more, you are an officer through and through.' Why, he thought, he might have been Edmonds addressing a headstrong young subaltern in 1901. 'You have not yet had the opportunity to prove your ability on the field of battle, but you can be sure that you will have such an opportunity soon enough, and I have no doubt at all that you will come through with flying colours. Resign, and you throw all of that away. Now tell me honestly, do you support Carson's stand?'

O'Dowd hesitated, and flushed. 'I think Ireland should be united and take its place alongside Australia and New

Zealand and Canada and South Africa . . . if it can be done fairly,' he agreed.

'Which is what everyone is trying to achieve,' Murdoch said. 'And what Carson and his fanatics are trying to prevent, regardless of common sense.'

'You spoke of democracy, sir. Sir Edward Carson surely represents the majority of Ulstermen.'

'I wonder,' Murdoch said. 'In any event, to say he represents the majority of Ulstermen and is therefore entitled to go his own way is like suggesting the MPs for the west country have the right to declare Somerset, Devon and Cornwall independent if they do not like a course undertaken by Westminster.' He could see that the young man was already half committed, however, and therefore virtually impervious to reason or logic, and so decided to try another approach. 'Anyway, how could you help Ulster's cause by resigning? Would you then join Carson's volunteers and become a rebel?'

'Good Lord, no.'

'Then what would you do?'

O'Dowd's shoulders rose and fell. 'I don't really know, sir.'

'Are your people well off?'

The young man shook his head. 'It was all they could do to put me through Sandhurst.'

'And you'd throw all that away?'

'How can I fight against them?' he cried.

'You will not be fighting against *them*. If we do have to move into northern Ireland we will be fighting against a few hotheads who will not obey the democratic process. Not your mother and father. And not any member of the civilian population who is not in arms against us.'

'They will all be against you,' O'Dowd said. 'Against us. Whether they are in arms or not, they will be against us.'

Murdoch frowned. 'Your parents?'

'I do not believe they will accept Dublin rule, sir.' O'Dowd's voice had dropped to hardly more than a whisper.

Murdoch sighed. 'Then it will be your duty to persuade them that it will not be as bad as they fear. I will arrange

328

leave, if you wish, for you to go up to Belfast and see them. You must do this, Harry, for their sake and yours. To leave the Army would be to ruin your career and their sacrifice. They cannot expect you to do that. And indeed, to stay with the Army is your best chance of affording them the protection they may need.'

'Even if I have to shoot some boyhood chum to do it,' O'Dowd said bitterly.

'If you have to do that, Harry, then he is no longer a chum,' Murdoch told him.

'Do you think you talked some sense into him?' Martin Walters asked.

'It is a quite tragic situation for a young officer to be in,' Murdoch said. 'From the way he spoke, I have a notion that his parents may even be actively involved in the Ulster movement. And yet he is a dedicated soldier who wants to do nothing more than serve his King and country and make his way in the regiment.'

'Well . . . we can't be held responsible for the sins of our parents,' Walters pointed out. 'Or there isn't one of us wouldn't be in the dock somewhere.'

'Agreed,' Murdoch said wholeheartedly, thinking of his own criminality as a parent. 'On the other hand, there aren't many of us who find ourselves in the position of having to arrest our own parents, either.'

'Good God, it could never come to that.'

'Nobody knows what it could come to, Martin. I hope to God our masters in Westminster sort the mess out before there is a tragedy.'

But they didn't. That same night the entire regiment was aroused by the sound of the shot which killed Harry O'Dowd.

Murdoch was horror-stricken. He felt like a murderer.

'Of course you cannot take responsibility, Murdoch,' Billy Hobbs argued. 'You did your duty, as the boy's senior officer, to talk him out of resigning.'

'Without realising just how much of a strain he was under,' Murdoch said miserably.

'You did your duty,' Hobbs insisted. Which was the official point of view. But it was none the less the saddest day of Murdoch's life when he stood with the colour guard beside Harry O'Dowd's coffin. The padre was uncertain as to the correct procedure in the case of a suicide, and Murdoch was prepared to pull every string he possessed to have the young man properly buried, but in the event the O'Dowds came down from Belfast to collect the body of their son. Walters had offered to do the handing over himself, but Murdoch refused to opt out of the responsibility.

'We have heard the Army may be sent against us,' Roger O'Dowd said.

'The Army is sent where the Government decides it should go, Mr O'Dowd,' Murdoch said. 'But I am afraid your son found the possibility too grave a responsibility to bear. I am sorry, believe me. He was a young officer of tremendous promise, and he was my friend.'

'Do soldiers have friends?' Mrs O'Dowd asked bitterly.

'Amongst each other, Mrs O'Dowd. I would beg you to believe that.'

'What a waste,' O'Dowd said. 'What a waste.'

Murdoch signalled RMS Yeald, and the colour party carried the coffin into the compartment. Then they stood back and saluted as the door was closed and the train pulled out of the station.

What a waste, Murdoch echoed.

Martin Walters insisted that Murdoch take a week's leave after Harry O'Dowd's death, and he went home to Broad Acres, where – like everywhere else in Britain – the news of the 'Curragh Mutiny' was the sole topic of conversation. Harry O'Dowd's tragedy was just one by-product of the whole miserable business. Lee did her best to make him happy, but he returned to Ireland still in a depressed frame of mind.

Indeed, O'Dowd's death cast a gloom over the entire regiment which was not easily dispelled. There were contributory factors. They had been on the Curragh too long. And there was no end in sight. Week after week drifted by, and winter gave way to spring and even summer, with the usual alarms from overseas, the usual now tiresome manoeuvres, under a new brigadier – Julian Byng, a son of the Earl of Strafford, very much an aristocrat but a capable and experienced soldier – and the usual letters to and from Bath. Lee even managed to come over to Dublin for a weekend in early June, and they were reunited for a couple of nights, but she could tell that Murdoch was an unhappy man.

He was the more unhappy because the whole thing had been so unnecessary. When Mr Asquith reintroduced his bill into the Commons, it had been watered down to such an extent that Ulster was allowed to opt out of the proposed Irish dominion for an indefinite period. This naturally did not please the Dubliners, and the wrangling went on, but the immediate threat of civil war seemed to have receded.

'So why can't we go home?' Ramage wanted to know.

'They'll move us eventually,' Murdoch told him. 'When they remember where we are.' He was more interested in the news that had just come through that the heir to the Austrian throne, the Archduke Franz Ferdinand, had been assassinated, with his wife, while visiting the Bosnian capital of Sarajevo.

'He had it coming,' Walters growled. 'If Austria wants to go around grabbing other people's territory, then they have to expect to put up with some knocks in return.'

'Hard lines on the poor Archduchess, though, sir,' Hobbs remarked.

'The Austrians seem to be blaming Serbia for it,' Murdoch said, studying *The Times*. 'Seems to me we could be starting on another crisis.'

He was far more accurate than he had intended to be. Three weeks later the Austrians bombarded Belgrade.

14
France, 1914

'The situation appears like this,' Martin Walters explained to his officers. 'Austria has apparently taken a very hard line with Serbia from the beginning, has entirely blamed the Serbs for master-minding the assassination of the Archduke. Apparently the man who fired the fatal shots, Gavrilo Princip, has been identified as belonging to a Serb secret society called the Black Hand – the whole thing sounds like something out of Sexton Blake, but they take these things seriously down in the Balkans. Well, anyway, the Austrians demanded virtual control over Serbian affairs until the business could be sorted out, and this the Serbs very properly refused. The upshot is that the Austrians issued an ultimatum. I must say, this sort of high-handed action is rather typical of the Austrians. But it was also a carefully calculated move.

'You probably know that President Poincaré of France has been on a state visit to Russia; well, the Austrian ultimatum was timed for delivery just after his departure, by sea, from St Petersburg, which meant that he could not be contacted and that therefore there would have to be a delay in any concerted Franco-Russian response to the Austrian move. But I'm afraid no one has any doubts as to what that response will be; Russia has made very clear her intention of opposing any infringement of Serbian sovereignty, which was what the Austrians were after. And now, of course, the ultimatum having expired, the balloon has really gone up.'

He paused to look over their excited faces.

'But does that necessarily involve us, sir?' Billy Hobbs asked. 'Even if Russia and Austria go to war?'

'No. Everything depends upon what the Germans do. If they refuse to get involved, well, then, the whole thing may simmer down. But the Kaiser's record in recent years hardly suggests that he will not want to become involved.'

'And if he declares war on Russia in support of Austria, then France will certainly come in,' Murdoch said.

'Oh, quite. The froggies are dying for a scrap, as usual, in any event. Especially with Germany.'

'But that still doesn't necessarily involve us,' Hobbs insisted.

'Agreed. But the Government feels that it must be prepared, *we* must be prepared, for whatever happens next. It may interest you to know that the Royal Navy, which has just completed its annual manoeuvres, has not been returned to a peace footing as is usual, but has been ordered to remain in a state of partial mobilisation. That is, the reservists are being kept with the fleet. Nor are the territorial battalions which are here with us being disbanded.'

'It all happened before, over Agadir,' Peter Ramage grumbled. 'Then it just fizzled.'

'Well, let us hope and pray that it just fizzles again this time,' the colonel said. 'Unfortunately, shots have been fired this time, and they weren't over Agadir.'

And there was hardly a man who actually wanted it to fizzle, Murdoch knew. They had been playing at soldiers for too long, watching the months and the years rolling by, performing duties which were as distasteful as they were unpleasant. They wanted to fight. Even more they wanted some relief from the unbearable tension of Ireland, the feeling that they were aliens in a part of their own United Kingdom.

And himself? He could not be sure of his own emotions. He wanted as much as any of them to be rid of Ireland, and manoeuvres, and peacetime soldiering. And yet he was haunted by everything he had studied over the past ten years, by South Africa, by the opinions of Harry Caspar – and by the feeling that once the tremendous latent force that was European militarism was unleashed against itself, it would not be a simple matter to confine that evil genie into his bottle again.

'Is there any chance of leave?' he asked Walters, when the meeting had been dismissed.

'I'm afraid not, as things stand at the moment. I am under orders to be ready to embark from Dublin at an hour's notice. Nor can I grant leave to any officer when there can be none for the men.'

Murdoch nodded. 'I accept that, I was actually thinking of the men. Some of them haven't seen their families for six months, and if we are about to be sent to Europe. . . .'

'It may not happen. In any event, they'd be separated from their families for longer than six months if we were sent back to India.'

The question was, what to write to Broad Acres, how much could he put on paper? Before he could decide, a telegram arrived from Bath:

WHAT THE HELL IS GOING ON STOP ALL MANNER OF RUMOURS STOP ARE WE AT WAR OR NOT STOP WHEN ARE YOU COMING HOME STOP HELEN HAS WHOOPING COUGH STOP DON'T TELL ME YOU GUYS ARE GOING TO FIGHT FOR SOME BALKAN COUNTRY WHICH I CAN'T EVEN FIND ON THE MAP STOP HARRY IS CROSSING ON THE NEXT BOAT STOP SAYS HE WANTS TO SEE YOU STOP WHEN ARE YOU COMING HOME STOP I LOVE YOU STOP LEE.

He smiled at her mixture of ebullience, indignation and concern. Theirs had been an odd marriage. They had been more fortunate than a good many army couples in being able to spend six years together instead of being immediately separated by an overseas posting, but even with three children under her belt, as it were, Lee had remained very much a bride. Presumably that was because she still found so much about English life, certainly as lived by the wife of a well-known and reasonably well-to-do Army officer, utterly strange. She always seemed to require to screw herself up to the required pitch before she could give orders to any of the staff at Broad Acres, and he would catch her looking at herself in the downstairs mirrors when she was wearing evening dress and awaiting guests for dinner with that quizzical expression of hers, as if asking herself, is this really me, standing here doing this, mistress of all I survey?

Equally she was given to gazing at him, when he was in uniform, clearly asking herself, am I really married to that handsome, famous man? She had never had to accept the fact that the uniform was for a purpose, that it might one day have to be taken away from her admiring gaze, and might return to her soiled with blood.

Now she would have to. And he had to tell her that, if he could. He cabled back: LETTER IN MAIL, and then settled down to try to explain the situation. He was worried about Helen, but there was absolutely nothing he could do about it, save tell her to trust Dr Williams and Sister Anderson. Having sent the letter, he waited and read the newspapers with the rest of the officers, and wondered what was going to happen next.

The situation ground on in a kind of inexorable dénouement. On the day Belgrade had been shelled, 29 July, there were the most frantic diplomatic manoeuvres, with all sides − except the principal protagonists, the Russians and the Austrians − calling for a conference and with Bethman-Hollweg, the German chancellor, cabling Sir Edward Grey, the British Foreign Secretary, offering to guarantee French territorial integrity, whatever the outcome of a war, if Great Britain would remain neutral. This was ignored, but by now the Kaiser, apparently thoroughly alarmed, was himself trying to bring about a meeting between Austria and Russia, and telephoning the Tsar Nicholas II, who was after all his cousin. This had the effect of delaying the threatened Russian mobilisation. But only delaying. The next day the Tsar, whose ministers had been in cabled consultation with Paris, hardened his attitude and decreed a general mobilis-ation, and at five in that afternoon Austria did likewise. On 1 August, both France and Germany ordered mobilisation, within minutes of each other, and later that evening Germany declared war on Russia.

The British Cabinet promptly responded by promising France to protect her coastline against naval violations, and a 'stand-by' order was received by all regular army units, but still the British carefully refrained from stating what their attitude would be to a general war. This developed within forty-eight hours, when Germany declared war on France as well. By then reports were already coming in of German violations of the Luxembourg frontier, and that they had demanded passage for their troops across Belgium. This being refused, the German army crossed the Belgian frontier anyway on the afternoon of 3 August.

Amazingly, it was not until two days later that Austria, who had instigated the entire crisis, finally declared war on Russia.

It was the invasion of Belgium which was the most serious aspect of the situation, from a British point of view. So far, nothing had happened to oblige the British to go to war. Germany and Austria-Hungary were preparing to fight France, Russia *and* Serbia. The odds in manpower were all against the central Powers, and so long as the third member of the Central Alliance, Italy, did not come in on the German side, Britain had every reason to sit on the sidelines – as she had during the Franco-Prussian War – and see how things went.

Except for Belgium. Great Britain had been one of the several Great Powers, which included Germany and France, who had in 1839 signed an international guarantee of Belgian neutrality, for all time. This had been all to the advantage of the British, for occupation of the Low Countries – the nearest part of Europe to England – by any hostile army was seen as posing a direct threat to the security of the British Isles; almost all the famous British European campaigns since the days of Elizabeth, and through Marlborough and Wellington, had been fought in Flanders – even Crécy and Agincourt had really been fought in support of a Flemish alliance. Thus since 1839 the possibility of having again to send troops to that rich, flat little country seemed to have ended forever.

But perpetual Belgian neutrality was also of the greatest value to France, now she was no longer the dominant military power in Europe. Her Belgian frontier was the only truly vulnerable part of her defences. Her eastern border was everywhere lined with high mountains, and even where the mountains ended, in the Belfort Gap, there was still very difficult campaigning country. The casualties suffered by General von Steinmetz in mounting a frontal assault upon the heights of Spicheren at the beginning of the war of 1870 had led to the removal of that officer from his command, and no one doubted that had the French been resolutely led the Germans would have been repulsed on the frontier and the unforgettable débâcle of the surrender at Sedan would never have been suffered. The French certainly had a resolute leader on this occasion, in Marshal Joffre. North-west of the Belfort Gap was the Forest of the Ardennes, which had proved difficult enough country to the Duke of Brunswick in 1792, and had been ignored altogether by the Germans in 1870, and was not going to be any the easier for them now. West of the Ardennes was neutral Belgium. It therefore had seemed apparent that the theatre of combat in the event of a fresh Franco-Prussian war would have to be the narrow north-eastern corner of France, the Belfort Gap, where the two armies would meet head on, and where German superiority in numbers would count for little.

Unfortunately, it now became obvious that the German general staff had determined not to become embroiled in one gigantic frontier battle in the east, but risk world opprobrium and violate Belgian neutrality, thus enabling their armies to sweep across the Flanders plain and invade France from the north. That this might well bring England in was hardly a matter for concern; the expeditionary force being prepared to move to France if necessary – in effect, the entire regular British army available in England – consisted only of five divisions, four infantry and one cavalry, which considering the scale of the German invasion, undertaken with some fifty divisions in several army corps, hardly seemed relevant. It would be a campaign like that of 1870 all over again, the French armies would be rolled aside, the British expeditionary force crushed flat, and peace would be dictated in Paris before the end of the year, at which time the Belgians could be paid compensation for any damage done and the matter forgotten. Similar frontier violations had long been part of military history, only to become important when the violaters *lost*.

Thus Martin Walters was in a grave mood when he called an officers' conference in the morning of 4 August, after he had attended a commanding officers' conference at the headquarters of General Allenby, commander designate of the cavalry division.

'I have to tell you,' he announced, 'that the Cabinet has issued an ultimatum to Germany, demanding the withdrawal of all troops from Belgian soil within twenty-four hours, or Great Britain will consider herself at war with Germany.' He paused, looking over the tense, expectant faces. 'I have further to tell you,' he went on, 'that the Cabinet does not expect that Germany will comply with this ultimatum, and that this regiment, and indeed the entire division, is under orders to embark for Le Havre at the earliest possible moment.'

Once again he paused, and Peter Ramage cried, 'Hurrah!'

'Hurrah!' the rest of the officers shouted.

Walters smiled. 'I am glad you feel that way, gentlemen. I have to say that I agree with you. Now, here are some details which may interest you. The entire regular establishment, less only training cadres, will be forming the expeditionary force. Sir John French will command. This is great news for me, and I know for all of you. General Allenby will command the cavalry, and the infantry divisions will be divided into two army corps, led respectively by Generals Smith-Dorrien and Haig. General Wilson has been made quartermaster, and will have responsibility for our arrival in France. And gentlemen, General Byng has been promoted to divisional rank, and we are to have a new brigadier.' He smiled. 'Well, not a new one. Brigadier-General Gough has been restored to his rank, and will command this brigade.'

'Hurrah,' Murdoch cried. 'Oh, hurrah.'

Again the command tent rang with cheers.

'There are two other pieces of information I have which

338

I know will interest you all,' Walters continued. 'One, it is reported that when it was suggested to the Kaiser that invading Belgium might cause Britain to fight him, he remarked that he was not afraid of a nation of shopkeepers with their contemptible little army. . . .' He paused to grin at them. 'I hope you will remember those words when you see a grey uniform in front of you. The other news is that Field Marshal Lord Kitchener has been appointed Secretary of State for War, with the duty of coordinating all military activities.'

This time there was a gasp. Kitchener had been virtually in retirement for several years.

'So you will see that we are deploying our maximum strength,' Walters told them. 'I may say that even Lord Roberts is going to play his part, old as he is. Now, as I am sure you all understand, there can be no embarkation leave, in this situation. Nor can we even tell our loved ones precisely where we are going, and when, as it is understood that there are several German submarines at sea which may well attempt to interfere with our transportation to France. I regret this as much as you, but there is no help for it. If all goes well, and we give the Germans a drubbing, then the whole business will be wrapped up by Christmas, which is certainly what the staff expects to happen. The regiment must be prepared to march to Dublin for embarkation the moment our transport arrives, except, of course, in the unlikely event of a German compliance with our ultimatum. As of this moment, even local leave is cancelled. I understand that our ammunition will be awaiting us in France. Are there any questions?'

'How soon can we hope to see action, sir?' Ramage asked.

'We will see action just as soon as we can get from Le Havre to the front line. Thank you, gentlemen. You may repeat everything I have told you to your men. Dismissed.'

The officers filed out, talking excitedly amongst themselves. Billy Hobbs hurried to his desk to start clearing up the various files and accounts, while Walters and Murdoch looked at each other. 'Well, Murdoch,' the colonel said.

'The big one. This time, really and truly, it would appear. Pleased?'

'I can still hardly believe it,' Murdoch said. Indeed, he was feeling a sense of shock. For all the Kaiser's sabre-rattling, the artificial hostility whipped up between the two nations, and, at a personal level, his own antagonism for Reger, he had never really expected Great Britain and Germany ever to find themselves at war. The two countries had been allies in many wars over the previous couple of centuries, and in fact, as far as he could remember, no British soldier had ever fired a shot against a German wearing his country's uniform: yet now they were going to face each other in battle.

Reger? Oh, he knew Reger would be there, with his Uhlans. Thank God little Paul was too young. But would this war lessen, or increase, the hatred the boy had been taught to feel for the British?

Walters, who of course knew nothing of Paul even if he knew something about Margriet, misinterpreted his expression. 'Of course,' he said. 'I know you are not Kitchener's favourite soldier. . . .'

'That's true enough,' Murdoch agreed.

'But on the other hand you are very nearly French's, so the two should cancel out. And French is in actual command in the field. If anyone can lick the Germans, he can.'

'Oh, indeed,' Murdoch agreed. And wondered why he felt so suddenly sceptical. That Field Marshal French could indeed beat the Germans? Or that anyone was going to beat anyone, in this war?

Predictably, that afternoon there was a telegram from Bath:

EVERYONE SAYS WAR MUST HAPPEN STOP ARE YOU COMING HOME STOP OR GOING TO FRANCE STOP PLEASE COME HOME FIRST STOP REALLY MUST SEE YOU STOP HARRY IS HERE ON HIS WAY TO PARIS STOP SAYS YOU AND HE MUST HAVE MEAL TOGETHER AT MAXIM'S STOP MAY COME ACROSS TO JOIN YOU STOP HELEN MUCH BETTER NOW STOP DO LET ME

KNOW WHAT IS HAPPENING STOP REPEAT DON'T REPEAT
DON'T GET YOURSELF SHOT AGAIN STOP I LOVE YOU LEE.

He replied in his usual style, LETTER IN MAIL. Then the
men and horses filed on board the transport in Dublin,
watched this time by cheering crowds, all antagonisms
forgotten in a common desire to fight the Germans. The
letter would have to wait until after they had disembarked
at Le Havre. In any event, thoughts of Broad Acres and the
dogs, of the children and his mother and sisters, of Lee
herself, had to be subordinated to concentration upon the
business of fighting and killing.

So now, he thought, to war. To that European war
everyone has expected for so long. To the sound of machine
guns and rifle fire, the shouts of brave men, the screams of
dying ones. But a war to be fought, in contrast to Somalia
or India or the veldt, in totally familiar surroundings, against
men as civilised as oneself, with the same essential values,
the same general historical backgrounds, the same hopes
for the futures of themselves and their families. That was
a reassuring thought. Less reassuring was the thought of
having to kill any such men. He felt almost like a novice
subaltern again; then he had wondered what he would feel
like when he saw a bearded Boer face in his sights. Tommy
Holt's death had ended that. Which one of his present
comrades would have to die before the killing instinct,
dormant now for seven years, would again be aroused?

The regiment disembarked on the morning of 14 August,
having spent a couple of bumpy days in the Western
Approaches and then the English Channel, but without
seeing a single German submarine. The transports had been
surrounded by siren-sounding torpedo boat destroyers,
which rushed to and fro at great speed with huge cascades
of water falling away from their bows, and overseen by the
huge, menacing, grey shape of a battlecruiser hovering on
the horizon.

In Le Havre, where they were greeted by cheering crowds
and a French brass band, their ammunition and remounts
were waiting for them; General Wilson had done his logis-

tical job well. Yet it was difficult to believe there was actually a war going on, because very little had happened in the ten days since the Germans had, as predicted, ignored the British ultimatum to withdraw from Belgium. Their invasion of that little country had apparently ground to a halt before the fortress of Liège, described as one of the strongest positions in Europe, and a French thrust into the Saar had also been checked, to leave the armies approximately where they had begun.

'These Europeans don't seem to know how to fight,' Ramage remarked.

But in France they were also greeted with stories of German atrocities in Belgium.

'Do you believe any of this stuff?' Walters asked Murdoch, handing him the newspaper.

'Not entirely. Maybe there have been one or two cases of rape. There usually are, when men get over-excited and manage to find a bottle. But wholesale shooting of Belgian civilians . . . the Germans are a civilised people.'

The rank and file certainly believed it. 'They are Huns,' RSM Yeald declared. 'By God, sir, Major Mackinder, I look forward to getting one of those bastards in my sights.'

The morale of the regiment was higher than Murdoch had known it since the day they began their railway journey north from Cape Town to fight the Boers. It was not merely the desire of professional soldiers to take the field after so long, or the euphoria of leaving Ireland and going on foreign service again – even if their foreign service left them closer to England than at the Curragh – they seemed genuinely imbued with a remarkable hatred of the German soldier, and indeed all things German, which had appeared virtually overnight. This would undoubtedly make them better fighting soldiers, he knew – but supposing the German soldiers felt the same way about the British?

The dragoons were the first cavalry regiment to arrive, and they found General Allenby and Brigadier-General Gough waiting for them, both impatiently anxious.

Allenby inspected the regiment as soon as it was disembarked. 'Good men, famous regiment,' he remarked tersely, shaking hands with Walters and Murdoch when the parade was completed. 'Now, gentlemen, I must ask you to move up to Le Cateau as rapidly as possible. That is the area of concentration determined upon for the British Expeditionary Force. Sir John French is already there with some advanced units. I'm afraid you will have to march it; the railways are entirely occupied with transporting French reservists to the colours.'

'I shall accompany you,' Gough said, 'if you don't mind, Colonel Walters?'

'We shall be honoured, sir,' Walters replied.

'The lancers should be here this afternoon, and they can follow on as quickly as possible.'

'I will see to that,' Allenby assured him. 'I may even come up with them myself. Better a brigade than nothing at all.'

'Are we going to move into Belgium itself, sir?' Murdoch asked. He had been studying the map, and Le Cateau was just inside the French border.

'I'm afraid you will have to ask Sir John that, Mackinder,' Allenby replied with a brief smile. 'He is presently coordinating our place in the scheme of things with General Joffre. Ah, here is Captain Desmils.' He greeted the red-trousered and blue-tuniced officer who had just arrived; his moustache was as bristling as any in the British Army, and his red kepi was laden with gold braid. 'Captain Desmils speaks perfect English, and will be your liaison officer with the local inhabitants. He also knows the route you are to follow.'

'Messieurs.' The French officer saluted. 'Shall we go and find the Boche?'

The regiment moved out that very afternoon, taking the road to Neuchâtel crossroads, where they would turn east to Amiens, Cambrai and then Le Cateau. 'That is Agincourt and Crécy country,' Murdoch reminded the junior officers. 'The British have been campaigning here for six hundred years.'

It was a magnificent march in the bright August sunshine. Huge crowds lined the streets, and even the country roads

343

were filled with pink-cheeked women and girls, gnarled old men, barking dogs and warlike young boys waving Union Jacks and cheering the English. Free wine was offered at every halt, together with apples and walnuts; bouquets of flowers were presented by pretty girls, who insisted upon being kissed. It became increasingly difficult to keep the men's minds on the tasks ahead of them, much less sober.

'Beats Somalia,' Ramage commented.

'Not even Cape Town was like this,' Reynolds remarked.

'Ah, but they know you have come to fight the Boche,' Captain Desmils explained.

It was indeed a pleasure to be in such a welcoming country, after the scowls they had experienced for so much of their time in Ireland, or the boos which were their last memory of England. The only unpleasant aspect of the march was the sudden deterioration of the news from the north.

The regiment marched about twenty miles a day, and thus it took them a week to reach Le Cateau, and it seemed that with every step the situation took a turn for the worse. On the evening of the sixteenth, when they camped outside St Saens, news arrived that the Germans had at last forced the surrender of Liège and were now set to burst into the remainder of Belgium – and then carry out the invasion of France. The Belgian army, under the personal command of King Albert, promptly fell back from the line of the Meuse, which it had been defending for as long as the fortresses held, to the area around the fortified seaport of Antwerp, leaving only holding forces to keep the Germans out of Brussels for as long as possible. This did not prove to be very long, however. The regiment marched by way of Poix on the seventeenth, through Amiens – and hysterical crowds – to Querneu on the eighteenth, and through Albert to the village of Bapaume on the nineteenth, when news came in of the Battle of Tirlemont, where the Belgians, although fighting desperately, were again defeated. Next day, 20 August, as the regiment arrived at Carnieres, within a day's march of Le Cateau, they heard that Brussels had been occupied by the Germans.

Nor was the news from the east any better, for it appeared that even the French armies were in retreat. It was easy to see that there was a great wave of uneasiness sweeping across northern France. People were openly packing up and saying that the Boches were coming, and there did not appear to be any way of stopping them; no one was offering free wine or bouquets of flowers now. The country east of Cambrai was full of British units, all marching on Le Cateau, but that evening a staff officer rode into the dragoons' encampment, to tell General Gough that the situation was changing far too rapidly for them to be able to wait until the entire BEF had disembarked and come up.

The regiment was commanded to advance immediately, in conjunction with all the available infantry, straight up and across the frontier into Belgium to take their places between the French 4th and 5th armies in holding the line of the Mons-Conde Canal. It was hoped that this left wing of the Allied armies would check any German flanking movement which might spread down through Belgium while the main French strength met their enemies in the Ardennes, where it was now supposed the Germans were about to launch their major offensive. That this possibility had been dismissed as most unlikely in pre-war staff talks no longer seemed relevant, nor the probability that the Germans would put their greatest effort into the swing through Belgium, not only because of the open country to be found in Flanders, but because, having decided to violate Belgian neutrality at all, *not* to use the terrain to their fullest advantage made nonsense of the action in the first place.

In any event, the word was now haste. It was a double march to Mons, their new assembly point, and it had to be done in twenty-four hours. The British Army, such of it as had arrived, streamed over the roads leading north from Le Cateau, through Denain and Valenciennes to Jemappes, marching all night, and arriving on the evening of the twenty-first, when they discovered themselves surrounded by pitheads and slagheaps; Mons was a mining town.

'Holy Jesus Christ!' RSM Yeald commented. 'Here we go again – shovelling coal.'

The good news was that the lancers were immediately behind the dragoons, and indeed they arrived at dusk, to provide at least the semblance of a brigade of cavalry.

'Now this,' Murdoch told the juniors, 'is Waterloo country.' For indeed the famous battlefield lay only just over twenty miles to the north-east, with Brussels only a few miles beyond that – and Brussels, they knew, was already in German hands.

Actually, there could be at last no doubt that they were in a war zone. The Belgian crowds who turned out to welcome them in Mons were enthusiastic but totally confused and indeed distraught at the way their country had yet again been turned into a cockpit. From the east there came a continual low growl which none of them had heard before, like an unending thunderstorm. The Boers had fired their Long Toms one at a time, and often with considerable time lags between each shot, as they had carefully chosen their target so as not to waste ammunition. This was non-stop firing, it seemed, as the French and German armies were locked in battle some sixty miles away.

The regiment arrived in the midst of the inevitable confusion which ensues when an army is thrust forward at great speed and sudden notice. Indeed, only a quarter of the BEF had actually come up by nightfall; the rest were still struggling along the roads from Le Havre. Gough's cavalry brigade was almost intact, but was given an encampment about half a mile back from the canal itself and protected from the north by a low ridge of land.

'They'll move us up to charge the Boche when the fighting actually starts,' Prendergast observed optimistically.

'Just as long as they do,' Ramage growled.

Late as it was, and exhausted as they were, there was still a good deal to be done. Murdoch and Hobbs appointed fatigue parties to dig latrines, the rest of the troopers got to work to pitch tents, and the farriers inspected the horses, which had suffered somewhat on the long walk up from the coast. Poor old Buccaneer was especially exhausted, and Murdoch realised that his favourite might have seen his last campaign.

It was after midnight before they finally turned in, and reveille was at dawn, only three hours later. But it appeared there were no orders, and no immediate sign of the enemy, so Murdoch rode up to the brow of the rise to discover what was going on.

He didn't much like what he saw. Before him the ground sloped very gently down to the canal itself, but the canal was neither very wide nor very deep, so far as he could make out. To their right there was a village, where from the flags flying, he assumed Sir John French had made his headquarters – those flags would be visible at a distance of several miles.

Beside the canal a road ran east and west, lined with elms, and these did provide an element of cover. The infantry was already deployed down there, having advanced from the encampments – like the cavalry behind the brow of the hill – to line the canal and face north. A wide extent of meadow gently sloped up again to another rise, where there were some more trees, and beyond the trees were the roofs of another hamlet, dominated by the church spire.

He walked his horse – a remount named Trajan, which he had more or less decided to adopt as a replacement for Buccaneer – down the slope to the nearest infantry company. 'How much water do you reckon there is, sergeant-major?' he asked the commanding NCO.

'Maybe five feet, sir.'

'You reckon the average German is more than five feet tall?'

The sergeant-major grinned. 'I do, sir. We'll have to hope he catches cold.'

There were also an inordinate number of bridges across the canal, which no one seemed to have thought of blowing up – they might not stop foot soldiers or cavalry from crossing, but should at least hold up wheeled transport, Murdoch thought, and then mentally kicked himself for a defensive mentality. If they repulsed the Germans, they would need those bridges for their own transport when they undertook the pursuit.

If they repulsed the Germans.

'At least that meadow gives us a good field of fire,' the sergeant-major observed. 'We'll be able to see what we're shooting at. Not like the bloody Boers, eh, sir?' He might never have seen Murdoch before in his life, but he recognised the South African ribbon, as well of course as the VC, and was proud to be seen talking to such a distinguished, and experienced, officer.

There was a toot on a horn, and an open car came along the road from the village, filled with red tabs and gold braid. Murdoch and the sergeant-major came to attention and saluted, and the car stopped to allow Sir John French to step down.

'Carry on, sergeant-major. Murdoch!' He shook hands. 'Good to see you. All well with the Regiment?'

'Looking forward to a fight, sir,' Murdoch told him.

'Well, I wouldn't be at all surprised if we get one. Reconnaissance indicates von Kluck isn't all that far away. And there's not a lot to stop him doing exactly what he wants. I've just come back from French HQ, and I'll tell you frankly, I don't like the situation one little bit. I suppose it would help if the froggies would learn to speak English. Half the time I simply have no idea what the bloody people are talking about. But I can tell you this: they're taking a mauling over there in the Ardennes, and are having to fall back from their advanced positions. So our job is to hold the enemy up while the froggies form a fresh line along with us and General Lanzerac over there on our left. What do you suppose that fellow is up to?'

He pointed with his swagger stick, and Murdoch gazed up at the lone biplane circling a few hundred feet above them, its engine making a noise like an angry bee.

One of the staff officers had levelled his binoculars. 'It's a Jerry, all right, sir. I can see the black crosses.'

'Having a look at what we're doing,' French grumbled. 'I don't suppose one of your people could drive him away, Manton?'

The colonel of the infantry battalion had arrived. 'Oh, indeed, sir. We'll let him know he's not welcome.'

Orders were given, and several marksmen were brought

348

up from the canal bank to aim at the aeroplane and fire. It was impossible to say if they hit it, but they must have come pretty close because after a few rounds the machine buzzed away to the north-east.

'Whatever is warfare coming to,' French remarked, 'when they can look down on us like that?'

'Not like the old-fashioned sort,' remarked another staff officer, pointing across the meadow beyond the canal, where several horsemen by the copse were obviously inspecting the British position through binoculars. Even at a distance they could be seen to be wearing coal scuttle helmets.

'Uhlans!' Murdoch snapped.

'Hm,' French commented. 'Well, we can't just let them count heads. Send a message to Colonel Bradstreet, Major Hopton, and ask him to dispatch a squadron of lancers to drive those fellows away.'

'With respect, sir,' Murdoch protested. 'The dragoons can do that.'

French grinned at him. 'I'm keeping your people up my sleeve as infantry replacements, Murdoch. God knows when the rest of the army is going to get here. And we could have a battle on our hands at any moment.'

It was a disappointment, but Murdoch returned to the hillock above the Westerns' encampments, and with the other officers stood and watched the lancers wading their horses across the canal and then setting off with cheers after the Uhlans – who allowed them to approach for a while, and then turned and cantered off. The lancers disappeared behind the copse and the next rise, there was a shot or two, and then they came back in some haste. It was not until dusk that news of what they had found filtered back to the dragoons; on topping the rise beyond the copse they had seen an enormous mass of German troops moving towards them: the captain commanding the squadron estimated not less than an army corps.

'How many men are there in a German army corps, Murdoch?' Billy Hobbs asked, as they ate their supper while the sun slowly sank into the west.

'About ninety thousand.'

'And how many men does French have here?'

'Well, there's one infantry division, certainly, and the better part of another, and one brigade of cavalry . . . say thirty thousand.'

'Long odds.'

Murdoch grinned at him. 'But we have the canal. All five feet of it.'

It was an eerie feeling to know that only a few miles away there was a huge enemy army – in fact, it was even more eerie to realise that this was the first time he had ever been about to engage a superior force, in real terms. The Boers had always been outnumbered, and if the Somalis had mustered ten to one against his squadron in the Togdheer, that discrepancy had been amply made up for by the dragoons' modern weapons.

Of course, the British force, small as it was for a modern army, was but a part of the huge French force to either side of them.

Indeed, red-trousered and blue-coated staff officers kept arriving at the British headquarters in a steady stream all evening, attempting to coordinate whatever strategy the Allies had decided to follow. They looked splendid when seen against the drab khaki-clad British – one of them was even a curassier, in burnished helmet and breastplate – but they would be visible for miles: a Boer sharpshooter would have been licking his lips.

There was also the sombre thought that these gaudily dressed but undoubtedly brave and competent Frenchmen had not managed as yet to check the German advance.

Martin Walters joined Murdoch for an after-dinner pipe. 'You've never smoked, have you, Murdoch?' he asked, stretching out his booted feet; they were sitting on camp chairs in front of their tents, while Reynolds and the colonel's batman, Harper, poured brandies.

'I enjoy an after-dinner cigar.'

'It's a great comfort,' Walters observed. 'Settles the nerves. I have a feeling that firing over there has died down somewhat.'

'Maybe. Just a little. But they're still fighting.' Murdoch pointed. The eastern sky, now that the sun was all but gone, was bright, as if the lights of a huge city were burning just over the horizon.

'Yes,' Walters observed. 'But it's definitely moved south.'

'Because the French are pulling back.'

'Yes,' Walters said again. 'Just as long as they don't pull back behind us.' He brooded for a few minutes. 'Have you heard from Lee?'

'Not yet. Have you had mail?'

'No, nothing's caught up with us, I suppose. What does she think about it all?'

'I have no idea. And I'd rather not find out, right this minute. I should think she's having kittens.'

'Yes. Did you know I was due to retire next year?'

'I seem to remember Judith saying something about it . . . oh, a long time ago.'

'I shan't now, of course. Unless this thing is over by then. It *will* be over by then, don't you think, Murdoch?'

It occurred to Murdoch that his commanding officer was nervous, and also, again with a sense of shock, that he had never actually followed Martin Walters into battle.

'I should think so, sir,' he said. 'If we stop them here, and then the Russians get going over in Poland, why, I should think even the Kaiser will be happy to sue for peace before he gets mangled.'

'Yes, I'm sure you're right,' Walters said. 'All we have to do is give them a bloody nose here.' He got up. 'I suppose we'd better turn in; they may be here tomorrow.' He took a couple of steps, and then stopped and looked back. 'When I retire, I'm going to become a pig farmer. That's something I've always wanted to do, farm pigs.'

Murdoch scratched his head. He could not imagine Judith Walters farming pigs.

Murdoch followed his colonel's suggestion and went to his tent as soon as he had finished his brandy and inspected the sentries. He slept soundly, and was awakened by a most unearthly noise, a high-pitched whining followed by an enormous explosion which shook the earth. He rolled out of his sleeping bag and sat up, pushing hair from his eyes, and gazed at a lantern, behind which was Reynolds.

'My God, sir,' the corporal said. 'My – ' his voice was drowned by another screaming wail, and another explosion.

'Heavy artillery,' Murdoch shouted above the din, reaching for his clothes and dragging them on. Cramming his cap on his head, he ran outside. It was very dark, although the village, perhaps a mile away to the right, was burning fiercely and sending a huge red glow over the pre-dawn sky. But the noise was very nearly paralysing. Apart from the screams of the shells and the huge *crumps* when they struck, there were men shouting, horses neighing and a bugle blaring.

'For God's sake stop that racket,' Murdoch bawled at Bugler Summerton, who was sounding assembly over and over again. 'We're all here. Sergeant-Major Yeald! Where are you, sergeant-major?'

Yeald came hurrying out of the darkness, also only half-dressed. 'Sir!'

'Casualties?'

'None as yet, sir. I don't think they're aiming at us. It's the village what's getting it.'

The German gunners had obviously laid their sights on those flags, Murdoch thought grimly. 'Very good, sergeant-major. Put extra men to guarding the horses. Captain Ramage!'

'Sir!'

'Find Prendergast and Pinder. We're reasonably protected by that hillock, save from splinters. Have the men lie down below the brow until the firing stops. Sergeant Alloway!'

'Sir!' The quartermaster sergeant came to attention.

'Have the pioneers strike those tents. They're only going to attract attention.'

'Yes, sir.'

Colonel Walters came hurrying up, straightening his tie. 'What in the name of God is going on?'

352

'The Germans are shelling our position, sir. Obviously they mean to advance.'

'What time is it?'

'Two thirty. It'll be daylight in another couple of hours.'

'There's another one.' Walters half-ducked, then stood straight again, giving Murdoch a somewhat shamefaced glance. But that his nerve was shaken was obvious.

'I think we should take cover with the men, sir,' Murdoch suggested gently.

They joined Billy Hobbs and the headquarters staff, near the brow of the hill, crouching behind some bushes and in a slight hollow, while the shells continued to scream overhead. Murdoch soon left them and crawled from group to group of troopers to reassure them. In fact, it was remarkable how little damage the shells were doing to their position – mainly, he supposed, because the Germans were indeed concentrating their fire on the burning village. However, he could not help remembering how the Boers had always come up, full of fight and apparently unscathed, after the heaviest British bombardments in South Africa. The noise remained ear-shattering and unceasing, and would, he knew, soon have its effect on morale: too many of the dragoons had never seen action.

'Why can't we fire back, sir?' asked Corporal Matheson. 'Don't we have any artillery of our own?'

'Indeed we do, corporal,' Murdoch agreed. 'But the enemy obviously don't have our position pin-pointed. It'd be a shame to tell them where we are, now wouldn't it?' He grinned at the anxious faces just becoming visible as the darkness began to fade. 'And if we did them as much damage as they are doing to us, it'd be an awful waste of ammunition.'

The bombardment stopped as suddenly as it had begun, and the silence was quite deafening. All sounds were for the moment blocked out by ringing in the ears. By now the darkness was definitely going fast. Murdoch stood up and looked down the slope to the canal, where the infantry had already been called forward to their positions and were lying or kneeling in a long line of hardly distinguishable figures

353

in the slowly lightening gloom. That they must have suffered some casualties was obvious from the number of shattered trees and the shell craters which dotted the ground; these had in places burst the canal bank itself, threatening to turn the whole area into a bog. He could see the busy parties of stretcher bearers, hear the cries and groans which seeped out of the morning.

'My God!' Walters was at his elbow. 'Look over there.'

Murdoch levelled his binoculars at the distant copse where the Uhlans had been seen the previous day, on a rise perhaps a mile and a half from the canal itself. As he watched he saw the entire hillside become covered with men, grey-clad troops, advancing in an orderly mass, bayoneted rifles thrust forward, spiked pickelhaube helmets making them appear almost like thousands of spearmen against the sudden red that filled the eastern sky.

'There must be thousands of them,' Billy Hobbs commented in an awed whisper.

Murdoch wondered if the Highland Brigade advancing on Magersfontein Ridge had appeared like that to the Boers.

There was a drumming of hooves, and Brigadier-General Gough himself galloped up to them; he had left his staff far behind. 'There seem to be a great number of those fellows, Martin,' he remarked to Walters. 'We need every rifleman we can get. Sir John would like you to take your regiment down to the canal, next to the Buffs.'

'Oh, indeed,' Walters agreed. 'Bugler. . . .'

'Let's keep them guessing, sir,' Murdoch suggested. 'The men are all standing by.' He ran off, sending Hobbs in the other direction, and within five minutes had all three squadrons ready. The horses were left under the care of half a troop; the other five hundred and fifty men, having abandoned their swords, moved forward down the slope to the canal bank. Here a gap had been left for them by the Buffs, the East Kent Regiment, who had suffered heavily during the bombardment and been ordered to close up. The two regiments greeted each other with affectionate chaff – they each knew the worth of the other – and then the dragoons prepared themselves for the coming contest.

354

'Easy now, lads,' Murdoch told the troopers, walking along behind them. 'Settle yourselves and take your time. Remember to pick your target and aim at it. You have all the advantage here, lying down while the enemy are standing up and advancing. Just keep your eyes on them and cut them down.'

He spoke quietly and confidently, and yet had a feeling of total unreality as he watched the approaching Germans. There could hardly be less than twenty thousand of them, he estimated, in virtual parade order, trampling through the grass and round the bushes. He did not suppose anything like this had been seen since Waterloo, when the French infantry had toiled up a hillside very like this to attack the British position. But the Germans were coming down the hill, and at Waterloo it had not been possible to kill a man at much over a hundred yards. This was 1914, and the Germans were already well inside the mile.

The British field guns opened fire, sending bursting little balls of smoke to explode over the heads of the advancing infantry. Even at a distance and without glasses it was possible to see men falling this way and that. But the advance never checked.

Gough had returned to be with them. 'I would say they are within range now, Martin,' he remarked quietly.

'Regiment will prepare to fire,' Walters said, joining Murdoch to walk up and down behind the men. 'Choose your targets. Take your time. Now, rapid fire at will.'

The rifles rippled, the Hotchkiss guns chattered; the entire British position erupted in flame and smoke. The day was now quite bright, although the sun had not yet risen, and the grey mass was starting to become individuals. It was also starting to lose its confidence as the bullets tore into it. Men fell right and left. It was impossible to accept that they were human beings, or that it was the regiment's bullets which were destroying them so easily. But they were capable of replying. As the line crumpled, men began to drop to their knees and level their rifles, and there were sinister thuds and crumps from all around them. The officers remained standing, of course – it was traditional in the British Army – but Murdoch thought it was a miracle none of them were hit, although of course the Germans were hardly in a position to take deliberate aim, under fire themselves and no doubt exhausted by their march.

Remarkably, they *were* still advancing, having fired off a volley, with the courage of brave and totally dedicated men, while the British, all along the canal bank, poured more and more fire into them. Murdoch saw Peter Ramage himself lying down with a rifle, firing with his men – he was almost tempted to do the same. The Germans struggled to within a few hundred yards of the water, and then at last began to fall back, leaving little grey clumps scattered all over the meadow. The British burst into cheers as the order to cease fire spread along the ranks.

'Coffee, sir?' Corporal Reynolds arrived bearing a tray. 'I added a little shot of brandy,' he said in a hoarse whisper.

'That was thoughtful of you, George. Colonel?'

Walters took a cup. 'Well,' he said. 'We certainly settled that one in a hurry.' He surveyed the meadow, now quite bright as the sun was up, and the dead and dying Germans. He turned his head as Hobbs and the Reverend Dai Llewellyn came up. 'Casualty report, Mr Hobbs?'

'Three men slightly wounded, sir.'

'It was like a miracle,' Llewellyn said. He was apt to get carried away at moments like this. 'One almost felt the beating of invisible wings above our heads. But those poor fellows . . . how many of them do you suppose have fallen for the last time.'

'One hell of a lot,' Murdoch told him. 'Have some coffee, padre. Billy?'

'Rather! I must say, the whole battle was rather like potting –' He gave a little gasp and half turned, while blood splattered the tunics of both Llewellyn and Murdoch. Then Hobbs slumped to the ground, the coffee cup rolling away from his hand.

'My God!' Walters said.

Murdoch knelt beside Hobbs. He had been shot through the head, and was dead. For a moment Murdoch felt quite numb. If they had never been the closest of friends, Billy

Hobbs was still virtually the first person he had spoken to on joining the regiment, and over the past few years he and Amy had often made up a four to play auction bridge with Lee and himself. Now, to see him lying there with his brains scattered across the grass . . . yet oddly, Murdoch felt no great sense of anger, merely an immense sadness, that Billy should have been the first member of the regiment to be killed in this war, and on Britain's first day of the war, virtually.

But it was unlikely that he would be the last.

Murdoch looked up at Walters and Llewellyn, both of whom were standing as if turned to stone, far more shocked than he was by the suddenness of what had happened. 'I think perhaps we should take some cover, gentlemen,' he suggested. 'Those fellows aren't bad shots, after all.'

The Germans attacked again, twice more during the day. They had obviously been given orders to sweep the 'contemptible' little British army from in front of them, and they were determined to do so. But it was impossible for flesh and blood to prevail against the hail of accurate rifle and machine-gun fire which played upon them as they came forward across the meadow. For all their immense training, their marvellous courage and determination, they simply had not gained the experience of ever fighting against well-trained riflemen – and, thanks to the grim lessons learned in the Boer War, every soldier in the British Army was a marksman, thus quadrupling the fire-power of the little force Sir John French had been able to bring into action.

The field marshal handled his resources with consummate skill, pushing up fresh units as they arrived to fill any gaps in the line, personally overseeing the disposition of the men and making them aware of his presence. When towards evening the Germans withdrew for what was obviously the last time, leaving several thousand casualties scattered across the once green but now brown and grey and red meadow, the British soldiers raised a great cheer.

'That's what we came here to do, sir,' RSM Yeald said. 'To teach the bastards a lesson.'

Murdoch went from squadron to squadron to discover the casualties. They had been quite amazingly light. Apart from Billy Hobbs, four men had been killed and a dozen wounded, only three of them seriously. He told Prendergast to form a burial party, and although the Reverend Llewellyn was not happy at such haste, the five men were interred immediately, each squadron being represented at the ceremony by ten men, while the work went on of preparing for the night; it was a close August evening, and Murdoch did not care to think what that meadow was going to be like in another twenty-four hours. Then he and Walters and the padre visited the wounded; the most serious were being prepared for despatch back to the base hospital in Le Cateau.

'Means a spell in Blighty,' Walters told them, lighting their cigarettes for them.

'Just as we were winning,' said Trooper Graves.

'You did your bit,' Murdoch assured him.

'Now I have to write to poor Amy,' Walters said, as they walked back to where the regiment was preparing dinner, leaving only sentries to watch the canal.

'Hobbs wasn't even really a combat officer,' Llewellyn remarked.

'I don't think this war is going to make much distinction,' Murdoch said, and then cocked his head. 'Brass.'

Two motor cars drew up, and the great men got down. 'Colonel Walters! Major Mackinder! My congratulations.' Sir John French looked tired but triumphant. 'Your men performed splendidly. In fact, every man in the army performed splendidly. I am proud of you all.'

'Will you join us for supper, sir?' Murdoch asked. There was an immensely savoury smell of chicken stew coming from Reynolds' cooking pot, and he thought it diplomatic to ask the field marshal to partake before French thought of asking where the chickens had come from.

'Why, that is very decent of you, Murdoch. Have you enough for us all?'

'I think so, sir.' Reynolds never under-catered.

They ate chicken and drank brandy, and enjoyed both

the magnificence of the evening and the euphoria of having achieved a complete victory; that the troopers also felt at peace with themselves and the world was evidenced by the cheerful chatter coming from only a few feet away.

'Damned bad luck about Hobbs,' French remarked. 'I am going to have to issue a general order requesting officers to take more care. Same thing happened in South Africa. Not that I want to interfere with an officer's duty, of course. His men have to see him. But there are limits.'

'Will they come again tomorrow, sir?' Walters asked.

'They may well, if they are foolhardy enough. But if they do, we'll kill some more. In any event, if the frogs have done half as well on either side of us, we should be thinking about counter-attacking by tomorrow afternoon. We should hear from them fairly soon.'

In fact, they had only just completed their meal and were lighting up their cigars when a staff officer rode into the encampment and dismounted.

'My God, Warrington,' the field marshal remarked. 'You look done up.'

The major's uniform was stained with dust and his horse was blown. Reynolds hastily gave him a glass of brandy, which he tossed off at a gulp. 'General Lanzerac is in retreat, sir,' he said.

French frowned at him. 'In retreat? No one told me he was planning to retreat.'

'The orders came through just after I reached him, sir,' the major explained. 'His people have been under heavy attack all day, and he is now pulling out, after having suffered heavy casualties. It appears the Germans got right up to the canal in the French sector and were only driven back after severe hand-to-hand fighting. They are still there, Sir John. I saw them, grey and red and blue, scattered around at bayonet range.'

'They wanted to fight with the bayonet,' Gough commented. 'No rifle fire for them.'

'And now they're pulling back, without informing anyone,' General Douglas Haig, commanding the army corps, commented in disgust. 'Damned frogs.'

'General Lanzerac is acting under orders from Marshal Joffre, sir,' Warrington said. 'He assumed you had received similar orders. The fact is, Marshal Joffre has ordered a general retreat, in the eastern sector as well. It has now definitely been determined that the main German strength is advancing through Belgium, that is, against the French Fifth Army and the BEF.'

Better late than never, Murdoch thought.

'By God,' French said. 'By God. Marshal Joffre's orders have certainly not reached me as yet. Well, then, gentlemen, we seem to have no choice. We will have to pull back. Immediately.' He got up, and the other officers rose with him.

'You mean retreat?' Colonel Walters asked. 'After winning such a clear-cut victory?'

'We can't take on the whole German army on our own, colonel. No, the BEF must withdraw. But we will do it as effectively as we can. Colonel Walters, I must ask your regiment to provide the rearguard, as you are mounted. Brigadier Gough, you will support the dragoons with the lancers if need be, but we are attempting to disengage with as little loss as possible.'

Gough nodded.

'Where are we going, sir?' Murdoch asked.

French gazed at him for a few moments, then he said, 'We will fall back on Le Cateau. The rest of the army should have come up by now. We'll at least have our full force in being.' He gazed at the dead Germans heaped on the meadow. 'Damned frogs,' he remarked. 'We could have held them here forever. Gentlemen, we have work to do.'

15

Le Cateau, 1914

The troopers were aghast. 'Retreat, sir?' RSM Yeald demanded. 'But we've just won a victory.'

'Tactically, sergeant-major,' Murdoch told him. 'Strategically, we seem to have taken a drubbing. But we're to guard the rear. Maybe we'll have a chance to give them another punch on the nose.'

The army began to pull out that night, moving as quietly as possible and leaving their camp fires burning so as to deceive the Germans into supposing they were still holding the line of the canal. It was all very reminiscent of withdrawing from in front of Magersfontein in 1900, only then the Westerns had been amongst the first regiments to leave. Now they were the last. They saluted the Buffs as the infantry marched out, equally confused and disappointed that they should be walking away from the scene of their triumph.

Brigadier-General Gough came down to say goodbye. 'You'll be withdrawn just as soon as the army is clear,' he promised them. 'If the Germans come again before then. . . .'

'We'll kill as many as we can,' Walters promised.

Gough shook his hand. 'Good man, Martin. But I have a feeling that after today's drubbing they may wish to rethink. Good luck, and I hope to see you by tomorrow afternoon.'

He walked his horse over the brow of the hill to where the lancers were waiting, and the brigade filed off. Darkness settled in, and the dragoons were left alone, save for the sappers who were mining the bridges.

The troopers lay amidst the now shot-torn trees, gazing

361

up the slope at the glow which came from beyond the next hill, where the Germans were encamped.

'Wouldn't it be a scream if they too had pulled out and just left their camp fires burning,' remarked Prendergast.

He was always an optimist, Murdoch thought, as he went back up to the top of the shallow hill behind which were their horses. He had a good view of the country in front of them, but found himself instead gazing at the five white crosses which had been erected that very afternoon.

Llewellyn was also there. 'It really upsets me,' the padre remarked, 'to leave them here to be overrun by the enemy. Do you think they'll descrate the graves, Murdoch?'

'They're supposed to be Christians,' Murdoch said. 'Anyway, Dai, we'll be back. No doubt about that.'

By midnight the sappers were finished their job and the lieutenant commanding sent them off, but he himself remained behind. 'I'm to fire the fuses,' he explained.

The night was absolutely quiet, save for an occasional shot from the German sentries. Whether there were actually French or British soldiers out there it was impossible to know, but Murdoch thought it was most unlikely. Dawn would be the decisive moment, but at three o'clock, while the night was still utterly dark, a horseman appeared from the south.

'Compliments of Brigadier-General Gough,' he said, 'and orders to withdraw rapidly.'

'Thank God for that,' Peter Ramage commented. 'I was beginning to feel quite lonely.'

'Quietly now,' Murdoch told the men as they filed past him to regain their horses. 'Not a sound.'

They mounted, and walked away from the canal behind their officers. Colonel Walters led, while Murdoch remained with RSM Yeald, Corporal Reynolds and six men to make sure there were no stragglers.

'Shall I fire the fuses now, sir?' asked the sapper lieutenant.

'Now or never,' Murdoch told him, and the boy scurried about. Apparently he had linked all the fuses to one central line, and he set it off before scrambling into the saddle.

'How long?' Murdoch asked him.

'About fifteen minutes.'

'Then we'd better not hang about.'

Half a mile back from the canal the rearguard waited for him, B Troop of Ramage's squadron, commanded by Ramage himself. These were the men who had been behind him when Murdoch charged the Mullah's army. They were the most reliable men he knew. But it was still a doleful march. Their way lay through Mons itself, and late as it was, those inhabitants who had not already fled turned out to watch them go, as all the previous evening they had watched the rest of the British army retreating. They were even more confused by the troopers, and they were resentful, too. 'Cowards,' someone shouted. 'You came here to fight, not to run away.'

From behind them came the dull bangs of the exploding charges. 'All right,' Murdoch said. 'The enemy will know we've pulled out now. Squadron will canter.'

They hurried over the road, many men half-asleep in their saddles as they had had very little sleep in the last forty-eight hours, watching the darkness fade to grey.

Just after dawn they were alerted by a warning from RSM Yeald, who was bringing up the rear. 'Uhlans!'

They drew rein and looked back, to see the horsemen on the next rise behind them silhouetted against the sunrise.

'They must have crossed the moment they heard those explosions,' Murdoch said. 'But they can't have got their wheeled transport across yet. I think we should discourage those fellows from approaching too close, Mr Ramage. A single volley should do it.'

'I'd rather give them a charge,' Ramage growled, but ordered his men to dismount and take aim. No sooner had they done so, however, than the Uhlans withdrew out of sight; they had had sufficient experience of British marksmanship at Mons.

Murdoch immediately despatched a rider to brigade with the news that the Germans were across the canal, and prepared to fight a rearguard action at any moment – but the enemy horse kept their distance and the infantry were obviously making slower going. However, it was obvious that von Kluck's entire force would soon be on their heels, and tired as the men were, Murdoch would not let them halt, even for a midday meal.

That evening they rode into the town of Le Cateau itself, having already passed the forward defences of the BEF, where men were hastily digging in and preparing for another battle. By now all the late units had come up – and they were back on French soil, with Paris itself less than a hundred miles behind them.

Brigadier Gough was waiting for them, to congratulate them on carrying out their task and to assign them to their cantonment area, which was behind the town itself and well sheltered by one of the many low hills which dotted the countryside. 'You're off for twenty-four hours, God willing,' he told them. 'Indulge in some concentrated rest and recuperation.'

Most of the dragoons were too tired even to pitch their tents, and Martin Walters decided not to force the issue that night. They all slept like the dead, and awoke at dawn to the sound of guns; the Germans had arrived.

The firing grew in intensity while the dragoons, well out of range, pitched their tents and made their camp as orderly as they could. Once everything was completed, Murdoch mounted Buccaneer and with Ramage rode up the slope to see what was going on. From the line of fire they could see that the Germans were apparently probing at the British lines, but not at this moment without too much determination, although they were keeping up a steady artillery bombardment. The British guns were replying with some vigour; white shell bursts could be seen scattered across the entire rolling green hills north of Le Cateau, but the town itself was suffering too, with several buildings burning, and a doleful stream of late refugees taking the road south. To Paris, Murdoch thought, and wondered what conditions were like in the city, now the war had suddenly arrived on its doorstep.

Later that morning the field marshal, accompanied by

364

General Smith-Dorrien, to whose corps the brigade had been attached, and Brigadier-General Gough, visited them. He congratulated them again on manning the rearguard from Mons, but also, in the privacy of the headquarters tent, imparted some grave information.

'There is no doubt,' French said, 'that *we*' – he paused to indicate that he really blamed his allies – 'grossly misjudged the German plan of campaign, and that by far the heaviest attack has been launched through Belgium, and now is brewing in front of ourselves and the French 5th Army. Marshal Joffre is transferring men as rapidly as he can from the east to our support, and I believe he is also trying to raise some new forces from the Paris garrison itself; obviously they will fight like the devil for the city. Equally obviously, I have no doubt he is seeking any possible means of launching a counter-attack. But whether such an opportunity will present itself I wouldn't care to say. What is certain is that we must hold here as long as we can, and at the moment we seem to be doing quite well.'

'When can we return to the line, sir?' Peter Ramage asked.

The field marshal smiled. 'You are a glutton for punishment, captain. Your men need rest. We'll send for you when we need you. Besides' – now the smile was touched with grimness – 'if we do have to pull out, we'll need another rearguard.'

Murdoch was actually quite relieved that they were not immediately required; he knew how exhausted both troopers and horses were. Far more exhausted, indeed, than on the march from Le Cateau north, because now they had the additional fatigue of belonging to a defeated army. That lay like a dead weight on their shoulders – especially as they knew that *they* had not been defeated.

Nevertheless, having rested, they had fallen to work to pitch their tents and dig their latrines with some broad humour. 'Never even had a crap in the last lot,' grumbled Corporal Matheson. 'Left it all bright and clean for the Jerries.'

'I suspect we'll be around here a while longer,' Murdoch

told him. He was more concerned about the horses, who had suffered terribly in their two forced marches in four days. A good number needed re-shoeing, and the farriers were hard at work.

All day the firing to their north grew in intensity as the German attacks grew heavier, but so far without making any great impression. It was a very odd feeling, to be enjoying a warm August afternoon, with the men lounging about in their shirt sleeves, and some of the younger troopers even engaging in a game of soccer, while a major battle was raging only a few miles away. And it *was* a major battle.

'Do you realise, sir,' Ramage told Murdoch, 'that now that the whole of the BEF is up, Sir John French commands a hundred thousand British soldiers?'

'I did realise that, Peter. Why?'

'Well, sir, he is engaged with probably twice that number of Germans. That must make this the biggest battle the British army has engaged in since Waterloo. Or indeed, in all history.'

'By Jove,' Murdoch said. 'But you're right. Wellington only had about seventy thousand at Waterloo.'

'And of those less than half were British,' Ramage pointed out.

Something to write home about, Murdoch decided, and that afternoon got down to a letter to Lee, although with the situation so likely to change for the worse at any moment, he didn't really know what to say. He had put away his pen and was having a cup of tea when there was a *toot-toot* of a car horn, and he looked up to see a Paris taxi-cab, of all things, bouncing across the field and stopping to allow Harry Caspar to get down.

'Harry!' He clasped his brother-in-law's hand. 'How the devil did you get here? I mean, why? I was on my way to see you and have that dinner at Maxim's.'

'Glad you can joke about it,' Harry said. 'Can you lend me ten quid? I didn't realise how expensive this ride would be.'

Murdoch only had five, so they gave that to the taxi-driver, together with a spare set of brass buttons Reynolds had managed to find, and the man departed, shaking his head and muttering about les Americaines.

'Now tell me,' Harry said. 'Is the situation as grim as it looks on the map, and from what everyone is saying?' He glanced at the hill to the north. 'And from what it sounds like over there?'

'It's grim,' Murdoch agreed. 'We can kill the bastards by the score, by the thousand, apparently, but they just keep on coming.'

'But you're making a stand of it here?'

'That's right.'

'This I have to see.'

'I'm not sure that you should,' Murdoch said. 'It's a little rough up there. And what Lee would say. . . .'

'Lee isn't going to know until it's over,' Harry pointed out. 'Come now, who's going to write you up so you get another medal?'

'We're all finished with medals for the time being,' Murdoch told him. 'We're the reserve.'

But he took Harry up to one of the forward positions, to look at the infantry crouching behind hedgerows and on reverse slopes, and to watch too, the German assaults on one or two advanced posts; they could even hear the shouts of the men engaged.

'Hell's bells,' Harry commented. 'Reminds me of Manchuria. The Russians slaughtered the Japanese just like that, but guess what? The Japanese won in the end.'

'Whose side are you on?' Murdoch asked.

The German attacks grew in intensity the next day; there could be no doubt they intended to take Le Cateau, because the town had grown up around one of the most vital cross-roads in northern France, the southern arm of which led directly into Paris. Now, even in reserve, life became very grim, as stray shells came over the hilltops to burst amidst the cantonments, scattering shrapnel in every direction, wounding men and lacerating horses, some of them so badly they had to be immediately destroyed, while keeping the rest under control was a task occupying half a squadron.

'Gee whiz,' Harry commented. 'I don't remember anything like *this* in Manchuria.'

The screaming of the dying horses was really pitiful.

'But then,' he added, 'the Japanese didn't go in for horses, much. Your people going to be able to take this?'

'Just as long as they have to,' Murdoch said. But there was no answer to being outflanked. General Smith-Dorrien returned to visit them that afternoon, accompanied as usual by Gough. 'The French are being pushed back,' he said. 'Oh, they're fighting magnificently; they know there's only Paris behind them. But there's not a lot they can do. They're taking the brunt of the attack, you see, simply because they aren't as trained to rifle fire as our chaps, and so the Germans regard them as a softer touch. Either way, we can't hold out here much longer. It is Sir John's intention to pull back this evening. This corps will cover the initial stages of the retreat, but when my infantry fall back tomorrow morning, I'm afraid the cavalry brigade will have to cover, as usual. Your prime duty will be to provide support for the regiment of horse artillery which is also going to remain as long as possible to hold the crossroads and try to keep the Germans from moving up too quickly. I know you will handle this responsibility as well as you covered the retreat from Mons. Good luck, and good hunting.'

Brigadier Gough gave a grim smile. 'It's nice to be wanted. You'll prepare to take your positions tonight.'

'At last,' Ramage said.

He represented the general viewpoint. The regiment was well rested, and the men were getting fed up at being strafed without even seeing their enemy. That night they moved forward, on foot, although the horses were led behind; the reason they were being given the rearguard was because they could retire more quickly than foot soldiers.

For over a mile they passed other British units pulling out, marching by on the trampled roads, and exchanging quips and banter. Many of the infantry were bandaged, but still carrying arms and anxious to resume the fight at the earliest possible moment. 'Just hold the bastards until we get dug in,' they called to the dragoons. 'We'll be ready for you. And them.'

One of Gough's staff officers was waiting for them about a mile south of the town, with orders to deploy to their right. Here they found several batteries of horse artillery already in position in a ploughed field, but what the rest of the army was doing it was impossible to say. The firing had died down with the darkness, and although Le Cateau burned fiercely and threw up an immense glow, beyond the range of the flames it was intensely dark, broken only by the occasional star shell sent up by the Germans.

'I gather we have to stay here for a while,' remarked Colonel Anstruther, who was commanding the batteries. 'I would let your men have a nap if they can, Walters.'

This was difficult, as throughout the night infantry filed by, stumbling over sleeping bodies, cursing and swearing.

With the first light General Smith-Dorrien appeared. 'We need twelve hours,' he said. 'You'll also bring those guns with you when you come, Anstruther.'

'Yes, sir,' the gunner replied.

'Good fortune.' He walked his horse off behind his retreating army.

'Coffee, gentlemen?' Reynolds was as ever on hand as the officers rubbed their unshaven chins and looked at each other. Reynolds as usual was immaculate.

'I think now is the time for you to pull out as well, Harry,' Murdoch said. 'This could be quite sticky. We could easily be overrun.'

'I wouldn't miss this for all the world,' Harry declared.

'Bit rough on Lee to lose both her husband and her brother on the same day,' Murdoch pointed out.

'I'll surrender,' Harry promised. 'And write her a letter from Berlin.'

By now there was sufficient light to see exactly what they had to do. The artillery had been positioned to the right of Le Cateau itself, about a mile back from the crossroads; they were emplaced behind a high, thick hedge, which left them totally concealed for the moment. The rest of the cavalry brigade, dismounted, was over to the left, covering several more batteries, and there could be no doubt that any force attempting to advance up the road was going to receive a very unpleasant surprise. But equally, there could be no doubt that the Germans *were* going to advance up the road.

Murdoch and Walters dismounted two squadrons and placed their men in the hedges, to either side of the guns. The third squadron, Ramage's, they held in reserve behind the next hillock, together with the horses.

The guns had also been concealed as well as possible from above, by branches and nets filled with leaves and suspended from long poles. This was very necessary, as the moment it was daylight several German aircraft appeared, flying low over the burning town and the fields around it, to discover if the BEF had indeed retreated. Murdoch could only imagine what Sir John French was thinking about this newfangled aspect of warfare, and in fact it was most disconcerting, as it entirely altered the age-old concept of concealment behind high ground if the enemy could determine your whereabouts and numbers at will.

The men obviously felt exposed too, and were with difficulty prevented from totally revealing their position by firing at the intruders, while they were all delighted when six French machines appeared to challenge the Germans. They watched in fascination as the biplanes wheeled and dived immediately above their heads, the observers firing at their enemies with rifles and revolvers, and there was a great cheer when one of the German machines was hit – or more probably, the pilot was – and it crashed into the ground with a huge *whoompf*, followed by a pillar of black smoke.

'Talk about the shape of things to come,' Harry Caspar commented. 'One day they'll think of mounting a machine gun in a plane, and then you'll see something.'

'Keep your head down,' Murdoch advised. He had been watching the road through his binoculars.

The enemy cavalry had been seen from time to time all morning, patrols appearing here and there, waiting to see if they would be fired upon. Now the patrols were probing further forward, into the burning town itself, and now too the heads of the German columns, massed as usual, were appearing over the furthest visible rise and marching upon Le Cateau.

'Won't be long now,' he muttered.

Colonel Anstruther was also studying the position through his glasses. 'I'm going to let them into the town, Walters,' he said. 'Can your chaps take care of any who come out the other side?'

'Oh, indeed,' Walters agreed.

Murdoch knelt between Ramage and Yeald to watch the German columns come on. He knew that within a few minutes he was going to witness carnage on a scale he would not have imagined possible a few weeks before – but he also knew, deep in his belly, that those men simply were not going to be stopped. His throat felt quite dry as he wondered how he would feel if commanded to walk into almost certain death.

The head of the column disappeared into the town, while the first of the Uhlans appeared on the southern side of the houses, slowly walking their horses up the hill, wondering what had happened to the British. Being human, Murdoch did not doubt they were praying that their enemies had fled in a rout, which was the only way this entire area would have become so deserted. And now the first of the marching soldiers appeared amidst the last of the houses.

'Fire,' Colonel Anstruther shouted. 'Rapid fire.'

The British artillery opened fire, those on the left of the road as well, pouring shells into the crossroads and immediately north of them at what, for the field guns, was point-blank range. The shells exploded, and the grey-clad men were tossed to and fro like chaff in a harvested wheat-field. The column dissolved, the men diving for shelter behind the rubbled buildings or into the ditches to either side of the road; while the dragoons and the lancers opened rifle and machine-gun fire on those who had already passed the houses, sending men and horses crashing to the ground, again driving the survivors to seek shelter in the fields. The noise was deafening, the rattle of the rifles and the machine guns comparing even with the heavier booms of the field guns, while smoke swirled and men screamed, and died.

'Holy Jesus Christ,' Harry commented, scribbling in his notebook as fast as he could. 'They'll never believe this back home. Never! Those guys must have a death wish. Can they possibly push you fellows away?'

'They can, and they will,' Murdoch told him. 'As long as they don't care how many of them get killed, they must drive us back eventually.' He went off to check the casualties, but these remained light, for the moment.

But the German guns had now identified the position of the British batteries, and while their infantry recovered and regrouped, they delivered a return barrage. It happened just as Murdoch had ordered breakfast, and made a mess of the meal. He could only thank God that the horses were over the hill and somewhat removed from serious trouble, for the batteries themselves were saturated with fire, and it was a case of lying flat and hoping that none of the flying shrapnel would find a target. Which it did, with unfailing regularity, as men cried and groaned, and it was necessary to direct the stretcher-bearers, themselves liable to death every moment, while aware of the deadly steel fragments flying in every direction.

Dai Llewellyn was a tower of strength, although within half an hour he was bleeding from three wounds. When Walters wanted to send him off with the wounded, he refused to go. 'Just nicks,' he said. 'I've suffered worse on Cardiff Arms Park.'

When the barrage finally ceased, Murdoch was able to despatch the more seriously wounded to the rear and the field ambulances, with orders to keep on going back to Paris.

Brigadier Gough rode over to talk to Walters. 'Can your men take much more of this, Martin?' he asked.

'I would think so, sir,' Walters said.

'I'd like to hold until dusk, if possible,' Gough said. 'That's perhaps another nine hours. But that's our best hope of getting the guns out.'

'Nine hours,' Walters agreed.

372

'Just so long as the ammo holds out,' Anstruther put in.

'Here they come again,' Harry Caspar cried, as the German infantry moved forward once more.

The gunners hurried back to their positions and poured more rapid fire into the advancing masses, to check them yet again, but now they were close enough to use their own rifles and, going to ground, kept up a continuous fire on the hedgerows behind which the British sheltered. The dragoons and the lancers replied with everything they had, but the casualties mounted as every so often a man dropped his rifle and collapsed on the ground.

'Hot work, for nine hours,' Walters said, wiping his face with his handkerchief.

'Begging your pardon, gentlemen,' said Corporal Reynolds, who was as usual dispensing hot coffee laced with brandy, with a total disregard for enemy fire. 'What are those people over there?'

Heads turned, and they looked to the right of the artillery emplacement where, about a mile away, a body of horsemen could be seen. Binoculars immediately came up. 'Uhlans!' everyone said together.

At that moment Gough himself galloped up. 'The French units on our right have pulled out,' he shouted. 'We will have to go too, without waiting for dark.'

'Could be a bit late,' Colonel Anstruther said. 'If those chaps get behind us.'

Gough peered through his glasses. 'God damn it,' he said. 'You'll have to wheel some guns.'

'That won't stop them,' Anstruther said. 'Not now.'

'With permission, sir,' Murdoch said. 'We have a squadron in reserve. It may be possible to disperse them long enough to get the guns through.'

Gough snapped his fingers. 'Do that, Murdoch. Colonel Anstruther, send a rider to Colonel Bretherton and request him to limber up his guns and move out as quickly as possible, and to Colonel Harris and request him to send two squadrons of the lancers to support the dragoons in advancing upon those cavalry. Then you limber up as well, and get down that road hell for leather.' He looked at Walters. 'Martin, the fate of the guns is in your hands.'

Murdoch was already running back over the hill to where Ramage was walking up and down, cutting at poppies with his sword in irritation, while his men sat on the ground and smoked. 'Action, Peter!' he shouted. 'Mount up. We have work to do.'

'Hurrah!' Ramage shouted back, and leapt into the saddle. Reynolds had run back with Murdoch, and now led Buccaneer forward. Murdoch would have preferred to take Trajan, but Buccaneer looked totally fit and rested and eager to go. He mounted, and found Reynolds as usual at his shoulder, along with RSM Yeald and Bugler Summerton.

'Now, George,' he protested.

'Could be the last time, sir,' Reynolds argued. 'If all the experts are right.'

Before Murdoch could remonstrate further, Martin Walters rode up. 'I've put Prendergast in temporary command,' he said. 'I'd not miss this for the world.' If he was certainly nervous, he was determined to overcome it, Murdoch could tell. 'Gentlemen?' He drew his sword.

He had forgotten the prayer, and Murdoch didn't think there was time to remind him. He drew his own sword, and the squadron moved out, harnesses jingling. As they emerged from round the hillock the artillerymen gave them a great cheer, as did their own comrades.

The Uhlans saw them at the same instant, and checked, for the moment uncertain how many men were advancing on them. But they certainly numbered a full regiment, Murdoch estimated, not less than five hundred men. Yet the squadron was already at the canter, while from behind them he heard the bugle call of the lancers, who were racing to their support.

'Bugler,' Colonel Walters shouted, pointing his sword. 'Sound the charge.'

The notes scattered across the morning, and the dragoons closed up into the two ranks they always employed. Swords were out and thrust forward, and the men roared and the

374

horses neighed as they raced at their enemies. The Uhlans hesitated, their brilliant helmets glinting in the sun, then responded to the challenge, lowering their lances as they moved forward.

'Mind those pig-stickers,' Walters bellowed, galloping ahead of his men. Murdoch moved up almost alongside him, carefully keeping a stride behind, as etiquette demanded, conscious of Reynolds and Yeald at his shoulder, with Summerton just behind. The Germans had no time to develop a gallop themselves. Their officers waved their swords as they got their men into a rough line, then the dragoons were upon them.

The first lance went over Murdoch's shoulder as he crouched over Buccaneer's head, and the man in front of them went down with a crash as the old horse performed his favourite shoulder charge. The jar nearly unseated Murdoch, but he recovered in time to cut at the next man to appear before him, thrust at the one after that, and then found himself on his feet as Buccaneer gave a huge gasp and collapsed. He hadn't been speared or shot, Murdoch was sure, but had suffered a massive heart attack and was already dead.

There was no time to grieve for the horse. Murdoch was surrounded by men and horses, jostling and yelling, neighing and prancing, while the dust swirled and made it difficult to tell friend from foe. Reynold rode over to give him a hand up, but was then dismounted himself as a horse cannoned into him and sent him tumbling to the ground. Murdoch grasped his arm to set him on his feet again, and saw Colonel Walters go down, a lance through his chest. He made to go to the colonel's aid, and heard his name called: 'Mackinder!'

He turned, and saw Paul von Reger bearing down on him, sabre extended to the full length of his arm. Murdoch leapt one way, and Reynolds the other, rolling over. Reynolds immediately drew the revolver he always carried and brought down the Uhlan colonel's horse with a single bullet.

Reger landed on his hands and knees, then regained his

feet, still grasping his sabre, face twisted in anger. 'You'd fight like a coward,' he shouted, glaring at the revolver.

Murdoch hesitated. But war could still surely be fought by gentlemen, he thought.

'Hold it, George,' he said, and stepped forward.

Reger grinned at him. 'I asked to fight against the British,' he said. 'I knew you would be there, old friend. Now I shall *kill* you.'

He lunged forward behind his blade, and Murdoch parried as best he could, and then again, as Reger kept on coming. Certainly the German was the better swordsman. But to fight a duel in such circumstances was impossible. As he turned to face his oldest adversary again, the lancers arrived to complete the defeat of the Uhlans. The new horses smashed into the heaving mob of men and animals and sent them every which way. A falling body struck reger on the shoulder, and he fell to his hands and knees again, but still retained his grasp on his sabre.

'Now, sir,' Reynolds called. 'You have him now.'

Murdoch hesitated. His instincts were to fight the duel to a finish. But this was, after all, war, not a private quarrel. He stepped up to Reger, his point presented at his exposed back. 'You are my prisoner, colonel,' he said.

'Major Mackinder! Major Makinder!' It was Peter Ramage, hatless and breathless, but still mounted, pulling his horse to a halt. 'Colonel Walters.....'

Murdoch turned and saw Martin Walters lying on the ground, blood streaming from his chest. In that moment he forgot about Reger, who was still turning to face him, and who had not yet agreed to surrender. Now he caught only the glimpse of the flying steel, heard the crack of Reynolds' revolver, and was then struck a savage blow on the shoulder.

He found himself lying on the ground, gazing up at Reynolds and the revolver; the batman's face was like a savage's in the paroxysm of anger which had swept across him. 'I got the bastard, sir,' he said.

'Don't kill him, George,' Murdoch gasped. 'Don't kill him.' Then he fainted.

*

Field Marshal Sir John French spared a moment to visit Murdoch in the base hospital in Paris. 'I think we'll have to get you a bar to that DSO,' he said. 'That charge certainly saved the guns.'

'Colonel Walters led that charge,' Murdoch reminded him.

'Oh, he'll get one too, poor fellow. Now you must rest up. You'll be home in a couple of days.'

'Home?' Murdoch demanded, trying to ignore the pain rippling through his shoulder. 'But, the regiment. . . .'

'Ramage can command it until you're fit enough to return. He's a good man, trained by you, of course.'

'The army. . . .'

'We'll hold. Somewhere. We'll hold. By God, they keep coming, but we keep knocking them down. They'll have to call a halt somewhere.'

'I can stay, surely,' Murdoch begged, looking at the doctor.

'You're lucky to be alive, major,' the doctor told him. 'If that sword-cut had been an inch or two to the left you'd be short of a head. As it is, you have a clean fracture of the collar-bone. A few weeks, and you should be fit for duty again. But right now, you're no use to anyone, and we have other wounded to attend to.'

'He's right,' Harry Caspar said.

'Tell me about the regiment,' Murdoch said.

'You took some casualties. But you sure put those Uhlans to flight. Took some prisoners too, including their colonel. Shot through the arm, he was, by your batman. Say, is it true he's the guy who got you?'

'I believe so,' Murdoch said. 'Is he going to be all right?'

'Now, I guess. It was all Peter Ramage could do to stop your men from lynching him.'

'Is Reynolds all right, Yeald?'

Harry nodded. 'Bugler Summerton bought it. And there's not too much hope for your colonel. But that charge! Maybe it was the last one ever. I sure mean to write it up. Give my love to Lee.'

'You mean you're not coming home with me?'

Harry grinned. 'I'm going to have that dinner in Maxim's, Jerries or no Jerries. What, miss this? Not on your life.'

Dr Abrahams had Murdoch's stretcher placed next to Martin Walters on the train to Le Havre. 'He asked to speak to you,' he explained.

'Murdoch,' Walters said. As he spoke blood bubbled from his mouth; the lance-head had penetrated his lung. 'Murdoch ... Judith. ...'

'I'll see her, Martin,' Murdoch promised.

'Had to go,' Walters explained. 'Had to go. You thought I was afraid, didn't you.'

'Good God no,' Murdoch lied.

'Had to go,' Walters said again. 'But Judith ... she won't understand. She didn't ever understand ... about death. Or about pigs,' he added after a moment. Then stirred again. 'Murdoch, Amy Hobbs ... I never did write to her. Murdoch. ...'

Murdoch held his hand.

'You oaf,' Lee said. 'Oh, you great oaf. Rushing off and getting yourself wounded again.' Her eyes were filled with tears. 'All to be a hero.' She kissed him for the third time, while Sister Anderson stood by to make sure she didn't touch the broken shoulder. 'To be a Mackinder!'

'That's the name of the game,' he said.

'Oh, sure. As long as you stay alive. Your photograph is in every newspaper. Charging Mackinder, they call you.'

'Martin Walters led the charge,' Murdoch reminded her.

'Oh, sure, and got himself killed.'

'While I get the credit. Have you seen Judith?'

She nodded. 'Poor woman, she hasn't really realised he's dead yet, I guess. But she'd like a word, when you're up and about.'

Murdoch nodded. 'I'll go see her. And Amy Hobbs.'

'Poor Amy,' Lee said. 'I'm so sorry for them both. I'm the lucky one. To have you home, reasonably in one piece.' She kissed him again. 'The children can't wait to see you.'

*
378

'We buried Buccaneer, sir,' Reynolds wrote. 'Full military honours. If I'd had my way I'd have buried that bastard Reger beside him. Or underneath him. Hope to see you soon, sir, and compliments of the regiment.'

Murdoch put down the letter and listened to the sound of rifle and gun fire, the cries of men, the shrill neighing of horses. Sometimes he even heard them in his sleep. His men were still hearing those things in reality, while he lay here in bed.

But how many times could he expect to be shot, and not killed? Would someone else say, 'Poor Lee, I don't think she realises he's dead yet.'

Lord Roberts came to see him. Bobs was now eighty-two years old, but as straight and spritely as ever, and, to Murdoch's amazement, in service uniform.

'I'm on my way to France,' he said proudly.

'You, sir? But . . . ?'

'Oh, they won't give me a command. They won't even let me fight. But they feel that my presence may encourage the troops. Not that they need much encouraging right this minute. You've heard the news?'

'No, sir.' He had, actually, but Roberts clearly wanted to tell him about it.

'Well, the newspapers are calling it the Miracle of the Marne. Not a miracle really, just good generalship on one side, and bad generalship on the other. The German advance, as was bound to happen, became somewhat disorganised, and so a gap was opened between von Kluck's army, the one your lads fought off at Mons and Le Cateau, and von Bülow's, next to him. Joffre spotted it, and moved troops into the opening. The BEF amongst them. They say he even used Paris taxi-cabs to rush men up to the front. Anyway, the Germans found themselves in danger of being taken in the flank, and went tumbling back. All danger to Paris is over.'

'And I missed it,' Murdoch said.

'The devil you did. Mons and Le Cateau may go down in the history books as British defeats, but they were superb defensive actions, which led directly to the counter-attack. Had it not been for people like you holding the Germans up twice in as many days, Joffre would never have had the time for his counter-stroke. Anyway, don't suppose the show is over, or even half over. Not by a long shot. The Germans are digging in right across Belgium, and they look as if they mean to stay, especially since they seem to have given the Russians a terrible thrashing in Poland. I felt all along that those so-called experts who predicted a short war were going to be proved wrong. You'll have time to return. If you want to. As a matter of fact, I have some personal news for you. Lord Kitchener has approved your promotion to lieutenant-colonel.'

Murdoch was speechless. If he had always expected to arrive at that rank, it had not been at the expense of Martin Walters' life.

'And, of course, you're getting a bar to your DSO,' Roberts went on. 'What I have to say is this, however. In view of your record, and the number of times you have been wounded, a place on the staff is yours for the asking. John French would be very happy to have you; he's said so.'

'And the alternative?'

'Why, to take command of the Royal Westerns.'

'I think that's what I'd like to do, sir,' Murdoch said.

Field Marshal Earl Roberts smiled, and shook his hand.

As soon as he was fit to leave hospital, Murdoch went to the prisoner of war camp where Reger was held.

'You'll find he's a surly customer,' remarked the officer in charge.

'We're old friends,' Murdoch said.

Reger was shown into the little interview room, and stood to attention.

'How's the arm?' Murdoch asked.

Reger moved his fingers. 'I can use it again.'

'Snap.'

'I would like to apologise, Major Mackinder. . . .' He frowned, as he saw the crossed swords on Murdoch's shoulder. 'Colonel Mackinder?'

'Happens to us all, in time, colonel.'

'My congratulations. I would like to apologise for wounding you when your head was turned. I had already started my swing before I realised that. I expected to die from your sword-thrust. I did not intend to surrender.'

Murdoch nodded. 'I had guessed that for myself. But now that it is over, for you, can we not shake hands and let the past be the past?'

Reger frowned again. 'You are doing this for Paul?'

Murdoch shrugged. 'Why, yes, perhaps I am.'

'And for Margriet?'

'For Paul,' Murdoch said carefully.

'He is a German, who will one day be a German soldier, who will then avenge me.'

'That's going to take a little time,' Murdoch pointed out. 'I'd like to think we could all be friends before that happens.'

'It will happen,' Roger said. 'You think it is all over, for me? I am nothing. It has only begun, for England and Germany. And Germany will triumph in the end. Then we will see about being friends.'

Murdoch sighed and stood up, but as he did so, he thought of the immense courage and determination of those grey hordes who had advanced into the teeth of equally determined rifle and machine-gun fire without flinching. 'We'll just have to wait and see,' he said.

Murdoch and Lee walked across the moors beyond Broad Acres. It was the most perfect September evening, with not a sound above the singing of the birds. 'But you're really going back,' she said. 'To all that mud, and death, and misery.'

'I have to,' he said. 'Much as I want to stay here with you and the children. Ramage and Llewellyn, Yeald and Reynolds . . . they're expecting me. Besides' – he grinned at her – 'Harry still hasn't given me that dinner at Maxim's.'

'But only the regiment matters,' she said.

His smile faded. 'Can you understand that?'

'Lieutenant-Colonel Murdoch Mackinder, VC, DSO and

bar, commanding officer of the Royal Western Dragoon Guards,' she said. 'Oh, Murdoch, I am *so* proud of you.'